HOT AS A PISTOL

Con Flannery raised his rough voice to a full-throated roar. "Listen to me, you storekeepers and moneygrubbers, and listen good! There's been talk around about my daughter. Gutter talk—you all know what you've been saying. There's talk about my daughter and a low, sneaking, bloody-handed son of a bitch with the name Ballard. Dirty men have come here to spread dirty money to see that she goes back to this man. You all think you're going to get rich with more dirty money if she does. But I'm here to tell you that if this talk goes on, a lot of you are going to get killed. And that, you half-men, is a promise."

WILD, WILD WOMEN

"I'd like to have a word with you, Saddler," Claggett said. "It's about the man you killed—Bullwhip Danner. He was a good man, in spite of everything, and you snuffed out his life in a drunken brawl. It's up to you to take Danner's place. Lead us across the Plains to California. I know you can do it. You've done it before."

"What makes you think that?"

"Sheriff Vardiman says so. He knows more about you than you think. How many times have you been across?"

"Only twice. You better get somebody else. I won't do it."

Reverend Claggett's face got angrier than it had been. "Are you deaf or still befuddled by whiskey? There is nobody else."

Hannah Claggett suddenly spoke up shyly. "Fifty young women are depending on you!"

Saddler Double Editions by *Leisure Books:*
A DIRTY WAY TO DIE/COLORADO CROSSING

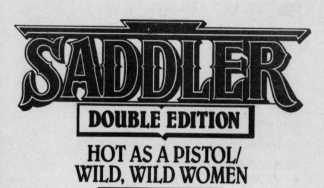

SADDLER

DOUBLE EDITION

HOT AS A PISTOL/ WILD, WILD WOMEN

Gene Curry

LEISURE BOOKS   NEW YORK CITY

A LEISURE BOOK®

August 1994

Published by

Dorchester Publishing Co., Inc.
276 Fifth Avenue
New York, NY 10001

HOT AS A PISTOL

ONE

Women have a way of getting me into trouble, but I give them a lot of help. This time though it was a fellow Texan who set me on the road to ruin. They called him Gentleman Johnny Callahan and we both came from the same part of West Texas, me from Jonesboro, Callahan from Dimmit. I had known Johnny most of my life, and while both of us had been raised by the ears, as they say in the Panhandle, I never brooded about it. My folks were poor but all right in their way, doing what they could for the kids. So being poor didn't bother me the way it did Callahan.

Years back, I remember him saying he would never, never again wear old clothes, any kind of hand-me-downs—no more patched overalls and broken boots for Johnny. He was going to dress like a gent, and he did, right from the day he got his first handful of folding money. I lost track of him for a few years; then I began to hear about him, mostly in Texas. After some false starts—running wet cows into Mexico, the finding of "stray" horses, and the like—old Johnny became a town tamer, a pacifier of little hellholes all over Texas. Not that John Callahan was a killer; he'd much rather cheat a man at cards than kill him. Naturally, in the line of work he followed, he had to douse the lamps of a few badmen, but backshooting and shotgunning wasn't much to his liking. Like I say, he did it for a living.

It went along like that for a while. I ran into him a few times, and while you'd have to stretch it to the breaking point to call us bosom pals, we got along well enough, things considering. We came from the hard part of Texas and away from there any kind of friendship counted for something.

The funny thing was that Johnny made a small but solid rep for himself, and then just dropped out of sight. He was seen no more in the fleshpots of Fort Griffin; they missed his nervy playing in the poker games of El Paso. After a few years, people began to say he was dead. There were more than a few daring liars who had seen him die, had witnessed his demise at the hands of any number of notorious desperados. Only one thing was sure, Gentleman Johnny Callahan was gone.

The last place I expected to find him was in the town of Dragoon Wells, in the Arizona Territory. I knew there was a town of that name three or four days ride from the Sonora border. Back in the '60's when the Apaches were running wild, with most of the men off to fight in Abe Lincoln's war, a few old codgers who had been dragoons in Alamo times stood off a whole mess of Indians and saved the town. Hence the name. All that stuff I learned later after I got to be marshal of the town.

I was on my way south to see what Mexico had to offer in the way of easy money. Dragoon Wells was on the way. Things happened and I stayed over and got into trouble.

I rode into town on a Sunday afternoon, and out on the edge of this benighted place some of the sports had a horse race going. On the bare brown hills surrounding the town were worked-out mines, the galvanized-iron sheeting of the buildings rusting in the sun. A second growth of brush was doing its best to cover the scarred hillsides. The sky was bright and clear, and it was hot. It didn't look like much of a town.

I was in no special hurry—my intention was to bunk in for the night, start again come morning—so I hung around for the races. I didn't get a good look at Johnny Callahan until he fell off the horse. That was right at the finish of the race. They were heading for the finish line and the rider who turned out to be Johnny was far in the lead, whacking his coal-black Arabian with his hat, urging the spirited critter to greater speed. There was no need to put all that distance between himself and the losers, but then Johnny always was a show-off.

That Arabian had his tail out straight as a poker and if he'd gone any faster he'd have been flying. He hit the finish ribbon like a bolt of lightning, and then it happened. Right at that instant some dog decided to commit suicide by running right under the Arabian. The dog got killed and the rider got thrown, as if pitched from one of those Roman catapults. He had a short, graceful flight and came down heavy. So heavy and hard you could hear his legs breaking above the groan that went up from the crowd. A few people stared at me as I drifted along to see the damage, but the main attraction was the bunged-up rider. He lay there cursing a blue streak, and when I got a better look I saw old Johnny Callahan.

I guess he was surprised as I was, though neither of us showed it. A glance passed between us before I turned away. Johnny had all the help he needed, and seeing there was a badge pinned to his shirt, I wasn't sure that he wanted to claim me as any kind of friend. Like Johnny, I had done a few lawless things in my time, but my efforts were more recent. As I went away from there I heard him yelling questions about his horse. I could have told him that the Arabian was still spooked but otherwise all right. What I didn't have to tell him was that he wouldn't be walking for quite some time.

7

Nothing is deader than a small town on a Sunday afternoon. This one was deader than most. Dragoon Wells had seen better days but not lately. It must have bustled pretty good when the mines were working; now it was just a town drowsing in the sun.

There were two hotels and one was boarded up, sun and wind taking their toll. The other hotel, right across the street, was open for business, but there was no mob of room seekers breaking down the door to get in. The door was open and I raised a man from the dead, namely the clerk from his Sunday afternoon nap, and got a key to a room for two dollars.

The clerk was interested in me, but not enough to start throwing questions. He turned the register on its swivel and gawked at my name before he settled back in his chair and spread a bandanna over his face. A potted palm and a lot of flies had died in the lobby; that's about all there was, and maybe the rest of the paying guests were at the races.

The room was No. 5 and there was a brass bed, the usual boxwood furniture. The flowered wallpaper was stained and faded. I had been in too many hotel rooms like this one; it didn't bother me. I put my stuff on the dresser and stretched out on the bed.

I hadn't been there much more than an hour when somebody rapped on the door. I knew it wasn't Callahan. A kid with arms and legs all loose like a rag doll came in.

"Marshall Callahan wants to talk to you," he said, shifting from one foot to the other. That didn't suit him; so he shifted back. "Quick as you can he'd like to."

"You sure you got the right room and the right man?" I wanted to know what name Johnny was calling me by. In the West a lot of wanted men go by the name of John Ryan. Not Smith—Ryan—and don't ask me why.

"You're Jim Saddler, ain't you?" the kid said.

I nodded. "Where do I find him?"

The kid said the jail. "He'd be obliged you came right

8

now," he said. "The marshal don't like to be kept waiting."

I found the jail without the kid's help. It had been built when the town was a town, intended to remain a town; a brick building of fair size, barred windows, iron banded oak door with old reward posters tacked up on both sides of it, a porch and a rocker.

A doctor was finishing up with Johnny when I went in. He was all splinted up and riding an old wheelchair with cobwebs still on it. A bottle and a glass stood on the desk with the usual lawman's office junk.

It was a good-looking jail; good looking as Johnny himself. The damn place was painted and swept out; the wide planked floor had been ground smooth and oiled until it glistened. It smelled of good cigars and good whiskey, none of that puke-and-sweat smell you get in jails. The desk wasn't the usual boot-scarred article but a heavy polished oak job with brass knobs for the drawers. The whole place gave me the feeling that old Johnny was doing all right for himself.

We just nodded. No hand pumping or back slapping. "Take a chair, be with you when the doc gets through."

I sat and listened and the doctor, an irritable old man, was laying down the law. "By rights you ought to be in bed," he said. "Why the hell do you want to sit a chair when you can be in your bed?"

Johnny said, "Cause I don't like bed except for two things. Right now I don't feel like neither. Now tell me the rest of it. Maybe I'll even believe you."

"Makes no difference what you do," the doctor snapped. "You got two broken legs. Nice clean breaks. You're young enough so all you have to do is let the bones knit. That's what you're supposed to do. Bang those legs around and you'll be walking on sticks the rest of your life."

"What's wrong with the wheelchair?" Johnny said.

"Not a thing when you're ready for it. My guess is you'll be glad to get to bed after a while. I'm leaving some laudanum if the pain gets bad. It's not whiskey, Marshal, you take it by the spoonful. Don't take too much, just what I said, or you won't have to worry about the legs or anything else. You'll be dead. Send the boy if you need me."

"Ain't this a bitch!" Johnny said after the doctor packed his bag and left. Johnny drummed on the splints with his fingertips. "What in hell are you doing here, Saddler?"

"The kid said you wanted to see me, didn't like to be kept waiting." I grinned at Johnny, his fancy duds still dusty from the fall, at the worried look on his lean, handsome face. Johnny must have some Indian blood in him. He's dark and has crow black hair with a shine to it. His light blue eyes were the Callahan part.

"I mean what are you doing in Dragoon Wells?" Johnny said. "You wouldn't be dodging the law, by any chance? For something big enough for them to start looking for you here? No need to get your back up about it, just asking."

"Nobody's looking for me that I know of," I said. "A few places I wouldn't be welcome, no more than that. Since you're asking, how about you? You haven't been heard from these last few years."

Johnny laughed and grimaced with pain at the same time. "Hell no!" he said. "It happened I found a good thing here and decided to stick with it. I'm a pillar of the community, more or less. There's some here wouldn't cry if I moved on, but never get up the nerve to say it. Others don't mind me; I do a good job for the town."

I looked around the well-kept office, at Johnny himself. "You look like you do a few things for yourself."

Johnny's smile was modest and that was worse than bragging. "A few creature comforts, Jim, old pardner."

My fur went up when I heard that old pardner stuff. Johnny is the kind who can be charming without being friendly, a good kind to watch out for. I was watching out real hard.

10

"You have something in mind, or did you want to talk about the horse race?" I enquired.

"What's your hurry? You sound like you're not glad to see me."

"Sure I am, Johnny," I said. "How the hell are you?"

"Got two broken legs," Johnny answered. "Otherwise good. How's about you?"

I told Johnny a few of the things I'd been doing. The big poker game I came out a big winner from in Sandstream, New Mexico. The rich girl I busted loose from a gang of outlaws in the Colorado mountains.

For a moment, Johnny looked homesick for the rootless life he used to lead. Then it passed as I knew it would. Johnny had that comfortable look that comes early to some men, even if they aren't married. When it isn't marriage it's money, and I had a fair idea that Johnny wasn't married.

"I don't know," Johnny said. "All this moving about, it's not all that great."

I didn't agree with that. I like to move around. "Looks like you're through with it," I said. "Me, I'm on my way to Sonora. I'll see when I get there."

Johnny wheeled himself around to the other side of the desk and pushed the chair out of the way. Then he got another glass from the drawer and filled that one and the one on the desk. It was Jack Daniel's, good stuff, no need of water. I got mine and knocked it back and got another one.

"That's what I wanted to talk to you about," Johnny said, getting out a box of long nines for both of us. We lit up and Johnny said, "Don't sound like you got pressing business in Mexico."

I can dicker too. "I'd like to get there," I said.

"Where the money is."

Johnny nodded and did the honors again. "That's the place to be. Of course there's money all over if you know how to get at it."

"And you do?"

"I'm getting good at it," Johnny said. "There's money here; you can have some if you like."

I said I'd like to get in the way of making some money. "What do I have to do to get it?"

"Work for me is what. I'm going to be needing a deputy. You could be him."

I had another drink to see if I liked the idea. I didn't. "I'd feel foolish," I said. "Look foolish, feel foolish. Thanks for thinking of me, but the answer has to be no. Look, old pardner, if you were in a real fix I'd probably help you out for old time's sake. You and me and the folks back home. But you're not. Tell me what's so hard about finding another deputy?"

"What's so hard? Hard as hell to find the right man. I need a man I can trust."

"What makes you sure you can trust me?"

Johnny smiled. "About this I think I can."

"You mean I wouldn't be after your job?"

"Exactly right. You'll never settle down and you know it. If you were a sensible man you'd find something the way I did. I do just fine in this village. The marshal's pay isn't too much, but I got a few sidelines. Got a handle on the poker games in town, faro as well. The man that runs a few girls upstairs over the saloon is kind of a partner. You could say I got a few investments here and there."

"What did you invest?"

"My goodwill," Johnny said, smiling. "No, sir, it's not what you're thinking. I didn't stomp in there and tell folks here's your new equal-share partner. Plenty of lawmen do that, but that makes for bad feeling all round. You do that to a man and he's going to have the knife ready for you if you stumble."

"You did more than stumble today. Where's the knife?"

Johnny waved away the smoke from his cigar. "So far it's only a small knife. Let me lay it out for you fair and honest. In some towns they got lawmen so mean, so crooked, the only way they can get rid of them is to kill

12

them. Hire some gunslinger just as bad to do the job. Hire him and hope he won't decide to take over where the dead man left off. You know me, Jim. I like money because I never had none. The thing is, I know how far I can go. I cleaned up their town for them and haven't robbed them blind. I faced the killers and did away with the ones that wouldn't run. No help in the doing of it, just me."

"But they still don't like you?"

"That's too strong," Johnny said. "I doubt they'd hire a gun to kill me. When I was taming the town I drew top wages. But I didn't hold them up for the same wages when the town got quiet. I got them together and said I was going to work for half of what I'd been getting."

I had to smile at Johnny's gall. "What had you been getting? Four hundred a month?"

Johnny smiled too. "Five," he said. "I'm a good man. Still, I did cut back by half. All right, I didn't lose anything after I started getting my contributions from the games and the girls, other things. Even got me a sweet little horse ranch outside town. You saw that Arabian I was riding today. That's just one of my fine animals."

"How much do I get?" I asked. I knew Johnny would try to beat me on the money, but I didn't want him to get too Scotch about it.

"A minute ago you didn't want the job."

"You talked me into it," I said. "How much is my share?"

Johnny looked at me with the suspicion of a wealthy widow, a rich fat lady of 60 faced with a man half her age who had just sworn his undying love. "Your share, as you call it, ain't half. If that's what you're thinking, then my answer is no. What did you have in mind, Jim, old pardner?"

There he went again. I did some adding and subtracting in my head, estimated how much Johnny squeezed from the pimps and the gamblers, then added about a quarter more than I expected to get. I gave out the figure, adding, "If you need me as bad as you say—" I didn't say the rest.

Johnny got ready to bluff it, then changed his mind. "The fact is, I do need you to back me. Not just back me, hold down the job for me. The doc was right about the pain. I don't know how long I'm going to be able to ride this thing. I'm going to have to work into it like the doc says. So it's bed for me, for a while. The minute that happens they're going to appoint a deputy of their own. I know how these fat merchants work. They'll hire some local shithead for less than half what I'm getting. Somebody tough but dumb they think they can handle. They could even promise him the job permanent if he can run me out of town. With me in this thing"—Johnny beat on the arms of the wheelchair—"that wouldn't take much doing."

"It could be done," I agreed. "What's your offer, boss?"

We beat on the money until it took a shape we both liked. I was to get half Johnny's wages, plus 20 per-cent of his take from the girls and the gambling, ten per-cent from the whiskey business. That was slow at times, Johnny swore up and down, and I didn't believe him but I took it. Nothing would be due to me from the horse ranch because it wasn't making any money.

Johnny set up drinks to clinch the deal. "A month here will set you up just fine," he said, losing his worried look. "And the nice thing about it, you don't have to do a damn thing. About the only excitement we see here is when some cowhand or farmer gets drunk. Then you lock him up, more than one if you're lucky, and collect a fine for drunk and disorderly the next morning. Collect the fine as soon as they open their eyes. Water's free but I don't serve breakfast. No, sir, and you can stop looking at me like that. It's none of your business what I collect from the town to feed prisoners. You get your wages and that's it."

I smiled at this guardian of law and order. "I didn't say

a thing," I said.

"You didn't have to. What the hell, the fines are just small potatoes. You'll get a fair shake from me and I know you'll give me the same."

"If the money adds up right."

"That's what I meant," Johnny said. "This is the tastiest little gravy boat you ever dipped into, old pardner. Make it look good for me and I'll never forget you. Don't get too rough with the people. They're good folks, most of them. Make your rounds on time, rattle the door locks on the stores, give them the feeling of being secure. That's what I do. You're going to get fat on this job, old pardner. You got anything else you want to thrash out?"

"One small thing," I said.

Johnny looked suspicious again. "What would that be, old pardner?"

"What you just said. That old pardner business. Do me a favor and drop it."

It wasn't costing money so Johnny smiled. "Sure thing, Deputy Saddler. Which reminds me, you got to swear and so forth. Then you get a badge."

I swore to uphold the laws of this and that. "You're supposed to keep a straight face," Johnny complained as he pinned on my deputy marshal's badge.

"That's asking too much," I said.

TWO

Kate Flannery came to town during my second day on the job. After that the job was never the same.

The first day was dead as dust. The only excitement was the look on the town fathers' faces when Johnny announced that I was going to be the new deputy. He asked for a meeting of the town council, so called, so he could give them the good news, and I have to say this for them—they didn't jump for joy. Far from it. There was a lot of throat clearing and sidelong glances before a burly banker named Dougal McLandress, a man with an air of importance as big as his belly, ventured the opinion that Marshal Callahan might have asked their advice before he pinned the deputy badge on me.

"What do we know about this man?" McLandress said, and those with nerve enough backed him up. Some of the town fathers didn't seem too concerned about me, and I figured they were the ones who didn't have to part with any money to keep Johnny in race horses. Even so,

16

there was considerable opposition to the idea of making me assistant lawdog of Dragoon Wells.

Johnny, the old West Texas fox, didn't get tough about it. I knew he would if he had to; at the moment, he didn't. "I'll stake my reputation on Jim Saddler," he said. "A finer man never lived than my friend here. Jim was a big help to me in the taming of many wild towns."

"Where was that?" McLandress wanted to know.

"All over," Johnny said before he went on to tell more lies about me. "You can sleep safe in your beds with Jim Saddler watching over the town. Jim Saddler will die on his feet before he lets any harm come to you."

"What can happen here?" McLandress argued. "Why not appoint a local man? Plenty men here could use the work." That was an appeal to local sentiment and the banker got some response. Some of the town fathers muttered for a while.

Johnny waited until they got through, then he said, "You raise two good points, Mr. McLandress. What can happen here, you want to know. The answer is, you never know. As soon as word gets out that I'm laid up, it could be that certain parties could take a notion to head this way. You ever notice they don't rob banks in busy towns, Mr. McLandress. The quiet towns they go after. It could happen. Then where would your local deputy be? Most likely he'd be dead and your bank would be empty."

McLandress grunted at the wound in his wallet. "The point is, you should have told us."

"I'm telling you now," Johnny repeated. "A local man wouldn't have the know-how, is what I mean. I'm not saying Jim Saddler is the only good man in the Territory. I'm saying he's good and he's here. Jim's my new deputy, gentlemen. I wouldn't trade him no matter what."

At last, the gloves were off and Johnny was showing how hard his fist was.

McLandress hooked his thumbs in his brocaded vest and rocked back on his heels, the very picture of a man of substance. It was plain that he was the most important man in that one-horse town; not getting his way didn't suit him.

"Then you won't reconsider?" he asked pompously, making the floorboards creak with his weight.

Johnny's light blue eyes hardened just enough to back up what he told the banker and everyone there. "Nothing to consider. Deputy Saddler's already sworn in. You're going to like him fine, you'll see."

Johnny didn't laugh until they got outside. "That's how you have to handle the sons of bitches. McLandress there would like to punch a hole in my kettle, doesn't know how to do it. Which doesn't mean he won't keep trying. You're here to see he doesn't. Now you can do what you like, I'm for bed. How in hell am I going to do a woman with these things on my legs?"

"Use your head, Johnny," I suggested.

"Like the New Orleans Frenchmen do?" Johnny sounded dubious about the idea. That would be his West Texas Baptist upbringing.

"Nothing wrong with it," I said, thinking of a few sweet little fillies who liked it that way. "You don't have to be French to like it. Make a trade. You do it to her, let her do it to you."

Texas may be a big state but old Johnny, the Panhandle shitkicker, hadn't been around that much. "You ever try it that way?"

"Anything worth doing is worth trying," I said. "First time I tried it convinced me."

Just then the loose-limbed kid came into the jail and said the buggy was waiting outside.

Johnny looked surprised. "What in hell are you talking about, Calvin?"

"Doc Kline said you'd be needing it along about now," Calvin said. "You don't want it?"

Johnny turned to me grinning through his pain. "That old quack knows too much. Anything comes up, send this fool out to fetch me."

18

"That's me he's talking about," Calvin said, holding the door open so Johnny could wheel himself through.

"You're on your own, Jim," Johnny said and went out.

I felt like a fool, honest I did. There I was with a star on my chest and a town to protect. I have nothing much against lawmen, nothing for them neither. Mostly, when I can do it, I keep the hell away from them, and it makes no difference to me if they're straight or crooked. I like them best when they're like Johnny, a little of both. If the story ever got out, me being a lawman, I would have to take a lot of joshing from the hard people I know. But, hell, I could always deny it; right then I was just interested in the money.

After I got my first look at Kate Flannery, money took a back seat. I opened the jail door and there she was, a vision with red hair in a green dress, going past in a new-looking black buggy with red and gold paint work. It glittered in spite of the trail dust, and so did she. Perched on top of her head was a dark silk hat the same color as her dress. If a swan could take human form, she'd be it; she had the same lift and curve of the neck and was proud as bejesus.

It was getting on toward sundown and the sun was a glow instead of a glare. She knew she was making an entrance, as the people say, and you never saw a nicer one.

A glossy black horse was pulling the buggy, and proud to do it. The gold glow of the sun hit her eyes when she looked at me. I had a feeling they'd be green, but that wasn't all of it. Anybody can have green eyes, but these were the real green eyes of a real redhead. You see eyes like that three or four times in a lifetime and you never forget them.

Women always know their good points and, while Kate had many, her eyes were the best. They flickered over me, deciding what I was in a glance; cool, scornful, they saw all they wanted to see. The people came out to gawk at her and with every good reason: Kate was

19

something to stare at, a woman to arouse hatred and envy in women, a woman for loveless, horny men to dream about.

I was proud of myself because I was the only one there who got a glance, an indication that I existed. Most likely that was because she hadn't seen me before. The others she ignored, as she sat in the spring seat, handling the well-trained horse with a queenly air. It was quiet, with the light about to go, but I could feel the excitement. She wasn't a stranger to these people, these dead-brained town dwellers. They knew her and didn't like her and some there hated her. I thought she was wonderful; that's how I am. I'm what they call a romantic, meaning that I'd rather look at a beautiful woman than eat dinner. This one was wild for all her ladylike airs. Her wildness came out and grabbed you, shocked you like a burn—a nice shock. I liked it at the time, and for all that happened later, I went on liking it. I liked it so much it nearly got me killed.

Then she passed from sight and Dragoon Wells was dull and dead again. Dust kicked up by the carriage swirled in the sun shafts of early evening. For a while there was nothing but the smooth noise of the passing carriage; after that was gone conversation buzzed up loud like disturbed bees. Whoever this green-eyed woman was, she was of some interest in my town.

My town! I liked the sound of that, if only in my head. There was no special reason to carry a rifle on my rounds, but I did it anyway, just to let them know. Now they had me to gawk at, though I wasn't half as pretty. They were still crowding the sidewalks, still buzzing when I went by. A few nodded stiffly, others just looked.

Dragoon Wells had been Mexican before it was American, and some of the old influence lingered in the wide plaza, the old Spanish church, the few dark faces left. The barbershop was called the City Barber Shop, Amos Parkins, *Prop.* A few streets straggled off the main drag, small houses painted white, some not. Everything was closed up except the three saloons, but business wasn't booming. A few horses were hitched in front. Along the main street a few shade trees were left. The ones I saw looked sorry to be there.

I made a tour of the town with everybody watching me. I don't know what they expected to see, but that's how they are in small towns. They say it takes man biting dog to make news in the big city; in a place like Dragoon Wells, dog biting dog is pretty hot stuff. Banker McLandress was out parading with his wife and daughter. I guessed she was his daughter, though there was no resemblance to mother or father. A good thing for her too. How these two lardy, suet-faced people ever produced a raving beauty like Laurie McLandress was one of the great mysteries of the world.

Of course she wasn't introduced to me by her first name. In fact, she wouldn't have been introduced at all if I hadn't pushed it. I think it would have pleased the fat banker if there had been a doorway or a side street to turn into, but there wasn't, and when I tipped my hat he felt he had to go through with it.

McLandress had a fat man's way of puffing out his words, as if he could never get enough breath. That gave him an abrupt manner of speaking that was just right for his natural bad temperedness.

"This is my wife and daughter, Mr. Saddler," he said. "Out for our before-Sunday-supper walk, as you can see."

I could see the daughter, all I wanted to see. Dragoon Wells wasn't such a dead town after all—two beautiful women inside of ten minutes. Not that Kate Flannery and Laurie McLandress had much in common, on the outside. Well no, I take that back. They looked different, but they had a lot in common. All beautiful women do, and I don't mean their looks, though everything else spins off from there. Laurie was dark haired and black eyed. Her eyes were not Spanish eyes, not black soulful eyes, but bright and clear, maybe a little hard. Her face was heart shaped and there was a sly, some would say mean, turn to her mouth. Her voice surprised me. It was Southern whereas her parents sounded like Yankees. It wasn't until later that I learned she had just come back from a finishing school in Charleston.

"And how do you like our fair city, Mr. Saddler?" she asked. Like her mouth, everything she said had a mean, humorous twist to it, and in a woman less beautiful, it would have been hard to take. But I'm a fool for beautiful women, and they can do just about anything to me except kill me.

"I like it fine, Miss McLandress," I said, wondering what she would be like in bed, then deciding that she need not be anything but there. I wanted to find out about the redhead in the buggy, but Laurie or her parents were not the people to ask.

She gave me the information anyway. "The town isn't usually this lively on Sunday evening," she said, smiling. "Did you get to see the reason?"

"Laurie!" old McLandress chided. "It's got nothing to do with us. Besides—"

"Oh fudge!" Laurie said, making "fudge" sound like something else. "The deputy is a man, isn't he? Did you see her, Deputy?"

"Would that be a lady in a shiny black buggy?"

"Well yes," he said, turning on her wicked smile again. "The *woman* in the buggy. How did you like her?"

In proportion, Mrs. McLandress was just as bulky as her husband, and a real stuffed shirtwaist. "Really, Laurie," she said. "I'm sure what the Flannery girl does is none of the deputy's concern. Isn't that right, Mr. Saddler?"

"Just as long as she doesn't break any laws," I said sternly.

Mrs. McLandress scolded Laurie for laughing in public. "There's nothing to laugh about," she said.

Laurie's bell-like laugh dwindled down to a smile. "You're wrong, Mama. I think what the deputy said is

very funny, and I think the deputy knows it's funny.
Don't you, Deputy?"

"Nothing is funny where the law is concerned, Miss
McLandress," I said as sanctimoniously as before.

That earned me a curt nod of approval from the
banker, more giggling from the daughter. "Marshal
Callahan is funny and doesn't know it. Mr. Saddler is
funny and won't admit it," Laurie said. "I like you better
than Marshal Callahan, Mr. Saddler."

All this was said in that apple pan dowdy voice that
seems made for pretty women with brains who don't
want to let on how smart they are. This one was bright
and catty, but with her looks and that husky voice I
forgave her everything, even for a few things that hadn't
happened yet. I had a feeling they would.

Laurie was whisked away to Sunday supper before she
had a chance to say anything else. I guessed she was all of
19, a full-grown woman where I was raised. Out in my
part of the country they are having their third kid at that
age. The man who got Laurie McLandress was in for soft
nights and hard days, for she had the look of a woman
who would drive a man hard, in or out of bed. She might
kill him young but he'd know he'd been alive. I wondered what she was doing in Dragoon Wells. From where
I stood she looked like a rose on a dunghill, as out of
place as she could get. I hoped she wasn't just home for a
visit. Of course there was always the redhead to think
about. Like they say, variety is the spice—and I was
feeling spicy as a stallion.

I finished my rounds without seeing any more pretty
women. Sure I saw women, but if you put pants on them
they could have been men. The West is hard on women,
and I'm not faulting them for having lantern jaws and
skin like cured cowhide. I know that many a good heart
beats behind a bony chest; usually I don't get to look that
far.

Johnny had asked me to look in on the poker games at
the Dorado Saloon, and that's what I did. Two middling-

stakes games were going, not bad for a Sunday night in the middle of nowhere. As soon as I pushed open the door a small, city-looking man wearing a candy-striped shirt with rosette armbands reached across the bar and insisted on pumping my hand. I guessed he was the owner and he said he was.

"Floyd Casey's my name," he said while he still had my hand. "A shame what happened to Johnny the Gent ain't it." He didn't sound too broken up about it.

"Terrible," I said.

Casey threw me a quick, foxy look which turned out to be the only look he had. "A few things maybe we can talk about. I mean later when you get settled," he began cautiously.

"I know what you mean," I said, giving nothing away. I knew what he meant. Johnny's partner in the girl and whiskey and gambling business was feeling me out for a double cross. Right then, that was as far as it got.

Casey reached under the bar and brought out his private bottle and set out drinks. That bourbon was so smooth it would have cured a sore throat. We had another one and Casey said, "You see a good-looking redhead in a buggy just now?"

"Kate Flannery?" I said.

"Not Carrie Nation," Casey said. "You get a good look at her? Sure you did. Ain't she something now. Wait till Johnny the Gent hears she's back in town. Of course forget you ain't from these parts and don't know a thing about it. I'm giving away no secrets when I say that Johnny used to be stuck real hard on Kate. Something went on between them, I don't know what. Before she had a big row with her father and run off, there was bad feeling between her and Johnny. Least they didn't talk but there was a time when they was thick as sour milk. Never did get to know who did the breaking off, her or Johnny. It'd be worth a man's life to ask him. Johnny's good natured enough, not about that gal though. I wonder what in hell she's doing back here. Always said not to me, she'd wash dirty shirts before she ever came back to Dragoon Wells."

"How long has she been away?" I asked, thinking I might as well get Casey's version of it. There were bound to be others. I got the feeling that this Kate Flannery, so beautiful and by all reports so ornery, was going to be trouble. Don't ask me how I knew because I didn't. It was just a feeling, but I've learned to trust my hunches in some things. Besides, I know women pretty good. I've known my share of them.

"The best part of two years," Casey said. "She was gone before anybody knew it. It came out though. One of the Flannery boys got drunk in town, unusual enough, they never come to town more than they have to. Later the talk was she'd hooked up with Peyton Ballard down in Mexico."

Now there was a name to wake up a conversation. "You mean the outlaw?" I asked, knowing there couldn't be two Peyton Ballards. Twenty years before, Peyton Ballard had been the most wanted Confederate guerrilla in the Southwest. All through the war he plundered and killed, waving the Stars and Bars all the time he was doing it. When Grant said the Confederates could take their side arms and go home he didn't include Peyton Ballard. Ulysses S. made it a personal order: catch Peyton Ballard and hang him on the spot.

"Some folks don't see him as an outlaw," Casey said, pouring whiskey. "The Secesh crowd think of him as a hard man in a hard time. But not a bandit. There's some that tried to get him a pardon so he can come back from Sonora."

Sonora was only a few days' ride from where we were. I said, "That where he is, the bloody-handed bastard?"

Casey pushed the bottle to me. "That's where he is, best I know. Makes no difference to me where he is, what he done. I'm in the saloon business, I keep out of wars. They tell me he stayed on in the Territory for a few years after the war. Rallied a bunch of die-hard Rebs, swore they'd never surrender. They swore they'd fight the bluebellies but most of the fighting was done in banks and stage robberies. Finally the army made it so hot for him he dodged on south and stayed there. Was rich when he left, is richer now."

"You think there's something to the story about the Flannery girl?"

"Could be," Casey said. "Here's how the story was told to me. Kate was traveling with some well-heeled Mexican who died or got killed someplace in Sonora. So she was stranded in some town and that's where Ballard found her. Maybe it was in Durango. That name comes to me. It's a big cowtown, so it figures Ballard would be there. He's a big rancher now, what I hear. More than a rancher, has horse herds and sells mounts to the Mex army. Mines, land, and such. Is a close friend of important politicians, both sides of the border. They say he'd still like to come back."

Casey stopped talking and looked at me, blowing a silent whistle as he did. "You're thinking the same thing, ain't you?"

"Maybe," I said, looking down at the badge on my chest. All of a sudden it wasn't a joke anymore. "Ballard has the name of holding on to what he thinks belongs to him. No need to get worked up about it, I guess. Likely enough it's just another wild story."

But the foxy little saloonkeeper wasn't fooled by my offhand manner. Grinning hard, he said, "That's what it is, just a story. Nothing is ever going to happen in this town."

He didn't believe it, and neither did I.

THREE

The smell of a woman's body can get me hard before you can count to ten. I opened the door of the jail and there it was in the darkness, faint but unmistakable, and it hadn't been there when I went out. It came fresh and clean through the cigar and bourbon smells. But I brought my gun out because a woman can kill as quickly as a man. I stepped in and away from the door, then Laurie McLandress said in that husky Southern voice, "Why don't you lock the door before you light the lamp. I already shut the shutters."

I touched the wick with a match and yellow light flared up. Laurie was behind the desk looking beautiful with a whiskey glass in her hand. I put the rifle in the rack.

Laurie said, "I haven't broken any laws and I haven't come to confess. Aren't you going to ask me why I did come?" She slid the bottle across the desk.

"You'll tell me when you get around to it," I said. Suddenly, I was as relaxed as she was. This was just a little sparring to be gone through. You ever see the way

27

pigeons mate? I guess everybody has. The female minces about with bitty steps while the male puffs out his chest and circles her, still pecking away but getting closer all the time. Pigeons know what they're doing, and so did we. However, this was a young lady of refinement, so I didn't just unbutton my pants. But that's where she was looking, unbuttoned or not. I didn't want to stand there bulging, so I sat down on the customer's side of my own desk.

"My father would kill me if he found me here," she informed me, not sounding too worried about it. It was hard to think of fat-assed McLandress killing anybody, but I knew he'd talk a lot. McLandress was the kind that couldn't say good morning without sounding indignant about it.

"Then we won't tell him," I said.

"Tell me about yourself," Laurie said casually, going at the whiskey again, drinking like a veteran. "If you don't mind, that is. I like to know something about a man before I get . . . confidential . . . with him. I have an idea what you're like. Why don't you tell me more?"

I told her what I was. That didn't mean that she wouldn't come back and say that I'd deceived her. Women do what they feel like doing. You have to be ready for it, as ready as you can. You're never ready enough.

I didn't make a book out of the telling and she liked that. Naturally I didn't tell her everything, just the good parts. "See, I was right," she said. "You're a wild, reckless man. You could be mean to a woman, but she'd have to provoke you. How would you like to be provoked?"

I stood up and she came around the desk to meet me. "I'd like it," I said. As I reached for her, she said, "We'll talk later, all right."

Anything she did was jake with me. I just didn't want her to leave. I didn't ask myself why she was there. It was enough that she was, soft and willing, and what else she

28

was could wait till later. What she did next hadn't been
learned in that Charleston finishing school. Her hand
went down to my crotch and she said, "Ah yes!" when
she touched it. Then she unbuttoned me while my hands
squeezed her rounded young ass. She took my cock out
and rubbed it gently while I unbuttoned the back of her
dress. It fell to the floor and she kicked it to one side. She
had come prepared: she was naked under the dress. I
stood there with my cock between her legs, running my
hands over her, and she said, "It would be ever so much
nicer lying down, don't you think?"

I picked her up and kneed open the door to the back
room and carried her in. It was a small room with a bed,
and I wondered if Kate Flannery had been there with
Johnny. I put her down on the soft quilt, and she pulled
me down after her. Now, she couldn't get me into her
fast enough; and she pulled my hands away and took
charge of my cock, guiding it in straight and true. She
was wet and I went in all the way, and her spine arched
with pleasure. I knew she wanted more than this; at the
moment it was enough. She came almost immediately
and that was just the salad.

Light from the office seeped into the room, and I could
see the sweet, sweaty shine of her soft young body. Her
polished black hair came loose and tumbled about her
shoulders, and her face was very young. But there was
nothing maidenly about what she did to me, or maybe
there was. It wasn't her first time and I was glad about
that. Virgins don't excite me the way they do other men.
She came three times before she whispered, "Please let
me feel you coming. Fill me up with your hot, sweet
juice." She gave little yelps of delight when I drove into
her and shot my load; she would have clapped her hands
if they hadn't been digging into my thighs.

We lay there, my weight on top of her slender body.
She begged me not to take my cock out of her, but to
leave it in her warm wetness where it would get hard
again in a little while. I was only too glad to leave it

29

where it was. Now and then she would contract her muscles down there and give it a squeeze that sent shivers up and down my spine. I groaned a little every time she did it and that pleased her because she knew how much pleasure she was giving. But she wasn't like some young girls who keep asking, "Is it good? Is it good? Am I doing it right?" She didn't have to ask anything because she knew it was good and she was doing it exactly right. I wasn't ready to go yet, but it was nice to lie like that.

Now it was her turn to moan as I sucked her soft yet firm breasts, sweet as cherries. "Oh Jesus!" she called out. "You're driving me crazy—but don't stop. Make me come, Saddler. Make me flow. I want it to pour out of me. I want you to think your cock is sliding in a bath of warm honey." She giggled at the thought. She was as horny as all get-out, but she was also young and full of mischief.

I was hard enough to start pumping again, so I pumped and sucked at the same time, while my hands kneaded her girlish ass. She locked her slender legs around the small of my back and ground her crotch into mine. I fucked her steadily, not brutally but steadily, drawing my shaft almost all the way out, then driving it to the hilt. The juice poured out of her until her pussy was sopping wet. A good sex smell was everywhere in the room, exciting both of us almost as much as the fucking itself, and it did feel like I was driving my shaft into a tight little tunnel lubricated with warm honey.

It was the best kind of what they call a honey-fuck—the kind where you're fucking somebody you really like and not some faceless whore you'll never see again. It was so damn good with her and could only get better. She hadn't sucked my cock yet, and I hadn't tongued her, but it was early and there was plenty of time for that. I kept on pumping, wanting to get the most out of it, wanting her to have the same intense pleasure. She took my face in both hands and held it, staring and smiling at the same time, as if she really wanted to see who was doing this to her.

She kissed me and put her tongue in my mouth. Doing that topped everything off, and she came and came and came, mumbling with her tongue still in my mouth. She had been wet before, but now the warm juice flowed out of her hot cunt and down her thighs. Now it was slippery between her legs and it couldn't have been better. There's nothing wrong with lust, and my cock got bigger, the wetter she got. Again she whispered that she wanted me to come and I needed no encouragement. I came until it seemed I could come no more. I felt drained and relaxed. This time I pulled out of her and we lay side by side. She closed her eyes and squeezed her legs together and sighed.

"I do that in bed at night," she said softly. "You won't think I'm bad if I tell you sometimes I get so excited I have to use my finger to make myself come?"

"Why should I think that makes you bad?"

"I just thought it might. My mother does and has warned me against it. I know she looks at my sheets for evidence of wetness. But I fooled her. Since she got suspicious, I've been putting a towel under me so I won't stain the sheets when I come. You know how wet I get."

"I do."

"You don't mind that?"

"Course not. It shows you've been having a good time."

"I like the way you say that: been having a good time. It sounds so nice and natural, as if there's nothing sinful about it."

"Sinful? That's foolish talk," I told her.

Laurie said, "You don't know my parents. Everything is sinful to them. Most dances are sinful. Most books are sinful. I once asked Daddy—he eats an awful lot—what about gluttony and he got mad. They've got sin on the brain."

"They must have done something to get you."

Holding onto my shaft, Laurie giggled. "I'll bet Daddy felt it was his duty. Do it, get it over with, but don't enjoy it. I'll bet they fucked with their nightgowns on. That's the kind they are. I love them, but they don't enjoy life. If they could only see me now."

"I'd just as soon they didn't." I was glad the iron-banded jail door was locked and barred. There would be no way to deal with old McLandress if he managed to break in.

"Don't worry about that," Laurie said. "They think I'm all tucked in for the night. Safe in my chaste little bed. Mother always warns me to say my prayers before I go to sleep. Well, you know what I think of that. Prick not prayer is what I think of before I close my eyes. The first time I saw you I knew you had a big one. I dreamt about you when I took my nap. Do you ever dream about pussy?"

"Sometimes I do," I said honestly. "It makes for sweeter dreams."

Laurie turned to look at me. "Do you ever come when you're having one of those dreams?"

Jesus! Such a conversation! "Not since I was a kid. Most kids have wet dreams. You stop having them when you get older and real life women are available."

Laurie giggled again. "I'm available," she said, and stretched out and took my cock in her mouth. She had a small tender mouth and my throbbing cock filled it completely. I don't know where a young girl like that learned to suck cocks so expertly. Maybe it came naturally to her. She sucked and used her tongue at the same time. I came and she swallowed it.

There was no awkwardness after it was over, as happens when strangers get to it without much love talk. Laurie sat up in the bed, groping in it for hairpins, while I fetched drinks.

"It was just fine," she said with hairpins in her mouth. I waited with the drink until she finished pinning back her hair. She smelled of clean sweat and soap and toilet water, and when I kissed her she smelled of bourbon. She told me that she had been born in Vermont, that the family came to Arizona because of her brother Tad's bad chest. Arizona hadn't helped Tad, and he had died. Old McLandress had been a banker in Vermont, and he followed the same trade in the Southwest. He was richer than people thought he was, Laurie said. Even if he lost half his money he'd still be rolling in green.

"I love my Papa and everything, but he's too strict," Laurie said. "That's why he sent me to that school in Charleston. Would you believe it, we're Scotch Presbyterians and he sent me to a school run by *nuns!* Next thing to a convent. I had to go to school with a lot of rich *Catholics!*"

"That's terrible," I agreed.

Laurie stroked me as if we'd been doing this for a long time. "Don't make fun," she said. "It was awful. The only fun I had was when I went over the wall after lights out. There was another girl and we'd go in the city—there are places, you know. Would you believe, a very, very handsome French teacher lost his position because of me. His apparatus was rather small. So he was not all that exciting. But you are. You are very exciting, yes you are. What's the use of living if you can't have fun. You think I'm terrible, don't you?"

I said not a bit of it.

"Well, I am glad to hear that," Laurie went on. "My father doesn't believe in a person having fun. We're not put on this earth to have fun, he says. My God! Now he's mad because I don't want to get married. You should see some of the men that come around, or he brings around. Oh I grant you some of them are pretty rich and one isn't bad looking. But you know, I'll be rich too when my father dies, but I just know the stuffy old dear will live practically forever. I keep saying to myself, if only you had your inheritance *now!*"

Sweet Jesus Christ! I was in bed with a girl who wanted to murder her old man! I asked her about it. She laughed

33

so hard the bed shook, and she pushed and tugged at me until I nearly fell on the floor. "You're crazy!" she laughed. "I wouldn't do *that!* You must think . . . oh, I don't believe it. No, no, I'm just talking about money."

"Sure you are," I said.

"The thing is, if I had my inheritance instead of having to wait for it, everything would be wonderful. Those men, I wouldn't even have to think about marrying one of them. It wouldn't even be dishonest, the money is mine anyway. It's in my father's will, the old darling. I saw it, he showed it to me. His entire estate is to be divided equally between my mother and me. Of course I'm going to need help."

"To do what?"

"Take the money out of the bank and get away with it. My father has more cash than he needs to cover it. So no one has to know. I'll just leave a note explaining everything. And I won't be greedy. I don't want more than I'm legally entitled to. My share will take care of your share. I have keys to everything."

My glass was empty so I drank from hers. "If it's that easy, why do you need me?"

"Silly! Of course I need you. You think I'd feel safe going away with all that money? A woman alone in this god-awful country. I'd be nervous, but you're not nervous. We could go away together I don't know where. You pick a place. What about Mexico City or Havana? The nice thing, we'd have the money and we'd have us."

"You forget I'm a lawman," I said, and we both laughed and hung all over each other. Sex may be the best fun you can have without laughing, but we were laughing too. She was crazy as a coot and she was close to being rich. Rich and one of the finest women that ever rumpled a bed.

"I'll have to think about it," I said.

"Oh shit!" Laurie said. "If you're worrying about Callahan, he'll be all right. He's like you, he gets along. I'm serious about this. I want to get away from here and

34

the only way is to have plenty of money. Don't think about Callahan, think about us. This is just the first time. It'll be better the next time and the next and—"

"I still have to think it over. I gave my word."

Laurie pulled away from me. "Don't take too long. You can't give me away because nobody would believe you. I had to say that. I like you *très* much, Saddler. I wish I didn't have to leave. I'll think about you in bed. I will, all night, I will. I may have to pleasure myself to ease the tension."

"Why not," I said.

FOUR

I *was sitting in the rocker on the jail porch and wonder-*ing how much loyalty I owed Johnny Callahan when three men rode in behind a skinny man driving a buckboard. There was something about the four of them that made me forget all about removing Laurie McLandress's inheritance from the bank.

The skinny gent in the rig touched his derby hat as he drove by, and I acknowledged it in a manner befitting a dedicated young lawman. There was something familiar about this mannerly gent, but it didn't strike me who he was until he tossed the reins to one of his companions and climbed down stiffly in front of the hotel. Earl Danziger, that's who he was, and a bigger conniver never drew breath. Everybody called him Earl, friends and enemies, and he had plenty of both. At some point a newspaper wag had written that Earl Danziger talked out of the four sides of his mouth. That about summed him up. Danziger wasn't just a politician, Danziger was anything that paid money. Danziger didn't steal with a

36

gun. He didn't have to. By itself his mouth was a deadly weapon, and it sure was a big one. I knew Danziger because he was from Texas, all over Texas, and maybe he'd even been born there.

At one time, every tree in Texas seemed to have a campaign picture of Earl Danziger nailed to it. Every tree, every barn, every railroad depot, stage station and ferry crossing had its picture of oily Earl. He got to be a state senator but got stuck there, and when there was a railroad scandal, instead of running for cover, Earl ran for governor. Brash was one of the less offensive words often used to describe the Poor Man's Friend, as he liked to be called. Most of the other names are too dirty to repeat. Earl was a briber, a go-between, a toady of the railroad moguls until he got caught with his hand in the honey bucket. He had two cracks at the governship and almost made it the second time around. If all it took was bribery, then Earl should have been Governor of Texas. Not so oddly, the voters liked him even while they were turning him down for the highest office in the state. Earl was a showman, a snake oil salesman who always provided good entertainment. When he failed to get elected he ran his own candidates and had some success. Then he made a fatal mistake, he elected an honest man who turned on him, denouncing him as a crook and a double-dyed villain. It got so hot in Austin that old Earl decided that maybe it was time to move on. Now he was here and he had company, the kind of company I don't like.

Whatever it was, Danziger's business must have been fairly important because ten minutes hadn't passed before he came out of the hotel, climbed in the buckboard, and took the road heading north with the three hardcases trailing behind. On the way out he doffed his hat to McLandress, standing on the sidewalk outside the bank. I went over to the hotel to make sure I wasn't mistaken. I wasn't. There was his name in a big round scrawl, showy as the man himself.

The clerk seemed to know who he was and that surprised me. "Where you been, Deputy?" the clerk said, appalled by my ignorance. "Mr. Danziger is just one of the biggest men in the Territory. Business, politics, everything. Told me to call him Earl right off. That's the kind of man he is, plain as an old shoe. Now I wonder what he's doing here. Some big deal, most likely."

"Where was he headed in such a hurry?" I asked, hoping I wouldn't get an answer I wouldn't like.

I got it after I persuaded the clerk, still shaken by his brush with the great man, that it was all right to tell an officer of the law.

"He asked me how to get to the Flannery place," the clerk said. "I thought that was kind of unusual but these big men never explain things. Never explain, never apologize, that's how these rich men get rich."

"That's all he said?"

"Mr. Danziger didn't say that. I didn't say he said it. I said he asked where the Flannery place was." The clerk smirked, the only way he could get back at me for asking questions. "Why don't you ask him yourself. That's not to say you'll get an answer. And don't ask me when he'll be coming back. Mr. Danziger didn't take me into his confidence."

I didn't have to ask where the Flannery place was located because I already knew. I had been asking about Kate Flannery in a careful way. I wanted to know what there was to know about her. So far all I knew, apart from Casey's gossip, was that she came from a big family of the wildest Irish rednecks in Arizona. Nobody in town had a good word for them, though I couldn't pin down what it was they had done. They kept to themselves, made no attempt to be neighborly, took no part in the life of the town. They bought nothing they couldn't make or raise on their own land: lumber, whiskey, iron work, bullets, preserved goods. They had fenced their land with barbwire hung with TRESPASSERS WILL BE SHOT signs. And that's where Earl Danziger, the man who never risked his own skin, was going. I thought I knew why, but there was nothing to do but wait.

I went to a four-stool eating place down the street run by a gabby old geezer with a stiff leg. While he was frying up some ham and eggs, I sounded him out on the Flannerys. It was hard to get him interested; all he wanted to do was gab about Earl Danziger and what he was doing in Dragoon Wells. For some reason he didn't like Danziger. I didn't ask him the reason.

"The Flannerys, they're half wild, nobody's got any use for them," the old gent said, turning the ham, then setting out a plate and hardware for me. "Old Con Flannery come here from Ireland about thirty years ago, maybe a bit more. Him and his five brothers was in the War, the Union side. Not a one of them got killed though I guess they was in plenty of battles. They got mustered out down South and drifted out here through Texas."

"How did they get so much land? They tell me it runs clear back into the hills."

The old man slid the ham and eggs onto my plate and pulled the coffee pot off the stove. "How did they get it? They took it, that's how they got it. During the war the country here went to wrack and ruin owing to the Apaches. A lot of folks just moved on. Some that went to war never come back. Old Con and his five hardcase brothers started putting a big place together out of the small spreads. I got to be fair to the man. He bought some of the land, but mostly he took. Took and hung on like a Boston Bull. Them Irish is a fierce bunch of wild men, afraid of nothing. Whipped the Apaches till they was afraid to show their dirty face in these parts. I guess the Flannerys did that. Be a liar to say they didn't."

The eggs were fried too hard but I was hungry after my night with Laurie. "Then what do people have against them? So far nobody I've talked to has accused them of anything but being independent."

"Well, that's it—independent," the old man said. "They're too god-blasted independent. It's like the rest

39

of us was just a bunch of trash. Who the hell are they to be so independent, a gang of half-wild potato-eating clodhoppers that probably didn't have a pair of boots till they went in the army. You think one of them'd walk in here and order a good meal like you just done? Not a chance. Don't spend a cent more than they can help. It's not like they's poor anymore, far from it."

"How many of them are there?" I figured that Danziger and his hardcases couldn't be far from the Flannery barbwire by now. "You make it sound like there's a separate nation out there."

"Too many for my money," the old man complained. "I don't know how many. Damned if they know themselves. Con and the four brothers all got married, had any number of sons and daughters, a powerful lot of sons. The sons are mostly growed and some of them has sons. If you're asking how many men out there can shoot a gun I would say probably twenty, give or take a few."

When that was out of the way I still had to wait. So I went back to the jail and cleaned guns that didn't need cleaning. The kid Calvin was cleaning the place and got in my way until I told him it was clean enough. He didn't like that and I told him he could dust and sweep twice as hard when Johnny got back. I whiled away the time by reading old wanted posters. A few faces were dead and I put them in the stove. Not much else happened.

Two hours later I suffered a disappointment when I heard Danziger and his boys coming back. I'd been hoping that Con Flannery and his Irishmen had dropped them in their tracks. When I got to the door I saw one of the hard cases was missing. So was Danziger's hat. They didn't come in as jaunty as they went out. It was a reasonable assumption that the missing man was dead. It was none of my business what he was; beyond the town limits killing was the county sheriff's concern.

I wondered if Danziger would come to me. Maybe he would. I did nothing but set a chair where I could watch the hotel through the window. Two boys from the livery stable came to take away the buckboard and the horses. The town dragged on through another dull day.

I was down to the stub of my second cigar when there was shouting down the street. It was trouble, the real start of the trouble. I went outside and a farmer with a chin beard was driving a wagon with a saddle horse tied to the tailgate. I went down to see what the farmer was hauling. I had a good idea what it was. The farmer halted the wagon in front of the jail and there was a dead man in the back of it. Danziger's missing gunman.

"Got something for you, Deputy," the farmer said in the unemotional way of farmers. "Found this man dragging from a stirrup a long way out. Dead as a nail before I found him. You'd be wanting to claim the body, I'd say. The dragging didn't kill him."

The farmer was right. There was a small hole in his forehead that must have killed him instantly. Then the horse spooked and dragged him.

"Never seen him before," the farmer said. "You know who he is?"

"Where did you find him?" I asked. "Was it out by the Flannery place?"

The farmer looked scared, no longer eager to be a part of it. "I didn't say the Flannerys had anything to do with this. Don't you go saying I did."

"Calm down, granger," I said. "You said on the road. The road is a public place. I'm just asking was it out by the Flannery place?"

"Close enough," he said cautiously. "Not too far from the main gate. Will you be wanting me for anything else? My name is Eben Linkhorn, everybody knows me."

I dragged the dead man out by the ankles and dumped him in the street and rolled him on his face. The back of his head was blown away. The farmer turned his team and drove off, and I dragged the body up on the porch and covered it with a blanket from the cells. People crowded around asking questions, but all the excitement wasn't enough to bring Danziger and his boys out of the

41

hotel. While I was tucking in the dead man, I took a gander at the hotel door. The only one in it was the clerk.

Calvin showed up and I asked him if the town had an undertaker. "Not anymore," he said. "The lumber man buries them now."

"Go fetch him," I said. "Tell him to take this thing out of here. No burying till I say so. The county sheriff may want to hold an inquest. Get it straight, Calvin, no funeral just yet."

The boy bobbed his head and hurried away and I went over to the hotel. No one was in the lobby except the clerk. "What's going on, Deputy? That dead man was with Mr. Danziger this morning. You here to tell Mr. Danziger? He's in the Governor's Suite. Second floor, end of the hall."

I found the door and knocked on it. One of the hard cases opened it a few inches and grunted. I took that to be a question. The hard case had one hand on his gun. Cigar smoke seeped out through the crack in the door.

"I want to see Danziger," I said.

The hard case didn't budge. I guess he thought he had to act tough in front of his boss, or maybe he needed the practice. Hard cases are better actors than actors.

"We call him *Mister* Danziger. What do you want?" Inside I heard the creak of someone getting on or off a bed.

You get tired of hard cases who try to look and dress the part. The real badmen don't have to bother. One of the deadliest killers I ever knew was a man in his fifties who looked like a mining engineer.

"My name is Saddler, I'm the law," I said. "Open the door or you'll be wearing it in a minute."

Then Danziger's voice called out from inside, "Open up, Lattigo. There's no call for any of that."

I went in and Danziger was stretched out on the bed, a long thin cigar tilting skyward from his loose, liver-colored lips. The other hard case was over by the window, hand on gun, looking my way. Bottles and glasses were in a polished wood box that hinged down in front, and when closed it could be carried by a handle. It was a big room with other rooms running off it. It was fancy but faded, and it looked like the governor hadn't been there lately.

Danziger had taken off his elastic sided shoes and was resting his feet on a pillow. When he held up his glass, the hard case by the window came over and filled it. Danziger watched me from the bed. "Something I can do for you, Deputy?"

"You're missing a man," I said.

"Thanks for telling me. You got anything else to tell me, seeing you're here."

Danziger had the hambone politician's flapping mouth. He didn't seem to listen to everything he said. I know that sounds funny, but maybe if you've been in so many of the same situations you just use the words you've used before. His words straggled out as if he found it hard to keep his mind on the proceedings. Everything he said had a tired tone, sort of sneering. I could see why the voters had shied away from him. The voters may be dumb, but they do show occasional good sense.

Danziger smiled encouragement. "I know you have something else to tell me. What is it?"

"Your man was brought in dead, a farmer found him shot," I said. "I sent the body over to the undertaker's. Will you be paying for the funeral, or will it go on the county?"

Danziger sipped his whiskey. "That's shocking news," he said. "Poor Andy. Of course, you know, I wasn't all that well acquainted with him. How about you boys? By the way, Deputy, I'd like you to meet Billy Rice and Harry Lattigo."

I knew that Billy Rice was a Texas gunman with a bad name in Brownsville and other places. I would have figured him to be older, but maybe he started young. He must have because he wasn't 30 yet. He was the one who poured Danziger's whiskey. He was dark haired and pale faced and wore dark clothes. He carried a short-barreled Sheriff's Model Colt .45 in a stiff holster. I think he was closer to his boss than the other gunman, a runt with mad-dog gray eyes and a down-home accent.

Rice nodded and Lattigo didn't do anything but stare. He hadn't forgiven me for our little chat at the door. Rice would be faster, that was pretty plain, which is not to say that Lattigo wasn't fast himself. But if it came to shooting, Rice would have to be shot first.

"How did it happen?" I asked Danziger.

He faked surprise. "You tell me, Deputy. Harmon, that's the dead man, decided he wanted to take a look at the country. We came on back and here we are. Who do you suppose could have shot him?"

"How about the Flannerys?"

"Never heard of them," Danziger said. "You boys ever hear that name?"

Rice and Lattigo said no. "I don't know what to tell you," Danziger said. "My guess is poor Harmon was done in by road agents, something like that."

"Don't take it so hard," I said.

"I said I was deeply shocked, that'll have to do," Danziger said.

"Maybe it will."

"Hey, Deputy," Lattigo cut in. "You're coming down kind of heavy for what you are. That's Mr. Earl Danziger you're talking to."

"I know who he is."

"Wait a minute, hold on there!" Danziger said without getting off the bed. He finished off the whiskey and handed the glass to Rice. "What's eating on you, Deputy? You come in here with a chip as big as a railroad tie and start throwing your weight around. You got something against my men? Against me? If we've met before I don't recall it. Did I do you some wrong? You asked questions and you got answers. You don't like the answers, should I make up new ones? We don't know

44

these Flannerys. All right, Harmon wandered off and got shot. Are you hinting we killed him? I think not, sir. You're the law—go catch Harmon's killer."

"Somebody stole your hat, maybe I can catch him at the same time." I thought that would get under his thick skin. It did.

Danziger swung his legs off the bed and sat up. Rice gave him a fresh cigar and a light. "Don't push it too hard, Deputy," Danziger warned, clouding up the room. "You have a lot to learn in the way of politeness, so why don't you save the tough talk for the Saturday night drunks. I'm a plain man, get along with everybody, try best I can. If somebody bothers me I tell them what I'm telling you: don't crowd me. I make a good friend and a bad enemy. Think about it, my friend."

Danziger lay down again and put his hands behind his head, the cigar tilted in his flabby mouth. Eyes closed as if he couldn't bear to see any more of the world's foolishness, he drawled out, "Harry, do a tired old man a favor. Go downstairs and find me something to eat. Then stop by the church and say a prayer for Harmon."

They were laughing when I left.

FIVE

Calvin was watching them load the dead man into a spring wagon when I got back to the jail. He wanted to know if he should dash out to Johnny's ranch to tell him about the killing and the strangers in town.

"You like the marshal, don't you?" I asked him.

"You bet," he said proudly. "Me and the marshal has been working together since my folks died four years ago. We get along good."

"Then stay away from him just now," I said. "He's got to let those legs heal up and that won't happen if he starts bumping about in that wheelchair. If something real bad happens, I'll tell you to go. Watch the jail till I get back. I'm going out to the Flannery place."

That shook him up. "Gosh!" he said.

It took about two hours to get to the start of their property, a swing gate in a barbwire fence that ran away into the distance on both sides. It was true what Casey said: they owned a powerful sight of land. It went all the way back to distant hills. On the gate was one of the

46

TRESPASSERS WILL BE SHOT signs, but nobody shot at me as I opened it. I guess the sign and their reputation for pugnacity were enough. My rights as a lawman ended the instant I crossed the town line; then I was just another trespasser. Even so, I hoped the badge would have some meaning to them. It was too bad they weren't nice law-abiding Germans instead of wild Irishmen. In this matter of shooting trespassers, the law was on their side. Good sense told me to turn back. I ignored my own advice and went ahead.

A good road started at the gate and went straight back through trees and a scatter of low hills. I got to the hills and through them without getting any extra holes in me. Past the hills was a wide, well-grassed valley with the silver slash of a small river in the middle of it. I don't know how many cows were down there—maybe 3,000 —and I figured that was just part of the herd. It was hot and quiet in the long valley, with no sign of a house until the road tipped up and went down again into another wide stretch of country. Then I saw a big sprawl of houses and buildings far off on the other side of a big pond that had been made by damming a creek. From where I was it looked like a town instead of a ranch. Smoke spiraled up into the hard blue sky and the screech of a sawmill was carried by the hot wind. In the sunlight the houses and buildings were a glaring white.

I started down the hill, a rifle cracked and somebody far away rang a bell. The bell went on ringing like a church calling the godly to prayer on Sunday morning. You couldn't have counted to 45 before men on horses, a lot of men and horses, were heading my way. I kept on going until a big-caliber rifle splintered rock in the road a few feet in front of me.

I expected them to come whooping but they rode in silence, all carrying rifles. Others, alerted by the bell, still clanging, rode in from both sides of the road. It was too late to run. If I did I'd be lifted out of the saddle by bullets. They got to me and some galloped past, heading for the main gate, as if to repel an invasion. They seemed to have a plan worked out in case of an attack.

The big man with the shaggy gray hair had to be Con Flannery. Cornelius Flannery, to give him his full name, had three inches and 50 pounds on me, a great brute of a man, straight backed for his age, somewhere in his late fifties. Three of the other men had the same height and powerful build, the same wide, sun-seamed faces. In town the people called Flannery "Old Con"; there was nothing old about him except his age. He sat atop a big claybank as lithe as an Indian and the good-looking Creedmore Sharps was small in his huge, work-hardened hands.

"Take his guns," Flannery ordered in a sandpapery voice that still had some Irish left in it. A younger version of the old man snatched my Winchester from the boot and got my beltgun. Every man there was mounted well, no nags for this mean-spirited bunch.

"You must be a fool," Flannery said. "It's a good thing for you you came in straight and in broad day. That's not to say you're going to ride out as cool as you came in. Mister, can I ask you a question? What do you think those signs are for?"

"I'm not trespassing," I said. "I came here to see Con Flannery. Is that you?"

"That's who I am. We're all Flannerys here, no strangers. You're a stranger. I don't know what you want, don't want to know. I don't talk to people less I have to do, and, Mister, I don't have to talk to you. Now turn that horse and get out before you get shot."

The young Flannery who took my guns had been looking me over. "Shoot him anyway, Con. He's up to something. This is Callahan's new saddletramp."

"Be off now," Con Flannery said to me. "You see how it is. The boys will ride with you. You must be lucky. You hear what I just said."

"I still want to talk to you."

"You don't listen, do you?"

"It's as important to you as it is to me."

"Nothing that you have to say is important to me, *Saddler*."

Word got around fast. They knew I worked for Johnny and they knew my name. "A man got killed this morning but that's not why I'm here, Mr. Flannery. If you shot a trespasser that's your business."

"Sure," Flannery said. "It's legal. I don't need you to tell me that. One more time I'll tell you—get out."

I said no and the Creedmore came up and pointed at me. It's a dandy, that Creedmore Sharps. Even going in, a bullet from a Creedmore makes a big hole. When it goes out it takes your spine with it. Flannery was right, I was a fool.

"Come along then," Flannery said at last. "It's bad luck to kill an idiot. That's what you are, Saddler. You had your chance and didn't take it. If I don't like what you have to say, it'll go hard on you."

"Fair enough," I said.

"Don't be so agreeable," Flannery growled. "You won't like it a bit."

The road ran straight down to the pond and around it to the other side. Cows grazed on the good grass, fat and slow moving. Far back were hills, beyond that mountains. Reeds grew along the side of the pond and cows stood knee-deep in the shore muck drinking water. For a while I couldn't see the main ranch because of the windbreak of trees. Then we were through the trees and I was looking at the best spread I'd seen for many a day. The big house was long and low with a Texas breezeway in the middle. Horses moved about in a long corral; a water tower and a red barn stood back from the house. In the distance there were other houses and barns. Flowers grew in beds in front of the house and under a shade tree, heavy and green, a swing creaked in the wind.

I got down and they took my horse and Flannery pointed me into the house. A trim gray-haired woman of Flannery's age looked at me from the breezeway before she went away. I didn't see Kate Flannery, but the door of the barn was open and the shiny black buggy was inside. Flannery didn't miss the look I gave it.

Inside, the main room of the house was long, dark and cool after the sun. It was sensible rather than fancy, no grand piano, no oil paintings, things favored by some ranchers who got rich. The floor was scrubbed white, bleached by strong soap, and sanded with fine white sand. Over the high stone fireplace hung an old regimental flag and the Stars and Stripes, a heavy saber in the old cavalry style, and a Navy Colt. Solid wood-and-leather chairs lined a dark dining room table on both sides. We sat at the table and Flannery said, "Get on with it."

I never saw a man more disinclined to help the law of the land. Con Flannery had a way of making everything he said sound final, like Moses setting the Israelites straight on this and that. That seemed to work with his kin, and they obeyed him without question, but I wasn't sure how far it would go with Earl Danziger and, the real threat, Peyton Ballard. It got very quiet in the big room.

"I know I'm not the law in the county," I said. He didn't comment on that. "But I'm the law in Dragoon Wells and that's where Danziger and his two gunmen are. This morning Danziger rode out this way with three men, came back with two. The third was brought in dead by a farmer."

"Make your point," Flannery said, looking at the reflection of his hands in the polished tabletop.

"I think Danziger came out here to say something you didn't like. Maybe he figured he could talk tough because he had the three gunslingers to back his play. He was wrong. You told him where to go and one of the hard-cases got shot when he reached. You could have killed all of them, but you let them go. Maybe that was a mistake, letting them go."

Flannery kept his hands still. "That a fact now?" he said. "It could have happened that way. This Danziger, what would he be wanting with me? You better answer that the politest way you know how. I do mean that."

I knew I could kill Flannery if he got mad enough to pull a gun on me. Then I could kill a few more Flannerys before they cut me down. There was no doubt about what the outcome of the fight would be. I'd be dead.

"Your daughter came back here last night," I said. Flannery's eyes didn't budge from mine. "I saw her myself on her way through town. I was told her name. It's hard to say what I have to say next, Mr. Flannery."

Flannery's voice was quiet, almost mild. "I'll decide how hard to take it, Saddler. What about my daughter?"

For an instant, I heard the rustle of silk in one of the dark doorways that led off the main room, and I knew she was there, listening. I don't know if Flannery heard it.

"They say your daughter is married to a man named Peyton Ballard, a rancher in Sonora."

Flannery found some grim humor in my delicate attempt not to hurt his feelings and get myself killed. "You can describe him better than that. Say he's a butcher and a renegade who's been trying to act like a gentleman. That's what he is, for all his money and influence."

Anyway, he hadn't denied it, so I guess the story was true. I said, "The way I see it, Danziger came here to persuade your daughter to go back to her husband. Ballard can't come himself or they'd hang him. So he sent Danziger as the go-between. Danziger brought along the three gunmen to give him confidence. One of them got shot, the rest ran. They looked like they'd been running when they got back to town."

"You tell a good story," Flannery said. "But you still haven't made your point, if there is a point. Is there?"

"Did it happen the way I just said, Mr. Flannery?" I asked. "Did Danziger come here to try to take your daughter?"

"If he did come, what has it got to do with you?"

"Meaning I'm not county law."

51

"The law's got nothing to do with it, county or not."

"If there's killing, the law has to get into it, Mr. Flannery."

What I said didn't bother him. "Any trouble comes up can be handled by us. That means me. You saw my brothers and the rest of our people just now. You think they're the kind to get scared because a few saloon thugs come here with their tied-down guns. We don't tie our guns down, Deputy, we shoot them. Another thing, you didn't see all of us. There's a few more up in the hills."

I had to admit that the Flannerys looked formidable enough. They could handle a lot more than Danziger and his two gunmen. But how much was a lot? Using Ballard's money, Danziger could buy all the gunmen he needed, more than he needed. This wasn't far from the border—what if Ballard decided to come himself? Word was that he had his politician friends scheming to get him a pardon, the only reason why he was trying to get his woman back the easy way. He could kiss the pardon goodbye if he came north of the border with his Sonora pistoleros. That was where the real threat lay, not in Danziger and his American gunmen. But they'd be bad enough, if they came in force, and I felt sure they would come, if something wasn't done about it. So far only one man had died; if the gunmen came, bodies would be falling like autumn leaves. Even so, Ballard was the man on my mind. Down where he was he could recruit the most dangerous men in the world, Mexican pistoleros. Men so mean, so empty of human feeling, that they'd kill a child for a dollar and a drink. They prowled the border country like wolves, half starved in their dirty though fancy clothes, their only trade murder for hire, and Peyton Ballard had the money to pay them all.

"You're thinking we can't take care of ourselves," Flannery said, staring hard at my expressionless face. "This talk is all just suppose. I'm not saying I have a daughter, I'm not saying she's here."

"You were in the war," I said. "What was the real

reason the Union beat the Rebs?"

"More men. Ah now, is that what you're thinking? You think they'd go to that much trouble?"

"Ballard's done worse in his time. Time doesn't change a man. Often he gets meaner than he was. If Danziger fails here, then Ballard will come. He'll weigh the pardon against the rest of it and decide the hell with it. You won't be able to handle him, Mr. Flannery. That's my answer. The town won't be able to handle him."

"Who in hell cares about the town?"

"I don't much, still they're people. What you need is help. I'd like to help any way I can."

I meant what I said, but the Irishman wasn't buying my wares. He raised his hand to stop me from saying anything more. "You've been telling me about Danziger, nothing I didn't know. The man's a public disgrace. Ballard doesn't need any explaining to me. I was a grown man before you were born, Saddler, so what Ballard was and is isn't news to me. But what about you? What do I know about you? Yesterday you weren't here and now you are. It's said that Callahan will vouch for you. That cuts no ice with me, more than the other way round. It could be that you didn't come to Dragoon Wells by chance."

"That's how it happened," I said, understanding his suspicion. A lot of people were suspicious about the way I came there.

"Nobody's calling you a liar, but you see my side of it. You could be working for Ballard yourself. You got here last night, Danziger got here this morning. All that could be more than a coincidence."

"Where does Callahan fit into this? Did Ballard send word to get his legs broken so I could take over?" I knew I had him there.

His smile had all the warmth of a judge's heart. "Maybe Callahan didn't plan to break his legs. That doesn't mean he didn't know you were coming. Maybe you and Callahan are part of it, maybe just you. I've got no reason to trust you, Saddler."

"What do you think I'm doing in Dragoon Wells?"

"For one thing, you're talking to me, something Danziger didn't get to do. You could be here to tell me what a bad man Peyton Ballard is so I won't get in his way. Answer me a question. When were you ever a lawman?"

Lying wouldn't get me anywhere with this hard-eyed man. "Never," I said. "This is my first time. That's not to say I won't do what I'm paid for."

"You have the look of a drifter," Flannery went on. "Nothing wrong with that by itself. I figure you for a gambler, a poker player. You play hard to win but you know how to lose. You lost here."

"What makes you say that, Mr. Flannery?"

"You bluffed your way in here, but a bluff can be called. I'm calling you, Saddler. Find yourself another game. This game is private, a family party you got no part in. Makes no difference to me if you're looking out for yourself or for Ballard. Here we are and here we stay. If Ballard comes here, here he'll be buried. That plain enough for you? You might tell that to Danziger so he can pass it along."

"I think he knows it by now."

"Pass along something else while you're at it," Flannery said. "A small bit of history. When me and my brothers came here there was nothing. During the war this was Secesh country, still is, a lot of it. We'd been good loyal soldiers but that didn't put meat on the table. We were Union men and Irish bogtrotters too, and that made us less welcome than we were. If the people had been friendly we'd have paid them in kind. They weren't friendly—anything but. What you probably didn't hear is they tried to run us out and that, my friend, was a terrible mistake. We don't own a blade of grass we didn't work for. Now we're rich—fools hate that word—so we don't have to be friendly. Leave us be, is all we ask. We fought whites and Indians and beat them and we'll do

54

the same for Ballard's greasers."

Once again I heard the rustle of the silk dress in the darkened hallway. I wondered what she thought of all this. There had been a big row with the old man before she ran off and married Ballard. It wouldn't be hard to quarrel with Con Flannery. There are some men who just know that God has given them the right to tell people what to do. Con Flannery was one of them, as bullheaded a man as ever roared out an order.

"It won't be any kind of fair fight. Your people may fight like wildcats, but there aren't enough of them," I said. "And from what I hear, you can't expect much help from the county sheriff. Don't you have any friends at all that will back you? You can't stand up to them by yourself."

Flannery looked around the big solid house and seemed to get reassurance. "My family are my friends, all I need. We'll make do, we always have. Everything in life is a gamble and so is this. You'd best go along now. Don't come back here—ever!"

"You mean I don't get shot?"

"Don't come back, I said. You may be all right, Saddler, but it's still none of your business. If you came out of real concern I appreciate it. But I'll say it again—don't come back."

I had an escort all the way to the gate.

SIX

When I got back to Dragoon Wells it was getting dark, and not being Saturday night, it was quiet. The brightest light was in Casey's saloon; the saloon was quiet like the town. The old geezer who ran the restaurant was closing up, but he unbolted the door when he saw me.

"Treat the customers right and they come back," he said. He thought opening for me entitled him to questions. I turned the questions aside and told him to fry up a big steak and charge it to Callahan.

"No offense, you better pay me. Callahan won't," he said.

I put money on the counter and asked how things had been going. There was no need to say what things because the whole town was still buzzing with talk of Kate Flannery having something to do with the dead man. It was suppertime for the town and I wondered what Laurie was doing. I knew I wouldn't throw her out of bed if she came over later after the town blew out the lights.

The door of the restaurant was closed and bolted; the place was empty except for us, yet the old man lowered his voice and looked around before he spoke. "One of them sidekicks of Danziger come over here to get food about the time you left. You'd think he was in some city, the way he bitched about my cooking. I guess they ate it all right. Later he come over for more."

The steak wasn't bad and I was hungry. "Then they stayed in the hotel?"

"One man didn't, he rode out about an hour after you left. Took the road he came in on, in a terrible hurry. Where do you suppose he went to?"

I knew as much as he did, which was nothing. After I finished the steak I went over to the hotel and got upstairs without waking the clerk. I think that man needed to get a lot of sleep. Lattigo opened the door and was as glad to see me as the first time. But there was no tough talk, and I was glad of that. It hadn't been such a good day and I was ready to break his teeth with my gun barrel.

"Deputy's here again," he said over his shoulder. Danziger told him to let me in. He sounded a bit drunk.

"What's it this time?" he asked looking at his hat. I guess he was thinking the hole in the hat could have been in his head.

I spun the hat onto the bed and it landed by his feet. "You forgot that when you were out to the Flannery place."

Danziger nudged the hat onto the floor, saying, "That can't be my hat, Deputy, got a hole in it." He laughed but Lattigo didn't.

The window was closed though it was a warm evening and the room stank of cigar smoke. Nothing had changed except that Danziger was more droopy eyed than usual. Still on the bed, a glass in his hand, he didn't look as casual as he sounded. His crinkly ginger hair was mussed and he combed it back with his fingers. Then he fixed his blue ribbon tie.

"But thanks for thinking of me," he said. "Hope you didn't go to much trouble getting it. By the way, how about a drink? We got off on the wrong foot this morning."

I'll say this for Danziger. He drank good whiskey. All his other good points escaped me. The slack-mouth son of a bitch pointed to his glass and Lattigo filled it. I got a full one too.

"To your good health, sir," Danziger toasted me.

"Mrs. Ballard sends her regards," I said, knocking back the whiskey.

"Hey, wait a minute, slow down there," Danziger said, putting his bare feet on the floor. "Don't just drink and run, Deputy. And don't tell me my whiskey isn't good—it's the best." I knew he was talking to give himself time to think. "What was that woman's name you just said?"

"Kate Flannery Ballard," I said. "Red hair, green eyes, nice figure."

"Yeah," Danziger said appreciatively though he was surely past the age when he could do anything active to a woman. If old Earl got a bone on he would need a lot of help. But there was fond remembrance in his drawling voice.

He looked up at me, still grinning. "You a friend of Kate?"

"From way back."

"You're a liar," Danziger said mildly, still grinning. "You may know what she looks like; that's all you know. Can't say I blame you for wanting to claim her friendship. You can't know her, Deputy. You haven't been in town much longer than we have. Fess up now."

"I like what I saw of her," I said.

Danziger watched me carefully, trying to size me up. He was a big noise in the Territory but he had corns and bunions like any old man. "That kind of talk could get you in trouble if it got back to the wrong man," he said. "Why don't you just forget about Kate. Be smart, do that."

The bluff was working, but I still didn't know where I was going. "I'd find that hard to do. I ha e a soft spot for ladies in distress, any kind of trouble. Apart from personal feelings, it's part of my job to look out for the taxpayers."

Danziger sidetracked for a while. He tried to sound casual, even friendly, but I knew his crooked brain was working hard to figure out what I wanted. I figured he would try the soft talk first, then rush in with the threats if that didn't work. He pulled his rubbery lips back in what he hoped would pass for a smile.

"This isn't much of a job you got here, is it?" he remarked, man to man, not offensive.

"I like the town and the pay isn't bad," I said. Out at the ranch Kate would be having supper or fighting with her father. I hoped she'd appreciate what I was trying to do for her, whatever it was.

"So you say," Danziger said. "But I hear it's just temporary till the marshal is walking again. You'll be looking for other work when he is. How'd you like to come to work for me?"

"Doing what?"

"What any man does that works for another man: what he's told. That's what Harry and Billy do. Job pays just fine, not that much to do. People don't bother me too much after I explain things to them. Harry and Billy back up my explanations. You could get used to it, Deputy."

I grinned at Lattigo. "I don't like to go about scaring the people. Besides, some of the little old ladies are pretty tough."

"Later for you," Lattigo said, his eyes measuring me for a coffin.

"You got enough nerve, that's for sure," Danziger said, smacking his lips over the whiskey. He must have been born poor, the way he enjoyed things so hard. "There's plenty of things you can do. Maybe it's just as well you don't work with Lattigo. You could get along with Rice,

59

never Lattigo. I'd be short a man in no time."

"It wouldn't be me," Lattigo said.

"Hush up," Danziger said. "These days I hang out in Tucson, a nice coming little city. Climate couldn't be better, not too much disorganized crookery. I could fix you up with a job as one of the territorial attorney's deputies. Pay's good because it's a political job. Not to mention the travel money and the fees. A smart man like you could advance himself in no time. How do you feel about that?"

"I'm thinking," I said.

Danziger studied the sticky end of his cigar. "It's not like you'd have to work. Only a fool works when he doesn't have to. That's the sweet thing about this job, no work. Yes sir, I'd say you'd make a fine territorial deputy."

I helped myself to more whiskey, and Danziger took that as a good sign. "Drink up, plenty more. How's Callahan?"

"Getting along good," I said. "You don't know him?"

"I know of him," Danziger said. "Like the rest of the people I thought he was dead. Then I heard he just lost his nerve, the reason he stayed on here."

Maybe Danziger was right about Johnny. I'd been wondering why he'd bury himself in a backwater like Dragoon Wells. It seemed to me that he had talked too much about the soft life of a small town lawman, all the money he was making, as if he wanted to convince himself more than he wanted to convince me. Or it could be that Danziger was hinting that I couldn't depend on Johnny, if it came to a showdown. It wasn't much of a threat. Johnny would be in bed, in a wheelchair or on crutches for a month or six weeks.

"Maybe I should be talking to Callahan instead of you," Danziger said. "Seeing as you just work for the man."

"I'm the boss right now," I said. "You better go on talking to me."

"Callahan could fire you, isn't that a fact?"

"He could. That doesn't say I'd go."

Danziger laughed a wheezy laugh, trying to get it out of his bony chest. "Damnedest lawman I ever saw. The town hires Callahan to tame the bullies, then when it's done he won't give back the badge. Now Callahan hires you and you say you won't go if you're fired. A lawless lawman, that's what you are."

So he wouldn't miss the point, I said, "I won't let the law get in the way of what I want to do."

"Which is?"

"Look out for the Flannery girl."

"I thought we were talking about your new job in Tucson. Suddenly we're back to what's none of your business."

"It's hard to stay away from it."

Danziger sighed, a grand strategist bothered by a lance corporal. "All right then, there it is. You know who Peyton Ballard is? All right, you do, who doesn't? I want to establish that fact." Danziger was like a lawyer laying a foundation, as they say. I guess he was some kind of lawyer. "It's important that you realize the sort of a man Peyton Ballard is. Don't talk, listen. On the face of it, it's a simple thing that happens every day and doesn't call for much talk. Mr. and Mrs. Ballard had a disagreement, a fight, and she lit out from home. Now she's back where she started only a lot richer than when she left. She didn't just take her personal things but a satchelful of gold pieces, Mexican Double Eagles, folding money, American, and a mess of jewelry. How much in all? More than fifty thousand, could be closer to sixty. The money is just part of it, but it is a big part of it. Ballard wants his wife back and he wants her with the money. To him it's one and the same thing."

"And she doesn't want to go," I said.

"That's what she thinks," Danziger said. "Being a woman, she doesn't know her own mind. Sir, she left a veritable paradise to come back here. In Sonora she lived

61

in a hacienda so close to a castle it didn't make any difference. Servants to wait on her hand and foot. The finest clothes. . . ."

Danziger talked on, enjoying his own windy statements. I was thinking about Peyton Ballard. As Danziger said, everybody knew who he was, hero or villain, depending on which side you favored in the Civil War. Even so, there were plenty of good old Rebels who despised him for what he was, what he had done. It wasn't the bank robbing and train wrecking that bothered them so much. For a time, right after the war, that sort of thing had been a national sport, like this new baseball. Ballard might have had his crimes forgiven if he hadn't burned out a townful of peaceful Germans in South Texas.

The men had fought for the Union and were back working their farms when Ballard and his Reb diehards swooped down on them in the dark, burning the town, shooting every man over the age of 14. That, at last, was the lump that couldn't be digested. It lay like lead in the belly, and it wouldn't come up or pass out the other end. Ballard knew what he had done, and knowing it, he got worse, and in the doing of it, he got rich. It took a cavalry campaign to drive him out.

"That's it in a nutshell," Danziger was saying. "Ballard wants his wife and his money, and he won't take no."

"Maybe he should come himself," I said. "Of course they'd hang him if he did. It'll take more than money to get him a pardon for killing those Germans."

"You're talking crazy, Deputy. What you're repeating is a pack of rotten lies. Sure Ballard did some wild things in his time. I'll bet you did a few. But he had nothing to do with murdering those squareheads. Fact is he's posted a standing reward of twenty thousand dollars for the apprehension of the real killers. He's not that far from catching them either. If you knew the money he's spent on detective agencies. As near as we can make out those squareheads were killed by Mexican bandits from across the river."

Danziger was getting worked up by his own words. He shook his head, saddened by the idea that people actually thought Peyton Ballard, landowner and friend of politicians, was an outlaw. "You don't think for a minute I'd be helping Peyton if any of this was true. For God's sake! Mark my words, Deputy, one of these days Peyton is going to prove his innocence."

I was watching Lattigo, not sure that he wouldn't make a try for me. Gunmen wouldn't be gunmen if they weren't a little crazy.

"That's interesting," I said. "But what happens if she keeps saying no? There's no law that says she can't leave her husband. She's not a Mormon or a slave."

Danziger considered that. "There's a law against stealing," he said. "What she took didn't belong to her. A husband's property doesn't belong to his wife and that, Deputy, is also the law. Peyton has papers to prove he owns everything she stole."

"Why doesn't he come here and make a charge against her, send her to the penitentiary? You know the answer to that as well as I do."

"I have another answer for it. You ever hear of something called extradition?"

"From here to Mexico? That doesn't sound too likely."

"Still, it could be done if one of Peyton's friends got as far as the Mexican president. President Diaz is a good friend of Uncle Sam. A lot of American capital is invested down there. Diaz could do some squeezing, as a favor. What's one woman when you're looking at big money?"

That was a new twist, one that might work. "Ballard would go that far? He'd end up owing a lot of favors, if he did. He'd have to spend more than fifty thousand to get the Mexicans to dance for him."

"You keep on missing the point no matter how hard I

prod you," Danziger said impatiently. "Forget about money, Peyton wants his wife back and he means to get her. I can't make that clear enough. Personally, I can't make that clear enough. The world's full of honey-fuck women with pretty faces and all you need is money to get them. No matter, it so happens that Peyton Ballard wants this one. I tell you she must be something for him to want her so bad. That's why I'm here, Deputy, to see that he gets her. Hell, it's not such a big thing, is it? Once she's back she'll see the sense of it."

"You're missing *my* point—she doesn't want to go."

"Oh Lord," Danziger said. "You keep saying that and I'm getting sick of it. She's going back, that's all there is to it. The reason I'm here is Peyton figured I could talk sense into her. If I do say so, I am known to have some powers of persuasion. Persuade, that's the word, not force. I'd hate for it to come to that."

It was time to say it, then see what happened. "That's the only way you're going to get her," I said. "You're right, I don't know her. But you're not getting her."

For once, Danziger wasn't faking his puzzlement. "I don't get it, Deputy," he said slowly, trying to be honest, which was very hard for him. "I could see it if she'd promised herself to you, if you'd stuck it in that sweet juicy crotch of hers. You haven't though, nor are you likely to. I hardly know her but I know this. You may have a big dingus on you, but it takes more than that to get Kate Flannery interested. I hear she likes a big cock, but even bigger money is what she wants. Hell, you may not even have a big enough pizzle—so why? I'd really like to know your reasoning."

Wearied by this gust of honesty, Danziger lay back on the heaped-up pillows and waited for my answer.

I said, "You're most of the reason, Danziger. Not all of it. I don't like the way you do things, with your bag of money and your gunslingers. If you don't like it you know what you can do about it." In a way, I hoped he would try to finish me, then and there. If Rice had been there I might not have been so eager. But I knew I could stop Lattigo with one shot, then do for old Earl with the next one. No doubt that wouldn't be the finish of it. Even so, Ballard might have trouble finding another go-between as slippery as Danziger.

"You'll get yours," Danziger said. "Not here though." I could tell he was nervous, knew what I was thinking.

I gave him more to think about. Why not, I was an enemy now. "If the girl wants to stay I'll see that she does. Try me and see how bad I can be. You may start the trouble here, but I'll finish it. You think because you have money and guns you can walk in here and take a woman who doesn't want to be taken. About getting her extradited to Mexico, you can try that too. You're a lawyer, you want to see what real law looks like."

Before Lattigo could blink I had the Colt out and pointing at Danziger's face. Lattigo blinked, so did Danziger. "This is the only law I care about, the only law you're going to see if you touch that girl. I'll kill you and I'll kill Ballard too, if he comes."

Danziger turned sullen, no more folksy smiles. "He will if he has to, Deputy. The door's always open should you change your mind. After it's shut, there's no way you can get in."

I holstered the Colt, still wanting to kill them. It came hard not to. It would clean up so much shit. When I think back on what happened later, it was too bad I didn't just go ahead and do it. Backing out of there, the last thing I heard from Danziger was, "No way you can win, Deputy. You don't have one chance in this world."

Maybe he was right.

SEVEN

I lay on the bed with my boots off and thought about Dougal McLandress's bad little girl. She was something to think about, that one. So saucy and clever, with a body just aching for cock. The thought of going off to Mexico City with her would cause me no pain. It wouldn't last but what the hell! Nothing lasts. But while it lasted, what a time we'd have. I've been in fine hotels in my time. I don't always sleep in jails or on the ground with a saddle for a pillow. A few weeks with Laurie McLandress would set me up for the hard life that is our lot. You bet it would.

I could see us in a swank hotel in the Avenida, that big wide boulevard in the center of the city, all flowers and palm trees, and mornings we could have breakfast with the French windows open, with the sounds and smells of the city coming through. In a hotel like that, the more money you pay, the bigger the beds. If I did it, if I went with her, we were going to need a big bed. Maybe we'd stay in bed for a week and have waiters come up with

66

thick steaks and cold champagne. Oysters on a bed of ice. Roast duck. Cold duck. But for me, the main course would always be Laurie.

If she dragged me to theatres, maybe I'd go. Maybe I'd even leave my beltgun at home. I'd buy something with a short barrel to carry in my coat pocket. A hotel like that would have big roomy bathtubs, and we'd get in there together, roll around in the sudsy water and do all sorts of exercise. She was 19 and she knew what she got it for. Oh Lord, did she ever!

I was good and horny when there was a light tap on the door. It was after midnight and the town had gone to bed. The tap came again as I was pulling on my boots. I went to the hinged peephole with a gun in my hand and saw a boy in a big hat looking up and down the street. I couldn't see the face under the hat. But when I opened the door it wasn't a boy—it was Kate Flannery!

Her eyes were emerald in the lamplight, clear and shining. Her red hair had been tucked up under the hat; some of it had come loose. I must have gaped because she kicked the door shut with her heel and locked it before I got a chance to say anything. She wore dark blue wool pants and a leather vest over a red shirt. She should have worn a green shirt to go with her eyes. It wasn't the time or place to tell her. Saying nothing, she went straight to Callahan's desk, opened the deep drawer and took out whiskey and glasses. When I saw the second glass I knew I'd been invited to whatever it was. In my own jail.

"I want to talk to you, Saddler!" she said in a hard ringing voice. There was no Charleston finishing school in this voice. It wasn't a country voice, but a voice of her own. Maybe there was a little Irish in it, though not what you'd call soft and sentimental.

"I'm here," I said. This one would have to be put in her place. That was the first thought I had the first time I saw her in the buggy. It would take some doing. I was ready to try.

She took her whiskey and walked around with it. I sat

down and let her walk off her impatience, her anger. At the door, she spun around and stared hard at me. "What kind of man are you, Saddler? Will you help me or not?"

"Help you how? I went to see your father. He said you didn't need any help."

She downed her whiskey and refilled the glass. This was the second hard-drinking woman I'd met in Dragoon Wells. "I know you came to my father's place," she said. "I heard everything you said. You knew I heard. It's true what you said. My father doesn't know what Peyton is like. You think you do?"

"I think I do. But you know him better. Sit down and don't be so tough. It doesn't suit you."

Getting a grip on her impatience, she sat down, and the rough range clothes didn't take away a thing from her. She was taller than Laurie, but wasn't much older. There was more of her to take hold of than there was with Laurie. It was six of one, half a dozen of the other. Both women were fine with me.

"I didn't mean to sound like that," she said. "I don't want to go back to Peyton, not now, not ever. Danziger is here to bring me back. My brother killed one of Danziger's men. Because of that my father, all of them, think they can stop Peyton when he comes."

"Then you have no doubt that he'll come. You'd know better than anybody."

"There's no doubt. Peyton will come after me and he'll bring an army. You've got to do something, Saddler. I listened to you while you talked to my father. He caught something of what you are. I caught more than he did."

"What am I, Miss Flannery?" I asked.

"A gunman, a gambler, but not the usual. I think you're a very hard man, Saddler, a resourceful man. You haven't spent your life in towns like this. You know how things are done."

"Like how to stop Ballard's pistoleros?" Laurie had offered me money, but this one kept a tight purse. There

68

was no mention of the long green. I hoped that what was between her legs was just as tight. "That could get me killed, Miss Flannery."

"You can stop that polite shit, Saddler, you've been fucking me with your eyes since I walked in here. You call me Kate. I'll call you Saddler. Jim doesn't suit you."

"I'll see if I can get it changed."

"Listen, you have to help me. How bad is Callahan? Callahan would help me for old times sake."

I said no. Callahan couldn't help her unless she rode away with him in the wheelchair.

"Then it has to be you, maybe it's better that it's you," Kate said, making everything sound final, just like her father. "Callahan isn't so bad, but he doesn't have your hardness."

I don't think she meant anything by saying I was hard. But I was getting hard in another way. The thought of the money Danziger said she'd taken from Ballard crossed my mind.

Instead of money, she offered herself. I was ready to take that, for openers. The money could wait until I was ready to bring it up. "I'll do what I can," I said.

"I hope I can repay you," she said. Now that kind of talk would sound perfectly natural coming from Laurie; from Kate it had a false ring, like a lead coin. She sensed that I was grinning at her and she looked up. "You can go fuck yourself, Saddler. Don't say it. You'd rather fuck me. All right, you can. I'm not good, I'm the best. You don't believe me?"

I made the Indian peace sign. "Enough of these questions and answers at the same time. It's like there's three people in here. You and your best friend and me. Yeah, I'd like to fuck you. I mean that sincerely . . . Kate."

"You'd be a fool if you didn't," Kate said, and we grinned our foxy grins. "It's a deal: do things for me and I'll do things for you. You'll like everything I do to you.

69

You think I'm forward, don't you?"

"Gosh no," I said. "However did you get an idea like that?"

She came up close. She had something in her hair that smelled good. "I'll show you how."

And she did. We went into Callahan's back room and into his bed. All thought of Ballard faded away as she let me take off her clothes. I like it when they don't help. I had to stoop to peel off her boy's pants, and when I got them open she gripped my head and pulled my face into her. Mom's Apple Pie! Sweet, tasty, warm! I wanted that as much as she did and she moaned as I found the right place. Her hands gripped my hair so hard that it hurt. It felt good. I widened her legs so I could get at her, give her everything, and her whole body shook as she came with quick contractions of her cunt muscles. I couldn't stand it any longer, I had to get into her. We tumbled into bed together and now it was her turn to pleasure me. I lay on my back with my bone up rock hard and throbbing, and she got on her knees between my legs and smiled at me over the top of it.

She knew how to tease, but she was enjoying it as much as I was. She licked her lips and then me. Then she took in the top and worked on that. I just about exploded when she did that, but she knew how to keep me from letting go. Compared to Kate, Laurie was just a novice with a lot to learn. Every time I was ready to let go she tightened her mouth until I was ready to beg. Then suddenly she climbed on top of me and put it inside her. We rolled over and I began to whack it into her.

There was something about her that made me want to be master. I sought to hold her down on her back and she fought me, wanting it and fighting it at the same time. We fought on, enjoying every minute of it, and I beat her. I was right about the hard doing of it, and when it was over at last and we lay together, emptied of lust and energy, she whispered, "You're a son of a bitch! No man ever did that to me!" But she smiled and asked me to get her a

70

drink of water, then a drink of whiskey. She drank the water first.

It was quiet in the back room of the jail, with no sound but the night wind whistling. I felt sorry for Peyton Ballard. He had to be missing what I just got. I wanted more and knew I was going to get it.

"I guess you wonder why I'm so horny," she said.

"I don't wonder about it. I guess you're horny because you're a horny woman." If she could be brash, then so could I. Laurie talked about sex with a kind of horny innocence. Kate was different; there was nothing innocent about anything she said.

She didn't like my remark and raised her hand to slap my face. I caught her wrist before she could do it. Red spots burned in her cheeks, and her green eyes snapped at me. "You're a fine one to talk, you big hot-cocked bastard. You're the kind that's horny all the time. You look like you'd fuck your grandmother."

I let go her wrist. "No slapping, you hear. You slap me and I'll slap you, only harder. And let's not get nasty about my grandmother. It's not ladylike."

That stopped her. No woman, not even the toughest whore, wants to be thought of as less than a lady. "All right," she said. "Just don't be calling me a horny woman."

I didn't remind her that she started it. I didn't want to fight with her. I wanted to fuck her till dawn. After a long silence she began to stroke my shaft, the old up and down friction, until it was standing again. Then she examined it as if she'd never seen a cock before.

"My but you respond so quickly. I'll bet that big thing of yours has been in a lot of women."

"That's what it's for."

"How many would you say? Make a guess in case you don't keep score."

I lay back like an oriental potentate and she stroked me faster. It certainly was a pleasure to lay back and take my ease while she did all the work.

71

"I would say about a hundred," I answered after pretending to think about it. "Maybe a shade over a hundred. But a hundred I'm sure of."

She was really beating my meat now, so hard that it was beginning to hurt. I don't know why she was mad about my 100 women. The count was probably right because I've fucked every kind of woman from good-looking paroled husband killers to Nob Hill society ladies and enjoyed every one of them. Kate could hardly have had that many cocks stuck in her, but it had to be a fair number.

"My but aren't we modest?" she said, her voice heavy with sarcasm. "And did they all tell you how wonderful you were?"

"Some did, some didn't. I don't look for praise."

"Stout fella," she said, a phrase she must have picked up from some English dude. "Well, I'm going to make you come all over yourself." She stroked me harder.

I reached down to stop her. "Ease up now. I can do that for myself. Turn over. I'm going to take you from behind. Put it right through your legs and into your hotbox. I'm tired and when I am I like a cushion."

She didn't protest when I turned her over, shoved it between her thighs and straight in where I wanted to go. I like it like that. You have the woman's ass under you and it *is* like a cushion. In an instant her anger was forgotten and her ass began to move under me. It squirmed as if it were alive. I wondered if old Peyton Ballard the bandit had ever done her like that. She tried to raise up when she came, but I held her firm for my own come. She shuddered under me. I thought she was going to cry, not from sadness but from crazy, wild happiness. Old Ballard, down in Sonora, knew what he was missing. No wonder he was breaking his balls to get her back. I didn't know if he loved her. Probably he did. Loved and hated her. Love and hate would go hand in hand with this dangerous woman. I don't mean she was murderous, just dangerous. A man who didn't watch himself with her would find himself in terrible trouble. But I have a weakness for dangerous, difficult women. All I ask is that they be beautiful and willing. She was both, but she was trying to trick me. To put it plain, I wanted some of the money she took from Ballard. I was like Laurie. I wasn't greedy. I didn't want anything more than half. I was taking a bigger risk than she was. After all, I'd lose more than my pride. The worst that could happen to her would be a speedy return to the ever-loving arms of her outlaw husband. But forget about everything but the money. I wanted some.

I started off with, "I could bring in guns of my own if I had some money. Nobody here is going to back me for what Callahan can pay, what I can pay. Even if I could find them the town wouldn't give me a cent. With money to show I could send a fast message to some hardcases I know in El Paso. They could get here fast before Danziger runs out of ideas."

Kate snuggled up to me. "I wish I had some. It's too bad I don't."

"What about your father? They say he's got plenty of green."

Kate's hand moved over me. "He won't give it to me. He thinks he can handle my husband. I'm afraid there's no money."

It was time to get to it. "I thought you might have some," I said, stroking her too. "It would help if you had."

Kate sighed and felt the outlines of my face. "You aren't handsome, but you'll do," she said, adding, "What makes you think I'd have money?"

"You might have saved some from the housekeeping money," I said. "A little here and there. It adds up."

Kate said, "Peyton has plenty of money, but he never gave me any. Oh, he'd buy me anything I wanted. All I had to do was ask, not even ask sometimes. But money —no. He knew I'd run away if he gave me money."

I said quietly, "Is that why you stole so much?"

I got a slap in the face for that, but it was more a token than a real slap. She felt she had to do it to show how outraged she was. "You son of a bitch!" she raged pretty convincingly. "I never stole a cent from that man."

"I shouldn't have said steal."

"It doesn't matter what you call it. I didn't steal anything. I left Mexico with nothing but the clothes on my back. A buggy, a horse and my clothes. Nothing else."

"Not even a few pieces of jewelry?"

She knew that I knew a woman would take jewelry before anything else. Maybe even before cash. "Well, yes, I did take a few pieces, but they belonged to me," she admitted, pausing to see how I took it. Then she went on. "They won't bring much. Jewelers have you at their mercy when you go to them to sell jewels. What I've told you is the truth, Saddler."

It was hard to think of this woman being at anyone's mercy. The role didn't fit her, like a 50-year-old actress playing a schoolgirl. "A little bird told me you got more than a few jewels, darlin'. Money and gold. Mexican Doubles, a whole lot of them, this little bird said."

"Go fuck yourself," Kate said. "You and your little bird! You've been listening to dirty rumors like the rest of them. My God! if I had money and gold, would I be here?"

"You might," I said. "Here you have some protection. On the move, Ballard would have detective agencies after you. They'd find you—a good chance of it—and then he'd find you. I think that's why you're staying on in Dragoon Wells."

"I don't like the way you're talking. It sounds as if you aren't going to help me. I thought you were better than that, Saddler."

That wasn't so bad. At least she hadn't accused me of tricking her into bed. "Look, are we friends or not?" I wanted to know. "Don't you want to share with a good friend?"

74

Kate rolled away from me and lay sulking. "Even if I had it, I wouldn't share it with you. One thing you're not and that's a friend. I'm not saying I have the money, but if I did, if I gave some of it to you—you'd probably run out on me."

She fought me when I tried to pull her close. In the end, she let me win. I said, "If you had money and you shared it I probably wouldn't leave you in the lurch. That's the truth, darlin'."

"Darlin', my ass!" Kate said. "What do you know about the truth?"

"As much as you. Truth's got nothing to do with it. I see it as a deal between two friends. I think I should get something out of it."

Kate reached for my crotch. It had only been a few minutes since our wrestling match, but I was ready to go again. "Isn't what you got enough?" she asked.

"I wouldn't give a damn if you didn't have money," I said. "But you do and I'd like a few dollars."

Kate laughed and stroked harder. "I can manage that much."

"More than a few," I said.

"How much more?"

"What would you say to half?"

"I'd say shit."

"So we haven't made any progress?" I said.

Instead of answering, Kate climbed on top of me, and for a while money was forgotten. But when it was over for the second round, we got back to it again.

"You could call *that* progress," Kate said, lying back with her eyes closed.

I felt like I'd been over the jumps and back again. "Why be such a hog about it?" I said, tired but happy. "It's not like you'll be left short. Half of fifty thousand is still a lot."

Kate opened her eyes and regarded me with deep suspicion. "How did you get that figure?"

"From Danziger."

"He's a liar and so are you."

"It's still a good deal," I said.

"What about a quarter share?" Kate said quickly, feeling she had worn me down. She had.

"A quarter share of fifty thousand?"

"A quarter share of twenty thousand. I have twenty, not fifty. That's five thousand."

"I know how much it is. I liked fifty thousand better. A quarter share of that is . . . ."

Kate said, "Take it or go fuck yourself. How much I have is none of your fucking business, Saddler. If I say I have twenty, then twenty it is. My friend, I put up with a lot to get what I have. If five thousand isn't enough for you, you greedy shit, then you can just pull your prick. What's it going to be?"

"Sold to the lady with the red hair," I said, reaching for her again. "I'll just have to trust you."

"Look who's talking," Kate scoffed. "You think I was lying about how hard it was to get what I have. My friend, after I had that fight with my father, I had to leave here with nothing. He thought I was still lying down for the marshal. I wasn't—we had a fight too—but my father thought I was. I told him to mind his own fucking business. I was free, white, if not twenty-one. After that I traveled all over, waitressing, clerking in stores. I was looking for a rich man, but the ones I found seemed to know what I was after. They'd buy me things, but no wedding ring. I got to know an awful lot about men, Saddler. Too much. When I met Peyton I was dancing in a saloon in Brownsville, Texas. Peyton isn't wanted in Texas so he could go there. I don't know how old Peyton is, over fifty anyway, but when he asked me to marry him I jumped at the chance."

"But you got to know him better," I said, ready to ward off a slap.

It didn't come. "That's what happened. Peyton isn't much good to any woman anymore. Maybe he never was. He was no good for me. He'd get in bed with me, usually drunk, and we'd try it again. Nothing. Then he'd get mad as if I was the cause. When he started to beat me I knew I had to get out. So I waited till one night when he got stinking drunk after another failure in the bedroom. Drunk, then cursing, then sleeping. I bribed one of his Mexicans to get me to the border. And here I am, sonny boy. If you double-cross me, I'll cut your balls off. Not that I want to castrate you, you rat. That's my story, shitkicker. I always shake hands when I make a deal."

We shook hands solemnly and she pressed herself close to me. "I only talk tough when I'm scared, Saddler. Right now, I'm scared to death. Promise you won't let Peyton get me."

I hoped I'd be alive to keep my word.

EIGHT

Bed didn't have much interest after Kate got out of it, but it was still dark and too early to get up. The sweet smell of Kate was on me and on the bedclothes. Our exertions had made a tangle of the bed, and it seemed a shame to straighten it, to put it back the same cold way it was before she came. I was getting fond of that bed and would always have fond memories of the two lovely ladies I'd tussled with in it. By itself, that made up for the trouble I was in.

I was in it, sure enough. I didn't think Danziger would try to get me in the jail if he hadn't tried it outside. Doing things the underhand way was more his style. A fixer and a crook wouldn't go against the law head-on unless there was some other way. I knew I'd been wrong in not killing him and I was taking my chances after that. But it was just as well that I hadn't. I couldn't kill him and stay on. Besides, it would be the finish of Johnny Callahan. Danziger's political cronies would see that the governor yanked him out of there, maybe put him on trial for conspiracy to commit murder. Then, too, I wouldn't be of any use to Kate, if I had to run. Ballard would send his gunmen, and that would be the end of it.

There was gray light in the window, but the town was still quiet. Thinking of Kate, I didn't blame Ballard for wanting her back. Any man with balls would want her back. I figured that Danziger wasn't too happy with the job he'd been given. There must have been a lot of money and a lot of threats to make him do what he was doing. All his life, Danziger had weaseled his way out of tight corners, always counting on his brain to survive. By the looks of him, it had worked pretty well in the past. Danziger wasn't the kind of man to believe in killing. It wasn't good business; besides, he probably didn't like it, like most sane men. Now, for the first time, he was mixed up in a dangerous game he couldn't quit. There were no strings he could pull to get him out of this one. Ten to one, Ballard had enough on Danziger to jail him for life. That and the money was why he was in Dragoon Wells. He would order killing if nothing else worked. But first he'd work with the money. I was sure of that.

The sun was warming the street when I unbarred the jail door and took a look at the town. Sun was full in the street by the time I dipped my head in a bucket of cold water and smoked one of Johnny's cigars. I didn't want to come back to any surprises; so I locked the jail and took the key with me when I went to eat at the old man's.

"Better have the steak and eggs instead of ham and eggs," he told me. I kind of liked the old gent, about the only man in town who wasn't looking daggers at me. "Don't want to try the ham on you. Don't look cured right. Not poisonous, just not cured right. I'll throw it in the pea soup. That ought to fix it."

Eggs, cracked into fat, began to sizzle. The old man made good coffee and the first hot cup burned away some of my gloomy mood. "Know any men I could hire as deputies?" I asked him.

The old man turned the eggs and came back with the

coffee pot. He was pretty bright for an old man who had spent his life frying eggs. "I'd have to say no, Mr. Saddler. A few days ago I would have said sure. Times are bad hereabouts, money scarce. A few days ago you'd be knee-deep in deputies. Not now, I'm afraid. Talk's been going round since that gunman got himself killed by the Flannerys. People know it's about that Flannery girl who won't go back to her husband. They's saying that's what she ought to do."

"Would you send her back?"

The old man said, "I'd have to say no to that. Of course, at my age there ain't much to be scared of. What can Ballard do to me, break my china? Kill me? I'm fixing to put a bullet in my head when I get too old to work. What do you think, Mr. Saddler?"

I got up and left him money. "I think you might send Danziger some of that ham. If you see a man looks like a deputy—grab him."

"Not a chance," the old man said.

On this morning at least, Danziger wasn't an early riser. Rice still hadn't come back to town. When he returned it wouldn't be escorting a new schoolteacher. My guess was that he had headed for the nearest telegraph office. That would be at the railroad, about two long days' ride from town. Danziger was sending for reinforcements. It couldn't be anything else.

I went back to the jail, and for want of something to do, I cleaned my guns. I was in the middle of it when I heard loud voices in the street. When I looked out it wasn't a lot of people. It was just Danziger flapping his mouth. All spruced up in a fresh suit, he was handing a line of bullshit to the banker, who was also the mayor. It wasn't a job that paid money, but McLandress liked it, liked the title. In the street it was hot and quiet and I could hear Danziger's every word. Most likely he wanted me to hear.

Danziger looked my way when I came out the jail door. Then he put his arm around McLandress's shoulder and said again that Dragoon Wells most definitely was a town with possibilities. McLandress, that sour, puffy man, wanted to believe what he was being told.

"I'm heartened you say that, Mr. Danziger," he said.

Danziger shoved on more horseshit, but even for him, flannel-mouth that he was, it wasn't easy to list all the wonders of Dragoon Wells. He did his best, and he was damn good at it. He stayed away from the cattle business because that wasn't too bad, and for smart ranchers like the Flannerys it was better than that.

Danziger turned his benign gaze on the dusty town. "I see this little city coming back to life," he declared. "Let me put it this way. My associates are definitely interested in what this town has to offer. You may depend on that, sir."

McLandress, already seeing a flow of money into his bank, liked everything Danziger was hinting at. But he was impatient to hear what it was.

"Pardon my reticence, sir," Danziger said. "But there are business reasons, if you get my meaning. At the moment it's confidential. If I disclosed my information before the time is ripe, other towns would be clamoring for attention. We can't let that happen, can we?"

Ever the man of business, McLandress said, "Absolutely not, sir. I understand perfectly. Perhaps a little talk later in my office. At your convenience, of course."

Taking the cigar out of his mouth, Danziger said with a wink, "It's a pleasure to do business with a man who knows business."

Danziger pretended to see me for the first time. "Good morning to you, Deputy."

He was in high good humor, and I guess he thought he had found a way to get around me. McLandress just gave me a stiff nod. Ah, I thought, if you only knew that I've been fucking your lovely daughter.

"What're you promising to do?" I asked Danziger. "Move the capital down this way?"

McLandress glowered at me. "We were having a

81

private business talk, nothing to do with you. I'd be obliged if you kept out of it."

Danziger grinned. He liked having me there. Lattigo was watching from the porch of the hotel. Danziger laughed at my little joke. "Afraid I don't have that much pull, Deputy. Tell you the truth, this snug little town would suit me fine. A country boy born and bred is what I am. Give me the quiet life, sir, good, hard-working people for neighbors. I ask you, what more could a man want?"

"You said it," I said.

McLandress wanted me gone. "I said this was a private talk. It concerns the very lifeblood of this community. Private, I said."

"Not the way Danziger yells, Mr. McLandress."

The banker bristled. "*Mister* Danziger," he said, climbing up on his high horse. "You have no better manners than Marshal Callahan."

Old Earl, friend of the common man, stuck up for me. "No need to call down the Deputy, Mr. Mayor. Like the man said, 'Call me by any name you like, just don't call me late for supper.' "

"Why don't you ask Danziger about the Flannerys?" I said to McLandress. "You know who they are?"

This time McLandress looked uncomfortable. "I'm not about to ask Mr. Danziger anything. He is known to me by reputation, which is more than I can say for you."

"Mr. Danziger is loved by one and all," I said.

Nothing I said bothered the man from Tucson. "If I didn't know you better, I'd think you didn't like me."

"Ask him about the Flannery girl," I said to McLandress.

"Absolutely not." McLandress was sweating in the hot sun. He turned away from me. "You feel like having that talk now, Mr. Danziger? Where we won't be interrupted."

"I wish you wouldn't stay mad at the Deputy," Danziger said, poking the banker in the ribs in his backroom way. "A good lawman is a little suspicious of everybody, even of a man like me that's known all over. About the talk, we'll have that later if you don't mind. I hope you got some good whiskey. To celebrate, I mean."

I don't think McLandress ever tasted whiskey in his life, but he managed a good-fellow smile. "It'll be there, sir. It's an honor to have you in our town, and I think I speak for the rest of its citizens. I'll bid you good morning."

Danziger smiled at the banker's back and then at me. Sweat trickled from his crinkly hair and ran into his eyes. He wiped it away and stuffed his handkerchief into his sleeve.

"How did I do?" he asked in a low voice.

"Pretty good," I said. "McLandress bit hard but you didn't pull too hard on the line, you shit-faced son of a bitch."

"It's too late to kill me," Danziger said. "You missed your chance up there in the hotel."

"It can still get done."

"I think it's too late. Soon it'll be later than that."

"Don't count on it, Danziger."

"But I do," Danziger said. "I count on money and then more money. Money solves all problems, cures all ills. It's what oils the wheels, makes the world go round. It's a powerful shame to waste it on just one woman. That's not for me to decide. I can call for more money than you'll ever see in your life. Why don't you start thinking the same way? Get yourself a wet tit and start sucking before the rush starts. Man, don't you see? No man can stand against the power of the dollar."

He wasn't saying anything I hadn't heard before. He was right about some of it, and we both knew it. But he didn't know me. I can be a mule. "You're wrong this time," I said.

"Don't be too sure," Danziger said calmly. "The only time I was wrong was when I ran for Governor of Texas. I didn't spread enough money around. I hedged when I

83

should have gone for broke. That was a fool thing to do—I could have made it back, and more, in no time."

"You're still wrong," I said. "I'm going to prove it to you."

Danziger wiped his face again. "I guess there's no good talking to you. Nothing personal, you understand, but I'm going to turn this town against you. First with promises, then with money. The money is how I hope to do it. Usually it's the start and the finish. And if you still doubt me, I'll tell you something else. I have to get that woman back to Ballard, and there's no ifs about it."

"You'd better start running," I said. "You're not going to get her."

"Run! You trying to be funny, Deputy." Danziger didn't laugh, didn't smile. "Where could I run that Ballard wouldn't find me?"

That night Danziger gave a party at the hotel. I didn't get an invitation, but that must have been an oversight. Anyway, I don't think lawmen get invited to parties. People figure they'll just show up. They don't get invited but nobody keeps them out when they come to drink the free liquor.

Killing Danziger and Lattigo still was a good idea, but it came to me that a better way would be for Kate Flannery to get the hell out of Dragoon Wells. No woman, no war. The more I thought about it, the better I liked it.

I sat on the porch watching things being carried into the hotel. A man from Casey's delivered a whole wagonload of whiskey and beer. There was even going to be food. I thought about Kate and didn't like the thought of having her gone. Yet I was willing to make the sacrifice. There were places she could go where Ballard wouldn't be likely to find her. Danziger thought Ballard was the Devil himself. I didn't credit him with that much power. I'd be losing money on the deal, but that would be better than all the bloodshed I saw ahead if she stayed. In the beginning, I thought there was a chance of making Danziger back down. Now I knew I'd be wrong. He couldn't. He was getting old and he wouldn't know how to run. I knew he would stay even if it got him killed. It probably would. Me too.

With Kate gone, all I'd have to do was wait around until Johnny got well. I owed him something. He hadn't given me the job to start a war. After he came back on his own two feet, I would head for the border. Kate was heavy on my mind, and it would take time to forget her. I'd manage to do that. So far though, my idea was all one sided. Kate wasn't a Flannery for nothing; there was a fair chance that she would tell me to go fuck myself. I grinned. I'd much rather fuck her.

I was still thinking about her when the band struck up over at the hotel. All the windows were open and the music blared out into the street. People passed the jail on the way to the party. A few nodded. It was getting dark and lights came on and people straggled to the hotel from all directions, stiff in their Sunday clothes. And it wasn't just a party for the town: people came in farm wagons and on horseback. I listened to the music for a while.

I had no idea how to get Kate out of Dragoon Wells. Sure as hell, her folks couldn't be talked to in any reasonable way. This time I'd get shot. I could rope her and tie her, but where would I take her? I gave up that idea, though I must say I liked it. I went inside and drank some of Johnny's bourbon and was ready for the party.

I corked the bottle and went to the door. The band sounded like a mechanical piano assisted by a fiddle, a banjo, a horn. It was pretty terrible. I gave it a while. No party ever gets going good until the first few bottles have been emptied. I walked down to the livery stable to have a look at my horse. Calvin worked there when he wasn't at the jail. He was sitting on a barrel trying to read a book by lantern light. The name of the book was *Great Captains of Industry;* Calvin moved his lips as he read.

Calvin slept in one of the empty stalls and his straw-filled mattress had been unrolled for the night. A plate of beans lay in front of him on another barrel, and now and then he reached out without looking and forked beans into his mouth. When I came in he put his finger in the book to mark his place.

"Who'd you say was the smartest—Diamond Jim Brady or Bet-A-Million Gates?" he wanted to know. To him it was a serious question.

"I think Gates has more money so that makes him the smart one," I said. "Besides, he doesn't wager as much as he lets on. Any strange horses come in today?"

"Nary a one," Calvin answered. "I'd of told you if there was. Just the regulars and yours."

Calvin told me he was planning to be a millionaire when he got old enough to do it. I said that was a dandy idea, so keep on studying the books. Calvin, eager to get back to his book, said he would. He was back in the dream world of millionaires by the time I left the stable.

In the days when Dragoon Wells had dreams of its own, the man who owned the hotel put in a ballroom. It wasn't any bigger than a country church; still, it was a ballroom. Now they had swept it out and opened the doors to let some air in. It opened off the lobby and the noisemakers were banging away when I got there. The clerk's face got as grim as the music when I walked in. I winked at him and joined the festivities.

People were dancing like people who hadn't paid for their liquor. Two of Casey's boys were behind a make-shift bar, planks laid across iron trestles, pouring as fast as they could grab the bottles. There were two punchbowls for the ladies, one with booze, one without. Men not wanting to wait for the bartenders were helping themselves to the whiskey. There was plenty of it, none of it Gilligan's Breathless.

Looking benevolent, Mayor McLandress was ladling punch for the ladies. I looked for Laurie but didn't see her, and there wasn't a Flannery in the room. Danziger was doing his damnedest to charm the bloomers off Mrs. McLandress. Lattigo was there too, never wandering far from his boss. The band cut loose again and Danziger led Mrs. McLandress out on to the floor.

McLandress spilled punch when he saw me. I gave him a wink and went to the bar for a drink. Out on the floor Danziger and the banker's lady were creaking around. I drank the whiskey, a fair bourbon, and poured another.

Danziger was manfully enduring the dance, a waltz, but he got out just in time before the band launched into what they thought was a polka. The men who owned the lumber company and buried dead gunmen came in with their wives. Danziger bowed to the undertaker's lady and whacked the undertaker on the back. The lumber man's fat wife giggled and said Mr. Danziger was a naughty man.

Danziger chucked her under the chin and turned to look at me, knowing I was an interested spectator. Not wanting to lose Danziger's attention, the fat woman clutched at his arm. It wasn't every day that a gallant like Earl Danziger blundered into her life. Still looking at me, Danziger squeezed her high on the arm. She giggled again and her husband broke out in a wintry smile.

"You're terrible, Mr. Danziger," the fat woman said.

Danziger told her to go and dance with her "beau." The fat lady didn't like that though she nearly laughed her fat head off. As the husband led her away, Danziger called out, "Till we meet again." The fat woman laughed and bullied her husband all over the floor.

"You're drinking—good!" Danziger said to me. "What do you think of my little get-together." He took my glass and went to get it filled, then came back with my drink and one for himself.

"I think it's a fine party," he said.

"You forgot to invite Mrs. Ballard," I said.

Danziger didn't answer until he stuck his face in his drink. "Wrong, my friend. I did invite her. I invited all the Flannerys. I thought we could talk this out over a few

87

drinks. Could be they'll show up later."

"You won't like it if they do."

Down at the end of the still dusty ballroom, the mechanical piano gave out a grinding sound as if it needed oil. The musicians played louder to cover it. They were game gents, those musicians, and while they worked their asses off for the dancers, one of Casey's boys brought pitchers of cold beer to the bandstand.

Danziger smiled at me, thinking he had it all wrapped up. "You'll be pleased to hear I decided not to move the capital from up north. Too much trouble. What I'm going to do is reopen the mines in this town."

"That'll take some doing," I said. "The mines are all played out. You saw the tip heaps when you rode in. That's all that's left."

"It can be done," Danziger said.

"They won't believe you," I said. "What was in the mines has been taken out. McLandress knows that, they all do. You can't mine what isn't there."

"Wrong again," Danziger said. "Those tip heaps, as you call them, are still full of valuable ore. In the old days they didn't know how to get everything out. Now they do. That's a fact, Deputy. Ask any mining engineer. They're starting to do it all over. It's going to mean new prosperity for this town."

"If it gets done."

"Well, yes, that's a consideration. They scratch my back and I'll scratch theirs. That's how it works."

Back at the punchbowl, McLandress was trying to listen; so Danziger raised his voice to a vote-getting level. "This town is going back on the map, Mr. Saddler. There'll be a new era of prosperity. You have my personal guarantee on that. Dragoon Wells is going to be one lively town."

"Livelier than you think," I said. "I don't give a shit what you do—you're not getting that girl."

The piano was beginning to sound like a keg of nails being rolled down a hill, and after trying to fix it, the hotel man pulled the lever that shut it off. McLandress jumped into the sudden silence and called on Danziger to make a speech. Acknowledging the applause, Danziger said he'd be glad to make a speech—"A short one, folks"—provided they didn't close down the bar. That got even more applause and Danziger went one way and I went another. Going out I snagged a full quart from the bar and went back to the jail.

NINE

Laurie was waiting for me in the shadows, and I put my gun away as she came out. She was wearing a caped coat with a hood over a flowered nightdress. Red sateen slippers peeped out from under the hem of the coat.

"I know," I said. "Your father will kill you if he finds you here. Why aren't you at the party?"

She was in a hurry to get inside the jail. "My father wouldn't let me go. He thinks I looked flushed. If he only knew what I'm flushed about. Maybe it's more than the flush. He said you were sure to be there, and he doesn't think I should be seen talking to a man like you."

I smiled at her. "Your father's right. Besides, I don't feel much like talking."

Laurie giggled. "Me neither. What have you been thinking about us? Have you decided? If I don't get out of this town I'm going to go crazy. What's taking you so long to make up your mind? Wasn't it good with me?"

I didn't know what to say. Most men would have grabbed her, grabbed the money, and been out of town inside of an hour. Nobody had to get shot—the money belonged to her, sort of. I liked this crazy girl, and it galled me to act like a shitkicker. Without the money she would have been dandy; with it she was a lonesome cowboy's dream.

Laurie came up close to me and I kissed her. "I'm going to be so good to you that you'll have to go with me," she said. "I'm going to break your back. That's a terrible thing to say, isn't it?"

"Sounds like poetry to me," I said, and we went in to bed like an old married couple. But nothing we did in there was old or married. I hadn't changed the bed-clothes since Kate, and Laurie sniffed suspiciously.

"You been putting something on your hair?" she asked, but her voice trailed off when I began to take off her clothes. The people at the party weren't having half the good time we were. She was right about the second time being better. A man and a woman get to know each other's bodies after the first time. She bucked under me as I put it into her, and she kept on bucking. God! She was a lovely thing, soft yet firm, strong but yielding, and I drove it in and out of her until her eyes were wild and when her climax came she shuddered her way through it, and then she had another and another. . . .

"We'll have years of this ahead of us," she whispered. I knew this wasn't true. Months maybe, but not years. No chance of that, even if I wanted to drag it out that long. But I said nothing. Laurie went on with, "Years of teaching each other, trying it in new ways, doing it in different ways. I have a French book my father doesn't know about. He'd have a fit of apoplexy if he knew I did. It has drawings. In one picture they're doing it dog-style. The woman gets down on her hands and knees and the man mounts her in that position. Does that sound good?"

"Sounds wonderful," I agreed.

"Want to try it?"

"Not right now. A cold, bare jail and a narrow bed

91

isn't the place for that."

"That's true. It would be better in a comfortable hotel room with thick, soft carpets and absolute privacy. Then we'll try it that way and all the other ways too."

"I'm looking forward to it," I said, which was no more than true.

"But we'll have to get there first," she prompted me, getting back to the subject of looting her father's bank. Her foxy little mind never strayed far from that. "We'll be off the same night we get the money. The money is mine by right. Anyway, what's my father going to do? Call in the Arizona Rangers to hunt down his own daughter? He won't do anything because there would be too much scandal. It could harm him in the banking community. If he can't control his own daughter, et cetera. And think of the fun the newspapers would have with him. My father is not a popular man—too tight with loans, too many foreclosures. We have nothing to fear, Saddler. A bank robbery without risk. I know you're going to say yes."

"I probably am," I said, thinking I'd be a fool if I didn't. But we didn't have to rush off that very minute. There was some unfinished business to be seen to. Business that was really none of my business. Still and all. . . .

At the moment my unfinished business was with Laurie. This time I lay on my back with my shaft pointing straight up. Laurie sat on it so it penetrated deep, and she gasped at the way it went in. I didn't have to do a thing. She moved her ass up and down. Her knees were on both sides of me, and she used them for leverage, raising and lowering her ass that way. She was young and supple and lightly built, so she was able to move without effort. Every time her ass moved down it seemed as if my shaft was sticking right up into her middle. It drove me wild. I squeezed her breasts at the same time, and she moaned as much from that as from her up-and-down movement on my cock.

"This position is from that French picture book," she whispered, hardly able to get the words out. Her face was strained but happy and full of healthy lust.

Hurrah for French picture books, I thought.

Now her ass was moving faster and faster as she worked up to her come. Then her ass came down hard and stayed there while she shuddered all over. She tried a few more up-and-down movements, but she was too weakened from orgasms to be able to manage more than a few. That was enough for me and I shot straight up into her. She came again and shook so hard I was afraid she was going to faint. But she didn't and after a while the trembling stopped and she smiled at me. Then she stretched out beside me in Johnny Callahan's bed and whispered, "It was so good I thought I was going to die."

"It wouldn't be a bad way to go. There's nobody like you, Laurie. I'm not just saying that."

"I hope not, Saddler. I feel as if I can do anything with you. And I want you to do anything with me or to me. I feel no shame with you."

"Why should you? You're a woman and I'm a man. We both like the same thing and there's no holding back."

She sounded serious when she said, "That's right. There's no pretending, no taking advantage. I don't know how honest you are about some things, but you're honest with me. Not once have you been rough with me."

"Why would I be rough?"

"Some men like to do it in a rough way. I know. I was with a man in Charleston—I was sixteen—and he used me like an animal. From behind, if you know what I'm saying. He just turned me on my face and rammed it in there. It hurt and if I cried he beat me when he finished. I shouldn't have gone with him, but I needed a man; and I knew him and I thought I could trust him."

"Stay away from rough men, men like that," I said.

"Oh I will, Saddler. From now on I'll stay with you."

"Good idea."

"They call that buggery, don't they?"

"They do, but you don't have to go on with this. You've told me and that's the end of it."

But she wasn't ready to let it go. You might say little Laurie had sex, in all its variations, on her feverish little mind.

"Have you ever been buggered, Saddler?"

"No," I said firmly. "I have not."

"It will be so nice in Mexico City," she said, abruptly changing the subject. I was glad of the change. Discussing buggery is not like discussing the weather. Give me the weather or the price of pork.

"Would you like a drink?" I asked her, and when she said yes I gave her a drink of Daniel's.

"Ah," she said, "not as good as sex, but good."

We lay quietly listening to the thump of the music coming from the hotel. "Don't take too long, Saddler, please don't," she whispered. "I know I said that before, but I feel the wildness building up in me and I have to let it go. If it can't be you, then I'll have to find someone else. I have to get the money before my father makes me marry some old geezer. Or some young geezer. He keeps talking about it. Then all my chances will be gone."

Right then I heard them coming. The music stopped and they were on their way. Laurie heard them too, men with loud voices. "Oh God! I have to go out the back way. Kiss me, Saddler, and please say yes."

The voices stopped before they reached the jail. I looked around to see if Laurie had left anything. She hadn't. Then McLandress yelled from outside, "You in there, Deputy?"

I yelled for them to come in. Whatever it was, Danziger was sure to be behind it. McLandress didn't come in first. Instead, a giant of a man I'd seen at the party opened the door. I had seen him glowering at me in the hotel, but put it down to nothing special. Now I knew it had to be more than that. He'd been drinking or dancing or both; sweat rolled off him like rain, and there were widening stains under the armpits of his heavy dark suit. His blond hair had been clipped so short in the Prussian style that his pink scalp showed through.

"Where's the Mayor?" I asked him.

The banker bulled his way through the crowd and came in followed by as many as could get in. I'd seen them before, the lumber company man and some others. None of them looked like working men; money-hungry smalltown businessmen is what they were. They shuffled in silently, and I knew McLandress was going to do the talking. Danziger had pulled the strings and here they were!

"You had more room back at the hotel," I said to the banker. I think I sounded friendly enough. I didn't have a thing against the stupid bastards. Money smells as sweet in my nose as it does in any man's, but I won't grub for it. That's what they were doing, sucking up to a schemer like Danziger.

It pained McLandress to be polite to me. The banker, being a banker, was the kind to make a sour face at a poor man's hello, then run to lick a rich man's boots.

McLandress cleared his throat noisily. "We've come to talk to you," he began. "It's time we had a talk."

I did my best to look agreeable. "What do you want to talk about?"

They mumbled back, some not liking me, some maybe even hating me because I was an obstacle that had to be moved and they weren't sure how to do it. I was standing between them and the money, and that's enough to make any businessman hate you. They believed all they had to do was to get rid of me and the money would come rolling in. Looking at the mealymouth bunch of shits, I was almost ready to concede that Danziger had more class. He was what he was and didn't pretend to be anything else.

Only the big man with the clipped head wasn't afraid of me, and I wondered again who he was. I knew McLandress was trying to work up enough nerve to tell me to quit, I was fired, or whatever. Before he spoke, the banker looked to make sure the big blond brute was still there. Then I got it. This was the man they wanted to put in as town marshal. After I decided that, I began to watch him more carefully. Rough stuff, if it came, would come from him.

"This has to be said, Mr. Saddler," the banker began, puckering his womanish lips. Behind him there was a murmur of agreement. I crossed my legs to make myself more comfortable, and wouldn't you know it, the rifle I held ended up pointing straight at the banker's jowly face.

At first, McLandress was like a rabbit looking at a snake. "Let me save time and say it for you," I said. "You want me to leave, but I don't want to leave. And maybe you want to know why I've been talking so tough to Danziger. Because he's a sneaking nightcrawler, is the answer. Danziger works for a man that burned a whole town and murdered its people. You want to hear more?"

"There's no proof of what you're saying," McLandress protested. "Anyway, the war's been over a long time."

"How long is long?" I asked them. I was talking to McLandress, but the question was for everyone. "There's no limit on what he did. That's the man you're pimping for, catching runaway women for. Slave catchers and pimps, that's what you are, all of you."

"We didn't come here to be insulted," McLandress blustered. "Least of all by the likes of you. You want to know how much we care about this Flannery woman? Not a thing—there's your answer. She was never one of us when she lived here. If sending her back means life to this town, then to blazes with her. To blazes with the rest of the Flannerys. They're no neighbors of ours. Mr. Danziger is about to give this town a chance and we're going to take it. I'll make it short—we want you to get out."

"Can't be done," I said, keeping an eye on the big man.

"You won't listen," the big man said.

"Then don't stand in the way," McLandress said. "Let things take their course. Nobody's asking you to hand over the girl. Keep out of it, that's all you have to do. That's what Callahan would do. I wish to God he was here instead of you."

"But he's not," I said. "Anyway, I don't know that he wouldn't do the same. That's not the question. I'm the marshal. You think I should let those bastards have the girl, go fishing or get drunk while they're taking her back to that butcher. No, sir."

McLandress sucked in so much air his lardy face turned red. He cleared his throat, getting ready to fire his big gun at me. The big gun was a weary-faced old man with Horace Greeley whiskers and a beaver hat. He trembled like a leaf—a drinker.

"If you please, Judge," the banker said, pulling him forward by a very frail arm. The old man jumped when his name was called and he dropped a heavy law book. When he got under the light I saw how old and poor he was, and how scared. McLandress grabbed the book off the floor and thrust it at him so hard he nearly knocked him down.

"Go easy with him," I said.

It was plain that the Judge hadn't heard a kind word for a very long time. Every miserable town in the West has a judge like this one.

"Thank you, Marshal Saddler, my name is Isaac Ferguson." He nodded at me and found it hard to stop once he had started.

The banker was puffed up like a rooster about to make a surprise attack on a hen. It's a wonder he didn't crow, and now that his jowls were red he looked very much like a rooster. I hoped he wasn't going to be too disappointed.

The Judge couldn't find his page and the banker had to help him. The book was the laws of the Arizona Territory and I knew what was coming. It didn't mean diddly-shit to me. The Judge found it easier to see after he finally discovered his spectacles in his pants pocket. They were dirty and one of the lenses was cracked down the middle.

Blinking at me, holding the law book in shaky hands, he told me I wasn't any kind of lawful lawman.

"Goddamn right," the big man said.

The Judge tried to bring the big man into focus. "Please don't interrupt, Mr. Dorfman," he said as sternly as his condition would allow. "I was about to cite the statute pertaining to the appointment of deputies and police officers of any kind."

The old man got started again and he read such and such, paragraph this and that. It boiled down that Johnny was required to send a letter to the Territorial Governor the day he appointed me. This had not been done, the Judge declared. Therefore, I had never been a legal deputy marshal.

"That's the law, Mr. Saddler. You notice that I address you as Mister instead of Deputy or Marshal. You have been holding office contrary to the laws of this territory. As an officer of the court—that's what a lawyer is—I direct you to surrender your badge and to vacate these premises. Forthwith, sir."

I grinned at the Judge. He was a drunk but I liked him. He reminded me of a drunken uncle who died by drinking from the wrong bottle. "You read that real good, Judge," I said.

The Judge was pleased, but the banker snapped, "Read it yourself if you want to. The law is clear. It should be, even to you. What are you smiling at? This is no joking matter. If you refuse to leave this office, if you defy the law, you can be arrested and prosecuted for—for what, Judge?"

The Judge had the charge on the tip of his tongue, but it must have slipped off. "For a lot of things," he quavered.

"Correct!" McLandress said. "That's what could happen to you. However"—the banker tried to sound reasonable, almost friendly—"there's no need for that. You had no way of knowing that you were breaking the

98

law. So we are prepared to be generous, Mr. Saddler. You've only been her a few days, but we're ready to pay you for the entire month. I think that's fair, don't you?"

"I think it's more than fair," I said. "Four thousand for four weeks is good pay in any army."

McLandress gulped, and his stinginess warred with the greed for Danziger's money. The figure I quoted was four times what Callahan got. "Come! Come! Mr. Saddler," he blustered. "We all know that Marshal Callahan agreed to pay you five hundred. Remember, you don't have to do a thing to get it . . . plus a little bonus for your inconvenience. What do you say to seven hundred and fifty dollars?"

I told them to go fuck themselves.

It got very quiet in the jail, and I moved the rifle away from McLandress until it was pointing at Dorfman, the man they wanted to put in as the new deputy. The Judge wasn't afraid of the rifle—maybe he couldn't see it—and neither was Dorfman. All the others wanted to run, and they crowded together like panicky sheep trying to get through the same small gap.

I expected to get fists from Dorfman—not talk. The Judge had read from his book, said his piece, and it hadn't worked. Dorfman moved out in front of the others. I told him to move back—the party was over. "Danziger's shindig is still going on," I said. "Go back and suck up some more."

Only a brave man or a stupid man would crowd a man pointing a rifle at his belly. The big man was both. There was a problem about how to handle him. I had to stop him if he kept coming. I could kill him with a touch of the trigger, but what would that get me other than blood on the floor?

Dorfman, the dumb bastard, told me that I had no right to stand in the way of the town's good fortune, and I guess the lumbering fool really believed that better times were just around the corner. "You ain't got no right to mess things up for us. People are out of work. Mr.

McLandress told you what we think, what we've decided. What do you care what happens to that woman? Let her go home where she belongs. What kind of a woman is she, running off on her lawful husband?"

I stood up holding the rifle. "Get out now," I said. "Just get out. There's your answer." I snapped the lever of the rifle, putting a bullet in the chamber. They turned and ran, and it was a good thing there were no women and kids in that crowd—they'd have been trampled. Only Dorfman stayed where he was.

"You too, squarehead," I said. "Don't get stupid. You'll have to wait for the next time Callahan breaks a leg."

"You're nothing but a smartmouth," Dorfman growled. "You wouldn't talk so tough if you didn't hold that gun."

"That's why I'm holding it. Get out quick."

Dorfman shook his thick head. "You're the one that's getting out, Saddler. You're through in this town."

I was tired of talking, and I didn't want to hear any more about people out of work. He was close enough to hit, so I hit him. The barrel dug in hard but it didn't knock him down, though it knocked the wind out of him. I upended the weapon and tried to get him with the stock. But he was fast and he clamped both hands on the rifle and would have tossed me along with it if I hadn't let go.

My gunbelt was slung over the back of the chair and as I turned he hit me with a punch like a mule kick that landed in the back of my head. Another man would have broken his hand but he didn't even grunt. He kicked me behind the knee while I was still falling. All I could think of was that handgun. I was close to grabbing it when the big man kicked chair and gunbelt clear across the room. I went over with the chair and he waded in with kicks. I took a flying leap and tackled him around the middle. When I got him I wished I hadn't. It was like trying to bring down a tree. There was nothing to hit him with but my fists.

We rolled on the floor and I tried to knee him in the balls. That didn't work either. He was up before me, grinning like a bastard telling me what he was going to do to me. He wasn't a flannelmouth, he meant to do it. I lowered my head and butted him in the gut. It was like using my head to batter down a door. My head hurt and it hurt worse when his big paws clamped on both sides of it. I expected a knee in the face, but that wasn't what he did. What he did was try to twist my head off my shoulders. I swear the son of a bitch lifted me off the floor by the head.

I don't know how big the bastard was, big as they come. He was at least three inches bigger than me and I'm six-one. In pounds he had me by 50 or 60. He lifted me and threw me like a sack of grain, but I didn't land as loose. My back hit the wall and I sat down hard. He grabbed up my rifle and broke it to bits on the top of the desk. He whacked until the barrel was bent and the desk was split. Then he threw the rifle away and came at me balling his fists, still talking. "I'm going to kick the living shit out of you. I'm going to kick your legs out through your back."

The only thing I could see was the broken chair. There was a leg with part of a rung still stuck to it. He didn't even try to stop me from getting it. He came at me with his hands out wide, ready to grab when I swung. I swung at his face and he blocked it but took a crack on the forearm. If it hurt he didn't show it. He didn't try to take the chair leg away from me, not at first. The next time I just feinted with the chunk of wood. He moved to block it and I hit him along the side of the head. His ear puffed up as soon as the blow landed. The mad grin on his face didn't change.

I got him with another crack on the head. I swung again and he blocked the blow with his open hand. His fingers closed like a steel trap. I hung onto the chair leg and he knocked me loose with a punch delivered by the other hand. He hit me on the shoulder with the chair leg before he tossed it away. He lifted his fists, huge and knobby, so I could see what he was going to use on me.

"These are all I need, little man," he said.

I went at him again using every dirty trick I knew. I know plenty of dirty tricks and at least one should have worked. He grunted when I landed a kick to his knee. That was all he did—grunt! Too much meat and muscle covered his bones to do any harm. Coming in hard, he crowded me against the back wall, making no effort to block the punches I threw at his meaty face. Then he started body punching, which was what I was afraid he would do.

The stink of sweat and liquor gusted in my face. My shoulder hurt like hell from the blow I had taken with the chair leg. He hit me again and pulled me away from the wall. A 1000-pound grizzly wouldn't have been any harder to fight. He grabbed me by the shirt and pulled. I went sliding across the top of the desk while some of the shirt stayed in his hand, and when I fell down on the other side he ran at the desk with both hands and tried to crush me against the wall. It was coming at me when I jumped on top of the desk while it was still moving and kicked him in the face.

His hands were spread wide pushing and his head was bent and the kick got him right under the chin and knocked him halfway across the room. I dived from the top of the desk, but he caught me in midair and threw me hard. I hit the stove and knocked the plate lifter and the plate from the top of it. Flames licked up as he came at me again. I knew he was boring in for the kill.

He ran at me and I sidestepped and tripped him in the direction of the stove. He yelled for the first time when his hands grabbed at the stove, and before he could turn I jumped on his back and forced his face down into the flames. There was a quick sizzling sound as the flames

102

burned off his eyebrows and the front of his hair. I jockeyed up on his back to get more leverage. I grabbed the back of his head and pressed it deeper into the fire. It was like riding a buffalo in its death throes. He screamed and kicked as the fire ate at his face. Then, screaming madly, he pitched me over his head.

I came down so hard I thought I'd broken my back but I hadn't and then I was up again. Dorfman heard me and ran toward the sound, but he couldn't see. His face was a mass of burned flesh and his hands fumbled at the air, as if they didn't belong to him. I dodged him easily and got my beltgun off the floor. A moment before I would have used it. Now there was no longer any need. He turned and lunged again and I hooked my toe around his ankle and brought him down with a twist and kicked him in the side of the head. I had to kick him again in the same place before he shuddered and lay still.

I figured McLandress and the town fathers hadn't gone far. They were out in the dark trying to sneak away, and it took a shot fired in the air to bring them back. "Go fetch the doctor," I yelled at them. "You pushed Dorfman into this. Get the doctor or I'll get you!"

I went back inside and closed the door. Dorfman lay on the floor like a dead bear. I bent down to look at his eyes, maybe he was blind. I hoped he wouldn't die.

The doctor came in after a while and looked at the wreckage of the office. "My God! Did you do that to Hansy Dorfman! I guess you did. I'll say this, he had it coming a long time. Many's the man I doctored that had business with that squarehead. Now it's his turn to need the black bag."

I drank whiskey while the doctor saw to Dorfman. The doctor took the bottle and poured a trickle of whiskey into Dorfman's blackened mouth. He began to groan and I asked the doctor if maybe I shouldn't put the irons on him in case he got lively again.

"Not necessary," the doctor said, drinking whiskey from the bottle before he handed it back to me. "Hansy

103

is going to be a good boy for a while. Fetch that lamp down close, will you? I want to see if he's blind."

I held the lamp while the doctor poured medical alcohol in a wad of cotton and dabbed at Dorfman's eyes. Then he threw away the dirty cotton and poked Dorfman in the ribs. "Try to open your eyes, Hansy. It's the doctor."

Dorfman's eyes fluttered open, and the doctor told me to turn the lamp down low. That done, he struck a sulphurhead match and moved it back and forth in front of Dorfman's eyes. The eyes, rimmed by black, followed the flame.

When the light was full again, the doctor had another drink of whiskey. "He'll be able to see and he never was handsome." The doctor was a sour old man full of mean humor. "Looks like I'm going to be busy with you around, Saddler."

I took the bottle back. "Busier than you think," I said.

"Well, I don't mind that," the doctor said.

TEN

I was trying to put the desk back together when Calvin showed up to do his sweeping and told me that Dorfman wasn't going to die. It was early morning and still cool. Calvin whistled when he saw the damage and went to the stable to borrow some carpenter tools. When he came back, he said, "Mr. Bush didn't want to loan them to me, but he did when I said you'd get mad."

"Do what you can with it," I said. I was back from breakfast and not in such a good mood.

Everything was getting too complicated for an old West Texas shitkicker like me. Like it or not, I was becoming too much a part of this half-forgotten town. If I had taken one of the nine other ways to the border, it would all be happening without me. A hundred to one, I'd never heard about what happened to Callahan, or Kate, or Laurie, or any of the others. The two women had me going. I had to choose between them, and then I had to choose between the one I wanted and Callahan.

Not that I trusted either one of them. They were just using me, trying to, to get what they wanted. But that's the way of women, yeah, and men, so I didn't feel put out about it. Anyway, there's no reason why you can't like someone you don't trust. Those old boys who wrote the Constitution had a good name for it—eternal vigilance. I would have to watch them so they wouldn't try to do me dirt at the wrong time.

I had been thinking about Calvin, the only person in town, apart from the old restaurant keeper, who didn't act edgy around me. I didn't count Laurie. She was too busy thinking about herself. At least she wasn't against me.

"You think Mr. Danziger has as much money as Bet-A-Million Gates?" Calvin asked, raising dust at the same time.

"Not even as much as Diamond Jim," I said.

Calvin collected the dirt in a dustpan and dumped it into the stove. "That's what I thought. Everybody else in this town thinks he's God Almighty. Mr. Bush at the stable is talking about fixing up the place for when people start coming back to town. You think that'll ever happen?"

"Not likely," I said. "If it ever happens it won't be because of anything Danziger does. He's just leading them up the garden path." I was still thinking about Kate. "How much do you know about what's happening?"

"More than you think probably. Mr. Bush don't talk about nothing else. It's like the whole town is holding their breath waiting to see what happens with that girl. Flannery, Kate Flannery. What's so important about her, is what I'd like to know?"

Calvin was still at the age when old Bet-A-Million Gates, with his millions made from barbwire, was more interesting than any woman, even one as great looking as Kate.

I had to make it sound reasonable to the boy. "She ran away from her husband because she hates him and doesn't want to go back. The husband wants her back so bad he's willing to do anything to get her."

"She must be a good cook," Calvin said. "You're in a fix, ain't you, Mr. Saddler. I could shoot a gun if I had one. I like Mr. Callahan, but I get along better with you. You don't keep forgetting my name like he does. You want help, I'm here all the time. Don't have to get paid more than I get now."

"No guns," I said. "You think you could make it to the telegraph line in a hurry? It's a good bit from here."

"Sending for the army, huh?" Calvin put away his broom and dustpan as if he'd never need them again. "That'll shake them up, if the army comes."

I looked at Calvin, with his gangling body and lank hair. No army was going to come, I told him. "Not their business. The Governor can send the Territorial militia. But you got to send him the message."

"Me!" Calvin's eyes danced with excitement.

"I don't know anyone else," I said. "The old man that runs the restaurant might do it, but he'd take a week to get there. It has to be faster than that."

Calvin didn't like the old man for reasons of his own. "That old man would fall off and kill hisself. I'll do it for you, Mr. Saddler, and I'll do it right. What should I tell the Governor?"

I said I'd write it out for him and I did. Calvin read it aloud:

"Governor William McReynolds—gosh!—Urgently request help. Regular cavalry or mounted militia. Expect attack by renegade Peyton Ballard and Mexicans. Definite proof they are proceeding Dragoon Wells this moment. Much bloodshed if help not received immediately. Signed James Saddler. Deputy Marshal. Dragoon Wells. Arizona Territory. Acting for John P. Callahan. Marshal.

"Gosh!" Calvin said again. "You think they'll come?

You make it sound like an invasion, Mr. Saddler. You really got proof Ballard and the Mexicans are on their way?"

"The last part, no. It's likely they'll come. I have to go on a good guess."

"That's lying to the Governor, Mr. Saddler."

"I'm lying in a good cause."

"You'll catch hell if the Governor sends the militia and there's nobody here but Danziger and that spook that follows him about. They could put you in jail for that."

I said, "Probably they could. It'd be better than having a lot of people killed. I'll let you in on a secret—they'd have to catch me first. You sure you want to do this? People are going to be mad at you when they find out. They will. I wouldn't mix you in but I can't go myself. Say no and it's all right."

Calvin was indignant at the suggestion that he wouldn't back me in time of trouble. "This is a chance to get my name in the paper. Local boy makes daring ride to save town, like they say. Words like that. Let me explain something to you, Mr. Saddler. It's important to get your name in the paper if you want people to notice you. I read once that's why Mr. Brady wears all them diamonds and stickpins and such. People notice him and write stories about him."

Calvin paused. "The only thing, I ain't got a horse."

"Take my horse but don't get rough with him. He'll go good if you tell him. Now listen to me. Watch out for hard-looking men when you get to the telegraph. It could be that Danziger has men, a man, posted there. One of his men, Billy Rice"—I described Rice—"rode out of here and hasn't come back. Rice is the smart one, that's why Danziger sent him, I'm guessing, to telegraph for more gunmen. Look around before you send the wire to the Governor. If it doesn't look good, ride on to the next telegraph station. They can't watch all of them. They could be watching the closest one."

Calvin was awed by the extent of Danziger's villainy.

"You mean they'd interfere with the telegraph operator. That's a federal crime, Mr. Saddler."

"That wouldn't mean much to these men. If they kill the telegrapher, who's to say who did it? Go on now. Stoke up on some grub and take bread and meat along. You won't be stopping to eat. When we go down to the stable we'll be talking about what you're going to tell Callahan."

"That's right clever, Mr. Saddler," Calvin said, taking the money I gave him. "Maybe I should take a gun along just in case."

I said no. "Don't try too hard to get your name in the paper. I don't want you getting killed over me, over this woman. I said no gun, and don't try to sneak one."

I wasn't sure that the stable man swallowed the story about Calvin riding out to Callahan's ranch. Calvin playacted a bit too hard. He did everything but walk to the footlights and whisper to the audience, the way they do. He looked too much like the bearer of great tidings, and I think the stable man caught some of that. I knew it might be edginess on my part, but to give Calvin a good start I hung around talking to Mr. Bush, who didn't want to talk to me. That meant he wanted to run to McLandress or to Danziger himself. And he did, as soon as I was back in the jail with the door closed. The stable man hurried past, darting nervous glances at the jail. Once Danziger heard the news, it didn't mean he would send Lattigo after the boy. If he did I would follow him and kill him. I'd shoot him out of the saddle without warning and leave him where he fell. It was something Lattigo needed and I was ready to do it for him.

The stable man didn't go to the bank but right into the hotel, which meant Danziger wasn't depending only on McLandress. Danziger would be playing the old go-between's game: telling one man that he trusted him more than another. In a few minutes, the stable man came out, looking pleased with himself, and went back to his work. I waited for Lattigo but he didn't show, and an hour later, still watching, I knew he wasn't going after the boy. That gave Calvin a start, and it saved Lattigo's life. For the moment it did.

The town was still quiet, but not for long. It came to life when loud yelling started at the far end of the main street, out past the sun-rotted bandstand where no band played anymore. My first thought was that Billy Rice had come back with a bunch of gunslingers ready to take on the Flannerys. Then I decided it couldn't be that because that wasn't the direction they would come from.

I went out to see what it was and there was old Con Flannery at the head of every man and boy in his family who was capable of shooting a gun. They were up on well-brushed horses, and you should have seen how that horse hair glistened in the sun. Every man and boy carried a beltgun and a rifle, and all the rifles were well-kept Winchesters. No old iron in this lot. Con Flannery was the only rider who wasn't carrying a repeater. He had the same Creedmore Sharps, the heavy rifle it was hard to miss with if you knew anything at all about guns. By the look of him, Con Flannery knew plenty, and if a man got in the sights of that rifle, he was done for. The Creedmore was good for 1000 yards, more if a man had the eye power to see that far. It was a favorite killing weapon of the Regulators, the assassins hired by the big ranchers to do away with small ranchers and farmers. It was a beautiful and terrible gun.

Con Flannery bulked up so big on his big horse in the lead that I didn't see Kate until they were well down the street. She didn't look any too happy and wasn't wearing the range clothes she'd come in the other night. Old Con had her riding sidesaddle, no doubt deciding that to fork a horse wasn't ladylike. But she was wearing a flat-crowned gray hat and boots instead of lady shoes and lady bonnet. The hat was cinched under her chin and tilted back on her head, giving her a reckless, defiant air. It was hard for her to hide that, and she wasn't trying.

They rode on in silence, with the whole town crowding

the sidewalks to gape. Nothing like this had ever been seen on a dull morning in a dead town. It was a show of force; all they needed was a flag to make it official. I heard the window of Danziger's room going up and knew he was watching. Everybody was watching and those that came late pushed through the others to get a look. The Flannerys weren't carrying jugs of coal oil; so the town was safe for now. That's no joke. They were capable of doing it, and might yet.

They kept coming, taking no heed of the hotel. They might have been riding through a ghost town for all the notice they took of the jittery citizens. I counted 20 Flannerys and 20 rifles. Impressive, on the face of it, and I had no doubt that they would put up one hell of a fight before Ballard's pistoleros cut them down. That's what had to happen, because courage and good intentions are no match for numbers and genuine meanness. Mexicans would die but Mexicans came cheap. Ballard could field 100 border gunmen for $5,000, maybe not even that much provided they could count on light-skinned women and plunder. To get the light-complected women they would do much more than kill a bunch of Irishmen.

Con Flannery raised his hand when he came abreast of the jail. The file of riders reined in, and if they feared an ambush there was no sign of it in their faces.

"Morning, Deputy," Flannery said.

"Sure is," I said.

"Not too hot."

"Just right. Anything I can do for you, Mr. Flannery?"

Con Flannery allowed himself a sliver of smile. "Nobody does anything for me, but I'm obliged by the asking. I'm here to say a few things having to do with my only daughter Kate. I guess you haven't made her acquaintance. This is Kate, Deputy Saddler."

I hoped Flannery meant what he said about me not knowing Kate. That Creedmore makes a terrible hole. Look at it this way. If a Creedmore can knock down a grizzly, what can't it do to a man? But I couldn't read a

111

thing in the Irishman's eyes.

"Miss Flannery," I said, formal as a real china teacup.

"Deputy Saddler," she said, giving nothing away. She was a lot better at playacting than Calvin.

That ended the politeness because the next instant Flannery raised his rough voice to a full-throated roar. "Listen to me, you storekeepers and money grubbers! Listen to me good! I won't say this but the one time. There's been talk going round about my daughter. This and that, gutter talk, no need to go into it. You all know what you've been saying. There's talk about my daughter and a low, sneaking, bloody-handed son of a bitch with the name Ballard. Some of you say she ought to go back to this animal. Dirty men have come here to spread dirty money to see that she does. You think you're all going to get rich with more dirty money if she does. If this talk goes on, a lot of you are going to get killed, and that, you half-men, is a promise."

Dust stirred in the sunlight and Flannery's voice boomed on, the words coming slow but stressful. "We came here today so you can take a good look at us. I ask you to think about it. Nobody's asking your help in this—I'd rather ask help from a rat—just stay out of it. Go about your grubby little business. Putting sand in the brown sugar is a lot safer than siding against us. Honest to God, I hope you believe me—it is. And for the man who came here with the renegade's dirty money, I want him to listen too."

Con Flannery turned his h rse and looked up at the open window of Danziger's room. "Hear me, Danziger," he roared. "I know who you are and what you are. Take your shitpants gunmen and get the hell out of this town. Crawl back to Ballard and tell him what he can expect if he comes here with his Mexicans. You don't like what I'm saying, come down and face me like a man. Borrow a weapon and we'll have it out. You and me, Danziger. Nobody's going to gang up on you. You want to be a man once in your life, I'll be waiting for you at the saloon."

Flannery turned back to me and you would never believe that he had been shouting threats. "It's been said, Deputy, and they can play catch with it for a while. If they side with Ballard after this, I'll flatten this miserable place. If Ballard can threaten to burn towns, then so can I. You know what I'd do, were I you?"

"What's that, Mr. Flannery?"

"I'd find another town to marshal in. This one hasn't much of a future. If Danziger can't find the saloon I'd take it kindly if you showed him the way. Deputy, what I told the town goes for you too. Don't take this job too serious. You're not the type."

Well, I'll be fucked, I thought. There I was risking my hide to keep his beautiful daughter from being handed over to Ballard, and here he was sticking out his jaw at me. I felt like I was getting it from every side. For sure I could get awful mad at the Flannery family, if I tried. It was still a good idea to get Kate out of there. There had to be places he couldn't find her. No detective agency is that good, or there wouldn't be notorious badmen still on the loose. They never did catch Jesse James, and they were looking for him a lot harder. Which wasn't to say that Ballard wouldn't spend money looking to find her. I would too. But what the hell! I was straining my brain for nothing. I knew she wouldn't go. Call me a man who didn't know his own mind, and you'd be right. I wanted her to go, I wanted her to stay.

About the only thing I could be sure of was there wouldn't be any showdown between Flannery and Danziger, who probably knew as much about guns as he did about ethics and honesty. Not a thing.

After Con Flannery left, all the interest in town was down at Casey's saloon. Up at the jail there was nothing happening. Sitting at the wrecked desk, I wondered how long the Flannerys would stay. Unless Billy Rice turned up with a pack of gunmen there wasn't much chance of a shootout. The Flannerys wouldn't shoot up the town— not yet. They had delivered their challenge, their warning, and now it was up to McLandress to sit in the game or get out. I knew Danziger wouldn't quit what he came for, but he wouldn't push it with the Flannerys breathing fire.

The door was open and Kate came in and sat down. Close up she looked better than ever, but the thought of all those brothers and uncles and cousins put a damper on how much I wanted her. It wouldn't have done me any good if I had been ready. She was all business today. I wasn't going to get a thing but talk. Not conversation— hard talk. I was ready to do some hard talking myself. Like how was I going to get paid for my part in the deal. If the governor sent the cavalry, and if he did it fast enough, the trouble with Ballard was likely to blow over. It was one thing to take on the Flannerys, but even the pistoleros would have no stomach for the Arizona Volunteers. As spit and polish soldiers they were rotten. All they knew how to do was kill. Most of them were rabid Indian killers and Mexican haters. It would please them no end to slaughter Ballard's private army.

Even so, they weren't there, and I was. My chances of getting killed were good. So I wanted to be paid. Kate must have known that because she started in on me before I could get a chance to start in on her.

"Never mind the money; you'll get your money," she said irritably. Like most redheads she was never far from boiling over. "What kind of plans have you made, that's what I'd like to know."

I told her about sending the boy to the telegraph station, after I went to the door to check for snoopers. "Not a word about that," I said. "You tell anybody and I'll leave you flat."

"I'm not too sure you won't."

"Maybe you should take your business to another store. This one is running out of everything."

"Son of a bitch! You know you're it."

"I'm glad we got that settled. I won't let them take you. You mind if I kill Ballard? If I could do that the

Mexicans wouldn't be so feisty with the money man dead."

Kate didn't even consider it. "All the better if you can do it," she said.

"It's something to think about if nothing else works. You'd be a rich widow if he hasn't changed his will. Are you in his will?"

There was real anger now. "None of your business, Saddler. What we agreed on is all you're going to get. Not a cent more."

"I'll get it when I get it," I said. "You won't like parting with the money, but you will. You want to know something else?"

"What's that, Saddler?"

I grinned at her. "I'm glad I'm not married to you," I said.

"I wouldn't marry you if you were good looking and owned a million dollars," Kate said.

Notice how all my women keep talking about money. You'd expect that kind of gab from the homely ones. Not so. It's the beauties who like to talk about the long green. Beauties are always greedy; they have so much, they want more.

"I'd have some money if you gave me some," I said. "And don't keep telling me I'll get it later. The later you spoke about the last time is now—where is it?"

Kate got up and walked around to remind me there was more than money in this deal. She swang her hips, as we say back home, and I had to force myself to keep my mind on business. With her carrying on like that, it wasn't easy.

She spun around with a swirl of skirts. "All right, you'll get a good part of it next time I come back to town. I had it ready today, but didn't want my father asking about it."

I knew that was a lie. Unless the gold was still in the ore stage, it would have made a nice small package. But no matter, she said it was coming.

Kate had nothing but scorn for my avarice. That was all right. Coming from a woman as greedy as she was, it was a sort of lefthanded compliment.

"Since you won't wait, won't trust me, it can't be all money," she said, sitting down again. She straddled a chair and rested her arms on the back of it, irritable as only a redheaded beauty can be. Dear Lord! I don't know if women know what straddling a chair can do to a man. I would say they do. This devil-woman knew it better than the rest.

"Listen to what I'm saying," she said. "If you're not interested, we can talk about politics."

"It can't be all in cash," I said.

"Some of it will be jewels," Kate went on. "I know what they're worth. You'll have to take my word for it. If you were willing to wait, you'd get a bigger share. That's what I think you ought to do. Take some cash now, then wait until I get away from here and sell the jewels."

"I hate to wait," I said. "We might get separated and I'd have to search all over for you."

She didn't miss the threat, fake though it was. Even if she double-shuffled me I wouldn't hunt her to the ends of the earth because of some shiny stones. If I followed her there would be other reasons. Like to get in bed with her.

Her green eyes snapped at me like pistols. "What are you going to do with jewelry? Wear it?"

I gave her my best shitkicker grin, knowing it would annoy her no end. "Golly no! I mean to sell off the dadburned stuff."

Kate sneered at me, knowing I had her measure and not liking it. These beauties hate to be figured; it takes away from their mystery.

"However did you get to be so lovable?" she asked. "It would be easy to hate you a lot, the way you are, what you are. Oh, what's the use of talking to a man like you."

"How much cash will there be?" The jewelry would be fine but not that easy to sell at a fair price. Any dealer I came to with jewels would know they hadn't belonged to

116

my grandmother no matter what sort of yarn I spun. I wondered if Kate would give me a bill of sale. Probably not. Anyway, I might have to show it to some sheriff, and if it went that far other things might be resurrected. So I'd have to go where the city burglars go.

"A third of your share will be cash," Kate said, and looked surprised when there was no argument from me. I knew she was hating herself for not having said a quarter. For a woman like Kate hating herself must have come as a shock; she knew she was the cat's ass. She was, and more.

I had a drink to celebrate the money I wasn't sure of. I tried to pour one for her, but she snatched the bottle away from me. Independent, that was my lovely Kate. She knocked it back like a cowhand at the end of a three-month trail drive.

"How does it feel to take money from a woman?" she said, showing me what the chair was getting and I wasn't.

"Not easy," I said. I had a few other things to say and would have said them if Con Flannery hadn't come in. The big Irishman didn't just come in. The door banged open and he filled the doorframe like a man of destiny in a full-length portrait; and it was just as well that he hadn't caught us doing it in Callahan's bed.

He wasn't like me. He didn't like the way his daughter was straddling that chair. "What are you doing here?" he demanded. Flannery didn't talk to people. He asked hard questions and demanded answers.

I could see why there was trouble between them, always would be while both lived. They were too much alike, and that's bad for fathers and daughters. There was no give, no tenderness, as there ought to be. Their lives were being wasted in a contest of wills.

"I asked you a question, Katie," Flannery said, feet planted like a man on a rolling deck.

"It's none of your fucking business," the man's daughter said, standing up to face him, sliding her hand into the side pocket of her skirt at the same time. I thought

117

the skirt sagged a little on the right side. Probably an ivory-handled .32. No pearl grips for this girl. Cheap and flashy, no class. Kate had class and I hoped she wouldn't shoot her father to prove it.

Flannery saw the movement toward the hideaway pistol, but that wasn't what stopped him from belting her. A fierce love seemed to vibrate between them; too late ever to be put into words. A shame the way things go.

Flannery stood aside and told her to get out. Kate approached him warily, her hand still holding the gun we couldn't see.

"Not because you say so," she said, and then she was gone and I was faced with a father's righteous wrath. I thought I was, but all Flannery did was stare at me for about half a minute. A long 30 seconds. Then, turning away, he said, "I still don't know what to make of you. I'll have to think about it some more."

I heard the Flannerys riding away.

ELEVEN

Calvin came back sooner than I expected, and he came back dead, roped across the saddle of my horse and covered with my blanket. As soon as I saw my horse I knew Calvin's body was under that blanket. Three Arizona Rangers brought him in, early in the morning, when I was coming back from breakfast. I got to the jail before they did and waited for them. Their starred badges glittered in the sunlight, and they took no heed of the people who came out to stare at the corpse of the orphaned boy who would never get to be rich and famous like Brady or Gates. I felt my gut turning to lead as they came closer.

They got down and hitched their animals at the jail post. McLandress was hurrying down the street on fat legs, puffing in his eagerness to get in a few licks at me. Right then I couldn't find any reason to fault McLandress. There was nothing he could say about me that I wasn't saying to myself. I had got a boy killed, a

119

poor kid who had nothing to do with any of it, and it was no comfort to wish it had been me instead of him.

Two of the Rangers were somewhere in their late twenties; their boss was about 40, long faced, wind burned, and he had the confident, settled look of a man who knew his business. Without the Ranger badge he could be taken for a cattle buyer or the foreman of a big spread. He moved slowly but not awkwardly: a man who saved his energy. He had big hands, and the handle of his short-barreled Colt .45 hadn't come from the factory. It was bigger than usual and curved back so it filled his hand in just the right way. The other Rangers had nothing remarkable about them.

"I'm Captain Wilkes, Arizona Rangers. I got a dead boy here. Where's Callahan?" The Ranger Captain didn't waste words, and he didn't jerk his thumb toward the corpse.

I told him who I was and he nodded.

"My men, Clagett and Lavery," he said.

I got nods from them.

"You know who he is?" Wilkes asked, lifting the end of the blanket from Calvin's face. He had been shot through the right eye. The other eye was open and the blood on his face had dried. I guessed he had been shot more than once, but I couldn't see the wounds. The rope—my rope—that held his wrists and ankles together went under my horse's belly. My horse whickered at me, nervous among strangers, nervous because of Calvin.

"Calvin Beamer," I said as Wilkes covered the dead face again. "Worked around the jail, the livery, got no family. Where did you find him?"

McLandress got there and let out everything he had been holding back for so long. "Arrest this man, sir. I demand that you arrest this man. He goes by the name of Saddler. Don't be too sure of that. Callahan, that's the Marshal, appointed him deputy without authority. Now he refuses to quit the jail, quit the job. He's holding office illegally. He's been threatening us with guns and he burned and maimed a man—arrest him right now."

Wilkes had clear gray eyes and they moved from me to McLandress, taking in his bulk and his mottled face. McLandress's face grew redder under the Ranger's casual gaze. There was so much the fat banker wanted to say. He wanted to get Callahan and me at the same time. He started up again, as if Wilkes hadn't heard everything he'd said.

"Be quiet, mister," Wilkes said. "The Governor can yell at me, nobody else. Anything you have to say I'll listen to later. Right now I'm going to talk to the Deputy and see what's what. So keep a lid on it, mister, you'll get your chance. Everybody will."

McLandress shut up but he didn't go away. Wilkes turned back to me. "You won't be needing that badge and rifle, Deputy. We're taking over from here on in. The Governor got a report there's big trouble fixing to cut loose down here. We're here to see it doesn't. Suppose you tell me what you know."

McLandress stood there, red faced with anger, while I told my side of it. I told Wilkes most of the truth, all the truth he needed to know. He grunted and here and there prompted me with a question. McLandress cut in when I told about Dorfman and the fight in the jail.

"You're saying this Dorfman didn't try to kill Deputy Saddler?" Wilkes said, eyeing the banker with natural dislike. He managed not to show too much of it.

McLandress blustered, repeating himself. "Mr. Dorfman was acting for the town," he said. "The Judge read the law and Saddler refused to listen. What Dorfman did was not attempted murder. Dorfman would have been the new marshal. In a way, that made him the legal marshal."

"Don't get legal, mister," Wilkes said, cutting off the banker's flow of words. "All that's for the courts to decide." He paused. "If it gets that far. It seems to me the Deputy had a right to defend himself. If you wanted law, you should have waited for the law."

I had been thinking about that. "You mind telling me how you got here so fast?" I asked. "The boy there couldn't have reached the telegraph line."

Wilkes hadn't been against me a moment before. He still wasn't but his voice got hard. Arizona Rangers, as good or better than the more famous Texas boys, don't think much of local law, crooked or honest.

"The Governor doesn't confide in me, Saddler," he said with a tight, faint smile. "He gives orders, I take them. You ought to be glad I'm here."

"Glad enough," I said honestly. "No offense. You won't be able to stop Ballard with two men. Ten Rangers wouldn't be enough."

"I got men on the way," Wilkes said. "We'll keep the peace here. If you want the boy, you can have him. If not . . . I guess the town."

I said I'd look after him. "How often was he shot?" I asked.

"Four times," Wilkes said. "One in the head, three in the body. We found him a day's ride from here, dead but the rigor had worn off. So he was shot long before we came on him. I have to say this, Saddler. You got that boy killed. No more killing is going to happen here. Now gather up your stuff and see to the boy. We're taking over the jail. This town is under Ranger law from now on. You got any objections?"

I knew Danziger was watching from the hotel window.

"Sure I have—Jarvis!"

They all went for their guns at the same time. Jarvis was faster than the others, but the other two were good boys. But I had the drop and I used it. I drew and fired and killed Jarvis with a bullet in the heart while his gun was just clearing leather. He staggered back, the gun dropping from his hand, his other hand reaching up to his heart and not making it. Getting the drop was what counted. I had talked them along, seeing them relax as the talk went on.

I fired the next bullet into the man beside Jarvis and

didn't wait for him to drop or die before I fired again. I gave him two and put two more in the other man. They'd hadn't fired a single shot, not even a close miss. The horses jerked away from the rack and one broke loose, heels kicking in fright.

I was down to one bullet in the chamber when Lattigo cut loose from the hotel window, jetting bullets at me, splintering porch wood and causing McLandress to scream like a woman. He was on his belly in the dust with his hands pressed over his face, begging not to be shot. I grabbed up the rifle and ran to the end of the porch and dived under the rail and came up rolling in the alley with Lattigo's bullets chasing me. I crawled up on the porch of the next building, and Lattigo blasted at me with his handgun. Bullets chipped the chairs on the porch, threw chips all around me, but I kept going. I got off the porch and lay under the overhang and reloaded the Colt. I knew he was reloading the rifle. There was yelling up at the hotel window and then it got quiet.

Lattigo's next rifle bullet gouged the heel of my boot without knocking it off. I threw three bullets his way to give me time to get to better cover. I got behind a pile of crates in front of the general store and his return fire didn't do any harm. There was no way to rush the hotel without getting killed. Lattigo would drop me before I ran three yards. I looked up and down the sidewalk wondering if one of the good townspeople might be ready to collect a reward by shooting me in the back. McLandress wouldn't do it. Gunning any man wouldn't come into his thick, righteous head. About Casey, the saloon keeper, I wasn't so sure. If he got rid of me he would earn Danziger's gratitude, for what it was worth, and he would get rid of Callahan, too. Getting shot in the back was something I had to risk.

Bullets tore into crates and I stayed where I was. Danziger wasn't shooting, not yet. A good chance he wouldn't join in. Lattigo was the one to get. He had already lost his life when he fired at me for the first time.

And I had to get him fast, then make preparations for the other men Jarvis had said were heading for town. I counted Lattigo's bullets when he cut loose again. He blasted without taking much aim. While he was reloading, I spotted a stack of new blankets lying behind the piled up crates. I picked it up and threw it. It didn't look anything like a man, but it was movement and Lattigo caught it on the fly. I fired while I ran and there was no return fire. Then I was down the street and halfway across it when Lattigo fired the bullets he had loaded. I knew he hadn't loaded all the way, not unless he was the fastest loader who had ever lived. Bullets kicked up dust, but I was down and away from him, and the angle for accurate shooting was bad. I fired at him when he leaned out, and he ducked back.

Now I was in a place where I couldn't see him and he couldn't see me. No one was at the windows or doors on the far side of the street. An alley ran between the hotel and the bank, but I stayed out of it. I didn't know Lattigo or how he worked. He was pretty good. I stayed where I was, to the side of the hotel, away from the big twin window, and waited for him to come to me. Time was on my side. Maybe it was. I didn't do anything when I heard the back door banging. There was no way to figure it. You could bang a door to make the other shooter think you had gone out that way. You could bang it and still go. I didn't hear any more noise after the door banged.

I knew Lattigo's horse was at the livery, but there were two dead men's horses still hitched to the jail rack. My horse stood fretting with the body still on it. Lattigo, unless he had gone out the back way, would have to make a break for the horses at the jail. He knew he couldn't give up. No jail for him. He was a professional gunman and knew how the game worked; knew I would shoot him in the back, kill him unarmed, if I got the chance.

I knew he could be getting away, that was the gamble. I could see the stable but I was a long way from it. He could snag a horse and boom out bareback, and at that distance there wasn't much hope of hitting a moving target. No matter. I'd go after him when I finished killing Danizger. They hadn't killed the boy, hadn't shattered his body with bullets, but they had to die for it. Somebody had to pay for poor dumb book-reading Calvin. If they didn't my whiskey would always have a bad taste.

By now most of my anger had gone away; but there was enough left to be merciless. Just then Lattigo came out the hotel door like a cannon ball. He dived into the street and came up blasting with the rifle, his head swiveling this way and that. He was backing away, the rifle ready, and he was turning to break into a run when he saw me with the stock of the Winchester jammed hard against my shoulder. God! it was good to kill that man. I was ready but still I fired faster than I had to. The first bullet ripped through his heart, and I shot him three times while he was falling. I jacked another shell and made myself stop. There was nothing to shoot at—he was meat!

I walked into the street and Danziger could have shot me from the window if he had the nerve. Lattigo was so dead blue flies buzzed in his leaking blood. Then I turned and looked up at Danziger's window. The window shade flapped against the bullet-shattered window frame. I wasn't watching my back anymore. Casey wouldn't try it now. I went in and the lobby was empty, dusty, flyblown, silent. On the desk the inkwell was spilled; the banging of the back door might have been the clerk getting out fast.

I went up and the door to Danziger's room was open partway. I stood to one side and poked it open all the way with the rifle barrel. At first I saw nothing and then I heard a snuffling sound under the bed. On the dresser Danziger's liquor case was split, broken by a ricocheting bullet. I raised the rifle and said, "Crawl out, Danziger. Crawl out or get killed where you are."

Nothing happened until the snuffling sound began again. I fired a bullet into the floor beside the bed.

Danziger yelled and came crawling out. They had cleaned the room for his arrival, but they hadn't swept under the bed, Danziger, the man who had dinner with the rich and powerful, was covered with lint and dust. It was in his crinkly hair and in his eyebrows. His nightshirt was torn where he had snagged it on some metal part of the bed in his hurry to get under it. His old man's rickety legs had blue veins like cords in the calf. There hadn't been time to get shaved or do anything before the shooting started.

Spittle ran from the corners of Danziger's loose mouth. "Don't kill me, please don't shoot. I told you I didn't want to be part of this. Ballard said—"

I raised the rifle and his body sagged even more. Danziger wanted to turn his back to the bullet. The son of a bitch wanted to turn his back. That's what he was mumbling, and he was turning when I lowered the rifle. No, I thought, this wasn't the way to do it. A quick clean bullet in the back of the head is better than most of us deserve. When the bullet strikes, the instant it smashes the skull, that's all there is. That's what the doctors say: no fading of the light. Bang! you're dead. I wasn't about to let Danziger off so easy, and I didn't give a shit how he got into it. How can a man be so scared that he starts something that goes along until a boy is murdered?

"Turn around," I said, grinning at him, enjoying his fear. Piss ran down his leg and made a pool on the floor. "People keep telling me I'm not the law, so I'm going to prove I am—I'm going to hang you, Danziger. If the Judge was legal enough to read me out of office, he can sentence you to hang. You're under arrest for murder, the murder of Calvin Beamer. Maybe there's a lawyer here that will defend you. You're a lawyer—you can do it. There's the door."

Danziger stepped out of the pool of piss. He still looked sick, but some of the fright had passed, and I could almost hear his crafty brain working again. But he was wrong, dead wrong, about thinking his way out of this. I wanted word of Danziger's trial and hanging to get out, spread far and wide, as far as saloon talk and newspapers could carry it. If it reached Ballard before he started, it might keep him from coming. I didn't think it would. But nothing would be lost except Danziger's dirty life.

"My clothes—" he started to say as the fear faded even more. It wouldn't have faded at all if he had known me better. He would have begged for a bullet and probably would when the noose hung over him.

I grabbed him and shoved him toward the door. "You'll go as you are. Let the town see how big a big man looks in a pissy nightshirt. We'll go down and you can make a speech. Tell them about reopening the mines— they'll want to hear that."

The street was filled with people, but it might have been empty, everything was so quiet. They must have thought Danziger had died when I fired the shot into the bed. Lined along the sidewalk, their faces looked like faces in old photographs, stiff and unsmiling, waiting for the photographer to squeeze the bulb. McLandress had gathered up some of his dignity and was waiting with the rest. His black suit was gray from the dust in the street. My horse came down the street when he saw me, still carrying the body.

I shoved Danziger into the middle of the street and he stood blinking in the sun. Gray hairs glittered in the ginger stubble on his chin. A sort of movement, an easing of tension, seemed to ripple through the people on the sidewalks. It stopped and there wasn't a sound.

I pointed at McLandress and the stable man Bush. "You and you, take the boy off my horse and do it gently. Lay him on the blanket and stand ready." I didn't have to raise my voice in all that silence. "There's going to be a funeral in this town and you're all going to attend. Hide from it and I'll drag you out. You're going to walk behind this boy's coffin and you're going to bow your heads and sing hymns. You're going to kick in the money for a real stone marker for Calvin Beamer. He wanted to be remembered."

An elderly woman spoke up from the front of the crowd. "We didn't kill him, Mr. Saddler. You don't have to drag me to his funeral. But I'll go. That doesn't say we had anything to do with this."

"Some of your men killed him, helped to kill him by standing by when this—this thing here"—I shoved Danziger again and he fell to his knees—"promised you money and that's all you could see. You knew God-damned well he was wrong, what he was trying to do with the Flannery girl. And don't tell me you sided with him because of Ballard. Ballard wasn't your first thought —it was the money. Take a good look at him now. Doesn't look so important, does he?"

The old man who cooked my meals spat close to Danziger's bare feet. "What're you fixing to do with him, Deputy? Turn him over to the law?" The old man grinned. "I forgot—that's you!"

I said, "What I'm fixing to do is put him on trial for murder. Trial starts right after the funeral. Danziger gave a party for you good people, now you'll give one for him. In the ballroom. Like I said about the funeral, everybody is invited."

The old man came forward and pointed to my rifle. "I'd be glad to lock him up for you. So's you can get on with the burying."

I gave the old man my rifle. "Don't kill him unless you have to."

After that I stood by while they took Calvin's bullet-wrecked body to the lumber man's laying-out room, a long high room behind his yard office. Five or six new coffins were stacked against the wall, all plain pine boxes without handles. "That one," I said, pointing to a bigger coffin standing by itself on a work bench. This one was made of dark wood and varnished to a gloss.

"That one's made special for Mr. Dirksen who is dying out on his ranch," the lumber man said.

"You can make another one," I said. "That one for the boy—the town will pay. Get on with it, no more talk."

There wasn't much laying out to be done on Calvin. They put him in the coffin and I took a last look at him. Before they screwed down the lid I sent the stable man to get the boy's well-thumbed book on rich and famous businessmen. I folded his hands around the damn fool book in place of a Bible. He didn't need it. He hadn't done anything to keep him out of wherever it was he was going—had gone.

"All right," I said.

Then the hearse took him out to the cemetery and we all walked behind it. Lattigo, still lying in the street, didn't get any attention. It was Calvin's big day, one they would always remember if only for the events that had brought it about. I saw Laurie in the crowd trying to push her way through the women so she could get close to me. She reached me and whispered as she walked along, eyes downcast.

"I heard what you said just now," she said. "Does that mean you won't be coming with me? I'm sorry about the boy, but I have to think about me. Just this morning my father was saying he'd better send me away. You know about that. So what's holding you back? You've done what you can and it's no use. Please give me an answer so I'll know."

Her father was looking our way with a puzzled look on his face. "I'll tell you sure after Danziger's trial," I said. "I won't let you down. You'll know in time."

Laurie, looking nervously in her father's direction, began to fall back with the women.

"You better not let me down," she said.

TWELVE

Danziger was behind bars and the old man was guard-ing him when I got back to the jail. It hadn't been a bad funeral. I had nothing to say about Calvin, not to the town of Dragoon Wells, and so I was greatly surprised when McLandress came forward and said he hadn't known Calvin except by name, but was sure he had been a good boy and the Lord was sure to forgive him for any small mischief he might have committed. The rest of them, standing on the hillside that ran down from the burying ground, listened with bowed heads.

That done, they shoveled Calvin under for keeps.

On the way back to town, McLandress walked along with me. I didn't tell him to fuck off because he had, in his clumsy way, done his best to say something for the dead boy. We walked in silence for a while. Then he said, "How did you know they weren't Rangers? You called one of them Jarvis, did you know him before?"

"Years ago back in Texas," I said. "Jimmy Dolan's

Saloon in El Paso, a big place, a lot of games going at the same time. I guess Jarvis never did see me. Jarvis was in a game with some hard cases from up north. Something started and Jarvis killed two men. Two shots, two men. He backed out of there before the law showed up. First time I saw two men killed that quick; so I remembered the man who did it. People told me who he was."

McLandress said, "But how did you know he hadn't joined the Rangers in the years since then? Plenty of wild boys turn about and become lawmen."

I grinned at the fat banker. "Jarvis did too many killings in those years. The Rangers check back on all the men that want to join. They don't do things like they do here."

McLandress was worried again. But he had nerve enough to say, "Maybe you're just as bad as he was."

"No, Banker," I said. "I'm no killer. You mean the way I gunned down Jarvis and his men. I got the drop, they weren't expecting it. What would you have tried to do—put them in jail?"

McLandress considered the question. "They wouldn't let you do that."

"Not likely," I said.

"Would you have . . . if you could?"

"No, Banker. Not after what they did to the boy. I figured they met him on the road and seeing their badges he talked too much. Maybe asked for their help. They killed him and brought the body back so they'd look like lawmen."

The banker's daughter, the lovely Laurie, hurried to hear what we were talking about. I guess she thought I was selling her out to her old man. Trying to match our short steps, she said, "That was a perfectly lovely funeral, don't you think so, Mr. Saddler. Father, you were very moving, the nice way you spoke."

"Hush up," McLandress snorted. "Can't you see we're talking."

"What about, Papa?" Laurie said, trying to link her arm with his. It was like a vine trying to grow up the side of a boulder.

"Town business, girl," McLandress said, disengaging her arm and telling her to go walk with the women.

"Be seeing you now, Mr. Saddler," Laurie called back to me.

"These terrible things, I don't know what to make of them," McLandress started off, fumbling for the right words. "All the things you said about Danziger and Ballard, they're hard to believe. You were a stranger to us—why should we have believed you?"

We were nearly back to town, passing the place where Callahan had broken his legs, where it all started. "You believe me now, Mr. McLandress?"

"I saw that dead boy," McLandress said. "It's funny. Nothing else you said made any difference. It took the boy to change that."

"And if Calvin hadn't been killed? What then?"

"I don't know. I knew you were right and Danziger was wrong. If the boy hadn't been killed I probably would have stayed on Danziger's side. The Flannery girl wasn't all that important."

"What about now?"

"You want an honest answer, I'll give you one. I wish she'd go away from this town. With her gone Ballard wouldn't burn us out. But we can't make her go; so Ballard will think we had a hand in keeping her here. So he'll burn the town or try to. Would you say that's right, Deputy?"

This was the first time McLandress had called me Deputy since the trouble began. "He'll try it," I said. "I'm still asking for your help. You sound like you're ready to give it."

McLandress looked at me. "There's an old and very good rule in business, Deputy. Cut your losses, don't invest any more capital when you're losing. That's what we've been doing with Danziger, and it's time we

132

stopped. We'll help you because it's the sensible thing to do."

You could hardly call that a heart-warming declaration, but it was honest. It was a banker's answer and I liked it fine.

We were in front of the jail and we looked at each other, two men who could never be friends. McLandress had a bulldog jaw underneath the fat put there by thousands of big dinners, but I knew he would keep his word once he gave it. That was the reasonable way to look at it. He might change his mind if Ballard rode into town on a donkey waving an olive branch and strewing $1,000 bills. And that, I was reasonably sure, was not about to happen. So poor old Calvin had done some good after all.

"I'll bring Danziger down to the hotel," I said. "That man has to hang."

"You want a suggestion, Mr. Saddler?"

"I'll listen."

McLandress said, "Don't keep telling people what to do. This is our town and we'll decide if Danziger is to hang." And with that he stumped on down to the hotel.

Danziger was still in his nightshirt and I asked the old man to fetch his clothes. Danziger gripped the bars of his cell, as if testing their strength. "You really mean to go through with this, Saddler?"

"That's the idea." I sat down and poured a drink. Danziger looked at the bottle and licked his lips. "No," I said. Then I changed my mind and filled a glass for him. He bolted the whiskey and held out his glass again. I took it and put it on the desk.

With whiskey in him, Danziger got a little cockier. "You know what you're doing is wrong, Saddler. I killed nobody, never carried a gun in my life."

I had another drink. "You brought Jarvis here."

"That was to prevent killing, not to start it," Danziger said. "You were supposed to get out; they were supposed to take over. I don't know why they had to kill the boy.

133

Maybe he tried to run."

"Calvin had no sense," I said. "There's nothing to talk about, not a thing. I told you to back off and you kept on coming. Now you're going. I'll hang you myself, I'm the law."

I got up and gave Danziger another drink. I wanted him to think about the things he'd be missing on the other side. This was a man who lived for the good things in life, but I knew he didn't enjoy them like a normal man. Danziger was a glutton for whiskey and rich food. He loved the appearance of comfort more than comfort itself.

"You're wrong if you think Ballard will get here in time," I said. What I did next was just for show. I reached into my pocket, which was full of cartridges, and took one out and held it up between thumb and forefinger. I turned the stubby brass cylinder before I dropped it in my lefthand shirt pocket. "That one is for you," I said. "That pocket is empty except for that bullet. I'll save that one for last. I'd save that one for you even if I had to face torture by not using it on myself."

"You're crazy," Danziger said. "You've been acting crazy all along. You won't take money and you won't run. That makes you crazy. Say what you want. Maybe I tried to buy you too cheap. No more bluffing, not now. Name a price and I'll meet it. How much?"

"You're wasting your time." When we weren't talking the big wooden clock on the wall made a loud tick. "Don't waste too much—you don't have much. You'll be dead in less than two hours." I knew what I wanted from Danziger, but I wanted to be sure of getting the truth. Faced with certain death, another man would be ready to tell the truth. It wasn't that simple with Danziger. Lying was natural as breathing to this man, and it was doubtful if he ever told the whole truth in his life. You would almost have to see and hear this man, to know what I'm talking about. No matter what, he would try to hold something back.

"There has to be something," Danziger said, sweat dribbling from his crinkly hair. In his face a muscle twitched that hadn't twitched before. The clock ticked and I heard the old man coming back with the clothes.

He came in and slung the clothes over the back of a chair. He hawked up a gob when he looked at Danziger but spat in the stove instead of on the floor. I told him to pour himself a drink.

"What's your name?" I asked him. "Sorry but I never did hear it."

He said they called him Dad Switzer and we said how-do, introduced at last. "You want me to start tying the rope?" he said.

"Have it ready," I said. "Tell McLandress I'll be there in a few minutes.

I pushed the clothes and boots through the bars of the cell, and when Danziger finished dressing ten minutes were left. I held up the key but didn't put it in the lock. "I want you to listen to me, Danziger. You get one chance to talk, tell me everything you know. One chance, then you hang. Convince yourself what I'm saying is the truth. There's no one here to help you, no politicians, no rich men, no Ballard. Keep it simple. What's Ballard going to do?"

Danziger started to tie his ribbon tie, but it would have felt too much like a rope. He threw it away and took hold of the bars again. "You'll let me go free if I give you what you want?"

I shook my head. "Not a chance. You can't murder a boy and walk away from it. The trade is, information for life in jail. You monkeyed with fake Rangers so you'll go before the Governor's Tribunal. You confess to me, you'll get life."

Danziger pretended to think about it. "That's not such a good trade. That the best you can do?"

I knew the son of a bitch was ready to jump at the chance, and being a lawyer, he knew that anything he told me, without witnesses present, didn't mean a fucking thing. Once he was lodged in the jail in the capital, he would start pulling strings to get out. He would call in every I.O.U. he held on every politician in the Territory. Getting Danziger where I wanted him was like trying to land a big trout with a thin line.

"Take it or leave it," I said.

"What's to say you won't double-cross me? You don't play by any rules."

I smiled, one bad man to another. "You can't give me money if you're dead. That's it, Danziger. I want something to ease my conscience for not hanging you. I'm not like you, I'm an honest crook."

Danziger smiled nervously, but he did smile. I guess he no longer saw the noose hanging over him. "Why not just settle for the money. Name a price, I'll get what you want."

I said no. It had to be jail. The clock began to whir as its metal insides got ready to chime the hour. "The hell with any more talk, let's go," I said.

"Suppose they find me guilty?"

"They will, but it's up to me to hang you. I'll get the Judge to set the time for tomorrow morning. We'll be long gone by then."

Danziger gulped and I hoped the habit of lying wasn't so deeply ingrained that it was impossible for him to tell the truth. "No more fake Rangers will be coming. Jarvis was all. If Ballard doesn't hear from me by tomorrow he'll be on his way. Jarvis was the last hope of doing it the easy way. Ballard will be here the day after tomorrow, maybe sometime late tomorrow if he pushes it."

It was my turn to be surprised, though I didn't show it. "Then he's already in the Territory. No other way he could get here that fast."

"Ballard figured he'd be spotted if he had led a big party across the border at the same time. That was smart, he probably would. Especially a big party of Mexicans. That would bring out the army in force. So he's been bringing them across five or ten at a time. At night, no show of force, no invasion. The plan was to make camp in a deep canyon not much more than a day south of here. You think you're doing me a favor. I'm doing you just as big a one. You won't be here when Ballard comes. He'll be mad and murderous, no more chance of a pardon after this. So all bets will be off. This will be the last time he ever crosses that border and he'll want people to remember it. You know what he said to me? He said, 'If it goes wrong and I have to come, Dragoon Wells will be just a name on a map.'"

I wanted to shoot Danziger in the mouth. Instead, I asked how many men Ballard had.

"I don't know that, can only guess," Danziger said. "Seventy-five is a good guess. Could even be more."

Jesus Christ! And every one of them a professional killer, men who had learned their grisly trade in regular and bandit armies. Mostly they'd be Mexicans but some Americans too. Americans rode with the Mexicans only by proving they could be worse than the Mexicans.

I unlocked the door for Danziger, and he said, "I'd like to be gone from this place." He didn't mean the jail but the town. He'd be gone all right, but not the way he intended. He was going to keep Calvin company for all time, because there was nothing I could think of that would cause me to turn him over to the Territorial Law, allow him to go on living. If I could get Ballard, then I'd get him; Danziger was here and he had to go first. I can't say I even hated the man. I was past that. He was filth that had to be washed away, a shithouse bucket that had to be emptied. A double cross? You bet it was. But of course Danziger knew none of that when I marched him down to the hotel at the point of my rifle. People who couldn't get into the ballroom lined the sidewalks to watch Danziger going to face justice. Lattigo's body had been taken away; there was a bloody patch where he had fallen. By now everyone knew the story—McLandress's doing—and no kind faces were turned toward old Earl. They liked him less when they saw he wasn't too repentant. Danziger thought that once again he had wormed his way out of a tight place. There was no point in telling him that he was walking to his death, with only a short layover in the make-do courtroom.

Why did I bother to go through with what I was doing? Stand him in front of a judge and jury and let them deal with him? Truth to tell, I didn't much care about the law, and still don't. My real intention was to put some backbone into these people for the fight that lay ahead. This was their town and I wanted them to remember it. Doing away with Danziger was the first step toward giving them back their self-respect. Once men have that they will fight to hell and gone.

What I had to do next was get the Flannerys to join in. There was no beating Ballard without them. How I was going to persuade them—persuade old Con, the only one who mattered—was still a question. As for Laurie there was nothing more to decide. In the years to come I would want to kick himself; there was no help for it—she would have to go without me. I would tell her the best way to do it, tell her to drop the idea of Havana or Mexico City. Go to New York and brazen it out, I'd tell her. Her old man wouldn't call in the law. It was a hard thing to have to do, to give her up. Did I love her? That's too complicated to answer. I don't stay with women for very long, or maybe it's the other way around. I don't have much to do with the faint-hearted ones; so there is no hard feeling when it's over. Women like that are always in need of a change of men, and I'm the same way about women. If you think it odd for a man to think about women on the way to a hanging that's how it was. But life would go on after Earl Danziger was dead. Fact is, life would be a tiny bit better for his passing.

Danziger balked some when he got his first look at the noose dangling from the hay hoist at the livery stable. It was a simple way of doing it. Danziger would walk, or be carried, up to the hayloft to have his necktie fitted. Then he'd be thrown out the door. There was a good drop, more than enough to swing him off in style. I didn't mind if he choked a bit when he ran out of rope.

Danziger looked away from the rope, his eyes begging for reassurance. He got a nod from me. I was done with lying to the sneaky son of a bitch. "Go in," I said.

They were waiting, all that could squeeze into the dusty old ballroom. Danziger had more people at this party than at the first one. People were there I hadn't seen before—but no Flannerys. I guessed Con Flannery had a spy in town; if so, old Con would know the whole story by now. On a fast horse it wasn't that far to the ranch.

The Judge's bench was the bandstand with a table and chair placed in the middle of it. Someone had hung a flag on the back wall, and the Judge was already in his chair with a Bible and the Laws of Arizona Territory in front of him. I could tell he'd fortified himself with a couple of big drinks, but that was all. The Judge had that normal, sober look that some drunks have in the first half of the day. He would do just fine.

McLandress and 11 men sat behind a trestle table to one side of the bench, and most of them I'd seen before. Bush the stable keeper was one of them. McLandress came over when I brought Danziger in.

"There's no lawyer for him. Wilcox said he was too sick to defend him."

Even then, Danziger had to show off. "That's all right, Mr. McLandress. There's not going to be any trial here."

The banker's eyes jumped to me. "What's he talking about?"

I looked straight at Danziger so there could be no mistake. "I don't know," I said. "It's got nothing to do with me."

Danziger swayed on his feet as if he had been punched hard and had just enough strength left to keep from falling. The color drained from his face and his slack mouth worked convulsively. "You dirty bastard—you lied to me!" Then he came at me with both hands, but

139

McLandress drove him away with his bulk and turned to stare at me again.

"He's crazy with fear," I said. "He'll say anything."

Maybe McLandress believed me. It hardly mattered. He wrestled Danziger into a chair on the other side of the bench, facing the jury table, and warned him to stay there or he'd be tied. When all that was done, he came back to me.

"You have to prosecute. There's nobody else."

I hadn't thought much about that. All I know about the law is not to get caught by it. I nodded and that made me a prosecutor.

The Judge liked having a courtroom to preside over. He wiped his spectacles and steadied them on his long nose. "I declare this court in session," he said. "This court, in special session, will hear the charge against Earl Danziger, the charge being murder, the murder of Calvin Beamer. You will act as prosecutor, Mr. Saddler?"

I stood up and said I would.

The Judge glanced over at Danziger. "And who will represent the defendant?"

Danziger got up too. "I will."

"Your honor," the Judge said.

Danziger said, "I will, your honor."

"Proceed," the Judge said, leaning back in his hair chair.

I kept to the facts. I told about sending Calvin to the telegraph line, the way he came back, the gunfight with Jarvis and his gunmen, the killing of Lattigo after he had opened fire on me from the window of Danziger's room. I testified that Danziger had confessed his part in the killing of Calvin Beamer.

Danziger jumped to his feet. "I did no such thing, your honor. This man solicited a bribe from me."

The Judge, glaring at Danziger, pounded the tabletop for silence. "Sit down, Mr. Danziger, you'll get your chance."

Then the Judge peered down at me. "Is that the

conclusion of your testimony, Mr. Saddler?"

I said it was and the Judge said I could make my closing remarks later. "All right, Mr. Danziger," he said.

Danziger walked up in front of the bench and looked around for something to lean on. Not finding it, he stood up as straight as he could. "With due respect, your honor, I submit that this court has no jurisdiction in this case. This being a Territory and not a State, this trial should properly be held in front of the Governor's Tribunal."

"Why is that?" the Judge wanted to know.

"Because Territorial Law states that any crime against the sovereignty of the Territory takes precedence over all lesser crimes. That includes homicide, your honor. I hereby plead guilty to the charge of conspiracy to cause three men to impersonate Territorial peace officers."

"I cannot accept your plea, Mr. Danziger," the Judge said. "The charge here is murder. We have only Mr. Saddler's word that the three men he killed were not real peace officers."

Danziger gaped. "But you just admitted his testimony."

"We heard his testimony, Mr. Danziger. The jury must decide what to do with it."

"But Saddler was telling the truth. The three men he killed were hired gunmen. I sent for them, sent a man to instruct them to pose as Arizona Rangers. That's what Saddler said, I'm saying it too. That makes it a matter for the Tribunal."

The Judge leaned forward in his chair. "This court is not inclined to believe Mr. Saddler's testimony. Not only is he the prosecutor in this case, he is also a hostile witness and shall be characterized accordingly."

"But he was telling the truth, your honor."

"The jury must decide that. At the moment I must decide whether there is a compelling reason why this trial should not continue. I am afraid that Mr. Saddler's testimony is not enough." The Judge cleared his throat.

"And neither is yours, Mr. Danziger. Obviously, it would be to your advantage to have this trial stopped. Therefore, since there is no reliable testimony"—I swear the Judge winked at me—"this trial for murder will continue. You may proceed, Mr. Danziger."

"Proceed!" Danziger was indignant. "This entire proceeding is irregular, your honor. The prosecutor is the principal witness against me. I demand a proper trial."

"No," the Judge said with no legal jargon added.

"I was given no opportunity to participate in the selection of the jury."

"Do you object to certain members of the jury? If so, I will take that under consideration, Mr. Danziger. You don't, then we will proceed. Your objections are overruled. Territorial Law states that certain formalities may be dispensed with when there is a state of emergency. One exists here, I believe. You will be seated, Mr. Danziger while Mr. Saddler makes his closing address to the jury. You may do that, Mr. Saddler."

Once again, I kept it short, and there was no legal language used. Danziger had convicted himself out of his own mouth, in his attempt to get the trial moved to the capital, and for once the jury members were hearing law talk they could understand. I said Danziger hadn't murdered the boy; that a man didn't have to pull the trigger to kill another human being. I was out of bounds when I told them they had to hang Danziger because this was their town and they had the say in it. No objection came from Danziger and the Judge didn't steer me back into narrow legal channels.

"It's up to you," I concluded.

I sat down and let Danziger run off at the mouth. He was talking for his life—already lost—and the Judge let him talk. If it had been a jury made up of strangers, he might have bullshitted his way out of it. But he was playing against a stacked deck. Still and all, he wasn't bad. The jury got a rundown on his whole career and all the important men he knew. They got the poverty of his early years; how he slopped hogs, taught himself to read. His old Maw and Paw were so goldarned proud when he got his lawyer's papers after reading law in some small-town attorney's office. Then they got the rest of it: the times he ran for Governor of Texas, the big men he helped get elected. He left out the railroad scandal, then remembered that he had nothing to lose by admitting to his part in it. He thought that was his trump card, the hold Ballard had over him. The threat of jail or death.

"I admit it, gentlemen," he declared. "In my time I have been a venal and wicked man, but I am no killer. Yes, gentlemen, I am guilty of avarice and bribery, but I am innocent of the crime of murder."

McLandress and the others didn't even retire to another room. All they did was put their heads together and whisper. There was a lot of solemn nodding and then McLandress stood up.

"We the jury find the defendant guilty," he said.

The Judge had just finished sentencing Danziger to hang—sentence to be carried out immediately—when a boy burst into the courtroom yelling, "The Flannerys are back! The Flannerys are back!"

THIRTEEN

The Flannerys were at the end of the street, waiting by the stable where Danziger was to hang. They sat on their horses in silence, spread out in a half circle so they wouldn't get in the way. Dangling from the hay hoist, the rope stirred in the hot wind that blew in from the south, and the Flannerys didn't stir when I brought Danziger out, with McLandress and all the others following along.

Before we left the court, I got bottle of whiskey from Casey and told Danziger to drink all he wanted. I watched while he emptied more than half a pint into his belly. Outside he asked for more and I let him drink. After that he walked pretty good, but not too steady. We went down to the hanging place with the whole town behind us.

Danziger got another drink and said, "I got to hand it to you, Saddler. You put one over on me that's never had one put. You think I'm afraid to die, you lousy saddletramp. At least I had a life, not like you. Gambler my asshole! You're just a fucking bum! You know how you're going to die! With nothing but the rags on your back. I'm dying a rich man and nobody's going to get a cent of my money. It's where nobody'll ever find it."

I let him talk. In a few minutes he would sound off no more. I didn't see Kate until we were close to the stable. She was in back of all the Flannerys but this time not sitting sidesaddle and not wearing lady clothes. She had on the range clothes she'd worn on the first night she came to the jail. Her face was drawn and white, but still beautiful. In a way, she should have been out in front of her kin. It was happening because of her, so she should have had a place of prominence right after Danziger.

Danziger saw her too and swept off his hat and nearly fell over making a bow. "Your husband misses you, Mrs. Ballard," he said. "You better hurry back to his bed and board." Danziger bent over laughing and I pulled him to his feet.

Con Flannery sat his big horse like a statue and the Creedmore Sharps was out of its scabbard. All the Flannerys had rifles in their hands.

"I heard you were going to do it and came to watch," Flannery said. "I guess you are."

Danziger was laughing again, about as drunk as he could get. He looked at Kate. "You fair to broke Peyton's back, missus."

Kate's hothead brother, the one named Emmet, started to bring out his gun. My gun was out first. "Try it, sonny," I said. "You can die too."

Hardly turning, Con Flannery backhanded his son across the face, all but knocking him off his horse. Then he looked at me. "We're still waiting."

I pushed Danziger toward the door of the stable. "Wait all you like, it's not being done for you."

Danziger went up the ladder by himself, and give McLandress his due, he climbed up too. Dad Switzer was standing by the open door of the loft and he reached out and grabbed the rope and brought it inside. It's hard to tell about men. Danziger held still while the noose was dropped over his head, then tightened and moved so the knot was behind his left ear. The whiskey had a lot to do with it, but not all of it. He ignored McLandress and Dad and aimed all his badmouthing at me. Some of what he said had truth in it, and you'd think because of that I should have enjoyed the thought of swinging him off. I didn't, and in the end I didn't have to. Suddenly, Danziger stopped talking and his face sagged like an old man going to sleep.

His voice came out in a surprised, "I'm going to die." He turned as if to escape through the open door of the hoist. Dad Switzer tripped him and he went flying out to the end of the rope. His neck cracked like a pistol shot and he was dead.

"I make a nice noose," Dad Switzer said in the same tone he used to praise his flapjacks. McLandress, white faced, didn't say anything. Dad said he would see to the body, and I went down to see what Con Flannery had to say. I was fresh out of reasonable words when I faced him again.

"You in or out?" I said. "There's no more time to waste in talk. If you're out, then get the hell out of this town. And I don't want to hear any more Irish bullshit about how unfriendly these people are. They're ready to stand up to Ballard with what they have. What the fuck are you going to do?"

"We're in," he said, looking at McLandress instead of me. "It's too bad the town has to suffer because of us."

McLandress didn't like to hear his town referred to in a pitying way. "You don't have to stay if you don't want. We can manage without you, Flannery." The banker turned and pointed to Danziger's body while Dad Switzer was still sawing at the rope with a clasp knife. Danziger's body dropped to the street. "We did that," McLandress said. "That's Earl Danziger we just hung. You think that didn't take some nerve."

Flannery spat. "Looked to me like he fell out that door."

McLandress refused to let go the credit. "With our rope around his neck, same thing," he said.

I got into the argument. "Save it for later," I said. "We have to talk about Ballard."

They followed me to the jail and I got out a bottle and poured a drink for Flannery, who took it without a word. I shook the bottle at McLandress and he hesitated before he said yes. Kate went past on her horse and I wondered where she was going. Laurie hadn't turned up at the trial or the hanging, but enough about my two ladies, I decided.

They got grim faced when I told them that Ballard was already on his way to Dragoon Wells. "We have some time," I said. "He may go to the ranch looking for your daughter, Mr. Flannery. Probably not. If he goes to the ranch and finds it deserted he'll burn you out. What about your womenfolk?"

Flannery drank more whiskey. "I sent them back in the hills when I came here. Kate wouldn't go, that's why she's along."

"Girls nowadays," McLandress said, shaking his head at the worry caused to fathers by young females of a certain kind—the kind I like.

"You said a mouthful," Con Flannery said, sliding the bottle to the banker.

I talked and they listened.

"First thing we have to do is keep Ballard from finding out that Danziger is dead. If he hears Danziger is dead he'll figure he talked. If that happens there won't be any way to lead him into a trap. A trap is our only hope. Any hope of getting help from the other ranchers?"

Con Flannery said not a prayer. "They're staying neutral in this. Hoping they won't get burned out too. Like you said before, what you see is what we've got."

"Then it'll have to do," I said. "Ballard won't expect anybody is going to fight him, so we're ahead there. Part of the same surprise. You sure you can talk for all the men in town, Mr. McLandress?"

McLandress was on his second glass of whiskey. "Call me Dougal," he said, making faces at the bite of the whiskey but enjoying it. "I can talk for the men that count. A few will sneak out, so we'd better post guards on the road to the south."

I said, "It's not likely they'll go that way, but we better send men out to watch for Ballard."

Flannery shoved his empty glass away from him. "You know there's always a chance Danziger was lying about the time. Maybe Ballard isn't as close as he said."

Kate Flannery passed the window again. I looked back to her father. "Maybe he hasn't even left Mexico. We don't know, so we have to figure he's right on top of us. Let's get to it."

Outside, McLandress surprised me by saying that he had been a militia major at one time. I knew the kind of officer he'd been, but I needed anything I could get. Flannery was different, a hardbitten man who had bulled his way through the bloodiest war fought on this continent. Flannery and his tough-looking brothers were going to make one hell of a difference. Even so, it was going to take more than courage to beat Ballard. Beat him hell! We'd be lucky if we could give him enough grief to make him head back for the border. If we could do that the town would be safe; an invasion of Arizona was going to get a lot of attention from the army.

We went out to get ready for a battle.

The first thing I did was to have Flannery and McLandress assemble their men in the hotel. Not all the men from the town turned up for the war talk, but the Flannerys were there, looking down their noses with the contempt ranchers have for town dwellers. I made no attempt to lessen the hostility between the two factions. It might make for a better fighting force, one side trying to show up the other. Using the lumber man's thick crayon pencil, I made a map of the town on the wall. I didn't have to rap for attention; their lives depended on it, they didn't have to be told.

I said, "We have to suppose Ballard will come in from the south. No reason why he shouldn't. They're a strong force and won't feel the need to be cautious. Danziger said Ballard is hopping mad. To a crazy man like Ballard that means killing mad. In one way that's good. It could make him careless. But it's going to be bad if we lose. You can't expect any mercy if you lose. Ballard will kill and burn until there's nothing left."

The Flannerys didn't budge, but some of the town men stirred uneasily, and I knew we'd be losing a few more men before Ballard got close to town. That was just as well; I didn't want to post men I couldn't count on. But for the moment the deserters stayed.

"We have to play hell with them, and we have to do it fast. If all we do is beat off an attack, then we're done for. Ballard will split his force and come at us from all sides. They'll bring along all the guns, all the ammunition they need. So we can't let it become a siege."

Bush the stable keeper glanced nervously at Con Flannery. "No offense meant to any man present, but I got a question that has to be asked."

I knew what was coming and it was better to get it out of the way. "Ask it," I said.

Bush said, "Would Ballard attack the town if his wife wasn't here?"

Con Flannery warned his people to be quiet. I was beginning to have respect for this big, bullying man.

"There's still time for her to go north," Bush said, fidgeting under the Irishman's stare. "If she started right now, with a strong escort, her family men, what's to stop her from reaching safety? There's an army post five days north of here. It seems to me Ballard wouldn't dare take his greasers that far north."

All their eyes moved to me. Some of what Bush said was true; it all depended on how close Ballard was to Dragoon Wells. Men were posted well south of town, and so far there was no sign of the approaching force. But it was hilly country south of where we were, and men would be hard to spot, even a large force like this one. My guess was that even if the Flannerys started now they wouldn't have more than half a day's start. Even so, the stable man had a point.

"Mrs. Ballard could do that, ride north with an escort, and there's a chance she could get away with it. There's the other chance that she'll be overtaken if she goes. What isn't a guess is Ballard will burn this town anyway. He's got nothing to lose. They can't hang him twice."

McLandress, the old windbag, sided with me. "No more of that kind of talk. Go on with it, Deputy."

I said, "We have to make sure they come in fast. Men have to be on the south road where Ballard can see them. They are to turn and run when they spot the Mexicans." It was hard to ask for volunteers, men who faced almost certain death. "They'll ride you down, the ones that go. If it's dark when they come you'll have some chance of getting off the road and hope they'll be more interested in the town. But the men who go will be the means of winning this fight."

Dad Switzer pushed his way through to the front. He said, "You remember the time I told you I wasn't afraid of dying because I plan to shoot myself when I get too old to work." Dad Switzer spat. "I just quit working—I'll go. Just don't ask me to run too hard."

Con Flannery gave me a grim smile. "I'd be more use here, but I'll go if you say."

"Not you and not McLandress," I said.

Kate's mean-looking brother said he'd go, but I turned him down too. The oldest of the Flannery brothers, a stooped man with lines of pain his face, said it was all right with him. He said he was sick and a widower, so he didn't care that much. His son, a rangy boy named Phelim, submitted that they might as well keep it in the family. His father, Conor, objected but the boy held firm. "They ain't going to run me down," he said, and we all wished he hadn't said it. He looked fast enough to run off into the dark, if they came in the dark, but there was no hope for his father and Dad Switzer.

I went on with it. "We hope it works and they come in fast fixing to level the town. We let them get about halfway down the street before we open fire. We begin firing at the south end of the street. Really throw lead at them down there. That way they won't try to turn. They'll ride on through to the north end and then turn. Only they won't get that far because of the trenches dug all the way across the street."

Con Flannery, the Civil War veteran, rubbed his face. "You're going to put us in trenches. That won't work, Mr. Saddler."

"Not men in the trenches," I said. "Pine boards at the bottom of the trenches with six-inch nails driven through and pointing up. That's the first trench. In the second and third, cheval-de-frise and rolls of barbwire. Two trenches north and south, coal oil for light."

"Sure," Con Flannery said. "The trenches just the right distance apart so a horse can clear one but not the next one. I saw that done in Virginia, not in a town though. The spikes on the cheval are going to play hell with the horses."

"And men. You land on a spike you don't get up again. The ditches have to be wide and deep, then the top covered with wagon covers stretched tight and anchored with long pegs so they won't pull loose. Then everything is covered with dirt and brushed smooth. It has to look right if they come by day. Won't make any difference at night."

"You got the alleys figured in this?" Flannery asked.

I nodded. "They won't try to get out through the alleys until they find the street completely blocked. To stop them from riding up on the sidewalks and porches and getting by the trenches that way, we have to block everything off with anything that can be moved. They'll have to turn to the alleys to get out."

151

McLandress wanted to demonstrate that he was as smart as the Irishman. "More cheval-de-frise in the alleys?"

"Coils of barbwire, everything in the stores, any wire you can find. It has to be spread high and loose so there is no way through. The harder they fight to get through, the worse off they'll be. And all the time we'll be pouring lead at them."

"By God! I'm beginning to feel sorry for the bastards," McLandress said, still feeling the effects of the whiskey. "They'll get such a trouncing they'll never come back to this town."

"No," I said.

McLandress lifted his bushy eyebrows. "No!" he echoed.

The Irishman knew what I meant, but didn't say anything. It had to be a slaughter, or as near as slaughter as we could make it. I hoped the men from the town would have the stomach for what had to be done. I figured the Flannerys wouldn't be squeamish.

"No quarter," I said. "That means we kill every man we can, wounded, unarmed, wanting to surrender—no quarter! They wouldn't show us mercy, but that's not the reason. This has to be total war. If too many escape they could come back. I want the name Dragoon Wells to spread fear clear into Mexico."

It's a hellish thing to see what whiskey can do to a banker. Seized by the spirit of killing, McLandress whipped an old Starr .45 revolver from the waistband of his pants and brandished it in the air.

"We'll massacre the greasy bastards! Remember the Alamo!" he yelled.

I went out with Con Flannery, and we were the last to leave. A sour smile twisted his face and his eyes were bright with the anticipation of the fight ahead. He was a strange man, always hard to figure.

"You really think we can do it?" he said.

It would be useless to try to bullshit this hard man. "If

we get lucky," I said.

The man- and horse-killing trenches were more important than anything else, and we got everybody digging and hauling dirt. It was a sight to see McLandress down in a hole digging with the poor men he would have snorted at a few days before. There was plenty of pick and crowbar work mixed in with the digging. In the early days, when Dragoon Wells was an ambitious town, they had dug up the main street and paved it end to end with rocks, then covered everything with a layer or gravel and dirt. Years and poor times had put holes and ruts in it, but it was still rock hard, and the only thing we could be thankful for was that it hadn't been paved.

It was the closest thing to the old frontier spirit that I had seen for a long time. Women and girls kept the coffee coming, and even Casey, the pimping saloonkeeper, was loading buckets of dirt. Over at the lumber yard they were nailing the chevals together, drilling holes in beer barrels from the saloons, malleting round staves into the holes, and then sharpening the points. The cheval-de-frise is one of the most terrible defensive weapons ever invented. No matter how you fall on it you get killed or wounded so badly that it doesn't make any difference. You can't rope it and drag it away because the rope slips off the greased staves. All you can do with a cheval is stay away from it, if you can, or die on it.

All the stores were open and nobody was making any money. Wagons loaded with great rolls of barbwire went up both sides of the streets. When they got to an alley or any space between the buildings, they dumped down rolls or wire and unrolled it. In the alleys rough barriers had been nailed together and the barbwire was coiled and strung across everything. Up and down the street came the sound of shattered glass as the windows that were to serve as firing positions were knocked out. The doors, most of them, were barred or blocked from the inside by furniture, and what wasn't used for that was dragged out to block off the sidewalks.

But everything depended on those three trenches. Four or five would have been better, but there wasn't time for that. The rocks from the street were piled along the sidewalks in front of the firing positions. The thing I feared most was fire; there was nothing that could be done about that, and it was too much to hope that part of the town wouldn't burn. It had to: Ballard would come ready to burn. I knew what Ballard looked like, and hoped I'd get a chance to kill him for Calvin. It was all Ballard's doing from start to finish. He wouldn't be hard to spot. Like all madmen he wasn't a coward and he wouldn't hide in a gully and let the Mexicans do the killing. He'd be right out in front of his private army, already crazy and now crazier because of a woman, and I wondered if Kate considered the many men who were to die because of her. Probably not.

For hours it looked as if we would never get it finished. The main street was like an upturned ants' nest, with the ants running every which way. But the thought of dying makes a man work harder than money ever can. They got the trenches finished and the lumber man's helpers began to drag the chevals over from the yard. Those damn things were our salvation; they gave me a cold feeling just the same. Flannery was down in the first trench setting them up, pressing down on the back spikes so they wouldn't move when men and horses came crashing down to their deaths. Jesus! I could just about hear the screaming of the horses.

Flannery got the first trench finished and moved on to the second while men stretched wagon covers and pegged them taut. They drove the pegs in close to the wide end and began to scatter on dirt, moving it around with brooms, covering everything. A man who was tired or plain clumsy nearly fell into the second trench and would have died if Flannery hadn't yanked him to safety by the collar.

They got the third ditch covered and dusted with dirt. One of the young Flannerys rode back from the edge of town and said it was quiet out there. I had one of them reporting every ten minutes. Dad Switzer and the other two men were out on the road, sitting there with bread and meat and water, not a hearty meal for men under sentence of death.

It was close to dark when we finished. I told McLandress to make sure the town didn't get too lit up. Too much light thrown up into the sky would alert Ballard long before he got close.

Next came the parceling out of guns and ammunition. Some likely looking men had old guns, or no guns, and that had to be changed, a cause for considerable grumbling. I had to take away a cared-for '73 Winchester from a very old man and give it to one of McLandress's tellers, a wiry man who had been in the army in Canada. There was a fair collection of standard weapons, rifles, shotguns and revolvers, but you should have seen some of the others. In that pile of old iron was a .22 caliber "bicycle" pistol, a one-shotter carried by Eastern ladies to discourage rapists from unwheeling them, or however you want to say it. Still, it was a gun and it could kill, provided you put the small caliber in the right place. I took it away from a small boy and gave it to a woman with a rock jaw and a build like a man. Yes, and there were swords and bayonets, pitchforks and sickles, carving knives and a Bowie knife with a broken tip. Nothing was refused, everything was handed out to the most likely fighters. I didn't see Laurie but Kate was all over the place. No one was going to take the .38 Colt Lightning, the fast firing double-action that was belted high around her waist. She had an '86 Winchester and the pockets of her wool shirt bulged with bullets. All the Flannerys had good weapons, all Winchesters except for old Con's Creedmore. The doctor was there with two black bags instead of one, and a basket filled with bandages. I didn't tell him there wouldn't be any doctoring done during the fighting. If it slowed down to that point, we would have lost, or would lose. A few faces were missing, nothing to be done about them, and it was hard to blame them for ducking out, though McLandress, who had been nipping again, cursed them for gutless cowards. The fat banker had turned into a regular fireater, now that he had cast off the starchy skin he had been wearing all his life. He even bellowed at his top sergeant of a wife when she suggested he drink black coffee and not get so excited.

And then, suddenly, we were ready. As ready as we'd ever be—and after that there was nothing to do but wait.

FOURTEEN

*K*ate had stayed away from me since she had come to town, and that was understandable, given the circumstances. But now it was quiet, and I was sitting alone in the jail, and still there was no sign of her.

Apart from the bank the jail was the strongest building in town, and as a defensive position it couldn't be bettered. That wasn't the idea—we were the attackers. The windows were too narrow to position a lot of men, and it wasn't in the right place. At the first shot far from town I would take my place with the others.

A woman brought me a covered plate of fried chicken, and still no Kate. Men watched the street and ate what would be the last supper for some of them. I had coffee going on the stove and ate the chicken while it boiled. The night wind was blowing outside and I felt cold even with the stove going. I heard one of the Flannery boys coming in to report to his father, who was down at the hotel. After that it was quiet.

McLandress knocked and came in with a flushed face

157

and an awkward look on it. The old fool had changed his black banker's clothes for his militia uniform of yesteryear. Needless to say, it didn't fit him, far too tight across the belly and hips. I guess he couldn't find the militia hat, because he still wore his banker's tile square on the middle of his head, as always.

We nodded and I wondered what he was up to. I knew it had nothing to do with Ballard. I pushed the bottle his way, but he submitted that black coffee would be better, after all. When there were cups of coffee steaming for both of us, he decided to dollop in a taste of whiskey, and I did the same. Only then did he start to inch his way toward the point of this get-together.

He started off by saying he was sorry we'd started out with bad feeling. I mumbled something appropriate and busied myself with coffee. McLandress took a long swig from his whiskey-laced java.

"You've been doing a fine job," he said. "Organizing the defenses and so forth. You know how it's done and you're doing it. If we succeed it will all be due to you."

I had $14 in my pocket, he knew how thin my roll was, so it couldn't be money. He had no way of knowing about the cash and jewels I hoped to get from Kate. And he was too friendly, however awkward, to be leading up to the money his daughter planned to lift from his bank. Which reminded me—where the hell was Laurie?

"No false modesty, sir," McLandress protested though I hadn't said a word. "When you first came to this town I didn't like you. Not so much you personally, but what I thought you were. Well, I was wrong, and I'm man enough to admit it."

I like a man who thinks he's so wonderful he can be humble. "What's done is done," I said amiably.

"You're made of the right stuff, I can see that now," McLandress said. "You've battered around a lot. Wild oats, sir. A man is all the better when he gets that out of his system."

I didn't like the way he talked about my oats in the past

tense. My firm intention was to sow a lot more before I got killed.

"A man with your character and resolution could be somebody in no time at all." McLandress took another belt of coffee and that put more fire in his face. "It isn't what a man has been but what he is now, if you follow my meaning. Of course you do." Then he gave it to me with both barrels. "My little girl Laurie is mighty fond of you."

It wasn't a joke because McLandress wasn't a joker. Humor was as foreign to him as a Chinaman would be to an Apache.

"A fine young lady," I said gallantly. "A credit to you and your lovely wife."

McLandress dismissed his lovely wife with a grunt. "About my daughter, yes and no," he said. "May I be frank, sir. How shall I put it? Laurie, though you'd never know it to look at her, is a little on the wild side. Heavens, I don't know where she got it from. Of course I have done a few wild things in my time. Haven't we all, sir?"

"A few wild oats," was the best I could come up with.

"Exactly," McLandress said. "Still, my little girl is a bit wild. When I say that I naturally don't mean—"

"Of course not," I said.

"I knew you'd understand. The fact is, she was always on the wild side. I thought that school in Charleston— cost me a pretty penny—would make her more settled. However, she returned with the same restless spirit. To come to the point, sir, I think she needs a husband."

"He's going to be a lucky man, whoever he is," I said with that gallows feeling that always comes over me, chilling my blood, when I'm threatened with matrimony.

"Not just any man, Mr. Saddler. Is it all right if I call you Jim?"

"That's my name . . . Dougal."

"The right man is what she needs, son. Laurie's had her pick of some fine men, most of them very well fixed, but none of them suit her. All she says is, 'Oh fudge!' when I bring some young man to the house for dinner. A young man, well not exactly young, came all the way from St. Louis, and she caused me great embarrassment by laughing at him."

"High spirits," I suggested.

"Exactly, son. Laurie says bankers and businessmen can go fly a kite, words to that effect. I think what she needs is a man who can tame her, if you know what I mean."

I did but I didn't say it because I didn't want to get into a gunfight with a banker. He didn't know what Laurie needed and neither did I. Laurie didn't. She knew what she liked but what you like isn't always what you need. His lovely little girl was hot as a pistol and no lone man would ever be enough to cool her down. Me, I didn't think she'd ever cool down; the fire between her thighs would never go out. I liked the thought and she would too, if she had known about it. Why shouldn't she stay randy as long as she had the will to spread her legs? I didn't say any of that to Dougal McLandress.

"Will you marry her?" McLandress held up his hand to stop me from talking. "I know this is sudden, but I'm convinced that you're the right man for her. There are differences in background, well yes, there's that, but nothing that can't be ironed out. Laurie hasn't any money of her own"—McLandress bore down heavily on this point—"and I am far from a wealthy man, no matter what you have heard about bankers. However, I have a modest store of worldly goods and am prepared to help my little girl's husband in every way I can."

"I'd be a washout at the banking business," I said.

McLandress looked startled as if he hadn't considered letting me get close to the real money. He trusted me enough to marry his daughter, but not to marry his money.

"To each his own," McLandress said, glossing over any talk of banking. "The cattle business, that's where you belong, son. Not a very large ranch, not at first anyway. Unfortunately, there isn't the money for that. But with a good woman at your side and plenty of hard work, you'd be a man of substance in no time. I won't press you for an answer, scarcely the time, is it, but I want you to think about it. Think of it, son, McLandress and Saddler, ranchers."

I thought about it after he took his rifle and went out. I didn't like it and Laurie wouldn't either. Not for me, the long back-breaking days in the saddle, the brain-boiling summers and ass-numbing winters. Worse than anything, I'd have Dougal McLandress both as partner and father-in-law. If we came through the fight with Ballard, the banker's whiskey-fired recklessness wouldn't last long. In a day or two, he'd be back to what he was, a smalltown banker. I knew Laurie would giggle when I told her, if I got to tell her, for only a dullhead like McLandress could see Laurie cooking and washing and mending, getting up in the dark to cook breakfast, falling wearily into bed after the last chores of the endless day were done. There wouldn't be much time, or energy, for Laurie to do the kind of things she liked to do in bed. I was thinking how crazy the whole thing was when there was another knock at the door. Whoever knocked had a light touch and I figured it was Kate. It wasn't, it was her father, standing in the doorway not like the wrath of God but like any other mortal. I waved him in and he asked if he could have a drink.

I gave it to him. "Nothing yet?"

"No sign of them. My boy Emmet just reported in. My brother and the other two are waiting out there on the road. They've been staring at that busted wagon wheel since it got dark." He turned the whiskey glass in his fingers, then without warning he said it.

"You've had to do with my girl, haven't you?"

I didn't answer and he went on without waiting for one. "I know you have. It's been in her face."

I said, "What do you want, Flannery?"

"Cool off," he said. "I'm not hot about it, why should you be? Men and women get together, it's the way of life. You like her or not?"

"I like her a lot."

"That's what I was afraid of."

"If I wanted to marry her I wouldn't ask you."

"Then you aren't going to marry her. You plan to go off with her?"

"If it's any of your business—no!"

Flannery drank the whiskey he'd been staring at. "That's good news . . . for you."

I needed the drink I poured. I was beginning to wish Ballard and his pistoleros would show up. "Meaning you'd try to kill me if I said yes?"

Flannery didn't rush in with an answer, but when it came I knew he meant it. "I'd just feel sorry for you," he said. "You'd be in plenty of trouble if you got tangled up tight with my Katie. You think it's funny, a father talking like this?"

"Not funny," I said. It was taking a turn I hadn't expected and didn't like.

"Call it odd then," Flannery said, filling our glasses. "Katie's a wild woman and she'll bring you down, if you let her. Other girls are wild and get over it. That won't happen with Katie. I don't say she's bad. There's something missing in her, that's all. I knew it all the time she was growing up. That's what all the fighting was about. Katie's trouble is she doesn't know what she wants. She says she does but she doesn't. I been sitting out there in the dark thinking about her, about you, this town."

"You came to it late," I said. "What difference does it make now?"

"Not much. But when I look at the townspeople out there it makes me feel bad. I had them figured for sheep, thought they didn't matter. Some of them are going to get killed because of my girl. I shouldn't have let it get this far. I should have forced her to go north with the boys along to protect her."

"That wouldn't be much better than Danziger. All along I've been telling people she isn't a runaway slave. Now I'm telling you. If she wants to stay in Dragoon Wells, that's what she should be able to do."

Gunfire erupted in the distance and we were on our feet and Kate Flannery was forgotten. It kept up as we ran to our positions and was still going on when we got there. The shooting stopped and then there was another quick spatter of shots. Nothing else after that. Our fire would be concentrated in two places, on both sides of the spike filled ditches, and at the only way out of town, the way they would come in. I looked down the street from a store window with all the glass knocked out, the resting place for the rifles clear of the jagged edges. The street was dark, with only a light showing here and there, but once the coal oil in the two separate ditches went off, there would be plenty of light to kill by.

Lights started to burn in some of the houses; that was the plan, to make it look like an alarmed town. Flannery and about half his men were across the street in the hotel; men were on the roofs on both sides. Outside of town horse hoofs thundered on the road. I began to count, knowing that one shot fired too soon would mean the end of us. Ballard's mind would jump to a trap; he would split his force and attack from four sides. I had made no provision for anything but an ambush; everything we had done depended on that.

The thunder of horses grew louder and on the night wind came the *yip-yip* cry of the Mexicans wanting to kill, loving the thought of killing. It sounded like an army was bearing down on us. I had been in plenty of fights, but you never get used to that sound. The thunder of the hoofs grew hollow for a moment; they were passing over the bridge that spanned the creek on the south edge of town. In a minute.

Then I saw the flare of their firebrands as they swept into the main street like a black flood. Seventy-five, hell! It was more like 100 Mexicans down there, and they came on like a force that couldn't be stopped. The howl of their bloodlust, their ancient hatred of gringos, filled the flame smudged night. A cold wind blew but there was sweat on my face as I steadied the Winchester and waited for them to get closer. I kept looking for Ballard in that first wild rush of men and horses, trying to pick him out from the oncoming torrent of noise and big hats and rifles.

They hit the first ditch at breakneck speed and men and horses plunged to their deaths in a welter of flapping wagon covers and gunshots and screams. I cut loose at the same time as Flannery across the street. Heavy fire broke out at the far end of the street. McLandress and the townspeople were driving them forward toward the death-filled ditches. Twenty-five or 30 horses and men were brought down by the first ditch, and those behind, driven forward by their own numbers and speed, piled in after them. Some jumped the first ditch and then hit the second. The coal oil beyond the third ditch licked up bright yellow and the flames were fanned higher by the wind. Some got across the first and second ditches by riding over the mass of dead and dying flesh. Not so many dead or dying Mexicans were tangled in the last ditch. No horse could get out of there, but men were crawling up the steep sides.

Then nine or ten Flannerys rose up from behind the wall of fire and drove them back, firing like infantrymen, down on one knee, levering and firing. From end to end the street was a screaming mass; rifles and handguns spat orange fire. A shotgun boomed one barrel, then the other. I killed five men with five shots and grabbed up another rifle when the pin clicked on empty. It was impossible to tell one attacker from another.

Now they were trying to turn, firing back as they rounded their horses short of the first ditch. They were still crawling out of the ditches, and I fired until the shots ran together, and still they came. I fired at a big man in a big hat and killed him, but he died yelling Spanish and I knew he wasn't Ballard. They were very good, the way they rallied. The wall of fire was weakening and the Flannerys moved through it firing as they came. The Mexicans rounded on them and cut a swath through their ranks with a heavy burst of fire.

At that point the Mexicans had a chance of breaking loose, but instead of going over the last ditch they turned back again, taking their losses, trying to overcome us with firepower. As they turned and came back, many on foot now, they poured lead at our positions. Bullets chipped stone close to my face.

A horseman galloped straight at the window I was firing from. I killed him and then the horse and the weight of their charge tore the window frame loose from the wood, and for a moment I was blinded by dust. I wiped dirt from my eyes and started firing again. Now they were trying to get out through the alleys and open spaces, and I heard them screaming in the dark as they galloped into the wire. The street was piled high with bodies, shapes, things still moving. A man was trapped under a horse, still firing with a pistol though his legs were shattered. I shot him in the head and the horse that pinned him jumped up and ran a few steps before it dropped again and died.

At the other window two men fell back and one was shot in the face and blinded and ran at the wall. The other man was dead. I grabbed the two rifles and moved out onto the sidewalk. A man running behind me was hit and fell down. He grabbed his leg and hauled himself up by holding onto a porch support. A bullet killed him as he swayed.

Across the street the Flannerys were coming from the hotel and on the roofs men were crawling their way closer to the alleys. A Mexican ripped by wire and slick with blood ran from the dark and was shot to bits. Two Flannerys dropped and then a third and I heard Con Flannery cursing the others forward into the fight. McLandress and the others were moving up from the

165

south end to close the trap, and the men on the roofs gave them cover as they came.

The last of the Mexicans, maybe 20, bunched up and were torn apart by fire until they reformed and tried to break out through the south end of the street. I yelled at Flannery and he turned, rallying his men, and now we had the last of the Mexicans between us. We opened fire as they charged at McLandress's town men. We closed in on them still firing, and when the guns were empty we pulled them down and beat and kicked and stomped them to death. Then with one last yell of defiance some of them broke through the mass of men and ran into the open chased by bullets.

Con Flannery looked at me, mad eyed with the joy of killing, and ran with his men following, through the hotel and out to the back where their horses were saddled and waiting. I heard them riding away as the rest of us got on with the killing.

I dropped my empty rifle and yanked my beltgun when Peyton Ballard rose up in front of me, the big Mexican hat cinched tight under his chin and hiding his face. He was wounded in the chest and holding a gun and was trying to bring it up to shoot. He fired and missed and the hammer came back under my thumb but I didn't fire. I dived at his legs and brought him down, and even with the wound he fought like a tiger. I still held the gun and I hammered at his skull until he went limp and I forced myself to stop. It was McLandress, smelling strongly of whiskey, of all people, who pulled me away from Ballard. I was smeared with Ballard's blood and I stood weak on rubber legs. McLandress got down beside the body and said it wasn't a body.

"He's alive, we can hang him," he said, turning his big white face to me.

Then I reloaded both rifles and we moved in after the last of the Mexicans, and they were game greasers and they all died well. Shooting broke out in an alley and a townsman, killed by a Mexican, bled to death with a

166

strand of wire dug into his throat.

McLandress, full of whiskey, was a wild man. Men who get a taste of killing grow to like it. "Some are still alive," he said, shaking with excitement. "We'll hang them too."

"Just shoot them," I said. "Only Ballard hangs."

And that's what we did, where we found them, and I had to keep some of the townsmen, the tame clerks and storekeepers, from killing them slow. It was no quick job: they were all over the place, mostly wounded. Men lit firebrands and the killing went on. We flushed them out, dragged them out, and killed them. Not a single man tried to give up—they were Mexicans! There was so much killing, and it had to be done. Shooting sounded from far away and I knew the Flannerys had caught up with the survivors, not all of them, of course, just most of them. A few would get away, and they would be hunted through the hours of darkness and long after daylight came. Even so, a handful would survive to carry the bloody story back to Sonora. I killed a man crawling under a sidewalk and then I stopped. I was sick of killing. Let the townsmen have their fun; after all, it was their town and their big night.

They killed the last Mexican when the sky was red with the coming day. The funny thing was he didn't have a mark on him; stunned by a fall from his horse, he had been out cold through the whole thing. Now he stood up on shaky legs and looked about in wonder at the bodies still being dragged and piled high for burial. Light was in the street and everything washed in red when he got up. He picked up his hat and his hand went down to his empty holster. He was young and his smile was apologetic and yet mocking. McLandress looked to me for guidance, no longer eager to kill, now that he had to do it in the full light of day. I nodded and Bush the stable man shot the boy from behind.

It was all over but the hanging.

FIFTEEN

We didn't wait for the Flannerys to get back—we just did it. Ballard wasn't like Danziger; he didn't say a word. No bribes were offered and no defense. It would have been useless, so he didn't try. Ballard looked older than his age, hollow eyed as if from no sleep or bad sleep, and as we walked him down to the livery stable he didn't ask about Kate. Where was Kate? Seven members of her family were dead, one as good as, and there wasn't a sign of her. Two women had been killed, but Kate wasn't one of them. I guessed she could wait.

We had the rope ready to be slung from the hay hoist when old Dad Switzer came limping into town, ragged and bloody but otherwise all right. The crowd assembled to see Ballard hanged gave way to let the old man through. He spat when he saw Ballard. He didn't say anything about the men who had been with him on the road. I knew they were dead, cut down in the first few minutes.

"Is this the great man?" the old man asked.

"This is him," I said.

Dad Switzer said he would take it as a great favor if he could hang this one. "I won't have to trip this one," he said.

He didn't. Dad and McLandress and Bush took Ballard up and he stepped out the window by himself. I don't know what I expected from Ballard, but I didn't get it. Nothing marked him for the notorious outlaw he had been. The years seemed to have worn him down; he didn't look like a well man, and it wasn't just the battle that had taken the life out of him. Liquor and sickness and age had done most of it; darlin' Kate had done the rest. And where in hell was that beautiful bitch?

They put Ballard's body with his Mexicans; he came last so he got the top spot. There was an argument about whether they should bury them in the cemetery. It didn't last long and they buried them in the cemetery, all in one big pit it took hours to dig. It didn't look deep enough to me, and I suggested that they dump in all the lime they could find. McLandress, sick-looking now, said that was a highly practical idea.

Con Flannery came back while we were standing over the graves of our own people. We hadn't buried any of the Flannerys; where they got planted was for Con to decide. He walked up and down the row of dead faces; two had been his brothers, men who had made the long haul with him. Con Flannery looked at them and that was all.

"Bury them with their friends," he said.

And then we straggled back to town. Our losses had been heavy enough, 19 men and two women; and as the townspeople walked back I saw that early grief was now replaced with quiet pride. They had done the impossible, all these ranchers and storekeepers. Old Dr. Kline had died of the excitement. It was a hell of a thing. Kate the beautiful bitch—where was Kate? She was free now, could go where she pleased and not have to think of Ballard. So many men had died because of her. Strictly

169

speaking, that wasn't true, yet men were dead. I had kept the faith with her, and now I wanted to be gone. Callahan and his Goddamned job didn't press too heavy on my mind. Besides, something bigger than a mildly crooked marshal's broken legs had happened in Dragoon Wells, and they wouldn't think much about Callahan for a while. Truthfully I was past caring what happened to Johnny; life was a prizefight and he would have to duck the punches or go under.

Some of the community spirit had worn off by the time the sun was hot in the sky. Everything passes, good fellowship quicker than anything else. Men stood staring at their shattered windows and bullet-broken furniture. Already there was squabbling about how the ditches were to be filled in and the street put back the way it was. A man complained that he didn't live at the end of town where the ditches were, the ditches that had saved his life. Casey was dead and I had been surprised to hear that. I had figured he would dodge out the back way. They say you should never get to know too much about a man you despise. Do that and you'll be forced to change your opinion. Maybe so.

Let them squabble. I was through with Dragoon Wells. All I wanted was a lot of liquor before I quit the town for good. But first—Kate. I would look for her when I had a drink, two drinks, probably more. I took off my badge and put in on the desk. Then I got sick of looking at it and threw it in a drawer. A little later I heard noise and went out to see what it was.

It was Kate—and Callahan! Kate was driving the fancy black-and-gold-trimmed buggy, and Callahan sat beside her like a fool, still in splints but livelier than the last time I'd seen him. Kate reined in the horse, but they didn't climb down. Con Flannery looked up from shoveling dirt, and that's all he did.

I went over. "You should have been here last night," I told Callahan. I was feeling mean.

"I'm getting out," Callahan said, shoving a roll of

money at me. I put it in my pocket without looking at it. "The job's all yours if you want it," Callahan said. "Kate and me are going up north."

I looked at Kate, so mean and beautiful. She was wearing the same green dress she came in.

"Congratulations," I said. Callahan didn't know what he was getting into. Or maybe he did, and didn't care. If he had lost his nerve, like Casey said, he had it back. Those two, Callahan and Kate, went back a long way, and there were things between them there was no knowing about. Could be they were wrong enough to be right together. Callahan hadn't always been a smalltown crook, and maybe a man still lived behind the dandy front. I didn't understand the man anymore than I understood Kate. Kate, I don't know how I felt about her. It was too late to ask her about the money. I couldn't and I wouldn't. Like the man said, I'd been had.

"Why don't you keep the job?" Johnny said, wanting to get out from under everybody's stares. No one came close, not even McLandress. Kate remained silent. "They never liked me," Johnny said. "After what you did, you won't have any trouble. Why didn't you let me know what was going on?"

"You couldn't have helped," I said. "Not your fault. I was busy." I looked around at the town I hoped I would never see again. "The town is better off without you— and me. They'll find a good man, they always do."

Callahan didn't say where they were going; up north was a big place. "We'd better be on our way," he said without offering to shake hands.

Kate spoke for the first time. "There's something in the desk drawer, Saddler. I left it there this morning. Goodbye, Saddler. Try not to get killed. There's only one of you"—she smiled a real smile—"and maybe that's a good thing."

Kate shook the reins and clicked her tongue and the buggy moved on. She didn't look at her father as they passed him. Flannery looked after her and went back to digging. The buggy went away and I never saw Kate again.

In the desk drawer I found the money she had promised. No jewelry, just bright Mexican gold pieces. The count was exactly right. The beautiful bitch had kept her word and I was a rich man while it lasted. I didn't feel bad about Kate. We had what we had and it was over. There was a note written in a strong bold hand with a forward slant. I grinned. Even her handwriting was tough, brassy, independent.

Dear Saddler:

You're too much man for me, so here's your money and good-bye. I'm going to think about you, you arrogant son of a bitch. But I have to find something safer than you. Grin all you like, turdhead, I'm going to try. If I fail, then fuck it. I'd have no chance at all if I stayed with you. You're bad and I'm worse, so you see it's hopeless. I'm going back to Johnny to see if he will have me. I will have a better chance with him. At least he's not crazy.

Kate

I was putting the money in my saddlebag when McLandress bustled in. The fat man was on his way back to being a banker. I knew there was going to be more talk about his daughter; it was far from what I expected to hear. My, he was all worked up.

"I want you to arrest my daughter," he said.

You can believe my jaw dropped when I heard that. "You know what you're saying?"

McLandress sat down heavily but shook his head at my whiskey. "Not arrest exactly," he said, a man much troubled. "Seeing that we have a sort of understanding about Laurie I can be frank with you. However, what I'm going to say must not get beyond this room."

"Never," I said.

McLandress nodded. "Laurie tried to rob the bank early this morning. My wife followed her and caught her opening the safe. She had an empty carpetbag, her intention was plain. My wife is watching her right now. She had to lock her in her room."

"You want me to have a talk with her?" I said sternly. "Make her realize the terrible disgrace she nearly brought on the family?"

McLandress was more banker than father. "Stronger than that," he said. "Threaten to send her to jail if she doesn't behave. As a matter of fact, son, this is a good time to start telling her what to do. As her future husband, that is." McLandress knew he was laying it on too thick, so he softened a little. "At heart she's a good girl, but he needs a firm hand."

"She'll get it," I said. "I'll go and talk to her right now."

"Good boy!" McLandress said. "Don't go easy on her, son. Bear down hard on her."

"You bet I will . . . Dad." I couldn't wait to bear down on lovely Laurie. She was a criminal, and I was going to tell her that the minute I got her into bed.

On the way to the house, McLandress said the joyriding was over for Laurie. From now on there would be nothing but solid good sense, plenty of hard work. After the wedding both of us would keep an eye on her to see she didn't stray into the pathways of sin and all the other things that make life worth living.

McLandress clapped me on the shoulder as we went into the house. "I'm never wrong about a man once I make my final decision," he said. "You're all right, son. Go on up now. Room's at the end of the hall. Mrs. McLandress and I will wait down here."

"It's best you don't come up," I agreed. Mrs. McLandress gave me a motherly smile that chilled my soul.

I knocked before I turned the key in the lock and went

in, and there she was sulking by the window. God! she was such a hot-crotch beauty, and still quivering with anger.

"You're a bad girl," I said with a straight face.

"Fuck you—you're the one that fucked it up! Why the hell didn't you come with me? Now I don't have a cent and never will. And what's this shit my father keeps talking about? You and me married, in the cattle business. You double-crossed me, Saddler. Let me down. If you think I'm going to live on some shitty little ranch, you know what you can do."

I grinned at her. "It's a good clean wholesome life," I said. "Working hard, raising lots of kids, watching them grow. Church on Sunday, box lunches in the afternoon. Forget about going to Mexico City, living in posh hotels, spending money in fancy stores, dining in big restaurants. You'll forget all that the minute we're married and have our own little ranch."

I think Laurie had been measuring the drop from the window when I came in. "I'd rather die," she said. "That's what I'll do—I'll drink poison. You'll be sorry when I'm dead, you big bastard!"

It wasn't the time or place, but I reached for her, and we grabbed at each other before we tumbled into her pretty canopied bed.

"Shush!" I warned her.

I reached for her and she pushed my hand away as if we were really married. "Oh, no," she said. "It was different the other time. You know I have no money, all you want is a quick poke."

"Well, it has to be quick, this time it has to," I said. "It's going to be hard, I'll just have to take you as you are. A poor penniless girl."

"Since when did you get so rich?"

"Since a minute ago."

Laurie let me do a few things under her dress. "You swear you aren't saying that just to get into my bloomers. That would not be the act of a gentleman. Go on—swear!"

I swore and then we made love and you'd never think there were two outraged parents waiting at the bottom of the stairs. When we finished Laurie snuggled up to me, still holding onto my cock.

"Don't get tired of me too soon, Saddler. It's all right when you do—I'll be all right—but don't do it too soon."

"The same goes for you," I said. "Of course you'll be all right. How could you help not be? You'll always be all right."

"I don't know that I like the way you say that."

"A compliment."

It was a compliment. No matter what happened Laurie would be all right. In the years to come, after I was gone and half forgotten, she would tumble out of a lot of beds. But she would always land on her feet. We would be good together, and we both knew it. I would do right by her in my own way; no harm would come to her and when it came time to break up, as it had to, I would see that she wasn't lacking for anything. The money from Kate would last a long time, even the way we'd spend it, and there would be more when that was gone. The world was full of money if you knew how to get at it. Laurie and I were friends, something I could never be with Kate; there's nothing better than getting into bed with a woman who is also a good friend.

"Now listen," I said when we had our clothes on and the bed was tidy again. "We can't go now or your folks will make a fuss. I won't go through that, even for you. Get packed but hide your bags until it's time to leave."

"Yes, sir," Laurie said, rubbing my yard through my pants. "When will that be?"

"As soon as it gets dark. I'll bring the horses around and you be ready when I do. How does Mexico City suit you? It's good to go somewhere without being chased."

Laurie smiled. "I want you to chase me a lot."

WILD, WILD WOMEN

ONE

I didn't know his name till I was ready to kill him. Bullwhip Danner is what he went by, and I still have the feeling that he had fashioned that handle for himself. But I suppose he had earned it over the years, leading emigrant wagon trains across the Plains to the West. It takes a lot of man to do that, and his passing was mourned by all who knew him, even those who hated his guts. I got plenty of dirty looks, for I was the one who finally put him under the sod. Of course, I knew none of that when I blew his lamp out. It wouldn't have mattered if I had known: there was no time to discuss his good or bad points.

The funny thing was, he wasn't even in the game that had caused the trouble. I'd been looking for some action. When a man folded and left the table, I'd asked if I could sit in. The others in the game gave me a quick look and, since I didn't look like a sharper—though I can be— they grunted agreement and I took the empty chair.

In those days Independence, Missouri, was full of strangers. Some of the men at the table gave their names, or at least names of who they claimed to be. Back then, Independence was the jumping off place for the wagons going west, and the once-quiet farm town was jam-packed with citizens of every immoral persuasion, from regular farm folk to New York City throat-slitters trying to dodge the hangman. It was a wild, teeming town of gamblers, drummers, gun salesmen, gold seekers, desert-ers, foreigners, escaped convicts, whores, pimps and clergymen. You could stay in a dirty room for the same price they charged in a big city hotel. The town had had its day and then had died, but when it had been strong there was none stronger.

There was plenty of money on the table, and I liked that. Only one of the gamesters was a farmer. I think all he had in the world was in front of him, and you didn't have to be a mind reader to know that he had sold his farm and was counting on going west a rich man. He wouldn't; they never did. He was losing when I sat in, and he went on losing.

The others in the game were town men of various kinds. They were used to gambling, and they won and lost, and didn't grunt any harder when they lost than when they won. All but one man, that is. He was a friend, or at least a partner, of the man I had to kill. No farmer, he had the look of a man who had done many things in his time, none of them all that well. I pegged him for a general wagon train worker, doing most anything that came up.

The card players who knew him addressed him as "Buffalo," but always with a trace of humor, and that meant he liked to think of himself as a hunter, a provider of meat for the westbound pilgrims. Maybe he had shot a few buffalo in his time; they're not hard to shoot for a man with a heavy rifle and a fairly steady hand. But I didn't see him as any kind of professional meat-killer, because the real hunters are a breed apart, silent men usually, restless and dangerous, slow and ill-tempered, hardly ever well-liked.

This little man was nothing like that. I don't say you have to be a big lanky man to kill buffs. It's just that a certain size as well as a certain temperament seem to go with the job. "Buffalo" looked and sounded all wrong for the work he professed to do. He was short and quick in his movements, and had a tight smile pasted on his face all the time he was playing. A mug of beer stood in front of him, but he didn't touch it except to wet his throat. I guess he needed to do that because he talked so much.

He drew my attention to the other man, the man who wasn't in the game, the man I ended up killing. I'd seen him sitting at the next table when I sat in but didn't think much about him. I think he must have moved the table with his belly, so he could sit in closer and listen to what was going on. What he was doing wasn't good manners, yet there was nothing he could be called down for. Even so, if there had been something to criticize, it wouldn't have been that easy. Because Bullwhip Danner was the kind of hunter the little man was not.

Back east in the Wild West magazines they have drawings of what they think various frontier types look like: the desperado with his villain's drooping black mustache; the cavalry scout with long, yellow hair and buckskins. Bullwhip Danner was a sketch of a buffalo hunter come to life. He looked intrepid, manly as all get-out and his keen blue eyes would have been just fine, if they hadn't been so dumb—and dangerous, because he knew he was dumb and didn't like it. Glancing over at him, I didn't doubt that he was a fine hunter; it was too bad he didn't stick to what he knew best. He was all wrong as a financier, a backer of poker games played by men smarter than himself. That's what he was doing, staking the quick-eyed, talky runt with the mug of warm beer.

I don't know where they hatched the idea, probably some night out on the trail. So many men have schemes and systems for winning big at poker and other games. They watch cold-eyed professionals beating the wheel or raking in pots, and think they can do it. They should know that it takes money as well as nerve to win big. And luck has something to do with it, too.

Buffalo was short on all three items. There was money

enough, but that's all there was. I knew there was nothing in reserve. A good gambler always has something he can dig up when a game goes against him. If he's known and respected, he can even go in the hole, because they know he's good for it. Buffalo had no such credit working for him. He also varied his play, and that didn't do any good.

After a while he started to sweat and stopped looking at his partner, who was putting away the whiskey pretty good while he watched his own savings go into other hands. The play went on, and I began to win. It took a while, but that's what happened. Nothing unusual about that; after all, gambling is how I make most of my living. I do lots of other work, nearly all of it dangerous, but given a choice, I'll take cards. When you play poker you get to work where it's warm, and when you're tired and rich enough or broke enough to quit, there is always a woman and a bed and a bottle to put life back into your bones.

I kept on winning. I could feel Danner's eyes boring into me. I had become the villain of the place; I was making off with all his hard-earned money. For a hunter like Danner, knocking down the buffalo is easier than rooting out stumps, about the hardest grind there is after plowing, but it's work just the same. In the old days, you could just set up a stand and kill the big bastards till kingdom come. Lately, though, with the herds scared off and thinned out, you'd have to work long days to put buffalo steaks on the table. And the folks won't eat the big critters with hide and horns and hoofs still attached. You have to do all the skinning, cleaning and dressing before the meat is ready for the stewpot or the skillet.

The game had been going on for a lot longer than the time I was in it. Two hours after I joined in some of the players got up to piss or stretch their legs. The farmer, gloomy as any failed man, stayed at the table and ate slices of hard-smoked ham, of which he had a good supply in both pockets of his canvas coat. I drank whiskey and bought a cigar from the bartender and felt pretty good.

The town of Independence and what went on there,

apart from the poker game, didn't mean a thing to me. I was on my way to this wild new town called Dodge City, in Kansas. They said it was going to be bigger than St. Louis in a few years, and I wanted to take some money out of the place before it got too respectable. It was just as well that I never got there, though, because not long after the time I'm talking about a new, hard-nosed marshal named Dillon came to town and put the lid on everything.

Buffalo had moved to the next table and was getting hell from his partner. As Danner saw it, Buffalo was a horse's cock and was playing his cards every which way but right. Now and then they stopped their argument and looked over at me. Buffalo just looked, but Danner glared. In the Southwest, certain Indian witchmen have the reputation of being able to put the evil eye on their enemies. I think Bullwhip Danner had been trying his level best to do that to me that day.

I guess the witchery didn't work, because when we pulled in our chairs and the game went on, I kept winning. The farmer was the first to drop out. He went off to be murdered by his irate wife or to blow his brains out. Getting the nod, Buffalo folded and left the table. He managed to get one drink from Danner's bottle before Danner grabbed it from him. The dumb son-of-a-bitch had failed to strike it big, and thirst was his punishment. I hoped Danner would leave himself when he finished the bottle. Instead, he called for a fresh one and proceeded to drown his disappointment. But his eyes grew angrier.

There was going to be trouble. How bad it was going to be depended on how hard Danner wanted to take his loss. Hard enough, I guessed. Guessed, hell! I knew how hard he was going to take it. What could I do about it? Not much. I don't work hard to win money just so I can give it back because some gent is unhappy. If some gaming gent loses big to me, then I'm always willing to stake him for a few hundred, if he isn't a professional, that is. Bullwhip Danner was all grown up and would have to make the best of it. Or the worst of it. I was ready for that, too. You have to be ready if you play for higher stakes than matchsticks.

Fact is, it wasn't all that big a game, certainly not the kind people hang around waiting to see who comes out winners. Other games were going on without any undue excitement. The other men accepted my winning streak with the customary calm of veteran gamblers. They bought drinks and so did I. Nobody likes to lose, but you can't win if you can't bear to lose. A few sour jokes were made about all the money I was taking in, but nothing more than that. When one man left to get some sleep, he said he was going to clean me out the next time we met.

An hour later I had a pile of money in front of me and the game was over. I don't know how much there was, maybe about $4,000. Not a bad day's work, but I've had better. Nothing happened until I began to shove the money together with both hands. That seemed to do it for Bullwhip Danner; it was the thought of all that money disappearing into my pocket that got him up on his feet. That by itself didn't mean beans to me, but then I saw the bullwhip.

It didn't hang from his holster behind the gun handle, the way some bullwhackers keep it. It hung from his belt, from a wide, steel hook set into the leather, and it wasn't just an ordinary bullwhip but the kind made from rhino hide. I don't know where they get the rhino hide they make them from, but they get made, and the men who carry them like to use them. These whips never wear out, and they never break, no matter how many years of use they get. You can kill with a whip like that—and I don't mean death by flogging. It's more like steel than hide and can lay open a man's throat as neatly as a deep knife slash. One or two slices across the belly, and a man finds himself holding in his guts. I once heard of a man who lost his cock and balls to one of those things. It happened in a gold camp in western Australia.

That story jumped into my mind when Danner spoke in what I took to be an Australian accent. You don't meet many Australians in this country. Those you do meet are always out in the West. Things get hot Down Under, and the West is the closest thing they can find to home.

Bullwhip Danner said, "You been having a right run of luck with the cards, haven't you, cobber?" "Cobber" was one of their words.

I stood up, having no mind to be bullwhipped sitting down. "Pretty good," I said, sure there was no way in the world to walk away from this. Honest Injun, that's what I wanted to do. I didn't know the man, had no quarrel with him or with his runty friend, yet I knew I was going to get to know them better. It was like when you're at a country dance and can't get out of dancing with your ugly second cousin. You dance, but you don't like it. You try to get through it as fast as you can. But this was one time when I couldn't do my duty and then duck out on the porch and drink from the bottle hidden in the rain barrel.

"Better than pretty good, I'd say." That was Danner's idea of clever conversation. Bad men in Australia must be the same as our home-grown bad men. Bad men everywhere seem to think killing is like courtship. It has to be done like the Virginia Reel, all the right steps in the right places.

I could have shot him. It would have saved me a deep gash on my right forearm. I'd had to shoot him anyway, but right then I thought I could face him down or put a bullet in his whip arm. I didn't pull a gun then because I keep my gun in my holster as much as I can. When it comes out, it comes out to kill. The killing habit is hard to break.

Anyway, for now it was just talk. Danner had a very loud voice that got on my nerves. Everyone seemed to know who he was, so I guess he had to put on a show. He was one of those hard cases who feel the need to explain why they're doing something bad. I prefer bad men who just do it because they feel like it.

Danner reached out and clamped his hand on the shoulder of his little friend Buffalo. He used his left hand, not the whip hand. It must have hurt, because Buffalo screwed up his mouth in pain. He smiled nervously when the big hunter let him go. Then Buffalo moved away and, still grinning, waited to see what was going to happen.

"I'm taking up for my friend here," Danner bellowed. "Bloody fool got himself into a poker game and got fleeced. 'Don't do it, Buffalo, old mate,' says I to him. Does he listen? Not on your tintype he don't. Well, says I to meself, I'll just hang about and see how the little fellow does. Sort of surprises me, is what he does. Ain't doing bad at all as long as he's handling the pasteboards with men he knows and trusts. Reg'lar fellers, you might say. Got a fighting chance, he does, till this cobber here shows up. Past that point, it's all downhill for old Buffalo."

One of the men who had been in the game, a tough-looking traveling salesman in a good suit, was standing at the bar with a drink in his hand. I remembered hearing him say that he was a drummer for a jewelry company in St. Louis. He knocked back his drink, but I knew it wasn't to give him courage. For a city man, he looked good and tough.

"What're you beefing about, my friend? It was a fair game." He laughed and reached for another drink. "I ought to know. I been gaming for years."

Danner didn't look at him. "Keep out of this, city man. This is between me and the sharper."

"Is that me?" I said. I should have shot him then. Men I know would have. Being called a sharper isn't the same as being called a cheat. Usually sharper means a man who gambles for a living but who doesn't advertise that fact with the black suit and fancy duds of the profession-al card mechanic. It means a lot of things to a lot of people. Sore losers hate sharpers—because they win.

"That's what you are, sharper," Danner said.

I still didn't want to kill him. You get tired of killing men for what they say. Besides, Independence, for all its temporary wildness, was still a farmer town at heart and had good, strong laws. I didn't want to hang around fighting bedbugs in the city jail while they got around to trying me for maiming or murder.

I was almost embarrassed by what I said next. "If your

friend thinks he's been dazzled, why doesn't he send for the sheriff? Let him decide."

Law-abiding me!

Danner laughed at that. He was drunk but steady on his feet. "Me and my friend are just simple wagon people," he said. "Guiding good folks to California is what we do for a living. My little friend worked hard for his money, sharper. No need for the sheriff to be called—just give it back."

It got quiet. "Not a chance," I said. "He lost in a straight game. Be smart—let it go."

My God, he was fast with that whip! If it had been uncoiled, I would have killed Danner when his hand moved. Instead, he sent the whip's length back behind him. People behind him scattered, and someone cried out in pain. Now there were just three of us in the center of the saloon: me, Danner, and Buffalo. Buffalo was on Danner's left, so he didn't have to move away from the whip. I wondered why he stayed where he was. I should have figured that the big, wild Australian was his only friend, if that's the right word for it. Maybe it was one of those strange partnerships: brute strength and weak brains.

"If that whip comes at me, I'll kill you," I said. "I won't wing you, not now. There's time to let it drop. You can't beat a short gun."

"So you say, cobber." The Australian knew how good he was. I knew it too. The whip handle in his hand was no less deadly than if he'd been gripping the butt of a gun. And still I didn't draw, because in a court of law it would be whip against gun. The prosecutor and the sheriff would check back on me and come up with some of the killings I'd done in my time, and when the law got through with me, I'd be marked as a killer who had gunned down a hard-working wagon-train man, whose only crime had been drinking too much liquor and a feeling that his friend had been cheated.

"You better pull on me," Danner said, his whip hand motionless, the rhino hide snaked out behind him. "Got you shitting your pants, don't I? You're thinking, will he go for my hand or my eyes? How about the jugular? I can cut it across so it'll gush like a broken pipe. What're you afraid of? But I'll tell you, cobber, no man can say Bullwhip Danner is an unmerciful cutter. Unbuckle your gun belt and your pants and shuffle over here with your unlawful gains. Do that, and maybe I'll give you a dollar for a drink."

I said nothing. I no longer wanted to walk away. Men have talked to me like that in the past; most of them are dead. A few I let live because they were just drunk, or foolish or crazy. You have to be careful about the men you let live. They have to be harmless or plain crazy. To kill such men does more harm to your reputation than letting them run off at the mouth. A dangerous man is altogether different; as a rule, you have to kill him, even if you don't especially want to.

I was in a bind, and good old Buffalo got me out of it by pulling a gun on me while I was watching the whip. Maybe the slug of whiskey made him do it. His hand snaked inside his coat and came out with a stubby revolver and he nearly got to fire it. My gun came out and knocked him down, but then the whip snapped my gun out of my hand with the force of a bullet. The whip cracked again and caught my gun while it was still skittering across the floor. I jerked my head to one side as the whip snapped straight at my eyes. It split the flesh on my forearm. Blood came with the pain, and I backed away with blood dripping from my hand, the whip snaking and snapping at my face. My ass hit the edge of a table and Danner yelled, thinking he had me where he could cut me up. The whip cracked an inch from my eye.

But then the city drummer yelled and threw me a short-barreled, double-action .38. The whip cracked at the gun as it sailed through the air. It missed. I caught it with my left hand and gave Danner four of the five small-caliber pills in the cylinder. You never saw a man more surprised, as all four bullets got him in the chest, in and around his heart. It was the fourth bullet that drilled through. Until then he was still moving at me, wounded but still on his feet. The one in the heart stopped him in his tracks, and he keeled over and died before he hit the floor. A foul stench filled the room as he voided his bowels.

But Buffalo wasn't dead. Though badly wounded, he tried to crawl toward the gun he had dropped. I got to it before he did and threw it away. The little man stopped crawling. His eyes rolled back in his head. Blood leaked from a hole in his chest, but no blood was mixed in the spit that dribbled from his mouth, so it looked like his lungs hadn't been damaged. I didn't care what shape his innards were in; if I hadn't been forced to fire so fast, I would have blown a hole in his head.

The drummer stepped forward to claim his gun, unmindful of the sour looks he was getting from the gamblers and the drinkers. I thought he was one dandy drummer; there was a real man underneath the big belly and the loud suit and the jowly face, baby-ass pink from hot towels in barbershops. I guessed he was a Jew. I didn't know much about Jews, but I liked this one.

Handing him back his .38, I said, "Thanks for the use of the weapon."

He said his name was Jacob Steiner, and we shook hands. "I could have shot him for you, but I thought you'd rather do it yourself." Steiner prodded the empty shells out of his gun and reloaded it before putting it in a shoulder holster under his coat.

Some of the drinkers pushed two tables together and put Buffalo aloft to wait for the doctor. His breathing was light and shallow. The blood from the bullet hole was dyeing his shirt a dark red.

Steiner told the barkeep to set out a bottle and clean glasses. "I should be buying," I said. "Who was that I just killed?"

Steiner slid the bottle towards me. "You mean you don't know? Me, I'm just a bauble salesman, but I know Bullwhip Danner. Knew him. They say he was one hell of a hunter and troubleshooter. He said it a lot himself. The name means nothing to you?"

Steiner drank good whiskey, and the bottle had his name on it—always a good sign. "I guess I heard it once or twice", I said. "How did he manage to live so long?"

Steiner raised his glass. "Your health, sir. Our late friend lasted so long because he thought he couldn't be killed by mortal man. I guess he'd been scouting and hunting with the wagons about five years. A determined sort of a man. He wanted to be a scout but didn't know beans about the country, being a foreigner. You know what the bastard did?"

"Bought that rhino whip?"

Steiner laughed. "I guess he brought that from Australia. What he did was to cross the Plains from California all by himself. Fought off Indians, got lost, all but starved. But he got to know the Plains pretty good. Folks here didn't take him too serious, him a foreigner. Then he convinced some hard-up train to give him his first job. The next five years he got as good as the best. Better, in his own opinion."

I grinned at the tough Jew. "You almost make me sorry I killed him, a man with such pluck and determination."

Steiner grinned back. "Don't be. That dead man was a son-of-a-bitch. No better man on the trail, but he was loud, stupid, and always looking for a fight."

I was thinking about the sheriff. He'd be there soon. "You know this town. How do you think this will go over?"

They said Jews don't drink. This one hadn't heard about that. He was putting two away for my one. "You won't even be charged," he said. "That doesn't mean they'll pin a medal on you. You'd think a brute like Danner wouldn't be popular. If you did, you'd be wrong. Bullwhip—such a name!—was what they call a colorful character. Besides, the wagon people need all the good men they can find."

Everybody turned to look at me when the sheriff and two hard, young deputies came in.

TWO

I got out of it, just like Jacob Steiner said I would. That fat salesman stood by me like a rock. It turned out that he studied law in his spare time—all those long evenings when the card games were over and he was holed up in some crossroads boarding house. The inquest was short and sour, because they didn't like Steiner and they didn't like me. Fishing for votes, the sheriff—a grimfaced oldster named Vardiman—made a lame effort to pick a few holes in our story. He managed to get in a few licks about stamping out lawlessness wherever it raised its ugly head. But it didn't work, and they had to let me go. Go! That was my main idea. When you kill a man in a town, it's best to be gone, unless you have some important reason for staying. I had nary a one.

As a town, Independence was busier than rich. You never saw so many restless farmers in your life. Outside of town were great parks of wagons forming into wagon trains. Many of the emigrant trains had already formed; whole counties of people were on the move. Not all the wagon people were poor, and many had left good farms to push off into the wilderness. California and Oregon were the two big places to go. I guess California had a magic sound to its name; more pilgrims were going there than to Oregon. Rumors of gold strikes persisted in spite of the fact that the big strikes of '49 were already history.

There was considerable politicking going on among the wagon people, too. Back home, men with strong wills or smooth tongues had been picked to boss the trains, and these same men expected to be the mayors or town fathers of the settlements they would found in the Far West. But some of the arrangements were changed or bent once they started out. All too often, by the time they got as far as Independence the bickering and the politicking had already started. It really got going when two smaller trains banded together for protection against the Indians and the outlaw bands that preyed on the trains far out on the trail.

All this was none of my business. I had been to California more than once and could pass up another visit. Let the sodbusters fight—I was going to Kansas, where I planned to do all my farming indoors at the card tables. After the inquest was over, I had another drink with Steiner and said I hoped I'd see him again some day, though I never expected to. He went off down the street carrying his two leather valises, and I went back to my rooming house to get my gear together.

While I was getting ready to go my landlady's daughter came in without knocking. She didn't have to knock: she'd been in and out of my room since I had arrived in Independence. And she always came to fuck. She was no kind of professional whore, or any kind of whore, though she might have ended up as one. I gave her more money than a working whore would make, and she took it without embarrassment. "Many thanks for the present, Mr. Saddler," she would say. I could never get her to call me Jim. Maybe that was because I was 38 and she was 18.

But she wasn't formal when we fucked; the difference in our ages was forgotten then. She fucked like a trooper and wasn't quiet about it either. When she was working up to her come, she gave out loud groans of joyful torment. When we had our first bout of sex, I was nervous because of her mother and told her so. I didn't want to get chased out of there by a carving knife or a shotgun. But she told me not to worry about it. Her mother had been a saloon girl in her younger years, and though she was long-retired she hadn't turned into a churchgoer, or any kind of hypocrite. Peggy—that was her name—said her mother's only regret was being too old to keep working the saloons. "She knows what I do," Peggy said, "and she appreciates the little presents you give me." After that I felt a lot better and I was able to fuck this nice, open-minded girl without looking over my shoulder.

There was none of the jaded whore about Peggy. When she got horny, and was really aroused, there was no faking. She loved sex, she said, and she loved to handle my cock, my magic wand, as she called it. When she sucked me off, and I came in her mouth, she swallowed it. According to her, come was good for a woman. It was better than a tonic; it kept a woman looking younger, and it was good for the complexion. I don't know where she'd read or heard such a thing, but she insisted it was true. True or not, it was a sure sign of affection. When a woman swallows your come it means she likes you.

I was just about packed when she arrived, but I didn't think I had to run out the door. She was wearing a dress of some thin material that did nothing to hide the curves of her lovely young body. Looking at her, my cock stirred and came to life. She had auburn hair, wide brown eyes, an oval face—her's was altogether a very pretty face. Her breasts were large for such a young girl. I knew what they looked like: I had sucked them many times. Suddenly I felt a strong need for her.

"You're leaving?" she said, looking at my bag. "I hate to see you leave." She sat on the edge of the bed.

"Better I moved on," I said. "That business with Danner."

"Yes," she said. "Danner had some friends, men as

dangerous as he was. They could come looking for you. I hate to see you go, but it's better you do. But they're not here yet, are they?"

That was what I wanted to hear. "No, they're not. You want to? I do. We have plenty of time."

"Yes, we do, Mr. Saddler. I'm already wet, and I can see you're hard. Sometimes at night when you're out gambling and I'm in bed by myself I have to squeeze my legs together, thinking how much I'd love to have your thing in me. But I never pleasure myself the way some women do with their finger or a cucumber. I think it's a waste."

"So do I."

She fondled my cock while I undressed her. She liked to be undressed by a man. When my pants were unbuttoned my cock stuck out like a flagpole. "Do you ever pleasure yourself, Mr. Saddler?" she asked. "When you're in some wild place and there are no women, do you . . ."

"It would be a waste," I said. And then I got the rest of her clothes off. There she stood, sweet 18, bright-eyed and ready for my shaft. She stretched out on the bed with her legs spread, a little trickle of joy juice leaking through her auburn beaver, and the sight of that drove me wild. I have to say women's beavers get me all heated up. I can't help it; it's the way I am. This was going to be our last fuck, so I wanted it to be a good one. Luckily, Peggy had the same idea.

I thrust it on into her and she gave out a groan of pleasure. She wrapped her legs around my back, which pushed me deeper into her every time I thrust forward. Soon she was so wet and I was pumping so hard that a sucking sound filled the room. Between groans and breathy sighs she called out, "Oh, Mr. Saddler, I'm going to miss your thing so much. Shove it into me hard, sir. In all the way, as far as it will go." Peggy reached down so she could touch my thrusting cock. That made me pump harder and harder, and she begged me not to let up.

If Bullwhip's friends had burst in at that moment, they would have had me dead to rights. But they didn't.

"Come, Mr. Saddler," she called out. "I want to feel your hot gush inside me." I geared myself up for my come and I came like a stallion. The danger I was in must have been part of it. I kept coming after I should have stopped. Her own come lasted a lot longer: one orgasm after another. It was so intense that her eyes rolled back in her head. I've never seen any woman have such a total orgasm. It was so deep, so complete that for a moment I was afraid she had lost consciousness. But she hadn't. After a few moments she opened her eyes and smiled up at me. Her legs were still locked around me, holding me in her. I couldn't have taken my cock out of her even if I had wanted to. But I didn't want to.

"Oh, Mr. Saddler, what am I going to do without you. I'm thinking of the long days and nights when I'll be without your cock, wanting it so bad, and it won't be here. It will be deep inside some other girl, and I'll be as jealous as hell. I'll pretend I'm that other woman and maybe I'll feel better. Promise you'll come back here some day. Please promise."

"I promise."

We both knew I'd never see Independence again. She left after a while and around about noontime the landlady, Peggy's mother, hollered up the stairs and said the Reverend Claggett wanted to have words with me. At first I thought it must be a joke, some old hard-assed friend full of whiskey was setting me up to have some fun. I had been stuffing the last of my stuff into my warbag when she wheezed upstairs and said the man of the cloth was waiting for me in her private parlor. There was a pretty young lady with him, the landlady said.

The landlady, randy old bitch that she was, guessed what was in my mind. She liked me for reasons too unpleasant to talk about. I think I was the man of her sweaty dreams.

"There's nobody holding a shotgun, if that's what's bothering you," she said. "Nobody—not even you— ever threw a leg over that young lady down below."

Heartened by the knowledge that I wasn't about to be threatened with a buckshot marriage, I went downstairs, and there was the Reverend Josiah Claggett and his pretty little daughter. The name suited the reverend, and his pretty little daughter looked like she had a sky pilot for a daddy, only more so. Hannah was her name, I was to learn later, and it suited her from the poke bonnet on her head to the rough farmer boots on her feet.

The father was grim, the daughter was pale—not just pale, but pinched and unhappy, as if she never expected to be anything but unhappy. That was a shame, because she was pretty, washed-out or not, and the tension inside her quivered like a wire. They stood like a father and daughter in a sad old photograph, and even the airless parlor with its overstuffed and never-used furniture might have been a photographer's studio.

"I'd like to have a word with you, Saddler," Claggett said.

"What about?" I didn't like the man. He looked like he had been born wearing a parson's black suit and flat-crowned hat.

"It's about the man you killed—Bullwhip Danner. He was a good man, in spite of everything, and you snuffed out his life in a drunken brawl. Have you any idea what you've done?"

"Sure," I said. "I killed Danner."

"You did more than that. By killing him you have set back the Lord's work."

"How so, Reverend?" I wished to hell he'd just of told me what was on his mind.

The girl had been staring at the floor as if she expected to find the meaning of life in one of the cracks between the boards. Now she looked up, more afraid of her old man than of me.

"Father," she ventured. "This isn't going to do any good."

Claggett said, "Hold your tongue, girl. I know what I'm doing."

I didn't like the way he talked to the girl. "What are you doing?" I asked.

At least that got a straight answer. "I demand that you take Bullwhip Danner's place. All the other reliable guides and hunters have been hired. Most of them. The few men left, we can't meet their price. It's up to you to take Danner's place. Lead us across the Plains to California. I know you can do it. You've done it before."

"What makes you think that?"

"Sheriff Vardiman says so. He knows more about you than you think. It's his business to know. How many times have you been across?"

If it hadn't been for the girl, I would have told him to go fuck himself. He looked like he took out a lot of anger on the girl. "Only twice. You better get somebody else. I won't do it."

Reverend Claggett's face got angrier than it had been. "Are you deaf or still befuddled by whiskey? There is nobody else."

"There's always somebody else," I said. "You'll just have to wait. You got this far, so what's the big hurry? You must be growing some green food while you wait." Any wagon train that had to lay over in some town usually plowed up enough prairie to grow potatoes and green stuff for the cookpot.

"We did that," he said. "That's not the problem. The problem is we must move on now."

"Why? Winter's over, no snow coming. It won't make any difference."

I was speaking the truth, and it wasn't the money or lack of it. I was going to Kansas to see what I could see. Going there was the best idea I could think of. A long, hard journey of more than 2,000 miles didn't appeal to me one bit. Out there on the trail there's nothing to do but work. At night you lie down too tired to talk, not that the talk is all that good, even if you feel like it.

A man like me can make good money on a train though. I didn't mind the Indians and the outlaws as much as the people I'd have to deal with in the train. Sure as hell, with this old buzzard leading it, it had to be a band of the godly and the saved. All friends of Jesus! Bosom friends of the Lord! I don't sneer at religion; I just keep away from it. I thought of the prayer meetings I'd be urged to attend. Hatchet-faced old ladies would make me presents of worn Bibles. They'd pray over me so loud I'd find it hard to sleep. And, Dear Lord, the monotony!

Hannah Claggett suddenly spoke up shyly. "Fifty young women are depending on you!"

Fifty young women! Hannah's pale blue eyes fluttered coyly behind her gold-wired glasses as she spoke. I knew she had taken my measure. I don't know what she thought of me, but I liked what I could see of her. It was warm in Missouri, but she was dressed for a blizzard, clothes on top of clothes—swathed in modesty from throat to toes. Not even a well-turned ankle was in evidence, as they said in the pink pages of the barber-shop magazines. But, for all the fearful, father-frightened manner she presented to the world, I knew there was a lively and lusty woman there, yearning to be free.

Reverend Claggett silenced his daughter with a glare that would have intimidated Lucifer himself. I wondered how the old Bible-thumper had gotten a bone on long enough to sire a daughter, but I was pretty sure he'd prayed for forgiveness the instant he rolled off his wife. That was the kind of man he was. Anything that made you feel good had to be wrong.

"What my daughter says is true," Claggett intoned. "Fifty young women were on their way to a better life before you killed Danner."

"What's stopping them now?"

He snorted. "I thought I made that clear. All the best men have been hired by other trains. The ones left—I can't pay the wages they want."

I liked Hannah Claggett, so I didn't tell her old man to go hang his Bible in an outhouse. "What you're saying is, I'm not one of your best men, so I'll be willing to work cheap. Why should I work at all?"

Claggett fixed me with a stern eye, completely sure that the Lord was right behind him. "Because it's your duty," he said. "Danner's life belonged to fifty young women, and you took it away. You have to do it for them."

Hannah blushed when I said, "I don't know that I'd be up to handling fifty women."

"I don't like your tone, sir," the man of God said.

"Why don't you climb down out of your pulpit?" I said. "Maybe I'll take the job, maybe I won't. Before I say yes or no, I'd like to take a look at your outfit. I know about the fifty women. Who are they, and where are they going? California is a long state. What part? North or south? The men you have, what about them?"

Claggett snapped his fingers at his daughter. I hated him for that. "Let's go take a look," he said.

Claggett's wagon park was about three miles outside of town, and they didn't call the big wagons prairie schooners for nothing. With the wind ruffling their white canvas tops, they looked like ships about to set sail. The difference was, this was the shoreline of a sea of grass. It stretched out beyond what the naked eye could see, beyond the power of the biggest telescope. I counted about 15 wagons. Other wagons were drawn up some distance away. I guessed they belonged to the Claggett train. Oxen wandered slowly inside rope corrals; cattle were penned in other enclosures. In the distance was another, bigger wagon train already on the move. Dust boiled up from the cow-cropped prairie grass. There was power and majesty in the size of the moving train and, no doubt, plenty of tough men with guts, yet it wasn't always the biggest outfits that got through.

Out there was some of the most dangerous country in the world: a terrible land of floods and prairie fires that could sweep through a train with the speed of the wind. Indians friendly one week were hostile the next. Renegades, white and red, prowled the limitless plains and lay in wait in mountain passes. Thrown together, burned and chilled, sick of the sameness of the food—when there was food—people's tempers flared and factions formed. No less than in any village, people took sides; old hatreds were revived, new ones created.

Reverend Claggett hadn't lied about the women. They were all over the place. A few men moved among the wagons. I counted five before I turned my attention back to the ladies. Claggett saw me counting and told me I could stop.

"I said fifty, and fifty it is," the preacher said. "I don't include my daughter."

Hannah darted a shy glance at me. "I've been saved for a long time," she said. I wondered how long it would take to unsave her. Call me a bad man if you like, but I think she needed to be unsaved, and needed it badly. She knew it, and so did I. When the time came, it would be good for both of us.

Claggett told her to go about her business, and she did. After that, the preacher and I walked around. Some of the girls bobbed and nodded at the old son-of-a-bitch, wanting to stay on the good side of him. Maybe old man Claggett was giving them a new start in life, but it was plain that few of them really liked him. It was easy not to like Mr. Claggett; for him the milk of human kindness had all gone sour. I kept telling myself not to be a horse's ass, and to climb up on my horse and head for Kansas. The whole thing smelled of trouble and I was going to be smack in the middle of it.

On the other hand, as I looked at those women, I wondered if my business in Kansas was all that pressing. Kansas wasn't going to blow away, and wherever men gather at a table, they gamble. It even came to me, as I walked around with Reverend Claggett, that I was good and sick of gambling. You sat at a table for 72 hours at a stretch, gulping boiled black coffee laced with whiskey, taking time out only to piss and eat. You bolt down plates of ham and eggs or eggs and ham because steak-eating is frowned upon during big games—takes too much time—and the nervous gamesters can't hold down all that meat.

A big Irishman was working on a busted wheel, and we traded grunts when Claggett said our names. The Irishman stank of whiskey. I guess the reverend put up with the boozing because the man was a hired hand, not one of the redeemed. He had big, nimble hands and handled his tools well, a man who knew his job. His name was Culligan. He looked like a bull buffalo wearing a derby hat instead of horns.

Yes sir, I decided, Kansas could wait. Out there on the

Great Plains I would become a better man. I'd breathe in good, clean prairie air, work hard and sleep sound. For once I would be doing a real man's job. Had they known about it, my folks back home in Jonesboro, West Texas, would have been proud of me.

We reached the last wagon, and Reverend Claggett turned to look at me, waiting for my answer.

I nodded. "I'll take the job."

Claggett frowned; with a face like his, that wasn't easy. "Remember," he said, "there can be no pulling out at the last minute."

Washing clothes in a tub nearby, a pretty, dark-eyed girl of about 19 hiked up her skirt to keep it from getting wet. She had lovely legs, strong and slender.

To the preacher man I said, "You can depend on me, sir. When I'm in, I stay in till the job's finished."

"Then we have much to talk about," he said.

THREE

Most of the talk was about keeping my hands off the women. I gave him a wise nod, but he kept on talking as if he hadn't noticed. Don't get me wrong. I wasn't going to try to ride all 50 women, but I wasn't signing on just for the wages. The women were there, and things would happen; that's as it should be. I'd get to them, or they'd get to me. Bedding down would be done, and not always in a bed or even on a blanket. Soft grass in a secluded place on a sunny day or a quiet night—what's wrong with that? If you can find something sinful in it, well, then you and me ain't never going to be friends. About his daughter I wasn't sure. I'd never been shot at by a clergyman.

"It's important that you pay attention to what I'm telling you," Claggett complained after we got settled in his wagon at a hinged, fold-down table. He set a jug of spring water on the table. I wondered where the Irishman hid his whiskey.

"I'm listening," I said.

It was hard for Claggett to get his voice out of the pulpit. I figured I'd have to get used to his way of speaking. "There is nothing so terrible in the sight of God as a fallen woman," he said.

Since God had never confided in me, I had nothing to say about that.

"Every time a woman desecrates her body outside the marriage bed, Jesus is crucified all over again. That is why I have made it my mission in life to lead wayward women back to the path of righteousness. My God is a terrible God, but He is also a God of mercy, provided the sinner is truly repentant. My mission is the salvation, the reclamation of the fallen woman."

I stared at the mournful old coot, hardly able to believe my ears. "You mean . . ."

"Exactly," Claggett said, knocking back spring water like whiskey. "With the exception of my daughter, every woman you have seen here today is in need of salvation."

"Did you say 'every woman'?"

Claggett waved away my thoughts. "It's not what you think," he said impatiently. "Not all have been women of the streets or the parlor houses, though many have sinned in that way. Some have served time in prison for theft, picking pockets, counterfeiting. Others are adultresses driven from their homes by grievously wronged husbands. Some are foreign women come to this country for reasons known only to themselves. However, it makes no difference to me—to Almighty God—what they have done, what they have been in the past. I, Josiah Claggett, will save them."

Looking at the man, I didn't know what to make of him. Of course he was crazy. I knew that. How crazy was what I wanted to know. How crazy was I, signing on to lead 50 wayward women across a continent? Maybe a dozen or so wouldn't have been so bad, but 50 bad girls seemed to be stretching it. Like all gamblers, I figured the odds, and that's what I was doing when the slim killer came up the step into the preacher's wagon. I was about to tell Claggett to find himself another man when the killer turned bright eyes on me. All it took was one look, and I changed my mind.

"What can I do for you, Maggie?" Reverend Claggett said to her.

"Well, you want your dinner or not?" Maggie O'Hara said. "If somebody didn't remind you to eat, you'd never do it. Here's beef stew the way you like it."

Maggie O'Hara, a stewpot in her hand, eyed me suspiciously as she ladled out stew for the preacher.

"You're forgetting Mr. Saddler," Claggett said.

"I wasn't sure he'd be staying," she said. "Is he?"

Claggett nodded, and I got a plate of stew. Mine didn't have as much meat as the parson's. Maggie turned to go, but Claggett called her back.

"Sit with us a while," he said.

Maggie sat down at the table and looked at me. "You ever know a man who called himself Langdon Moore?"

"Not that I remember," I said. "Any reason I should?"

"You'd remember Langdon," Maggie said. "Big feller, with a droopy mustache. Was from New Hampshire and talked like it. Was a bunco artist till he started blowing tin cans. Blew one too many. Got caught in Cairo, Illinois. Used to have an advance man who sort of looked like you. I never did get a good look at him. Always coming and going through some back alley."

"It wasn't me," I said.

"Old Langdon's doing twenty years for bank robbing because of that man. They were in it together, but this man turned state's evidence."

I finished my stew. "Where were you at the time?"

"Maggie was in Sing Sing prison for life," Reverend Claggett said.

I knew they didn't give women life for bank robbery, so it had to have been murder. I wondered what kind of murder, but didn't ask. I didn't say a thing. Maggie didn't either. Instead, she smiled at the preacher.

"You don't mind if I tell Mr. Saddler, do you?" Claggett asked her.

"Hell, no!" she said, then thought better of her rough language. "Of course not. You're the one who got me out."

Claggett said, "Maggie worked for a certain parlor

house in the Tenderloin district of New York. In the course of her sinful employment, a young man attempted to go beyond the bounds of, er, ordinary sins of the flesh. In spite of her nefarious trade, some good remained in Maggie, and she refused. This young man, God rest his wicked soul, grew violent and proceeded to beat her. They had been drinking champagne, and she killed him with the bottle."

"They *are* heavy," I said, keeping up my end of the peculiar conversation.

That got Maggie's Irish up. Her blue eyes crackled with cold anger. "Maybe I'd better tell it, Reverend. Our friend here will understand my language better than yours."

Reverend Claggett stared at what was left of his stew. "There's no need," he said.

"Begging your pardon, but I think there is," she said. "It was like this. I worked for Big Flossie for nearly a year, and nobody beefed about not getting what they paid for. I was saving up to get married, get me? Lots of high-toned gents wanted to set me up, but that wasn't for me, and I didn't want to marry some flatfoot or bartender neither. So I decided to sell it for a year—a year was the limit—then I'd take my roll and maybe go south or west, where nobody knew me. I was going to catch some nice man—catch him and be a good wife to him—and what's wrong with that?"

"Not a thing," I said.

Maggie wasn't so pretty when she got angry. "I was just two months short of my year when this young son-of-a-bitch come in one night and started asking me to do things I don't like."

"Unspeakable things," Claggett murmured to his plate.

"Saddler knows the names for them," Maggie said. "Well, I just worked there and didn't want to make trouble, so I told him to go talk to Flossie, and get some other girl who would give him his wish. But no, it was me or nothing. One more time I say no, and that's when he got rough. My rich admirer said he'd mark me up so bad

I wouldn't be able to sell it on the Bowery. He started in to do it, and I beaned him with the bottle."

For a moment, I thought she was going to cry, but she was past that. Claggett leaned over and patted her hand; I liked him a little better after that.

"I always did have lousy luck," Maggie said. "I had to go and kill a politician's son. Anybody else, Flossie could have fixed it for the police to toss him in the river. But the thought of dumping Tim Hanrahan's son scared the pie out of her. Flossie got the police in on it, and they all decided I'd have to go down for it. Flossie wouldn't even pay for the lawyer, which is the way it works out when one of the girls gets in trouble. I had to use every cent I'd saved. This lawyer, Grandy, tried to make a deal for manslaughter. No deal, said the district attorney, saying what Tim Hanrahan told him to say. So they made it murder, and I got life."

I looked at her. "Why are you telling me all this?"

"So you won't get any ideas about me because of what I've been. I wouldn't kill you with a bottle, Saddler. I'd shoot you dead!"

Reverend Claggett reasserted his authority. "There will be no more of that talk," he said. "What happened to you in New York will never be mentioned again. Now, get on with your work, Maggie. We'll be leaving here at sunrise."

After she left we sat in silence for a while. Then Claggett said, "I suppose you're wondering how I got her out of prison."

"Tell me, if you want to."

"It won't hurt the girl, and it will explain something about me," he said. "To you I'm just a Bible-thumper, a Holy Joe, a sky pilot. Such names don't bother me."

"Get to the point, Reverend."

"The point is, sir, I get things done. I don't give up. Faith can move mountains. When it doesn't, I find a way to get around them."

"You must have pushed hard to get the girl out of Sing Sing. How did you even hear about it?"

"One of the girls the police forced to perjure herself at

Maggie's trial told me about it. I found her in McGurk's Suicide Palace on the Bowery. Maybe you've heard of it?"

I had. It was the last stop for whores in the final stages of disease and despair. For some reason the management didn't seem to mind too much. Maybe the whores bought drinks for the house before they swallowed a fatal dose of carbolic acid.

"I had gone there as part of my work," Claggett went on. "She was dying, but I rode with her in the ambulance. Before she died she told me about Maggie O'Hara and the trial rigged by Hanrahan. And"—Claggett allowed himself a wintry smile—"she told me about Tim Hanrahan himself. It seems he liked the things his dead son had liked—the beating, the cruelty. She said Flossie could tell me the rest."

"But you didn't start with Flossie?" I was beginning to get an odd feeling about the Reverend Josiah Claggett. I knew I had never seen him before, but he reminded me of someone. I couldn't remember who.

"No, I started with Hanrahan," Claggett said. "He owned a building, published a newspaper on Park Row. I went there and was told to write a letter requesting an appointment. They assured me that I would get an answer. No, I said, I didn't have time for that. I said I'd just write a note and let them take it in to the great man. They laughed, thought I was crazy. You think I look crazy?"

"A little," I said. "You got to see Hanrahan?"

"Indeed I did," Claggett said. "When they let me in, he locked the door. And while I sat there he burned the note I had sent him. I had written the dead girl's name on it, and other things I'd rather not talk about. What did I think I was doing, he wanted to know. I told him I had a signed statement from the girl at McGurk's. I said her handwriting and signature could be verified. She had worked at one time for some lawyers on East 17th Street. Hanrahan wanted to know where this statement was. Where he would never find it, I said. He said he could beat it out of me, or have it done. I said he could try that.

He walked to the telephone on the wall and began to crank the handle. Then he changed his mind. I think God must have stayed his hand."

"God—or something else," I said, still trying to place this man's face.

Claggett ignored my remark. Outside, the wagon train was coming to life, the way a train always does when the long journey is about to start. Women called back and forth, and the penned cattle bawled restlessly.

"Hanrahan asked me what I planned to do with the girl's statement," the preacher said. "Give it to a rival newspaper? No, I said. New York newspapers are filthy rags. What I was going to do, I said, was to print up tens of thousands of copies of the girl's statement and throw them from the top of the highest building in the city. The wind would do the rest."

I stared at him. "You've got plenty of nerve, Reverend."

"You don't need nerve if you're not afraid to die. Oh, yes, he offered me money. Said the statement was a lie, but he was a businessman and had to protect himself. No money, I said. Just get Maggie O'Hara out of jail. How on earth could he do that? Find a way, I told him. Try hard, I said. That's where we left it. I was to come back the next day at the same time and he'd let me know what could be done."

All I could say was, "I'm surprised you're still alive."

"I came close enough to not being," Claggett said. "It was getting dark when I left Hanrahan's office. That's a business district down there, and the streets are quiet when offices and stores close for the night. Instead of going back to my hotel, I went for a walk over toward the Brooklyn Bridge. By the time I got down to the streets below the bridge, three men were following me. The street was empty, and they walked down the middle of it. I stopped, and so did they. Then one of them said I was under arrest for the murder of a prostitute the night before. As the man spoke, he began to draw a revolver from a shoulder holster."

The man of God paused to drink water. Then he looked at me. "I killed him first. God forgive me, I killed all three of them. Nobody saw me do it, but it convinced Hanrahan. He got the girl out."

The man seated across the table from me was at least 65-years-old, gray-bearded and stooped, his long narrow face seamed and burnt by the sun. I don't know why I hadn't noticed his hands before: long and supple in spite of his age. I'm not easily surprised, but now I was.

"You can't be *Josiah* Claggett," I said. "It's been thirty years since—"

"No need to feel awkward about it, Saddler. Most people don't even remember the name. Most people think I've been in my grave for many a year, and that's all to the good. You weren't even born when they put me in jail. I did eighteen years before they let me out. What makes you remember me?"

"Maybe because you were the first of the fast guns." Josiah Claggett's career as a gunman had started before the Civil War, at a time when handguns used percussion loads instead of cased shells. They said he always carried a couple of extra loaded cylinders to give him an edge. In his time, he had been the most feared outlaw on the old Santa Fe Trail. I never did hear how he got started on the wrong road. Most badmen have somebody to blame, but then most badmen are liars. More than likely, Josiah Claggett had never felt the need to cook up some woeful tale of injustice. Not that it mattered much: he had been as bad a man as ever had lived.

"I did what I did," Claggett said simply. "I did it because I wanted to do it. Satan had a firm hold on me in those years. I was possessed by the arrogance of the devil himself. No man could kill me, no prison could hold me, and even when they shot me full of holes and threw me in a cell, the fires of rebellion still burned bright. No matter how long it took, I vowed to break out and kill the men who had betrayed me for the reward money. It took them three years to break me. I raised a sledgehammer to brain a guard, the worst of the lot, when suddenly I felt my arms grow weak and a great peace come over me. I dropped the hammer and fell to my knees and began to pray."

"What did the guard do?" I asked.

"He fired at me—fired twice and missed. I tore open my shirt and told him to fire again. He didn't. Instead, he yelled that I had gone crazy, so they locked me up with the crazy men."

"But you got out."

"It took nearly a year before they put me back with the rest of the prisoners. For a whole year I lived with the scum of the earth, with men so vile that the other prisoners would have killed them if they'd gotten the chance—child-killers, madmen who craved the taste of human flesh, rapists, defilers of animals. But to me all were children of God. I swore that if I ever got out, I would devote the rest of my life to doing good. And— miraculously—I did get out after another fifteen years in that place. The world had forgotten me. I became a preacher and married a good woman and began my new life's work. You've seen my daughter Hannah, my only daughter."

Something warned me not to ask about Claggett's wife. All I knew was that she had been a good woman. I wondered where she was now.

Outside, it was dark, and the cook fires were going. Looking at Reverend Claggett, I began to wish I'd gone to Kansas.

FOUR

The women were gathered for supper when Claggett and I climbed down from the wagon. In the circle of fires they were something to see: women of all shapes and sizes, ranging from plain to pretty, and all young. Yankee twangs mingled with Southern drawls. I heard women speaking in French, German and Italian; the other languages I had to guess at. The whispering and giggling stopped as soon as Claggett appeared, and they waited for the old reformed killer to say grace.

Mercifully, he didn't thank the Lord too long or too hard. Then, while the women ate, he told them about me. I was to be the new hunter, guide and man of all work. If it came to wrongdoing, I was to be the constable, and Claggett the judge.

Then it was my turn to talk. Now, I like women and I wanted to tell them nice things, but that wasn't part of my job. The men I had seen earlier were there, but the only name I knew was Culligan's.

I told the women what they had to expect out there on the Plains. Rules would be laid down, and they would have to abide by them. Once a wagon was assigned to a place in the line, that position could not be changed, no matter how much dust they had to eat. The wagons were to travel in two lines instead of one. That way the cattle would have more grass to graze on. "Other trains have gone ahead of us, so there won't always be that much grass. We'll maintain an even pace, so that one line of wagons doesn't fall behind the other. When it starts to get dark, the two lines of wagons are to draw in close. If an attack comes, we'll be able to form a defense much more easily."

One of the men stood up, and some of the women turned to look at him. He was about my age. I wondered what a sailor was doing in a wagon train. His heavy coat was double-breasted and made of rough blue cloth with brass buttons. Instead of a peaked cap he wore a gray, uncreased farmer's hat, new-looking despite the dust on it. Somebody had given his face a few lumps not too long before, but it must have been one very tough man, or two or three smaller ones, who had done the beating. This sailor had the look of a man used to giving orders without the easy air of command that comes from being an officer. First or second mate, I figured.

Before he could say anything, Claggett held up his hand. "About time you men were introduced." He nodded at the whiskey-swilling Irishman. "You already met Rix Culligan, our wheelwright and carpenter. His job is to keep us rolling, and there's few that can do it as well. Rix will tell you so himself."

The preacher's humor was feeble, and it didn't do a thing to clear the tension from the air. Some of the hostility came from Culligan, and an uncharitable view of his fellow man seemed to come easy to him. I guessed he liked nothing but his work and his whiskey, and a very occasional cheap whore. There might be trouble with Culligan because of his drinking, but he'd have to push it hard before I killed him. First rule on a long cattle drive is never kill the cook, but in a wagon train a wheelwright is even more important. Culligan grunted at me in his eloquent way.

Claggett indicated the seaman. "This is Thomas

Iversen, late of the good ship *Savannah*. He was waylaid by harbor thugs in Baltimore and missed his sailing. His ship is going around the Cape, then to San Francisco, where he'll join her again."

"Glad to know you, Iversen," I lied.

"You too, Saddler," the sailor said, knowing that I wasn't buying his story. A fast ship—I had heard of the *Savannah*—would reach California long before we did. He could have signed on another vessel or gone overland by way of Panama. But what he was up to was none of my business, as long as he kept it to himself.

The preacher pointed to a third man, a soft-looking man in his late forties. He looked more out of place than any of the others, and it wasn't just the well-tailored city clothes rumpled and dirtied by camp life. More than anything, it was his air of unease—and the twitch in his face that he tried to quiet by touching with a forefinger that betrayed his nervousness. The prairie wind and sun had blistered his face; his fair, freckled skin was the kind that never takes a tan. His upper lip had that slight bulge that comes from wearing a heavy mustache for many years. Now the mustache was gone. Beside him sat a very young girl, slightly built, wearing a wool shirt, canvas trousers and soft, mid-calf boots.

"We're lucky to have a real doctor with us," Reverend Claggett said. "Say hello to Dr. Culkin Ames of Lancaster, Pennsylvania." Claggett touched his hatbrim with his finger. "I'm forgetting my manners. The young lady with the doctor is Miss Isabel Ames, his daughter."

We did some nodding and bowing. Ames was fidgety but friendly—almost too friendly, too eager to please someone he didn't know. Isabel murmured something I couldn't hear. I suppose it was a polite howdy-do. She was young, but there was a coolness about her that didn't go with her years. And even in the firelight she bore no resemblance to her father. That was just as well for her.

"Where are the other men?" the reverend asked Culligan.

"Seeing to the cattle. You want me to go get them?"

Claggett said no. He turned to look at Iversen, who

was still standing. "Just don't forget who's captain of this ship," the preacher reminded him. For an instant I got a glimpse of the mean man he had been so many years before. How much of the meanness was hidden behind the mild, carefully-phrased words, and the relentless determination to do good?

Iversen backed down under the hard eye of God's agent on earth. "Nobody's questioning your judgment, Mr. Claggett. All I want to know is what this man Saddler is going to be. No denying we need a scout and meat-provider, but what's all this about giving orders? Saying how this and that is to be done? These two lines of wagons, for one thing—lots of wagon trains leave here the way I always seen wagon trains move. Answer me that, Saddler."

"You don't listen, commodore," I said.

Now it was my turn to get a hard eye from the preacher. "Let's have none of that. I told you the man's name. It's Thomas Iversen."

I saw no reason to back down. "How's this for an idea, parson. Why don't you let Thomas Iversen take you across?"

"I could do it," Iversen said. "It could be done with a compass. They do it in the North African desert all the time."

I turned back to Reverend Claggett. "Why don't you rig up some sails while you're at it? Good luck, friends and neighbors. I'm going to Kansas."

I was surprised when Culligan spoke up. "The compass idea is bullshit. It would work well enough on the Plains, but once you hit mountains you'd never get a true reading."

"I'm still going to Kansas," I said.

"You gave your word," Claggett said, getting in my way. When our eyes locked for a moment, I knew the meanness in him was far from gone. "You signed on, you have to go."

I knew he was packing the short gun with which he had killed the three city detectives. I was sure I could beat him, but you never know about these things. "Nobody makes me do anything, not even you," I said.

Claggett said quietly, "I could."

"What happens if you're wrong?" I didn't want to kill this strange, God-fearing man. Still, if I let him back me down, nothing would go right after that. It's too bad the world has to be ruled by force, but that's how it works.

I don't know what changed his mind, whether it was God or good sense. "What is it you want?" he said. "Say it now, because there isn't that much time left."

My hand had been close to my gun, and I kept it where it was. "I want to run this train my own way. You can question my judgment, but no one else can. If I don't like what you say, I'll tell you. I can't see that it's going to work any other way. Besides Culligan I'm the only one who's been across. I can't do Culligan's work, and he can't do mine. So there's nothing to argue about there."

I stared at the sullen Irishman. "You think we're going to have trouble?" I asked.

"Only if you make it."

"That takes care of that," I said. "The rest of the men will take orders from me. You're part of that, Iversen. I don't know what you did at sea. On this voyage I give the orders."

Dr. Ames's crop-headed daughter spoke up in a cool, flat voice. "What about my father? Will you give him orders, too?"

The doctor looked away, as if he wanted to hide. He had a high, prissy voice. "It doesn't matter, dear. I'm sure Mr. Saddler knows what he's doing."

"Does he?" she said.

The dark-eyed girl I had seen earlier at the washtub was still showing more of her legs than she needed to, now that the laundry was done. She had a devilish look about her that I liked. A trouble-maker to be sure, but for her I could forgive just about anything. "I'll bet Mr. Saddler is a fine doctor," she said in a Southern voice. Maybe she was from New Orleans. "In point of fact, he can doctor me any time he has a mind to."

I guess Isabel Ames had to stand up for the medical profession. "I'd expect that kind of talk from you, Flaxie

Cole. That kind of talk and nothing else."

Flaxie Cole smiled sweetly. "Is that a fact, now?" she said. "Why don't you take your middle finger in the bushes for a while. It'll relax your nerves no end."

Dr. Ames had to use all his flabby strength to keep his daughter from springing to her feet. "Please, ladies," he said. "Why must there be all this fighting?"

It didn't do any good. "Because Flaxie Cole is a dirty slut," the doctor's daughter yelled.

Maggie O'Hara took the Southern girl's side. "Don't you call my friend a slut, you finger-fucker!"

The two tough girls, the New York killer and the New Orleans whore, threw their arms around each other. The Reverend Claggett looked stricken, as if God had forsaken him in his hour of need. I glanced over at Hannah Claggett, sitting by herself. Though her eyes were hooded in modesty, there was an unmistakable glitter of excitement behind the gold-rimmed glasses.

Reverend Claggett came out of his shock. "Stop it!" he roared. "Get down on your knees this very minute and beg the Almighty's forgiveness!"

Rebellion still flared; it took the threat of expulsion to get all the women in the praying position. I don't pray much, so I stayed on my feet, doing my best to fit in by bowing my head. Many other heads were bowed, but not Flaxie Cole's. She looked straight at me, and her thoughts were not on the hereafter. Neither were mine.

My thoughts, God forgive me, and I'm sure He will because they say He ain't such a bad feller, were all on Flaxie Cole. She was offering it to me on a plate, and I was hungry. I think there was a touch of the Creole in her. She was dark enough for that. The French girls of New Orleans know why nature put that sweet little beaver between their legs, and they treat it with tender loving care. So do I. Of course, all women know what they have it for, though it seems to come as a surprise to certain young ladies. But not in New Orleans.

Reverend Claggett droned on, imploring the Lord not to be too hard on the ladies. Yes, they had sinned in the past, he admitted, but all that was over. Their wanton ways and wicked lives were behind them. The trouble was that the devil was trying to make backsliders out of them. But, declared Reverend Claggett, the Devil didn't have a chance. They had him on the run and would drive him back to the fiery pit, where he belonged.

We all said "Amen" when the preacher got through with his speech. Flaxie Cole said it too, but she smiled all the while.

After that the meeting broke up and quiet descended on the wagon train. It had been a lively session, but I was glad it was over. Reverend Claggett looked tired and somewhat confused, as if he couldn't understand why he had failed to get a stranglehold on the devil.

Claggett and his daughter traveled in their own wagon, one of the biggest in the train. Its sides were built higher than usual, and Hannah's bunk was set off behind a wall of thin pine boards. Hannah was a grown woman but the preacher snapped his fingers at her as if she were a wayward child. "Get to your bed, girl," he ordered.

The firelight glinted on the gold rims of her glasses. I felt sorry for her in her shyness and loneliness. Life had dealt her a poor hand when it gave her Claggett for a father.

"I'm not sleepy yet, Father," she said. "I'll go in a while."

The preacher's eyebrows lifted in surprise. I think he detected a faint hint of rebellion in her gentle voice. I know I did.

"Do what I tell you," Claggett said. "We have a long, hard journey ahead of us."

The look in her eyes seemed to say that her whole life had been one long, hard journey. But then she smiled, as if she had decided something of great importance.

"Good night, Mr. Saddler," she said.

"Good night, Miss Claggett," I said.

I was glad when the train settled down for the night. It stood on an elevation in the prairie. From where I was I could see the lights of the town. Then, one by one, the lights winked out, and all around me there was nothing but the darkness and the night wind. The wind smelled of grass and cows and women. I noticed the woman smells more than the others.

I could have bunked in with Iversen and Culligan, but it would have taken a blizzard to make me do that. The guard had already been set for the night, so I could sleep. When I finally felt like it, I took my blankets and settled into a grassy hollow some distance from the camp. The sky was dusted with stars. It was quiet except for the movement of the cattle in the pens. I lay on my back, staring up at the sky.

Then I heard her coming, her bare feet rustling in the grass as she made her way from the wagon she shared with Maggie O'Hara. She moved in the starlight with slender grace, a bottle in her hand, but I wouldn't have minded if she'd brought only herself. But to have Flaxie Cole and a bottle of whiskey and soft grass under us—what more could a man ask for?

Flaxie's Louisiana voice was as smooth as the bourbon in the bottle. I flipped back the blanket and made a place for her, then covered us again. I tell you, it was nice under that blanket, with the night breeze blowing and us warm as a basket of kittens, the bottle passing back and forth between us.

"Oh, Jesus Christ, it's good to be with a man again!" Flaxie said, blowing her bourbon breath in my ear. "I'm so sick of women I could scream. I could scream fit to bust my brisket."

"Don't do it," I said. "You'd wake the padre, and I like your brisket just the way it is."

My hand was on her crotch as I said it. She was wet, and I was hard. She had long, lovely slender legs. I loved their smoothness. I cupped my hands under her young, rounded, almost boyish backside and let her do the work. It was like Culligan and his wagon wheels. I never interfere with people who know their work. And Flaxie certainly did.

She couldn't have been a parlor-house girl for very long, because she was small and strong and tight down below. She didn't push me in with a single thrust. She worked me in little by little, inch by inch.

"Oh, my God, isn't there any end to it?" she gasped happily. We were happy and a little drunk and didn't do anything for a while except lie there, my length inside her and her muscles contracting and letting go. Then we began to move, and oh what a sweet fuck that was! My face was buried in her long black hair. When we began to move faster, she wrapped her legs around my back. When she did that, our pace quickened and our crotches grinded together. My cock was sweet and slippery as warm honey.

She came, and then she came again. It felt good to feel her coming with me stiff and hard inside her. She was a gentle girl, and I liked her very much. She needed me as much as I needed her. It had been a long time since I had been with a girl I liked as much as this one. The wind blew colder as our fucking went on, but under the blanket we were moist and warm.

We were out under the stars, but we were as comfortable as if we were in a big, soft bed. The grass smelled sweet under us. It was a chilly night, but it was cozy with the blanket on top of us. We lay side by side, her left hand playing with my cock, my right hand playing with her cunt. Her beaver was sweet and soft and moist and she groaned when my middle finger probed into her. Her entire body seemed to vibrate when my finger put gentle pressure on her clit. Here was a beautiful girl who loved sex in all its variations. She touched my hand and said, "Down there—would you. Please do that to me."

I didn't need to be told what she wanted. I moved down under the blanket and buried my face in her muff. She smelled as sweet as the grass. My tongue went into her and she drummed her heels on the ground. The wagon train was only a short distance away, but Flaxie and I were in our own private world. I tongued her and she kept begging for more, and I gave it to her.

My tongue excited her so much that she began to cry out and, much as I hated to do it, I had to shush her. We were in a hollow and that made her cries seem louder than they were. I suspected that Reverend Claggett, the old jailbird, was a light sleeper and I didn't want to find him standing over us with a gun in his hand. We were breaking his principal rule—no sex—and he would be breathing hell and damnation if he found us together. And what I was doing to Flaxie would make him even madder than if he found us just having ordinary sex.

Flaxie was quieter after I shushed her. There was no more crying out—she groaned but not loud enough to be heard by anybody. The joy juice flowed out of her as she came over and over. I kept tonguing her through her orgasms and she grabbed my hair so hard I thought she was going to tear it out. Finally, she used both hands to raise my head from where it was. She pulled me up beside her. My mouth was wet and she kissed it, tasting herself. "I'm so happy," she said. "I've been wanting that from a man for such a long time."

"It's a long way to California," I said. "We'll have lots of nights like this. This is just the beginning. It will get better and better as we go along."

"Yes it will," she said, but I sensed a note of hesitation in her soft voice. At the time, I failed to understand what her reluctance meant, but I let it go. We were having too good a time to spoil it with doubts and questions. When she was ready for it, I rolled her over and took her from behind, my cock pushing between her legs, burying itself in her cunt. I love doing it like that. You have the woman's soft ass under you like a cushion. I spread her legs a little so I could get in all the way. I think it was the angle that made it so pleasurable. My cock brushed against her clit as I pumped in and out. My hands were around her breasts, squeezing them gently. She groaned as my fingers rolled her nipples between them. She raised her ass as I pumped harder and faster. She came before I did and the way she shuddered under me made my cock swell so large that I was afraid I couldn't go on without hurting her. But her come had made her so wet she was dripping and my cock slid in and out as easily as before. I wanted this fuck to last all night, but finally I couldn't stand it anymore and I shot my load into her. She gave a loud cry before I could stop her. Then she remembered

where we were—the dangerous situation we were in—
and she was quiet.

I rolled off her and we lay together under the blanket,
looking up at the stars. It was colder now. We had been
there for the best part of two hours, but though the
blanket was thin and old, we were very comfortable.

"This is very nice," Flaxie murmured, as if it needed
saying. "You know, I haven't done it out of doors since I
was fourteen, in Louisiana. My cousin was the same age
and we did it in a meadow under a tree. You don't mind
me telling you that?"

"Not a bit," I said honestly. "Your cousin was a lucky
boy. To be so young and have such a lovely girl."

"I am a good fuck, don't you think?"

"None better. I wish we had a wagon of our own. We
could fuck all the way to California."

"The jolting of the wagon would probably make it
better," Flaxie said. "We'll be together as often as we
can, but we have to be careful."

"Yes. Claggett is a big problem."

"Claggett isn't the only problem, but I don't want to
talk about that. It would spoil what we have."

With everything drained out of us, we lay in each
other's arms and slept for a while.

FIVE

I don't know how long she had been gone when I woke up. But I didn't feel or hear a thing until that razor-sharp knife nicked my throat. It was the bourbon plus my sweet fucking with Flaxie that had put me out. Along with cold steel and a warm trickle of blood, there was the strong, soap smell of Maggie O'Hara. Maybe the time in jail had made her fussy about staying clean; I had noticed how nice she smelled the first time we met.

There was nothing I could do about that knife; with her kind of background, she'd know how to use it. Still fogged with bourbon and pleasantly worn out from Flaxie, I preferred to think it was all a mistake. I didn't get the smallest chance to say that. The knife point drew a little more blood. One thrust or slash and I'd be finished.

"Don't talk, just listen," Maggie warned me.

It smelled now like she'd been into the bourbon bottle like the rest of us. Looked like I had fallen in with a bunch of hard-drinking women.

"You don't have to nod or do anything," Maggie said. "What I'm going to tell you will not be repeated."

Just like the snake oil salesmen say. Except that Maggie O'Hara wasn't selling anything but instant death. I didn't want to buy that, so I held still.

"Stay away from Flaxie, and that means tonight and every night and forever," Maggie said, holding the knife where it was.

If she meant to kill me for sure, I would have tried to take it away from her. The chances of doing that weren't good, though, no matter how desperate I was. I didn't know how much bourbon she had taken aboard. I guessed a lot. The knife was one of those things with the blade edged on both sides. It came to a needle point at the end, and it wasn't made for anything other than killing. Some tough women carry razors, but this one had a man-killing knife. For sure, she was good and mad.

"Flaxie belongs to me," she said, this beautiful tough girl who had done time in one of the toughest prisons in the world. "Touch her again, and I'll kill you. One way or another, I'll kill you. I killed one man, so killing another won't be any harder. If I can't use a knife or a gun, I'll poison you. I'll grind up glass so fine you'll never feel it in your grits. You hear me, shitkicker?"

At least I was breathing through my mouth and not through a hole in my throat. She held the knife back about a quarter of an inch. "I didn't know she belonged to you," I said truthfully, my mind flashing back to all that hugging and snuggling when they took sides during the argument earlier in the night.

I had run into a few women like Maggie in my time. Some liked to enjoy sex with women like it was the most natural thing in the world. Others learned it along the way. Maybe the time in jail had done it to Maggie; or could be it had been the year working in the parlor house. I began to get the feeling that the killing of the man with the champagne bottle had been no accident, after all. But it wasn't the time or the place to ask questions.

"I'd kill you right now, if we didn't need you," she said. "If it wasn't for that, you'd be dead. Who'd know, who'd care?"

"I'd care," I said.

"You wouldn't know," she said. "But we do need you, so I'll let you live. Look at Flaxie again, though, and you're a dead man, whether we need you or not. I had her coming along just fine, and you had to show up. You and your smooth talk, filling that poor kid's head with lies. She's still too young to know what men are like. But she'll learn. You feed that kid one more drink, and I'll dig your grave. That's a promise, shitkicker."

I made a feeble effort to defend myself. "Flaxie brought the bottle," I said.

I felt the prick of the knife again. "That's right," Maggie said in a deadly whisper. "Put the blame on *her*. I'll bet you cooked up the whole thing with her. Got her to get me drunk so I'd be sleeping sound when you sneak off to fuck with her. I thought there was something funny when she suggested that we have a few drinks. I thought it was because she was so happy we were finally heading West. Just the two of us out there, making a new life. Answer me, bastard!"

"I didn't know. Honest Injun, I didn't," I said, not sure that a sudden surge of anger wouldn't drive that knife into my throat. Once again I wondered if I could grab the knife before she drove it all the way to the hilt.

But in spite of the knife, I felt a sudden longing for her. Call that crazy, if you like. They say a man shoots his wad when he's hanged; maybe what I felt for her then was something close to that.

"You know it now," Maggie said. "Flaxie is mine, every soft inch of her belongs to me. Those last few months in Sing Sing, I used to dream about a girl like Flaxie. There were plenty of cunts there and I'm human . . . but it was always someone like Flaxie I dreamed about. I'm telling you all this so you know I mean it about killing you. Crazy! I even knew what she looked like. I knew her so well I drew a picture of her on the wall of my cell. The bastards made me wash it off, but they couldn't wash it out of my mind. I could pleasure myself with just her picture in my mind. When it looked like I'd never get out, I made a knife from a piece of hoop iron and planned to finger myself one last time and then put the knife through my heart. But I got out the night I was going to do it."

The bourbon was wearing off. There was a note of sadness in her voice. "She's all I've got. If I don't have her, I don't have anything. You couldn't understand feeling like that about a woman."

I didn't know what to say. Any answer might be the wrong answer.

"'Course you couldn't," Maggie answered for me. "All men see women as something soft with a furry hole in the crotch." Anger replaced the sadness in her voice. "I don't care what you do to the rest of these cunts in the train. Fuck yourself blind, for all I care. Just leave my girl alone. It'll be the death of you, if you don't. Keep your distance, and we'll manage to get along fine."

Maggie stood up. I reached for my gun and found it wasn't there. She pointed to where it lay glinting dully in the moonlight. "I emptied the shells, too," she said. "Want to make a try for it?"

I didn't. Then she surprised me by reaching into the pocket of her skirt and producing a half-full bottle of bourbon. "That's what's left of the whiskey Flaxie fed me. It's all yours, you son-of-a-bitch. Funny, isn't it? Me giving you something instead of taking something away."

I figured the whiskey wasn't poisoned, so I uncorked the bottle and took a deep swallow. If I didn't watch myself, I was going to turn into a drunkard, all these ladies feeding me whiskey. But I sure as hell needed that drink.

I looked up at her. "What did you come to take away?" I asked.

"Your cock!" she answered.

I finished what was in the bottle and went back to sleep. Yes sir, I would have been better off in Kansas.

No other visitors came to call during the night.

In the morning only the nick in my throat remained to prove that the whole thing hadn't been a nightmare. First light was breaking over the wagon train, and people were stirring, eager to start, but apprehensive about what lay ahead of them. I can hardly be called the rooted, home-building type, yet the sight of a wagon train about to move always stirs my blood. Others had crossed the plains and the mountains, but no crossing is ever the same.

At first there was some fog. But it soon blew away and the sky became vast and blue and cloudless. On this first morning of the great journey there was no dawdling over breakfast. A few miles away the town of Independence was white in the morning sun. I noticed that some of the women looked at it in a lingering way, and for some their courage faltered as they thought of the life they were leaving forever.

I hitched the bandanna higher around my throat to hide the small knife wound. I wasn't likely to forget the woman who had put it there. There had to be some sort of reckoning with Maggie O'Hara. I didn't know when or where it would come. Nonetheless, there would be trouble with her, if not for me, then for someone else. At that moment, I had no idea what I was going to do about her.

After the morning meal was over and the cookfires covered with dirt, we waited for Reverend Claggett's command to move out. Surprisingly, he hadn't done that much preaching, as if he had worn himself out with his exhortations of the night before. Me, I wanted to be gone as quickly as possible, because once on the trail, there would be plenty of work to do. I was more concerned about the water barrels than anything else. Winter was over, and the warm spring wind would blow the Plains bone dry. At the moment there was plenty of meat, but salted meat sours in the stomach before long. Part of my job was to put fresh meat in the cook pot or in the skillet.

Contrary to what some people thought, we weren't about to journey into the garden of plenty. Far out on the Plains the buffalo hunters had thinned out the herds, taking only the hides, leaving the meat to rot. The

Indians often slaughtered more than they needed, to keep the encroaching whites and enemy tribes hungry. People still talked of wild turkeys, but it had been years since I'd seen one. So I would have to hunt what I could find; the ladies would eat it and like it, or go hungry.

Culligan climbed down from his wagon with Iversen behind him. The Irishman looked no angrier than usual, which meant that his hate was for the world and for no one particular person. I had seen him checking the wagon wheels the day before. Now, sullen or not, he walked the length of the train doing it again. He was a man you couldn't like but could respect. I had no way of knowing how good a fighting man he was; time would tell that, too, for there is no crossing of the Plains without its share of fights. Looking at his bristly red face with its bull-calf brow and pugnacious jaw, I guessed Culligan wouldn't back down when the going got tough. Thomas Iversen, though, was an unanswered question. A man good at some things is no good at others. I think he saw himself as one hell of a fine fellow. Maybe he was, in some ways; the long journey would decide his merit.

What none of them were counting on was the distance they had yet to travel. I'd been across and it was still hard to say what it was like. It often feels as if the Plains have no end. There seems to be no boundary to the country out there, no place where you can say for sure it will stop. And then, for much of the crossing, there is the sameness to be faced day after day. Of course, there are landmarks, but mostly there is monotony. In the end, it gets so you welcome any change at all, anything that stands out above the sea of grass. Maps don't seem to mean anything; distance loses meaning. You travel for days and nothing changes.

As I watched the preacher walk back from the head of the train, I wondered if any of them, other than Culligan, knew what they were in for. Their greatest enemy would be loneliness, which may not sound right with so many people traveling together. Yet it's true: the endless journey forces people in upon themselves. They wonder what they're doing, where they are, and what's going to happen to them. Far from home, the poverty or misery of home begins to seem not so bad after all.

Loneliness and the ever-blowing wind are what I remember about the crossings I've made. The wind is always there, hot or cold, and it saws at the nerves as nothing else can. In the face of the prairie wind, friendly men turn silent and rush quickly to anger; animosities emerge that remain for life.

Of all the people here, only Hannah Claggett seemed peaceful. There was a strange serenity about her that made me wonder. She brushed her hair and coiled it in that schoolteacherish way of hers. She smiled at me and said good morning as if we were meeting on some village street. But I knew she wanted cock—needed it. And I liked her very much.

Maggie O'Hara, standing beside her wagon, stared at me and said nothing. Flaxie looked at me and then looked away. I wondered how the night had gone for them. Flaxie was subdued, almost frightened in her manner. Thinking of the double-edged knife, I hardly blamed her. All I wanted Flaxie to do was to stay away from me. A pity—but I didn't want to have to kill Maggie O'Hara. That's what I would have to do, if she pulled a knife on me again. It was a shame about Flaxie; no matter, I would have to make do with the other 50 women in the train. Forty-nine, to be exact, for it wasn't likely that Maggie would ever join me under the stars.

The cattle were to be handled by an old geezer I hadn't seen before. He came loping along on a good-looking bay and introduced himself as Kiowa Sam Jaspers. The boy with him I took to be his grandson, but old Sam announced with some pride that the boy was his son. I wasn't sure if I believed him, but they did belong to the same family. There was no mistaking the potato noses and long-lobed ears.

Sam said the boy's name was Cyrus. "A good lad, but not too bright in the head," Sam said. "Don't have much to say neither. Ain't that so, boy?"

"Sure is," the boy said.

Sam informed me that he had been raised by the Kiowas and knew their customs and language. That was a safe thing to say, since we weren't going anywhere close to Texas. Maybe he really had been raised by the Kiowas. Anything was possible. But I marked him down for a liar and hoped he knew more about cows than he did about Kiowas.

"You know much about Kiowas?" the old man asked.

"Not many in my part of Texas," I said, thinking that when you have to work with a man, it's best not to show him up as a liar, if you have no special reason for doing so.

"Then you'll hear many good Kiowa stories before this journey is over," old Sam said.

Not if I can help it, I thought.

I had been looking at the boy called Cyrus. His quiet tongue would be a mercy on a long trip; on the other hand, a lame-brained boy in a wagonful of young women could be a problem. I didn't know how old he was, maybe about 16 or 17, but plenty big for his age. The boy's lack of brains wouldn't bother some of the ladies, if they got hot enough between the legs on cold nights.

I motioned Kiowa Sam aside and said, "That boy ever been with a woman that you know of?"

"Never has," Kiowa Sam said. "I ought to know. I been looking after him all his life." The old man laughed. "That don't mean he won't get the itch one of these days."

The boy seemed to have taken a fancy to Hannah Claggett, maybe because she was the only one who didn't talk to him as you would to a dog. I didn't want this lamebrain to be her first man. I gave Kiowa Sam a look that stopped his smile. "Tell Cyrus to wait till we get to California. You tell him, because it's your place to tell him. If you don't, I will."

The old man's seamed face grew ugly. "Maybe you will and maybe you won't."

"Meaning what?"

"Meaning you wasn't doing so bad last night with that Southern gal. That one's a woman-licker, case you didn't know."

Well there was no profit in beating hell out of an old man. He wore a gun, a good-looking old Scofield .45 six-shooter in an oiled holster with an open end. The long-barreled Scofield had the front sight filed off so it wouldn't snag on the leather when it was yanked from the holster. When you see a man with the front sight of his pistol filed off, it means he's a braggart or one hell of a shot at close range.

I looked from Sam to the hulking son. Best I could tell, Sam was past the age for women. The little pot belly that hung on his skinny frame said his main pleasure in life was the cook pot. Besides, he'd been guarding the cattle, and there was no reason why he should come spying on me and Flaxie. So it had to be the boy, hot in the crotch and wanting to know how a real man did it to a woman. That in itself wasn't so bad: Boys like a free show so they can brag about it later. But there was something about this muscle-bound lout that bothered me.

"You mind your business, and I'll mind mine," Sam said. "That boy is my business. Yours is to get these whores to California."

"Ladies, old man," I corrected him. "We got nothing but ladies on this trip."

Sam spat. He wasn't much afraid of me. Maybe he was too old to care. I didn't care either. I'd kill him if I had to.

He stared at me, a concerned father. "Then what's my boy to do if he gets the itch on the way across?"

"You ever live on a farm?" I asked Sam.

"I been on one. What's that got to do with it?"

"Tell your boy to do what farm boys usually do when their pants get too hot. Bossy won't mind."

What I was saying was nothing but the truth, but Kiowa Sam didn't like it.

"You calling my boy a calf-lover, Saddler?" the old man asked. His hand moved slightly closer to his holstered Scofield.

"Nobody says he has to fall in love with the critter," I said.

Sam laughed, and I knew he would use what I'd said in one of his stories years hence. If he lived that long.

Just then Reverend Claggett raised his hand, and the wagon train pointed its way west.

SIX

A bugle blew, and we were off to the land of the free. Some trains are so well set-up, so well planned and organized, that you think nothing can stop them. Most of these outfits are bossed, sometimes owned completely, by rich men with visions of model communities dancing in their heads. Often these rich organizers and visionaries have been soldiers in their time—officers naturally—and they think they know how to do it. Many of them do. They see an overland trek as just another military maneuver, the movement of a large amount of goods from one place to another.

But our train did not make an impressive sight. This was no rich overland train, and there was no uniformity in its appearance. It had been put together by Josiah Claggett's iron will. I guessed he'd had no money of his own, so he must have set up the train with donations. He was a hard man to say no to.

The wagons had been standing for so long that grass had grown up beside the wagon wheels. But the wheels began to turn when the bugle blew. Kiowa Sam did the bugling, though he wasn't very good at it. I was glad to see so many oxen pulling away. Those big bastards are slow and dumb, but they get you there. They're more like slow-moving machines than animals and their meat isn't all that hard to take. Given a choice, I'll take ox steak over horse steak. Mule meat, even stewed soft, is pretty bad.

Reverend Claggett drove the lead wagon in the right column. Hannah sat beside him, prissy but pretty in the bright morning light. She was sewing a patch on one of the old man's coats. Some of the women knew how to handle wagons already; some didn't, but before we got to California they would all know.

Most of the wagons were Conestogas, those big landships that had originated in Pennsylvania more than a century and a half before. They had to cross rough country, and they were built to take it. Usually they were about 27 feet long, 11 feet high, and the real big ones could go as heavy as 4000 pounds. That's one big piece of work, and it could take four or five men two months to make one.

The bed was boat-shaped, the center sagging, the ends arched upward. This was no whim on the builder's part. If the load shifted, it shifted toward the center. This helped on the upgrades and downgrades. It was especially meant to keep the load from shifting back toward the endgates on steep grades. If that happened, you'd have your belongings strewn all over the trail.

I'm going into all this detail because the Conestoga, like the buffalo, is vanishing from the West. Oh, you still see some in the wild places. Most of the ones you see are old. Ours were old then, had made many a crossing, and had had the sides gouged by Indian lances or splintered by riflefire.

The heavy chains that held the endgates in place rattled as we moved off. A light morning wind filled the wagon covers made of white canvas or homespun; they were puckered by a draw rope that held down the ends. The ends were lashed to the wagon sides.

Iversen drove none too expertly, while Culligan walked forward on both sides of the wagons, not inspecting every wheel as it passed but always aware of what was happening. If we didn't get through, it wouldn't be because of Culligan, sullen and ill-tempered though he was. There was no need to be so careful on the first stage of the journey. All the same, he was. I respect a man who knows his job and does it well.

Some of Culligan's truculence came from pride in his work; the rest was Irish. This bull-browed boy had an awesome responsibility. The wagons had to move and keep moving. They carried immense weight, and their underpinnings had to be seen to constantly. Heavily ironed and braced, the bolsters and the axles were of hickory; the hubs of sour or black gum were almost impossible to split. The rims of the wheels were any-where from two to ten inches. A four-inch rim was the usual size, and the front wheels were, as a rule, about a foot smaller than the back. Heavy iron tires, usually two half-circles of iron welded tight, held the wheel together. To put a good wagon together took as much blacksmithing as woodworking. Like all good wagon wheels, they were dished out slightly. Most Conestogas were painted in the national colors: red, white and blue. The running gear was red, a Prussian blue body, and a white canvas top. The colors of our wagons, however, were somewhat faded.

Maggie O'Hara, originally a farmer's daughter, han-dled the wagon as well as any man. No doubt the daily grind of prison life had toughened her body, though I must say there was nothing hard about it. Idly, I found myself wondering how many men had stuck it in Maggie in her time. I guessed a few hundred, at least. I found myself thinking about Hanrahan's dead son. The man must have been mighty peculiar to want to do other things to Maggie besides fuck her in a nice, natural manner. Yet, in a way, I understood. There was an arrogance about her that could get your hackles up—and your cock—just by looking at her. Maybe I was being swell-headed, but I figured she wanted a strong man to subdue her, and hadn't yet found him.

Flaxie Cole sat beside her on the wagon seat, dark and

demure, not daring to look my way. It had been so good under that blanket on the grass in the moonlight. When she first came to me, bare feet rustling in the grass, I had looked forward to many such nights. Damn it to hell! I had no mind to tangle with her jailbird "husband," not unless I wanted more trouble than I was ready to handle.

I rode along by the wagons, checking the gear. Culligan, mindful only of his own job, showed no interest in what was being carried. Except for a grand piano, we had just about everything else with us on that trail. Most wagons had tool boxes affixed to their left sides in back of the lazyboard, which pulled out in front of the rear left wheel. In such boxes you'd find the usual gear of a frontier freighter: hatchets, axes, an auger, different kinds of nails, extra rope, linchpins, kingbolts and strap iron. In the big boxes there might be the wagon jack, but as a rule, it was too big to fit into the limited space. Big, heavy, and clumsy, its usual place would be hanging from the rear axle, alongside the tar bucket with the pine tar to lubricate the wheels. The jacks worked with a lever handle, much like an ordinary pump handle. They had to be damned sturdy to lift a wagon weighing three or four tons, and sometimes more.

I myself was concerned about water. You'd think a sea of grass would have a sea of water under it. No such thing. You found water where you found it, when you were lucky. Sometimes the Indians poisoned the water to spite each other as much as the invading whites. It was even said that some wandering white gun-runners sold the poison to the Indians. It would, I thought, be a pleasure to hang a man like that.

Independence dropped away behind us. There were no more backward glances. The women knew there was no turning back. A wagon train may be slow, but the big wheels turn, and the old life falls behind.

The water barrels were lashed good and tight; I found them well-banded with no leaks. Water meant everything. You could root and scratch for food, manage to survive on things considered inedible, but you had to have water.

This was our first morning out. Enthusiasm was strong. Kiowa Sam and his lamebrain son Cyrus were seeing to the cattle. Cyrus was as slow in movement as he was in speech; he did his job well when Sam told him how to do it, or reminded him of something he had forgotten. Now and then his work took him too close to the Claggett wagon. I didn't like that, but for the moment it wasn't important enough to do anything about it. Claggett took no heed of him, staring straight ahead, as if he could see all the way across the continent, even through the snowy wall of the Rockies.

Hannah Claggett always smiled at Cyrus as he came close to the wagon. Every time she did so, he blushed like a dude with a bad sunburn, but here was no bashful swain, I decided. The shyness was genuine enough, but what would happen when Hannah realized that she had been leading on a possibly dangerous fool. Maybe she did know it: figured she'd get her first poke from somebody harmless.

Maybe I should have kept my broken Texas nose out of it. But something warned me that Cyrus was trouble. On a remote ranch with somebody to keep the blinkers on him, he might have lived out a useful enough life, buggering a few lambs to while away the lonely hours. But he wasn't on a·ranch. I didn't want to tell Claggett about it, because that would make trouble for the girl. I didn't want to have to kill Cyrus, something I most certainly would have to do if he attacked her. Sometimes, on a long journey, you have to shoot or hang a troublemaker. It can be a tonic for everyone who witnesses it. But that's usually when you have to deal with a lot of would-be hard cases. On this trip most of the witnesses to Cyrus's death would be young women.

Cyrus's way of getting close to the Claggett wagon was to maneuver a stray in that direction. I knew it was no accident after it happened for the second time. At the moment, the cows were well watered and well grassed, so the wandering off was the fool's idea of being clever. The next time he did it, I kicked my horse and rode up close. I got a remote nod from the preacher and a smile from

Hannah. She had been smiling at Cyrus too. Cyrus wasn't so glad to see me, so I got nothing from him.

"Having trouble with the cows, is that it?" I said, nodding at the half-grown calf.

Cyrus turned sullen at being called down in front of his lady love. "They run off," he said. "They do that, I come and fetch them back. That happens."

"That happens too much. If you can't run a smooth herd in this country, what's going to happen when we hit rough country?"

"I know my work, how to do it," Cyrus said.

I turned my horse toward the wagon and saw that Kiowa Sam was watching from where he was with the rest of the cows.

"Then do it," I told Cyrus. "Another thing. Next time a cow strays, tell him to pick another wagon."

Cyrus had a lame brain, but part of it—the crafty part—worked well enough. "They follow up this wagon 'cause it's in the lead."

"Have a talk with the cows," I said. "Tell them it's against the rules to bunch up at the lead wagon."

Cyrus's slack mouth hung open. "That's crazy," he said. "How can I talk to cows?"

Kiowa Sam was nosing his horse through the small herd, trying to hear what was being said.

I had to say everything plain in the end. "Keep your strays away from this wagon, Cyrus. Do that, or I'll set you to riding drag."

Cyrus didn't like that; it was the worst job in a train. Some trains don't even bother with a back point man. Usually the people in the last wagons watch the country behind them. When it's flat country, you can see far enough to spot trouble. We might do it later when we got into broken country. At the moment there was no need. But I was ready to make a job for Cyrus, if I had to. The man who rides the back point has to swallow the dust kicked up by the train. There is no one to talk to, no company at all. And in hostile country you're an easy target.

"You got no right to do that," Cyrus said.

"Sonny," I said, "I can do just about anything I please. Now get the hell away from here and stay away."

Cyrus rode back to have a confab with his father. I looked at Hannah Claggett; her eyes were wild with excitement. Two men had been quarreling over her! Hannah was a bright, if peculiar, girl. She knew the whole thing had nothing to do with stray cows. Damn it to hell! I felt like a fool, trading hard words with a lamebrain about a mad minister's bespectacled daughter.

"Don't you think you were a bit hard on Cyrus?" Hannah asked, her eyes merry. "You'd really do what you said you'd do?"

I should have caught on sooner, but I can be slow. Hannah thought I was jealous. Not true at all. I fully intended to throw a leg over her, that is if I didn't have to risk a bullet from the preacher while I was doing it. But jealous—no! Hell, I wasn't even jealous of Maggie O'Hara, who was doing all those peculiar woman things to the sweetest little furry beaver in the whole train. Well, no, the sweetest little beaver in the train belonged to Maggie herself. I was as sure of that as I am that I'll never die in bed—if I'm lucky, I won't. I didn't give a damn about all the men who had been in Maggie's life, or in Maggie herself. But that was just dreaming. Flaxie would have done fine. Take it from me, she was sweet as a nest of wild honey.

I expected trouble with Kiowa Sam, but it didn't come just then. All he did was whisper to Cyrus; after that they stayed with the cows. No more strays found their way to the Claggett wagon.

"Well, would you do that to Cyrus?" Hannah asked again, matching her needlework to the jolt of the wagon. She was very good at it.

The man of God hadn't been paying much attention. Now he glanced over at me. "Do what?" he asked.

"Make Cyrus—Kiowa Sam's son—ride drag. We're going to have to do it some time. Not always Cyrus, of course, but the men have to get used to the idea. I know it's a tough job, but he's young, and it won't kill him.

Make a better man of him, in fact."

Hannah was trying to hide a grin.

Claggett's eyes turned back toward the horizon. "I don't mind the idea," he said. "Sam can handle the cows by himself. Sam was the one I hired for the job. He gets wages, food, and a place to sleep, not the son. Sam said he'd look after him on the way. I couldn't see the harm of it. What good are we, if we don't show some Christian charity?"

"Amen to that!" I said, and the strangled sound Hannah made turned into a fit of coughing.

When it subsided, she said, "Must be the dust." She turned her eyes, now calm, on me. "Don't you think there is a lot of dust—or something—in the air, Mr. Saddler?"

I returned her calm look. "Sometimes a walk in the damp night air helps a sore throat, Miss Claggett."

"Yes," she said. "I might do that."

I knew she would and hoped it would be tonight. Poor old Cyrus! He wasn't going to be the first after all.

SEVEN

That first day, because it was flat, grassy country, we made a good 20 miles. Men, women and animals were rested and eager to get on with it. In the days to come, our pace would slow down to as little as ten miles a day. It was an old story for me. But for now all was well: good country, weather as fine as fine could be. Our pace was about two miles an hour, as we didn't want to push the animals hard. Mules make better time than oxen, but oxen outlast mules. It still was cool enough to keep moving all day, but there would come a time when it would be best to travel only in the mornings and late afternoons. During the real hot part of the day we would eat, sleep, see to repairs, and make plans—all the things that have to be done during an overland crossing.

That first day we made good time and corralled by a creek with not a tree in sight. This wasn't dangerous country, so we didn't corral in a circle. Instead, the two lines of wagons were pulled in to form an oval protection of a sort. It was quiet along the creek as the wagons settled in. The women, silent for most of the day, piled down from the wagons and began to talk as if they had just been given permission to do so. The sight of the clear, running water cheered them. Droves of them went downstream and began to wash off the sweat and dirt of the day. You could hear their laughter and the splashing of the water as darkness gathered. Nothing cheers me more than the sound of a woman's laughter. I hated to think that some would never make it to California. But there was no getting around the fact that some would die.

I walked the train and counted people and animals. No one had wandered off or ducked out along the way. Some of the women were coming back from their splash in the creek. Maggie O'Hara was with Flaxie. Dr. Ames sat by a cookfire and waited for his daughter to get back. I wondered what he was so nervous about. They don't have alligators in streams in Missouri. Something was going on between the doctor and his daughter that I couldn't quite figure out.

After the reverend intoned grace, we went at the grub like the hungry folks we were. Everybody ate in a big circle, and I got to sit close to Hannah Claggett. The preacher man did not seem to notice. I saw Kiowa Sam and his lamebrain son staring at me. Culligan ate and smoked a cigar at the same time. Iversen just sat and ate. It would have been a pleasant moment, if not for the danger in the air. I knew I wasn't imagining it. It was faint, but it was there, and I wondered if Maggie had changed her mind and decided to kill me after all. You never know what women are going to do. If you did, they wouldn't be half as exciting.

Sam and Cyrus were a threat and made little effort to hide it. I ruled out Reverend Claggett because he had no immediate cause to kill me. Culligan just wanted to do his work and get drunk in his wagon at night. Iversen? I didn't know a thing about Iversen except that he was a liar. The talk about rejoining his ship in California was horseshit. But that was his business. Dr. Ames didn't come into it at all. Now and then his crop-headed daughter glanced over at me, always with plain dislike. It hardly mattered what she thought of me. Maybe she didn't like Texans.

The women were tired and rightly so. There wasn't so much enthusiasm now. All they wanted was sleep, and for the moment enough men were there to stand guard so the ladies could get their rest. At that time outlaw gangs still ran in Missouri, but their interests lay in trains that ran on rails. Few bandits bothered wagon trains; it wasn't worth the bother.

As the women drifted to their blankets, I called out the men who were to stand guard. I was to take the watch with Culligan. After that Iversen and Dr. Ames were to look out for marauders. I didn't think there would be any. Kiowa Sam and Cyrus were to take the last watch, then catch up on their sleep in a wagon after we started out again at first light. It was a standard plan of guard against night attack. In time, some of the women would have to do guard duty with the men.

It got very dark and quiet. Below the camp the creek bubbled along. Culligan took one end of the train, and I took the other. Nothing happened until a woman screamed in her sleep and I ran to her wagon with the Winchester in my hand. Culligan came fast from the far end of the train. But it was just a nightmare, and after the woman spoke to me in some foreign language, I patted her on the head and she went back to sleep.

Fifteen minutes later we were relieved by Iversen and Ames. Iversen handled his rifle as if he knew how it worked. I wasn't too sure about the nervous doctor. He held his rifle like it was hot to the touch. What surprised me was that his daughter went to stand guard with him. Nothing in the rules said she couldn't do that, so I didn't say anything. Culligan climbed into his wagon, and I heard the pop of a cork.

So far, so good.

I was tired but not sleepy enough to sleep. I manage to get along on short rations of shut-eye. A light drizzle grew heavier, which was typical weather for Missouri at that time of year. I didn't want to bunk in with Culligan and his cigar and bottle, so I was making up a place to sleep under the wagon when Hannah Claggett came up silently in the darkness and whispered to me.

I was surprised and said, "Why are you up at this hour?"

She didn't answer that. "You're not going to sleep under there are you?"

I pointed toward the floor of the wagon above my head. "The air is better."

"Oh, that's terrible," she whispered. "Come and talk in my wagon until the rain stops. You'll catch your death down here."

Well, of course I wouldn't. "What about your father? Won't he object to midnight callers?"

Hannah knelt down on the wet grass. "He won't be back for hours. Every night he goes off by himself to pray, usually until the middle of the night. It's all right. You can come with me. I won't take no, and I mean it. It isn't right."

Hot damn! I'll take a chance on anything, even a bullet from a killer-preacher's fast gun. But I did feel kind of peculiar. I crawled out from under the wagon, and there wasn't a soul in sight except for Hannah. She wore a quilted nightcoat over a long nightdress, and she smelled good.

Faint light showed from the preacher's big wagon. Hannah told me to stay in the shadows while she went inside and turned the lamp wick down all the way. After that, hardly a glimmer showed. She leaned down over the swung-down endgate and took my hand, and I went in.

I had been there before and knew what it looked like. The fold-down table had been put up flat against the wall and hinged. The preacher's bed hadn't been made up. Hannah led me into her tiny cubicle at the far end of the wagon. It was big enough for a slim girl; with the two of us in there, it was like being crammed into a packing case.

I expected to have to do some fooling around with this girl. No such thing. She peeled off in the darkness and helped me to unbutton my pants. My she smelled sweet with her clothes off! It was dark in there and at first I couldn't see an inch of her, not a curve, but as my hands roved over her young body, I knew I had been right all along. This girl was made for poking and wanted it badly.

Her bed was hardly more than a bunk, and not a soft one at that. It couldn't have mattered less. Nothing was said and nothing needed to be said. Her young mouth was sweet and strained with longing, and when I reached down and touched her, a shudder ran through her body. I wanted to shush her when she whispered, but she said there was no need. Her father did the same thing every night, prayed far into the dark hours.

"We'd hear him coming, the way he walks," she whispered.

After that, I decided to hell with the reverend. This girl brought out the best in me; wanting her so much made me hard as a rock.

She touched it and rubbed it until it was my turn to shudder. "Gracious! It's so big." she said. "I had no idea. Please put that into me."

I did. It went in smooth and easy, all the way to the hilt. Her back arched like a cat's and I drove my cock in and out of her like it was a steel rod. I seemed to get bigger and harder as our fucking went on. She knew nothing about men; she wanted to know everything. My balls fascinated her, and she whispered in that school-girlish voice, "To think the whole world starts here. Amazing! Astonishing!"

Fact is, I hadn't given the idea much thought. I knew men and women fucked, and sometimes there were babies. "That's how it all started," I whispered back.

"But it's all so wonderful," she said. "So wonderful and beautiful!"

I pushed it in all the way, drew it out to the tip, then drove in again. "It can be," I said.

"Is it like that with me?"

"What do you think?"

"I think I can't bear to stop."

She had come so many times that she was quivering with exhaustion. I came twice and wanted more of her, but men have certain drawbacks. You have to wait for a while. With me—no brag—it doesn't take that long to get hard again. Truthfully, I just wanted to stay in her, to enjoy the feeling of being in her, with her soft young body under mine. The feel of her and the smell of her was enough for me. Our bodies were damp with clean sweat, the kind that comes from good fucking.

"I don't want to stop either," I said, "but what about your father?"

"Don't worry," she said. "He won't be back for ages. I ought to know. I've lived with him all my life."

The way she said that had such a sad sound. When he did return, we didn't hear him until he was climbing up over the endgate of the wagon. Her hand clamped over my mouth, though I wasn't about to say a word. I didn't know what to do, so I did nothing.

Reverend Claggett, no longer young, groaned as he made up his bed. The floor of the wagon creaked as he knelt beside it. Then we heard him say in that doomsday voice, "Oh, God, speed us on our way, I beseech You. The years have passed, and You have redeemed . . . and yet . . . and yet . . . Please help me, oh Lord, for I am the lowliest of sinners. I am beyond my depth, oh Lord, as if things are happening that I cannot understand."

Moments later he lay down and began to snore like a woodcutter. The noise filled the big wagon. I felt Hannah shaking under me. I thought she was crying or trembling with fear. Then I realized that she was laughing.

"What's so funny?" I whispered.

"Gracious! You've gone all soft," she murmured. "I'll have to help you, won't I?"

Together we got it rock-hard again.

And the reverend snored on.

I had two problems to think about. The floor of the wagon wasn't solid but planked, and it creaked when a man's weight was put on it. I'm a shade over 190, and that's plenty of pounds. Old Claggett was snoring, but I was ready to bet that he was a light sleeper. You form habits early, and Claggett had been an outlaw and jailbird for about half his life. I was pretty sure he'd get kind of mad if he caught me sneaking out of his daughter's cubicle in the middle of the night. Saying that I'd come to tuck her in wouldn't get me far.

Apart from that, it was a cold, rainy night outside, and if I left Hannah's bed I'd have to spend the rest of the night in Culligan's wagon, or under it. The idea didn't appeal to me. Along about now, Culligan would be at the bottom of the bottle or starting on a new one. Liquor was forbidden on the train, but when you're as big as Culligan you can do a lot of things you're not supposed to. As far as I knew, he didn't drink during the day, just at night after the wagons were corralled. Truthfully, I didn't want to sleep with Culligan, or even close to him. So, I stayed where I was and hoped for the best.

And I got it. There is nothing like being in bed with a soft, warm young woman on a cold, wet night. You can listen to the rain dripping and be glad you're not out in it. Naturally, Hannah wasn't wearing her gold-rimmed glasses—I'm not sure she really needed them—and in the dim light that filtered into the cubicle she looked different, younger and somehow full of mischief. She looked like a kid who had gotten away with some prank.

After the reverend climbed into the wagon I was nervous for a while, but Hannah whispered that it was all right. I wasn't so sure, but then I decided the hell with it. There's no spice in life without danger. Hannah's bed was narrow, but it was big enough when I was on top of her. She was a virgin, but she took to sex naturally and without a trace of awkwardness. With Claggett snoring only a few feet away we couldn't go in for any fancy fucking, much as we both wanted to, but man on top of woman, or the other way around, is fine with me.

Hannah was a virgin and very tight, so I had to push hard. But the friction made it that much more exciting. She had strong muscles down there and she used them to drive me wild. It was a cold night, but sweat still glistened on her face and body. She felt slippery under me. Instead of locking her legs behind me, she spread them as wide as the bed would allow, making it possible for me to plow her deep.

By now I was past caring about the Reverend Claggett.

I didn't know about the doctor's daughter, but I was pretty sure Hannah was the only virgin in the train. Now I don't go looking for virgins, but it can get you bone-hard when you know you're giving a woman her first fuck; what they lack in experience they make up with lots of energy and an eagerness to please.

Hannah didn't close her eyes but watched my face as I fucked her, as if she wanted to be sure that her body, her tight cunt, pleased me. I couldn't have been more pleased. She got wetter and wetter as I fucked her steadily but gently. I knew she wanted this to be a wild fuck, but we didn't dare. She was wild enough though, raising her ass off the bed and grinding her crotch into mine. Her ass was small and round and firm. I have large hands and they held the twin globes of her ass tightly.

"I like everything you're doing to me," she whispered. "I've often wondered what it would be like. But it's better than anything I ever imagined. Do you like it as much as I do? Do you like the way I fuck?"

She said the word shyly. It was funny to hear it coming from her. Just saying fuck seemed to get her even more excited and she whispered a lot of other forbidden words to me. Cunt. Balls. Cock. Hard-on. I don't know where she had heard them, but they must have been in her head for a long time. I guess that's what happens to a cock-wanting woman when she's been kept down too long.

"Shoot your load, Jim," she whispered. Another bit of naughtiness. I came like a firehose.

I liked her, everything about her. I didn't want to settle down with her on some farm, have her call me in for supper, or smile at her across the candied yams, but I liked her.

Claggett snored on. I hoped he wasn't keeping God awake. Hannah and I didn't need any of God's help. Hannah was more excited by the proximity of danger than I was. I get enough danger in the kind of work I do. More than that is like getting too much on your plate. But Hannah kept coming back for extra helpings. Man, that girl was starved for sex.

You never saw a girl with such stamina, such energy. There's a saying that such and such a woman can go all night. This one could. Her enthusiasm was catching, like speaking in tongues at a revival meeting. Claggett snored on, and I plowed his daughter. I guess we'd be at it still, if first light hadn't thinned the darkness to gray. Preacher or no preacher, I had to get out of there.

It was the longest sneak I took in my life. I had to go out over the endgate of the wagon. I was closer to the driver's seat, but that was sprung and would squeak like the devil. If Claggett heard that, he would draw and fire without asking questions. I had no mind to kill the old man; by his rules, I was in the wrong. So I went by way of the endgate.

Not much light showed yet, just gray streaks in the sky. It would be more than half an hour before the first of the sleepers blinked awake. Sam and Cyrus were on the last watch of the night, but I saw no sign of them.

I would have to go the next day without sleep. Fine with me. I was feeling all right, the way you ought to feel after a good night with a woman. Sure, I was tired. No, not tired exactly, just droopy and relaxed, all the tensions gone. I wondered if there would be other nights with Hannah. It was hard to tell. I hoped there would, because it had been one sweet ride.

The light was slightly brighter and I was rolling up the bedroll under the tent when I heard the scream. It was high and terrified and despairing. I knew it was Hannah. I dropped the bedroll and ran. I didn't give a damn now about her father. If I caught him beating her, I'd kill him.

I got to the Claggett tent as people tumbled from their wagons. Their faces seemed to know that this wasn't the foreign woman with the nightmares. And somehow I knew it wasn't Claggett in trouble.

People ran behind me to the tent. Whiskey-sick or not, Culligan was right behind me with a rifle. I dived into the bed of the wagon and found Claggett tearing at the thin wood partition that separated Hannah's bed from the rest of the space. The preacher had a gun in his hand. Hannah's bare feet showed beyond the end of the partition. They kicked convulsively, but the screaming had subsided.

Claggett, in his panic, was doing no damn good. I shoved him aside so hard that his back hit the far sideboard of the wagon. Culligan, stinking with whiskey, pointed at the twitching feet. "The girl must be having a fit," he said. "We got to keep her from swallowing her tongue."

I knew he was wrong when I heard the rattle for the first time. The Irishman heard it too, and his mottled face turned a blotchy white. "Dear, sweet, Jesus Christ!" he said. "It's like being in a coffin with a rattler."

I pointed, and without a word Culligan ripped the hinged table from the wall and shattered the thin wood in several places. Then he ran at it from the side and knocked the whole thing down. Maybe he was too full of whiskey to be scared. Maybe he was just a tough man. The rattler, full-grown and thick-bodied, struck at him from close to Hannah's neck. The fangs struck wood and I blew the head off the snake before it could strike again. It dropped off the bed and writhed on the wreckage on the floor. Culligan stomped it to a pulp with iron-shod heels. Then he scraped the thing to the endgate of the wagon and kicked it out. Reaching into his coat pocket, he took out a pint bottle of whiskey and handed it to me. I pushed it aside, but he drank from it himself, his face still blotchy with shock and disgust.

Hannah was dying. Nothing could save her. She had been bitten in the face and neck, and the punctures in the big, throbbing neck vein were going to kill her. By now the venom had been carried to all parts of her body. Just then Dr. Ames climbed up with his little black bag. I didn't need the professional and sorrowful shake of the head to know that Hannah would be dead within minutes.

"All I can do is give her an injection to kill the pain," Ames said.

"Then do it and get out."

I knelt beside the little bed where we had spent such a good night together. Culligan climbed down and shooed the others away, then lowered the drop cover. Claggett seemed to be fresh out of prayers, for which I was glad. I might have slapped his face if he had dared to pray over this sweet, young girl. All the preacher did was sit and stare at the floor of the wagon.

The morphine Ames gave Hannah took its effect quickly. She opened her eyes and looked almost happy. It didn't matter to her that her father was there and could hear everything she said. She was past caring about the preacher and his terrible God. She knew she didn't have more than a few minutes, and yet it didn't seem to bother her.

"What do you think it'll be like on the other side?" she asked, smiling. "You think there's anything at all?"

I had no answer for that. "If there is, we'll have a get-together," I said. "I'll be along one of these days. We'll all be along pretty soon."

I thought she was going to say something else, but she didn't. She just smiled and died, still holding my hand. I hated to see her go. I had to loosen her hand to get my own hand away. I didn't look at Claggett.

Outside, the others waited for news of her death. I told them to look after her. Culligan handed me his bottle in full sight of the preacher. I took it and drank deeply. The bottle was empty when I finished.

"I'll see to the grave," Culligan said. "She was a nice little woman."

The Irishman had small, quick, clever eyes. "What are you going to do?"

He knew what I knew. "Look for Cyrus," I said.

Culligan turned away. "That's your business," he said. "It could be Cyrus. Him or the father. They have it in for you, boyo, so keep a good lookout. I been across the Plains more than a few times, and Sam has stories to go with the rest of him. Nothing you could prove to the law."

"I won't worry too much about the law," I said. "Where we're going there is no law."

EIGHT

The women who were preparing Hannah's body for burial were foreigners, German sisters in their late twenties. They looked capable.

I was certain that Cyrus had thrown the snake into her bed just after I'd left. I wondered why he hadn't done it while I was there. My guess was that he considered it less risky after I'd gone. Besides, the rattler could have struck at me instead of Hannah, because I had been on top of her. Her body had been covered by mine.

I had no hard evidence against Cyrus, just a suspicion. Some suspicions can be trusted though, and I trusted this one. Cyrus had to be done away with; all that remained was to decide how to do it.

Some of the women were crying, though they couldn't have known Hannah very well. Soon there would come a time when death wouldn't move them to tears. All the women looked at me as Culligan went to dig the grave. Dr. Ames had gone back into the wagon to look at Hannah's body with his daughter. There was hardly a time when she wasn't with him.

But they looked at me as if they expected me to do something. That meant they knew about Hannah and me—our night together. In a small town it's hard to keep anything a secret; a wagon train is worse.

I was sure Cyrus had tossed the fat-bodied rattler into Hannah's bed. It must have taken him some trouble to catch one that big, because the snake that killed Hannah was about as big as they come. Those big old snakes are wary, so Cyrus must have had to use all his idiot cunning.

The horror of it all made me shudder. A full-grown rattler thrown suddenly in darkness; the squirming, rattling reptile landing in the darkness on the girl's naked body. Perhaps happy and fully at ease for the first time in her life, she must have been drifting off to sleep when it happened. Maybe, at first, she thought it just a nightmare, the onset of a bad dream. Then came the horror. It was real, and it was happening to her. There had been no escape, walled in as she was by the wood partition built by her goddamned madman of a father. Maybe the first scream came even before the rattler struck. The vibration of the scream had drawn the snake's attention to her face and throat. In the first dim light of dawn, she must have been able to see the evil head of the angered reptile, as it drew back to sink its fangs into her flesh. Thrown or dropped from the front of the wagon, it must have landed on or about her face and throat, for all the bite marks were in that part of her body.

But it was the fangs puncturing the jugular that had done her in. When you get it there, you're as good as dead. Nothing helps. The blood flows too fast through the jugular; a frail girl like Hannah didn't have a prayer.

The fact is that frailty or strength has nothing to do with it. It's unusual to get snake-bit in the throat, but I've seen it happen once, and I'll never forget it. It happened when I was just a kid and working with a big cow outfit in Texas. In most outfits, the trail boss won't stand for dangerous horseplay. So, you'd have to call discipline lax in this outfit I worked for. One night after supper some fool thought he'd stir up a little excitement by tossing a rattler into a group of men sitting around the fire. He hooked the snake, not a big one, with a stick and tossed it in with a holler. Instead of some sensible man shooting the damn thing, the rest of them started slinging the snake back and forth. The snake kept getting madder all the time. The fools playing the game used sticks like the first man, and it went pretty good for a while. Then one young fellow tried to hook the snake with a stick that was too short. He had to stoop to get at the rattler and got fanged right through the jugular. Far from puny, he was a big brawler of a man, the kind that boasts he can rassle grizzlies, uproot trees and the like. Didn't matter a good goddamn, not in the end.

That ended the game, then and there. He knew what the bite meant, and so did the others. He was still on his feet, and stayed there for about a minute, but they knew they were looking at a dead man. Nobody blamed anybody. They caught him before he fell and made him as comfortable as they could. Somebody dug out a bottle and fed him as much as they could. They got about half a pint into him before his throat muscles stopped working. Then his lungs stopped sucking air and he died.

Hannah Claggett was the second human I'd seen die that way. It was no accident, no stray snake drawn into the wagon by the need for warmth. No matter what they tell you, snakes are shy creatures and stay away from people as much as they can. I had heard of snakes crawling into wagons in freezing weather, but the weather then was good, almost warm. Anyway, the pine partition that shut off Hannah's bed was twice the height of the wagon side. That made it about eight feet high. No snake had gotten over that alone.

Kiowa Sam came up to me, making sympathetic sounds. He wouldn't have done that if he hadn't known about Hannah and me. At the same time, there was something in his voice that made me want to kill him. I don't even know what I'd call the sound he made. The treacherous old man told me that I shouldn't have climbed into bed with his idiot son's intended woman. That was part of the sound. The rest of it was a sort of

wary defiance—daring me. For Sam that was a bad
mistake: to take me for a reasonable man. I wasn't
feeling reasonable. Cyrus was going to die, and not even
the reverend was going to have any say in my decision.

I looked at Sam, at his dirty, patched buckskins and
broken teeth. The only thing about Sam that seemed to
be in complete working order was the big Scofield
revolver. Just as good as the Colt .45 in many ways, the
Scofield had never caught on like the Old Equalizer. It
didn't have a graceful look, nor the sleekness of the Colt,
but that didn't keep it from being a fine shooting iron in
the hands of a man who knew how to use it.

The job had to get done, and there was no point
trading talk with Sam. "Where's Cyrus?" I asked point-
blank. "Everybody showed up but him."

Sam gave me a sly grin. "Guess he's taking it real hard,
what happened to the Claggett girl. Had a special kind of
a fondness for that one, he did. Used to talk about her to
me. Cyrus knew he wasn't like the rest of us, figured he
didn't want to stay out in the world all his life—his way
of putting it. I got a bit of money socked away, and he's
all the time saying why don't we give up this life and get a
little ranch far from people? Cyrus figured the Claggett
girl, shy and all, might be the right woman for him. A
good, quiet, shy girl not like the rest of these—"

"Ladies!" I finished for him.

"Your word, not mine," Sam said. "Cyrus figured the
Claggett girl had a wish for him, too. She smiled at him,
and always had a cheery hello when he came around."

"Rounding up the strays."

"The boy's way of courting the girl; only way he
knowed how. Wasn't no harm meant by it. You warned
him off. Cyrus didn't like you doing that, but he did what
you said anyway. I told him the same, 'Don't make no
trouble.'"

"Everybody ran to the Claggett wagon when she
started screaming. Why didn't Cyrus come too?" I
asked.

Sam had an answer for everything—he thought. "We
was just going off night guard when it happened. Cyrus

went a few minutes ahead of me. Must have fell right asleep. By the time he waked, it was all over for the poor girl. A damned shame, is what it is."

Sam winked at me. "Course she's just the first on this trip. Poor things, they ain't all going to make it. You'll be fine, though—young, and well set-up like you are."

I restrained the urge to draw and kill him. "You have anything to do with Cyrus murdering that girl?" I asked him. "I think maybe you did."

Sam showed the right amount of surprise. "That's crazy talk, that's what it is," he said. "Didn't I just tell you he had a big fondness for her, hoped maybe she'd be his woman? You been drinking that Irishman's whiskey, Saddler? Say a thing like that!"

"Answer the question, Sam. I won't ask it a third time."

Sam kept his gunhand still while he carved up the air with the other. "O' course I didn't have nothing to do with it. Snake crept in there and stung the child. Nothing makes murder out of that. The snake's dead, and you can't ask the snake. Ain't you never heard of a person being snake-bit before?"

"Just like that, only one time. This time was a murder, and you or Cyrus did it. Either he did it by himself, or you thought it up for him."

"Why'd I want to do that for?"

"You look like a mean man. A mean man'd murder a girl with a snake. Answer the question, or do something about it."

Sam must have been fast enough in his day. Against somebody else he might be fast enough to get by. For an instant, I thought he was going to go for his gun. It was in his mean nature to go up against a faster and younger man. But maybe he saw something in my face, in my eyes, that forced him to hold back

"I had nothing to do with nothing," he said.

"You better speak the truth."

"Who's to decide what I'm saying isn't true?"

"I'll decide it. Call Cyrus here, and we'll have this out. Try a sneak on me, Sam, and I'll shoot your eyes out. Get him here. Don't go yelling—fetch him quiet."

In a few minutes, Sam came back with Cyrus. He was red-eyed and shaking. Sometimes killers who murder on impulse are like that. They do it, and then they're sorry for it. But when I saw his naked hate for me, I knew for sure he had killed the girl.

He stood beside his father, taller by a good ten inches. I felt no pity for the murderous fool. No law says an idiot has to be good-natured like people think. I didn't care how he died, just as long as he did. Even so, I didn't want a hanging.

"Well, go ahead and ask him," Sam said.

"What's he going to ask me?" Cyrus said.

"Did you kill the girl with the snake, is what he's going to ask you," Sam said.

"I didn't kill nobody," Cyrus said.

I couldn't see any gun on Cyrus. It was likely that Sam wouldn't let him carry one. He might have a knife though. I would have to watch for that.

I pointed at Cyrus. "Hold up your hands one at a time. Sam, if you don't like that, you can try to stop me."

"Not me," Sam said.

At my direction, Cyrus held up his right hand, and I smelled it. The smell of the snake was still strong on the skin. I didn't ask to look at the other hand. Snake smell isn't something you can smell from a distance. It isn't that strong, except at first, and then it fades. But the fading takes a while. You can't get that smell any way except by handling a snake. A snake gives off a musk, a stink, when it finds itself in danger. I wondered if Cyrus had used a forked stick to pin the head of the big rattler before he grabbed the back of the head. That was one way to do it.

"You stink of rattlesnake," I said. "You did it."

"The boy's always fooling around with snakes and wild critters," Sam said.

Cyrus spoke suddenly. "She could have been my woman. I know she could. Why'd you have to come along and spoil it? She smiled at me. You wanted her for yourself. Not to make a good wife out of her, like I would have done. All you wanted was to use her like a cow. I seen you sneaking with her into that wagon. If I'd had a gun, I'd a shot you, and Hannah'd still be alive. All the time you was in there with her, I had my ear to the sideboard. I heard all the things you was doing to her. Things she was saying to you. After that she wasn't no good as a wife to me. That's right—I threw the snake in there."

Sam said, "You goddamned fool. That wasn't the way."

"You know what has to be done," I said to Sam. Cyrus stood and stared at the gun in my holster.

"You can't do it, Saddler." I guess Sam had some feeling after all. "He ain't never been right. Even a judge would just lock him up."

"No judge here," I said. "I'm the judge."

"Look," Sam said in a voice close to pleading. "What's done is done. Nothing can bring the girl back. I'll take Cyrus far away from here. We'll go far back in the hills and never see a soul. Not a human, man, woman, or child."

"You won't be around that long," I said. "I don't want some other girl to die because your little boy here gets jealous. I'll give you this much—I won't hang him. The only question is—do you kill him or do I?"

"Kill my own son?"

"Makes no difference to me. He has to die."

Cyrus said, "Who's got to die?"

Sam thought for a moment, then nodded at me. "We're just talking, boy. You walk over behind that wagon with me."

"All right, Pa," Cyrus said.

I waited with the .44 cocked in my hand, not at all sure that Sam wouldn't try some last sneak trick to save the idiot. If he came back with a gun ready, I'd blow his brains out.

I waited until a single shot rang out, then I moved away from where I had been standing. Sam came out

from behind the wagon with the big Scofield in his
holster. People came running at the sound of the shot.
Reverend Claggett came first. Culligan came too, but I
noticed that he didn't hurry. The women were excited,
and some were crying again.

"What happened?" Claggett asked me.

Sam answered, looking at me, "My boy Cyrus started
fooling with my beltgun and shot himself dead—an
accident. You know, that poor boy never had a chance in
this world."

"A boy like that shouldn't have the handling of guns,"
Claggett said. "We'll bury him with my girl."

It made no difference but I couldn't let it go. My voice,
hard and cold, stopped Claggett and turned him.

"Sam will want to bury his boy by himself," I said.

"What did you say, Saddler?"

"They weren't kin, so it's better that way."

Sam nodded, his eyes hating me.

"Anyway you like," Claggett said, but I knew he wasn't
buying everything I was selling. Without another word,
he climbed into the wagon where the foreign women
were readying Hannah's body for its last rest.

No one offered to help Sam with the grave. It couldn't
have been more than a shallow grave, because he was
back in less than half an hour. The others were gathered
by Hannah's grave while Claggett read over her. Culligan
was burning her name into the headboard of her grave.
The smell of the burning wood and the hot iron were
strong in the quiet morning air. Culligan had to put the
iron back in the fire several times before he got all of
Hannah's name and her dates on the heavy slab of wood.

I kept my eye on Sam while I listened to the preacher's
droning voice. There was no emotion in it: she might
have been anyone. Some of the women cried. I looked up
and saw Maggie O'Hara staring at me. I couldn't be sure
how much the others knew about Cyrus's death, but
somehow Maggie knew everything, and for the first time
there was something other than dislike in her eyes.

Sam didn't attend Hannah's funeral. It might have got

him killed if he had. The mourners dispersed, and I found Sam waiting for me after it was over. I don't know whether Sam was grieving over his son, or just full of hate for me. Same thing, I guess. I couldn't blame him, but that made no difference either. Sam had to be gotten rid of, and now was the time.

"You made me kill my own boy," Sam said, as if I didn't know it.

"You had a choice, and you took it. Now, get out."

I don't know why Sam looked so surprised. "I signed on with Claggett to see his cows to California. We made a deal. All right, Cyrus killed the girl, and I killed him. That was a deal too, and I kept it. You figure I'm going to assault some of your ladies, is that it? Them days is behind me for good."

"Get your gear and get out," I said. "If you're still here fifteen minutes from now, I'll kill you."

This time Sam's anger won out over his caution, and his hand went to his gun belt. The draw he tried for would have been good for a man half his age. The Scofield has a long barrel, but it came out fast. But before it did my .44 Colt was cocked and aimed at his heart. Sam stopped his draw before the muzzle of the Scofield quite cleared leather. Still, it was a good draw. If he had tried to complete it, I would have put one through his heart, another one in his face.

The Scofield dropped back into its oiled holster without making a sound. It was all over in seconds, and no one had seen it except Culligan, who was putting away his tools, and Maggie O'Hara.

"You still have fifteen minutes," I said. I knew I should have killed Sam then for the good of all mankind. The old man stank of a bad life—the smell of a man who didn't know good from evil. Maybe I'm not tough enough, but I had just forced a man to kill his own son, and that's a hard thing to do. I knew I was making a mistake in letting him live, but I went ahead and made it. I hoped it would end there, but in my gut I knew it wouldn't. Call me a fool, and you'd be right.

Sam looked at me for a long, hard moment before he turned away and went to collect his gear. What he was doing was burning my face into his memory.

"You're riding high now, Saddler," he said. "But everybody stumbles, and I'll be there when you do. You'll never make it."

After Sam left, Culligan came up to me. "I saw that bit of business with the guns. Why didn't you kill him when you had the chance?"

"I'd have to explain why I did it. That would dirty up Hannah's name."

"In a way it would," the Irishman said. "But she's dead, and what harm could it do her? We're alive, and Kiowa Sam is on the loose."

"To do what? A while back you hinted something about Sam. Say it straight, for Christ's sake."

Culligan said, "There was no proof against him. That's what Sam said. But the fact is, two trains Sam herded for never got to California. The wagons were looted and burned, young women stolen, guns and money—everything—taken. Funny thing was Sam and Cyrus survived both times. The first time Sam's story was that him and Cyrus was miles off, catching strays when the attack came. They got back too late, when everybody was dead except the stolen women."

"What about the second train?" I was beginning to wonder if I should go after Sam, but he was out of sight. Out of sight and maybe waiting with a long gun.

Culligan padlocked his tool chest. "Sam's story was that they quit the train because of the leader's making fun of Cyrus. They quit the train and let it go on from there. On the face of it, both stories could have happened the way he told them."

"What're you saying?"

"I knew the leader of that train, the second one. His name was Jonathan Bass. A better man you never met on this earth. Making fun of a half-witted boy was the last thing he'd do."

I said, "These burned trains. Were there any dead

bodies besides the wagon people?"

Culligan spat. "Both times a few dead Indians. Another funny thing. Most of them were shot in the back. So tell me, Saddler, what do you think of all that?"

"You're right," I said. "I should have killed him when I had the chance."

NINE

We made good time crossing Missouri. No brigands, no attacks of any kind. Except for the remnants of the various outlaw gangs, hunted by posses and spied on by the ruthless Pinkertons, Missouri had left its wild days behind.

I wasn't out to blaze any new trails. The old Oregon Trail had proved itself a good way to go, and that's how we were going to go until it came time to branch off at Fort Bridger, right smack on the Utah-Wyoming line, and head southwest to California. Wyoming came after Kansas and Nebraska. And after we passed Fort Bridger into Utah, we would still have to cross Nevada, east to west, before we got to California.

Now, if you study these trails on a map, they look simple enough; the lines appear to be direct—the easiest way to get from one place to another. But a land trail is far from being a railroad line. You don't just sit a seat and let other men do the work while you sleep, eat, drink, play cards and smoke. A map can indicate a desert or a stretch of mountains or badlands, but that doesn't tell you what they're really like. A map can't tell you a thing about the heat, drought, blizzards, Indians, or outlaws you might encounter. A map has no way of telling you about the regions where half the rodents carry bubonic plague. A child, or someone else, can pick up a baby squirrel or prairie dog, get a bite, and kill off a whole train. And then there is typhus and cholera.

But Missouri was fine. I expected Claggett to come around asking questions about why Kiowa Sam was no longer with the train. He didn't, and I was glad he didn't. I wanted to put Hannah and her death behind me. It was just one more of those things that smudge the clear picture of a man's life. Come to think of it, Claggett didn't have much to say about anything, at least not to me. He wasn't a stupid man; he had figured things out. Now he drove the lead wagon by himself, offering to share it with no one. There was some squabbling among the women and the days began to drag. They always do, except that with this train it happened faster than usual.

Sometimes I found women looking at me—or at Iversen. Culligan's only love was his work and his whiskey, so he was out of the running. Reverend Claggett was as remote as God, or at least as the prophet Abraham. As the days dragged on, I found Flaxie Cole staring at me again, and Maggie was not unmindful of this attention. I did my best to keep away from them both. Flaxie never spoke when I approached their wagon. Maggie was always civil enough, though never without a touch of sarcasm in everything she said. As long as she left it at that, it was jake with me.

Iversen was getting a big play from the ladies in spite of the preacher's warning, and I couldn't blame the man for going around with a confused look on his face. A well set-up man, he must have had his fair share of women in his lifetime. Here he was with more women than he could handle and couldn't do much about it. For a while, not knowing the facts about Maggie and Flaxie, he seemed to concern himself with their well being, always coming around with a cheery hello and what he considered to be the right tone of light talk. I was all set to warn him off, not that I liked him much, but that was before somebody—Maggie, no doubt—set him on a straight course. After that he stayed with the cows and did his other day-to-day chores. But I wasn't completely sure that the trouble had passed. Set a girl like Flaxie down anywhere in the world, and there is going to be trouble.

After Hannah's death I didn't feel much like women for a while. That was the oddest thing, because I'm always interested in women, all races, shades and colors. But then my old lightning rod dangled in my pants. I knew memories of Hannah would fade along with the guilty feeling I had about her. And then there would be another woman.

I was more concerned about Kiowa Sam than I was about Iversen's balls, or my own. If the sailorman lost his *cojones* to Maggie's double-edged knife, that would be too bad for Iversen. The wagon train would sustain the loss. Usually, when you lose your balls you lose your life. However, we did have a bona fide doctor in the train, so it was likely that Iversen would continue to live, ball-less or not.

I had been on several crossings of the Plains, but this was the first time I had run into this particular situation. Usually, nothing happens to a man who kills another man who has been trying to get his wife's bloomers down, especially if he has been warned about it. In a way, Maggie and Flaxie were man and wife. Most definitely Maggie was the man and carried both knife and revolver and knew how to use them.

Kiowa Sam stayed in my mind most, but finally I stopped cursing myself for not having killed him. What I had to do then was watch out for him day and night. Not in Missouri, though; the law was too strong there and most of the hideouts were well known to the law. No band of marauders could operate there without being spotted, except maybe the James Gang, who were local heroes. Kansas and the bottom end of Nebraska were safe enough. I felt sure that if trouble came from Sam, it would come in the wastelands of Utah or Nevada.

From Culligan's stories, it looked like Sam and Cyrus

had been working with renegade bands with strongholds
far beyond the reach of the law. Long before an attack
came, the marauders would know every detail of the
wagon train, right down to the number of guns and
cartridges. They would know what was of value and what
was not. All but the poorest emigrants had some gold or
greenbacks socked away to help them get started in the
Promised Land. It must have looked pretty foolproof to
Sam. Who in hell would suspect a gabby old man and a
lamebrained boy of working with merciless killers?

Everyone would be murdered except the young wom-
en and girls. And young women, the younger the better,
were as good as gold in the Far West. Better, in fact, since
a gold bar is cold to the touch and doesn't have legs with
a hot furry hole between them. Some of the women
would be doped and sold to the Chinese whorehouses in
San Francisco. Some would live out their short lives in
cowtown brothels.

So this train would be like a gold mine on wheels to
Kiowa Sam and his partners. There could be more than
one gang, but I didn't think so. Sam was a vicious and
foxy old man and would work with men he knew and
could trust in a business way. Half a hundred women and
all young! It would be like heaven on earth to Sam. All
those furry holes! All that money!

Once we reached Fort Bridger I was going to ask for an
army escort. There was no guarantee that I would get
one. The army has a lot of ground to cover, and a lot of
bad men to deal with. As I said earlier, the Indian
situation was like quicksilver—never steady. It wouldn't
take an Indian war to wipe us out. A band of renegade
braves thirsting for whiskey, white women and blood
could do it. They did it all the time. Some got caught,
and some didn't. In the old days they blamed half the
wagon train massacres on the Mormons, and indeed they
had wiped out a few trains of unwelcome settlers, but no
one believed that kind of guff any more. Except for a few
Mormon-hating diehards, that fear was a thing of the
past.

I was betting on Utah or Nevada; the spirit of a train

was at its lowest point when it got that far west. Nevada was worse than Utah and not because it was farther along the weary road. Nevada was bleak and bitter, sun-blasted and pitiless. You could travel for days and not see a patch of green. Much of it was desert, and the mountains looked like drawings of what mountains are supposed to look like on the moon. What water there is can be expected to be alkaloid.

Yes, Nevada was a good place to ambush a band of tired people. I wondered if I could hire a few men along the way. I'd do it if I could, if they looked right. But no more beached sailors and jittery doctors. I would take all the Culligans I could get, but men like Rix Culligan are hard to find. Smart wagonmasters hire them on as soon as they get the chance. But such men know how valuable they are, and that makes them difficult to deal with. Like buffalo hunters, they're a breed apart.

I thought about taking the old trail that cuts down into Nevada from Nebraska without going through Utah. In the old days it had been busy enough, but for years the Overland had been established as the main route to central California. I gave up the idea of the old route for three reasons: it was rough travel; it would add time to the crossing; and they'd be scouting us days before the attack. A man, a few men, can dodge off into the wilderness and get lost. How in hell do you keep a wagon train from being spotted?

A lot would happen. I was sure of it. We crossed into Kansas some miles south of Junction City—a collection of unpainted frame buildings trying to look like it had a future. If there had been enough good men along, I would have thumbs-downed the idea of going into the place. At that time it had a bad name all over the West. Law there was lax and rich at the same time, which gives you some idea of what it was like. It was a favorite haunt of killers, cow thieves, army deserters, and tinhorn gamblers. As a sin town it wasn't as well advertised as other towns I've been in. Still, it was pretty bad.

Claggett argued about it, but finally gave in. "The women stay here with the train," he said.

I nodded agreement to that. I knew as well as he did that some of the ladies might be tempted to go back to their old line of work. Besides, to bring a wagonload of women into a town like that was asking for the worst kind of trouble.

You should have heard the complaining when the women heard I was going to town by myself. Isabel Ames, the doctor's daughter, wanted to go along and got snippy about it when I said no.

"Then bring back the latest newspapers," she insisted.

"If they have any," I said. "Maybe they do at that. There's a small army post close by. I'll see what I can get you." I wondered what kind of news she was trying to catch up on.

Dr. Ames put in his two cents and said he'd be obliged if I looked for some papers. It was a puzzle to me why they hung around together all the time. Of course, they had their own wagon, a big new thing with a snowy canvas top, but most folks who travel together make a point of splitting up now and then, a sensible thing to do. But not this family, not this father and daughter. I noticed that she had the habit of ordering him around, and I don't mean in the affectionately bossy way some girls have. What I mean is, she told him what to do. They kept to themselves and rebuffed all attempts at friendliness by the other women in the party. Personally, I didn't give a damn what they did, as long as they didn't make any trouble. Yet I have to say this: I didn't like either one of them.

I rode a few hours north into Junction City. Riding in, I couldn't see any reason why they had decided to build a town there. Maybe they had cut cards as a way of deciding where the townsite should be. In the distance, close enough to see, was the small army post.

The town had one short main street with narrower streets branching off it. In the town square a bandstand had been left unfinished, as if the carpenters had downed their tools about six months before. There were a lot of saloons and gaming houses. The town had two churches, but they didn't look too prosperous. One was painted white; the other wasn't painted at all.

Most men with work to do don't hang around saloons early in the morning, so I went to the saloons to look for the unemployed. The place I went into first wasn't too big or too fancy, because men looking for work wouldn't have much money to spend. You could gamble or drink there, but no food was available. There were girls to be had, too, if you had the money. Suddenly I felt like having a woman, a bought-and-paid-for saloon girl, one I could enjoy without Reverend Claggett thumping me on the ass with his Bible.

For so early in the day, the place was well-filled, but a few empty tables were left. I got a mug of beer and a man-sized glass of whiskey and sat down to look over the ladies. Nearly all were the usual, worn-out whores you find working in cowtown saloons. All but one, that is. That one was young, barely in her twenties, and pretty enough for any man who wasn't looking for the impossible. I gave her the nod when the man she was feeding drinks to at a table fell asleep, his head hung over the back of his chair.

I liked her smart, sassy, don't-give-a-damn look. More men than women have that look, but a few women have it too. She sat down and jerked her thumb over her shoulder toward the snoring drunk at the other table. It was hard to place her by her accent. I guessed Pennsylvania.

"I want a drink," I said. "You'll be wanting to drink with me."

"I've never had a real drink in my life," she said. "I don't like whiskey. If you order champagne, it'll be hard cider with that gas blown through it to make it fizz. That all right with you? I'll make a dollar if you buy that."

I pointed to my empty glass. "Fill that with bourbon. Order a bottle of champagne for yourself. You can drink it. I won't."

No waiters worked there; the saloon girls served the drinks in low-cut dresses that were supposed to get the customers excited. It would be good to go upstairs with this young girl. A friendly business transaction and nothing more. Nobody would get killed while we were going at it, or after we finished.

She said her name was Rita when she came back with the drinks. The so-called champagne was uncorked, and she drank some of it. "Hard cider isn't so bad. It's the cold tea I hate. If you know how much cold tea I've drunk in my life."

"You want a slug of bourbon?"

Rita shook her head. "Tried it back home in Lancaster. That's in Pennsylvania. Not bourbon, home brew. No difference to me. I plain didn't like it. You from the wagon train parked south of here?"

"How did you know that?"

"Somebody told me. That's how I know. Funny you're the only one that's come into town."

I told her why I was in Junction City. "I could get by with two good men. Two of the men I had lit out, leaving me short."

Rita raised her glass of bubbling cider. "You're looking for good men. You're not about to find them here, Saddler."

"Not a one?"

"Not that I know of. You're looking for men of all work, am I right?"

"That's the kind."

"What about taking me along with you?"

"Can't do it," I said. Then I explained something about Reverend Claggett and his ideas.

"I heard something about that, too. That's the real reason you didn't bring the train into town," she said.

I grinned at her open, country face. "That's the real reason I can't take you along. What you do is fine by me, but Claggett would turn a cold eye on you. You don't have that determined-to-be-saved look about you."

Rita laughed. "Does it show that much? You're right, though. I don't want to be saved; I want to be rich. Frisco is the place for that. There's so much money out there—some of it has to stick to my little fingers."

"It might at that," I said. "The only question is, what're you doing in Junction City?"

"It's hard to get on a wagon train if you're by yourself," Rita said. "A boy I knew back home in Dutch country—I was his intended and all—was in the Army. He said he'd send for me soon as he made sergeant and was allowed to have a wife on the post. That was five years ago, and finally he wrote and said it was all right for me to come. My father was close to dying, so I couldn't leave right off. When I finally got here, I found my darlin' Hobart had deserted the army and gone off with some other woman. No way to chase after him, so I went to work at the only work there was 'cept dumping slop jars in the hotel. I been here only six weeks, and I guess they like me pretty good. But where I want to be is Frisco, make some money, open a real fancy house of my own. A reliable establishment with a good reputation. No wallet stealing, no drunk rolling. Rich men like to go to a house where they know they'll be safe. Trouble is, how in hell do I get there? Railroad stops short of here to the east, so that's no good. Wouldn't stand a chance trying to make it alone."

I could tell it wasn't just another saloon girl story. You get to hear hundreds. As a rule, the money is never for themselves; it's to cure consumption or fix up a clubfoot. This girl was telling it straight, and I knew it.

"If you've been here for six weeks, you should have enough to get back to Pennsylvania. If you don't have enough, I have a few dollars that aren't working for me at the moment."

Her eyes opened wide. "You mean you don't even know me and you'd give me money?" She clicked her fingers. "Just like that."

I grinned. "A few dollars is what I said. Enough to get you home. After a while it would be like you'd never been here. Who's to know?"

Rita's laugh was harsh for such a young girl. "What home? My father is dead, the farm belongs to my Uncle Herman now. So, what in hell would I do there? Work as a hired girl for Herman and his hairy paws that kept getting all over me when I was a kid? Thank you—no!

What I do now suits me fine, but for me it's just a beginning. By now I know all the tricks of the trade and am ready to teach other girls the things they don't know. Like I said, Saddler, I don't want to be saved, I want to be rich. I'm smart enough to do it. I'm not PD—that's Pennsylvania Dutch—for nothing."

She got up to get me another bourbon. When she brought it back, I said, "I'd like to take you on the train, but the train belongs to old man Claggett." I thought for a moment. "Maybe there is a way you could go. Pretend to be saved. Act demure, and maybe you'll get there."

Her eyes flared with sudden anger. "You mean act like a hypocrite!"

I shrugged. "I'm not telling you to do anything. It's a way to get to California, is all. Not all the way to Frisco, but close enough."

She reached over and covered her hand with mine. "I'm not mad at you, Saddler. I just can't do it. I want to be what I am. You want to do me a favor, and I'm thankful for it. I just can't do it. I'll just have to find another way."

"We could have a lot of good nights between here and California."

"You're beginning to sound horny. Are you? You're sitting down, so I can't see."

"Very horny," I said. "I'm ready to go upstairs, if you are. The offer of the money is still good, however you go west. Look, I'm no Holy Joe like Claggett, and I'm not out to make over the world. Be what you want to be, and let anyone that doesn't like it—"

"Piss against the wind," Rita said and laughed.

"You'll have to be older, fatter and jollier before you can get away with talk like that in San Francisco. Now, let's get up those stairs and into a soft bed. For that kind of fun there's nothing better than bed."

I placed both hands on the tabletop and was about to get up. Something in Rita's face stopped me. "What's the matter?"

The glance she gave the saloon was casual, but it didn't

miss anything, not even the drunk at the next table. She
laughed and smiled at nothing. "They want me to help
them kill you," she said.

"Who does?"

"I never did get the name," Rita said. "But the old
man that hired the two gunslingers to kill you was old,
with dirty-looking buckskins. Old but with a springy
walk."

I didn't need to be told Kiowa Sam's name. Sam
wasn't dumb. He figured I'd ride into Junction City
looking to hire a few men as replacements.

"You know who he is?" Rita asked, smiling hard.

"I know him," I said. "The name would mean nothing
to you. He still in town?"

Rita said no. "He hung around a whole day, searching
for the right men for the job. The Rainey brothers, twins.
I entertained both of them a few times, 'specially Bud,
and he was the one that got me into it. Fifty dollars, he
promised me. Gave me ten for a start."

"You'd never collect the rest of it," I said. "Now, how
was this killing to be arranged?"

Rita's smile was so rigid, it must have hurt her face.
"Seems like this old man figured you'd enjoy a woman
before you went back to the train. Old man said you have
this weakness for good-looking women. I guess that's me,
'least in this miserable town. They must be terrible
afraid of you, Saddler. I mean, the old man is. The
Rainey brothers wanted to have it out right in the open,
figuring you wouldn't have a chance against them. The
old man said they'd just get killed if they tried that. No
money changed hands till they agreed to do it the sneaky
way."

I finished the dribble of whiskey in the glass. "Which
of the sneaky ways is that?"

Rita said, "This is how it's supposed to work. First, we
have a few drinks down here and then we go upstairs to
my room. The Rainey brothers are waiting in a room
down the hall. We get up to my room, and you get your
clothes off. You have no way of knowing that somebody
is out to kill you in this town, so you just peel off. You

don't wear your gun to bed, do you?"

"Not usually."

"Nobody does. That's what they're counting on. Once you're peeled off, I get this sudden idea to go down and get a fresh bottle, because you're fixing to stay a while. You see how it works?"

"You go out, the Raineys come in, blasting. You know them to carry shotguns?"

"Can't say what they carry besides their pistols. Shotguns, yes, that could be it. You think you can beat them to it?"

"Looks like it, now that I know about it. After it's over, what happens to you? You'll have sided with an outsider against town people."

Rita stopped smiling. "I don't know what's going to happen to me. I hadn't thought about it. I just can't let them kill you like a sick dog. I guess I'll find my way someplace."

I squeezed her hand. "Little sister," I said. "You're going to California, and you're going with me. The hell with the preacher. If he doesn't like it, he can take the ladies to California all by his lonesome. As soon as this is over we'll be on our way."

"All this killing talk is making me very horny," Rita said. This time her smile was real.

I smiled back. "We'll have plenty of time on the trail."

TEN

The bustle of the saloon went on as we went upstairs. The hallway, lined with narrow doors, was dark and quiet. It was a bright day outside, but here oil lamps threw only dim light in the hallway. All the doors were open but one. I figured that's where the Rainey brothers were. I walked in front of the girl, ready to draw and fire, because there was no way to be sure these two-bit killers would follow the old man's plan. One or the other might get brave, and then the killing would start.

Rita's room was five doors down from the door they were watching from. It wasn't locked, and we went in and closed the door. Once inside, we did a little play-acting for the Raineys. I grabbed at Rita, and she giggled the way whores do. I sat on the bed, and it creaked. I dropped one heel on the floor, then followed it with the other. Then I eased myself off the bed without making much noise. I fixed up the bed with a jail dummy and moved over against the wall, the Colt cocked and ready in my hand. There would be no time for reloading. Three bullets apiece would have to get the job done.

Rita pulled on an imitation silk robe and said in a loud voice, "What you need, sir, is some good whiskey to put life in your bone." That done, she opened the door and closed it with a bang. I heard her going downstairs in the quiet that followed.

They came in without using the door handle. The door was just a flimsy sheet of wood and one kick knocked it off its hinges. A sawed-off shotgun blasted the pillows covered by sheets on the bed. Two blasts, one right after the other, and the bed burst into flames. I blew a hole in the shotgunner's head as the other shooter reached around him and opened up with a handgun. I had to give him four of my remaining bullets before he was driven back from the cover of his brother's body and slammed against the far wall. In death they didn't look much like twins. The one with the shattered face could have been a twin to anyone.

I stepped over them and went downstairs into the suddenly silent saloon. I reloaded and all the chambers in my Colt had live rounds in them again. I wasn't looking for any more trouble, so I slid it into its holster. Everyone stared at me, but no one tried to stop me. Maybe some of them knew what had taken place. Maybe the Rainey brothers weren't all that well-liked in town.

I went out after Rita and put her up on the horse in front of me. No bullets chased us as we rode out of town. Then we put distance between us and the town, and when we topped a rise the wagon train lay drowsing in the sun.

Halfway between the rise and the train a varnished buggy with a broken wheel stood by the side of the road. A stocky man with a derby hat pushed far back on his head stood looking at it. Even at a distance there was something familiar about him, but it wasn't until we got closer that I recognized him as Jacob Steiner, the drummer who had saved my life by tossing me the .38 back in Independence. I caught the flash of field glasses from the wagon train.

I climbed down, and so did Rita. She looked surprised

at the way I thumped Steiner on the back and wrung his hand. "What in hell are you doing with a busted buggy in Kansas?"

Steiner smiled all over his broad face. "A good question. But the Jews have a saying for everything. The answer for this situation is—everybody has to be somewhere."

Steiner doffed his derby and clicked his heels when Rita climbed down from my horse.

"You know this crazy man?" she asked, smiling.

"You bet I know him," I said. "He sided with me when everybody else was wetting their pants with fright. I'd be dead now if not for him."

Rita held out her hand. "You're all right with me, Fritz."

Steiner winced. "Please, young lady, the name is Jacob. Jake, if you like."

Rita said, "Then Jake it is."

Instead of shaking Rita's hand, Jake bent forward to kiss it. Rita blushed and then laughed. "Back home in Pennsylvania they'd think you were crazy if you did that. You ever been to Pennsylvania?"

Jacob Steiner sighed; it was the sigh of a man whose life had been bumpy. "There is no eastern or southern state in which I have not been. You see before you the Wandering Jew."

I cut in. "You wandered a bit too far this time, Jake. Now, what's the real answer to the question?"

"You mean what am I doing in Kansas?"

"I mean this part of Kansas."

"Trying my luck," Steiner said. "You remember I told you I was a bauble—jewelry—salesman when we met in Independence?"

I remembered. "Has something happened to change that?"

"Most definitely," he answered. "You can't sell jewelry if you don't have it. Shortly after leaving Independence, I was held up on the road and had everything stolen. One of the highwaymen fired a bullet into the wheel of my buggy. Knowing it would come apart sooner or later, I bound it with wire and hoped for the best. I hoped in vain."

"So I see," I said. "Men that sell whiskey and jewels, watches even, get robbed all the time. But don't you work for some company back east?"

"Unfortunately, I am my own company," Steiner said, sighing hard. "I have had many companies. However did the rumor get started that all Jews are sharp traders? I'm so goddamned tired—excuse me, miss—of trying to sell things. Sometimes, I'm just plain tired."

I had one of my great ideas. "How would you like to go to California, Jake?"

Steiner's fat face quivered with excitement. "You mean, cross the Great American Desert with the rest of you?"

"It's not really a desert," I said. "Come with us, or I'll stake you to get wherever it is you want to go. Chicago. St. Louis. New Orleans. New York."

Steiner smiled. "I owe rather a lot of money in two of the cities just mentioned. Besides, I like the idea of going to California. At least it's one place that I haven't been. Perhaps my luck will change out there in the Golden West." Steiner sighed, a sort of habit with him. "I could use a change, believe me."

"Then let's go," I said.

We took the horse, none-too-well-nourished, and left the broken buggy where it lay on its side. "How I hated that thing," Steiner said as we walked down the long hill toward the wagon train.

The whole train came out to stare at the new arrivals. Reverend Claggett came forward as if to ward off evil.

"What have we got here?" Claggett asked without as much as a nod to my friends. Claggett's attitude got my back up. I consider people who risk their lives to save mine to be friends.

"What we have is two people," I said. "There were no men in Junction City worth a damn. I was lucky enough to run into Mr. Steiner here. He'll work his passage or pay for it. That depends on what you want him to do."

"More than that depends on it," the preacher said

abruptly. "Nobody gave you leave to hire a man like this."

Steiner's face grew red. "A man like what?"

Claggett took a hard look at Steiner. "I know who you are," he said. "You helped to kill that man back in Independence. But that's not the reason. They said you were a peddler of trinkets and baubles. Rubbish sold to gullible, foolish women who should buy food for their families."

"I wasn't that successful," Steiner said. "Anyway, I'm out of the jewelry business. You need a man, and I'm willing to work hard."

"At what?" Claggett was determined to be unpleasant.

"What Mr. Saddler tells me to do. If I have to take orders from you, I won't go."

I almost gave out one of Steiner's breathy sighs. I was breaking my ass to get Steiner to California, and here he was back-talking the boss man.

Claggett had been listening to Steiner's faint German accent. "What country are you from?"

"I had the misfortune to be born in Germany," Steiner answered. "At the moment I'm from where I'm standing."

"What faith are you?"

"I, sir, am a Jew. Does that fact bother you?"

To my surprise Claggett shook his head. "I am well-versed in your faith and have much respect for it. My questions to you are put man-to-man. Take this any way you like. To me you look like a man who has never done an honest day's work in his life. I'm afraid I don't want you, Mr. Steiner."

Rita had to get her oar in. "Why don't you give your jaw a rest, preacher?"

I shushed her, and she took heed of me. I wanted to get Claggett straight about Steiner. Before I got a chance to talk, Steiner said calmly, as if playing a trump card: "I was one of the best riflemen in the German army. Does that make a difference? You're going where you'll need all the marksmen you can find, or so says Mr. Saddler."

Claggett looked at Steiner. "You'll have to prove that,

about being a crack shot. I never heard of any Jews in the German army. I didn't know they took them in."

Steiner smiled bitterly. "We're not that anxious to be conscripted, but they take us just the same. When I got the letter to report for service, I immediately took a train for Hamburg. If that boat had sailed on time, I wouldn't have served at all. Alas, they caught up with me, and I became a German infantryman. There was a black mark against me right from the beginning. In time that changed slightly, when they were forced to acknowledge my ability with a rifle. I was assigned to a company of sharpshooters but remained a private during my military career of two years, three months and six days."

Claggett was puzzled. "What kind of an enlistment is that?"

"Not the usual kind," Steiner said. "I made my plans, and then I deserted when we were on maneuvers close to the French border."

"You ran away," Claggett said, but I knew that was just for effect. The preacher didn't want to give in too quickly.

"As fast as I could," Steiner said. "And I'm still a crack shot."

Claggett turned to me. "Give me your rifle," he said. I unsheathed the Winchester .44-.40 and handed it to Steiner, who said he hadn't handled a lever action before. I showed him how it worked by jacking out all the shells and reloading.

"I think I can manage it," he said.

"We'll see about that," Claggett said to Steiner. "Set up a target at a fair distance."

"There's no need for that," Steiner said. "A few tin cans thrown in the air will do. Anything will do."

Culligan came forward with a small, badly rusted bucket. "This thing is past fixing. How's about that?"

"It will do, but throw it far," Claggett said.

"I'll throw," Culligan said, holding the bucket by the handle.

"I'm ready," Steiner said.

Culligan whirled the bucket with a powerful hand until

it became a blur. Then he released it. It sailed up high and out far. Steiner didn't try for a shot until it reached the apex of its flight and began to fall. His first shot hit it dead center, spinning it off to one side. He jacked a shell, fired, and hit it again. The bucket was close to the ground when he put a third bullet through it.

"Is that good enough for you?" he asked Claggett.

"If you're hungry there's food on the fire," the preacher said, his way of saying that Steiner was hired.

Now came the harder part—Rita. I said Rita had saved my life back in town and that was all the reason I needed for letting her join the train. "She'll pay her way and won't make any trouble for anybody. She won't be part of the train, just a passenger."

"You'll have to repay her some other way," Claggett decided. "You have plenty of money from that poker game, and you have wages coming as guide. Use some of that to show your gratitude."

Rita flared up, as I knew she would. "This Holy Joe talks like I'm not even here."

I told her to shut up.

"Money isn't what she needs," I told Claggett. "She got to Kansas all right. That's not to say she'll get out again. This country is crawling with men that would delight to take her prisoner. Apart from that, she wants to go to San Francisco."

"To do what?"

Rita cut in with, "To mind my own business. That's why I'm going to Frisco."

Claggett's mental torment was crazy but real. "I'd be doing the devil's work if I took you to California. I know you mean to continue your life of sin. Listen to me, girl, Jesus Christ died on the cross for your sins."

"You got it wrong, padre," Rita said. "I wasn't around at the time."

Claggett shook his head in disbelief. "You mock the crucified Christ! But there is time to repent, even at this moment. I mean only the best for you. Kneel with me, and we will pray together." Claggett's voice grew shrill with fervor. "We will pray and beg the Lord's forgiveness. Then you will set out with us on a new life filled with decency and hard work. Answer me, girl!"

I didn't expect Rita's answer to be as strong as "Fuck you, preacher," but it was.

Claggett's face turned white with anger. "That settles it; she's not going," he said. "Do what you like about the money. Just send her away from here."

Push had come to shove. It was time to say it. "If she goes, then I go with her. Try to pull that shoulder gun on me, and I'll shoot the fingers off your hand. Make up your mind."

Claggett knew he was beaten. Hiring Steiner was a stroke of luck, but even a crack shot wouldn't make up for the loss of a guide and hunter.

"You'll be responsible for her," Claggett said, turning his back. "This is the second time you've made me back down, Saddler. No matter how it goes, there won't be a third. I mean that sincerely."

I knew he did. Claggett was sincere about everything. If he brooded about me flouting his God-given authority, it could come to killing long before we reached the California line.

"My God! What a picklepuss that old man is," Rita said. "If I had a face sour as that, I'd wear a mask."

I was sick of all the bickering. "You don't have to talk tough all the time," I said. "I don't know what goes on in Claggett's head, but I do know he's trying to do some good. Maybe he's going about it the wrong way. That's not for you to decide. So, keep a damper on that fuck you talk and maybe—just maybe—you'll get to California, Rita. What's your last name, anyway?"

"The name is Halsmann, and from now on I won't say anything stronger than 'darn.' That mild enough for you?"

"Fuck you, Miss Halsmann," I said, grinning at the sassy farm girl from PD country.

Rita bobbed up and down. "Well, I certainly hope you will, Mr. Saddler. If your prick is as hard as your jawline, we'll have a great time."

Just then Maggie O'Hara came out from the train and

looked Rita over at close range. I guess she liked what she saw. Maggie ignored me, at least at first. "You're welcome to bunk in our wagon," she offered. Her freckled Irish face had the expression of a hungry man staring at a porterhouse steak. "We have a real big wagon, and there's lots of room. Is it a deal?"

I expected to hear some strong language, but all Rita did was to smile sweetly. "Thanks, but no," she said. "I talk in my sleep the whole night long. You'd never get any rest with me aboard."

Maggie knew she had been pegged for what she was. "Oh, that wouldn't bother us. Why don't you give it a try?"

Suddenly Rita dropped her ladylike act. "Find somebody else to diddle and lick," she said.

Without thinking, Maggie placed her hand on the butt of her gun. "You've got a dirty mouth on you for a rube," she said. "I'm sorry I even asked. Who in hell wants a dirty whore in their wagon!"

"You do," Rita said. "You try to come at me unawares, and I'll break your darned neck." Rita smiled at me when she said darned.

Maggie was furious because I was there and could hear everything. "If I wanted you bad enough, I'd take you, rube. I'd take you, and there isn't a thing you could do about it."

Then it was my turn to get it. Maggie said, "You stay out of woman-business, Saddler. I figure you already turned this girl against me and Flaxie."

I was tired. It had not been a good day, by any means. "You're wrong about Flaxie. I like your wife very much."

Once again, it got close to killing between us. I wondered if Jake Steiner could juggle eggs or do card tricks. Anything to ease the tension that never seemed to go away.

"One of these days . . ." Maggie said as she walked away.

"I hope not," I said after her, watching her back, because I wasn't sure she wouldn't whirl and fire. She was capable of it. She was capable of anything. The thought of what she'd be like in bed continued to gnaw at me.

Rita looked at my face, and her eyes were troubled. "Would you really have shot her? Killed a woman, I mean."

I nodded. "If I had to. It may come to that before it's over."

Rita looked along the line of wagons. In a few minutes we would be on the move again.

"Just one big, happy family!" Rita said.

ELEVEN

We crossed the line into Nebraska at a place called Fairburn, keeping to the Oregon Trail until we reached the South Platte. Nothing much happened on the way through Nebraska. A few years before, Nebraska had been full of hostile Sioux ready to take on the Army or anyone else who trespassed into their territory. The grassy plains of Nebraska had been nourished by the blood of red men and white.

It had taken a merciless campaign by Colonel Mac-Kenzie, a merciless man himself, to enforce an uneasy peace on the Sioux. Feared even more than the Indian-hating Custer, MacKenzie's cavalry, supported by infantry, swept through Nebraska like fire and sword, burning and killing without discrimination. MacKenzie vowed to pacify the Sioux even if it meant wiping out every man, woman and child. Now, a few years later, Nebraska was peaceful.

Now and then a small band of Sioux would come to trade for salt or sugar. I told Claggett to let them have the salt for nothing. Buffalo were getting scarcer all the time, and they needed salt to preserve what meat they had.

Whenever such a band came to the train, they let it be known, well in advance, that their intentions were peaceful. They always, or most always, carried a flag of truce and kept out of rifle range until we waved them in. But even then, no doubt thinking of MacKenzie, they approached warily and were elaborately polite. They were fascinated by a whole wagon train of women with just a few men to protect them. I doubted that they had ever seen anything like it before.

They were peaceful, but I watched them just the same. One band larger than the others wanted to know if we had any whiskey. I was firm about that. No whiskey, I said, now or later. Not for gold, not for anything. I explained to their leader, who spoke halting English, that Reverend Claggett was down on whiskey and wouldn't be caught in the same territory as it. I guess one look at Claggett's Old Testament face convinced them that I was telling the truth. We gave them salt, and they rode away into broken country. That night I doubled the guard, thinking they might decide to come at us in the dark, but the night passed quietly.

It was good to have Jake Steiner along; at last here was a man I could talk to. I liked Culligan better than I had at the start of the trip, but we had no words to trade. At some point in his life the Irishman had decided to live as a loner, even in a crowd. I was pretty sure he hadn't been born that way; something had changed him, but what it was I had no idea. It must have been something bad, because most Irishmen are friendly enough. Culligan worked and drank and slept. I can't say honestly that he ever got completely drunk. If anything happened in the night, he could rouse up as quickly as any man in the train. Sometimes I thought it was odd to be with so many people I knew nothing about.

Jake Steiner was the only one there who didn't seem to lie. Of course, maybe everything he told me was a lie, but I didn't think so. He sure as hell hadn't lied about being a crack shot with a rifle.

I paid passage for Rita in a wagon with two hard-faced young women. They needed Rita's money—my money

—and they took it, but didn't talk to her. Rita didn't give a damn. She had a one-track mind, that girl. She was going to get rich in Frisco, and nothing was going to stop her.

I guess Steiner and Rita were the only real friends I had in that train. Steiner was the most talkative son-of-a-bitch you ever met, yet I never tired of his stories. He never repeated himself, and he had been a lot more places than I had, and that's saying something because I've been all over. I've been a drifter all my life, but Steiner had me beat hollow. He had spent two years in South America looking for emeralds.

"They called them Green Fire, but they didn't burn for me," Steiner said. "One time some old Indian fraud told me about a place far back in the jungle where the green rocks were thick as fleas on a mongrel. I gave him money and other things, and indeed there were green rocks when I finally got there. Unfortunately, that's what they turned out to be—green rocks. By then I knew what emeralds didn't look like. Then, one morning I woke up and decided that God hadn't intended for me to find emeralds of any size. If he had, I would have been born with emeralds in both baby fists."

So far, that had been the story of his whole life, always coming close to what he thought he wanted, then having it slip from his grasp at the last moment. There was some bitterness in him, but not much. He took life as it came, and mostly it was hard.

"I don't know why I can't make a go of something. I know I'm smart enough, and some of my ideas aren't bad."

"Maybe what you need is a partner," I said that night as we watched for Sioux. "Don't look at me, Jake, because I'm not the partnering kind. Don't need to be, the way I make a living. I can make my way with a gun and a deck of cards. You, you're different. You're a born businessman, only you get it wrong somehow."

Steiner sighed. "I know you're right, but good partners are hard to find. I had a partner once in New Orleans, the coffee business, and he robbed me blind before he took off for parts unknown. Since then I've been wary of partners."

Somehow my idea of a partnership got into Rita's mind. I know I didn't mention it to her, and I'm pretty sure that Steiner didn't. Rita liked the tough, fat Jew right from the first day they met on the road from Junction City. Back in the old country, Steiner had gone to a good school before the army grabbed him. He spoke German, French and English; his years in South America made him fluent in Spanish as well. All this impressed Rita, who had never been out of Lancaster, Pennsylvania until she went to Kansas. Jake had read a lot in rooming houses all over the world, and there wasn't much he didn't know.

Little by little, it came out that Rita could barely read English. She could struggle through a printed page, but for her it was rough going. To make up for this, Steiner elected himself president of a one-woman academy, and at night when he wasn't working or standing guard, he huddled by the fire with her, going over her spelling and grammar. The hardest job he had was to make her stop talking dirty. Rita was a foulmouth. Every other word was "fuck" or "shit" or "balls." Steiner stopped her every time she came out with a mouthful, and he kept on doing it.

Everybody except Culligan regarded them with suspicion and hostility. They were having a good time together, and that annoyed most of the ladies, Maggie O'Hara most of all. It bothered Iversen, too, that he couldn't seem to get Rita interested in him. Lord knows he tried, and her indifference must have come as a slap in the face, for he was sort of a handsome fellow, kind of dumb, but handsome. I knew that many of the other ladies would have welcomed the chance to get in bed with him. But he wasn't horny enough to go against Claggett's orders. No sex with the "saved" women was the preacher's rule, and Iversen obeyed it out of fear.

The fact is, there was good reason to be afraid of

Claggett. Claggett was a fierce man and probably more than a little crazy. Anyway, Iversen, a sailor by trade, was no kind of gunslinger. He wouldn't stand a chance if he crossed the preacher, though I had no doubt that he was handy enough with his fists. But there would be no fisticuffs with Claggett. Iversen would get a bullet in the heart, and the train would move on.

Trouble between Steiner and Iversen was inevitable. I saw it coming, but there was nothing I could do about it. Both were big, tough men with hard lives behind them. It wasn't my place to tell them what to do. Claggett was the chaplain of the outfit, not me, but he didn't seem to be aware of what was developing. I couldn't take sides in it, though I liked Steiner a lot more than Iversen.

Steiner did his best to keep out of Iversen's way, not an easy thing to do, the way we were thrown together day and night. Sometimes Iversen would mimic Steiner's accent, making it sound a lot more Dutchy than it was. In fact, Steiner spoke the best English in the whole train. When Iversen made fun of his accent, Steiner pretended to take it as a joke. But that didn't work.

The hornier Iversen got for Rita, the more hostile he got towards Steiner. The poor, dumb son-of-a-bitch did everything he could to make her notice him. He was good with his hands and worked like a bastard to make a braided rawhide belt for her. I'd see him working at it, late at night by the fire. In the end, it didn't get him a goddamned thing. One morning, while Steiner was sleeping in Culligan's wagon after standing the last watch, Iversen presented Rita with the belt. His seatanned face flushed red when she said thanks, but she didn't need a belt.

Iversen had been a lot of places, but that hadn't taught him manners. He flung the belt in the fire and said, "You'd take it quick enough if that fucking foreigner Jew gave it to you."

Rita gave him her sweetest smile. "Yes, I probably would. But he doesn't have to give me a thing. Look, Mr. Iversen, there's no need for this. We're going to be traveling together for a long time."

"That we are," Iversen said, watching his present burn and curl into ash in the fire.

By now we were well out on the Overland Trail and making fair time. There were some delays, mostly caused by broken wheels. But our luck was holding, and it continued to hold as we moved along just north of the Wyoming line.

The worst delay came when it rained for two whole days and everything turned to mud. Winter was over, but the rain came down in cold, gray sheets that chilled the body and numbed the mind. There was nothing to do but keep on going—because that's the principal rule in a crossing of the Plains—keep moving, no matter what. Finally, the rain let up and the sun started to dry the land again. It was good to see the sun shining on the wet grass early in the morning.

Our destination, for the moment, was Fort Bridger, in the southwest corner of Wyoming, the last army post we would come to before we reached California. For hundreds of miles past Fort Bridger there was nothing but desert and mountains and semi-arid plains. Out there was where the real danger lay.

Past Bridger the Overland Trail took a slant to the southwest, rough traveling all the way. I still figured Nevada as the place for a possible attack. The Army patrolled the northern part of Utah, so that made Nevada the logical place for Kiowa Sam to come at us. I felt it in my bones, the way an old man feels his aches on a damp day.

Some of the women could shoot, but most of the foreign and city women had never handled a gun of any kind. I went from wagon to wagon, talking to the women who said they could shoot. I warned them not to waste time bragging and lying. It could get them killed; it could get us all killed. If they couldn't shoot, it was best to give their weapons to the women who could. I found a few Southern mountain women who knew rifles and was glad to get them. I divided up the weapons, giving the nervy city women the handguns.

That evening, still about 40 miles from Fort Bridger, I told them what they could expect if they were captured. I couldn't tell them to end their lives with their last bullet. People cling to life as long as possible, even if the only way to do it is being chained to a bed in a dirty whorehouse in Chinatown or Juarez. Steiner and Rita sat together listening to me, while Iversen stared at them from the far side of the fire.

Claggett prayed for divine guidance. I would have settled for a Gatling gun or a troop of cavalry. Claggett's praying did nothing to cheer us up. He said the important thing was to die with a clear conscience and love for the Lord in your heart. He urged the wicked amongst us to repent while there was time. I guess that meant Rita, Steiner, Culligan and me. It was strange, and somehow heartening, to see Steiner and Rita exchanging smiles in the midst of all this gloom.

I had given up any ideas about Rita and me after she became friendly with Steiner. I had been looking forward to some good nights with her. Now, somehow, that didn't seem right. I could manage until I found another woman, a safe woman who wouldn't bring on a showdown with Claggett. That was the last thing I wanted, and I was ready to go womanless for the rest of the trip, a horrible thought though that was. I just wished Iversen would take the same attitude; but he was doing no such thing. The stupid son-of-a-bitch wanted to poke Rita and meant to do it.

Except for those who had to stand guard, the women drifted off to their wagons to sleep. I could have slept before my watch, but I didn't feel like it. Instead, I sat by the fire and poked at it with a stick. Rita had gone to her wagon, and Steiner was guarding the cows. We were in high plains country, and the night was cold. I put more wood on the fire, wondering how many of us would have to die. Some of us would. That had to happen, and there was a fair chance that none of us would make it to California.

Claggett's preaching hadn't put me in a gloomy mood. I was already in one before he started mouthing off to

God. I knew God would get good and sick of Claggett, if ever he got to heaven. I felt there ought to be something I could do to get these people through. Right then I couldn't think of a goddamned thing, though. I sat there until it was time to stand my watch. As I sat in the darkness, I felt the restlessness of the women sleeping uneasily in their wagons. Nothing happened during my watch, and I was gloomy as ever by the time it ended.

I was bedding down for the night in a sandy hollow near the wagons, when something happened to cheer me up.

TWELVE

This time no knife blade nicked me awake, and there was no surprise because I saw her coming. I was surprised but not the way I was with Maggie. It was Rita. She came down into the hollow with no attempt at concealment. She was a tall girl and threw a long shadow in the moonlight.

Without a word, she got under the blankets with me and bundled us up good, because the night was chilly. "This sand is a lot softer than that wagon bed," she said. "You worry too much, Saddler. You ought to be asleep by now."

I wanted her very much, but I had to speak my mind. "You don't have to do this. You don't owe me a thing. I thought you and Jake—"

"You bet your life we have something," Rita said. "We have something now, and it's going to get better if we manage to stay alive. I owe you more than you think. There's only one thing. This will be the first and last time for us. You understand what I mean?"

"No," I said.

"Jake says it's all right," Rita said, unbuttoning my

pants and fondling my cock. It came up hard and straight as a flagpole.

"Jesus Christ!" I said. "You mean you talked it over with him!"

Rita squeezed my balls gently. "Of course I talked it over with him. I saw the way you looked tonight, all down-hearted, no woman to bed with, and I said straight to Jake, 'Jake, I got to do something for Jim Saddler. He's gone out of his way to show kindness to a whore and a Wandering Jew, and it ain't—isn't—right for him to look the way he does.'"

Rita had my pants off by now. My shirt followed. "What did Jake say?" I asked.

Rita laughed softly. "Jake said he was thinking the same thing, only there was no way he could say it to me. Jake said you were a good friend; it was only right to cheer you up. Listen to me—it's all right. Jake is a man of the world, and he's making me a woman of the world. Jake wants me to give you the best time you ever had in your life."

I started to unbutton her dress. "You convinced me," I said.

My rod was like iron as I drove into her. God! How I needed to do that. Rita knew all the tricks, but this was no mechanical whore I was bulling but a real woman. She was a tall girl, so I was able to suck her breasts as I went in and out of her. She groaned as my tongue tickled her nipples. Jake Steiner was a lucky man. At that moment, so was I. She gasped as she came. She was one of those women who come quickly and easily and can go all night with the right man. This might be my last fuck on earth, I reasoned, and I put everything I had into it and into her.

All the tension of weeks of danger had built up in me, begging to be released. I felt my balls tighten as I got ready to shoot my load. When I did, I shuddered from head to toe. It was that good! As my juice volleyed into her, I felt the band of tension that had been squeezing my head loosen up. I felt like I would never stop coming.

"Don't take it out yet," Rita said gently. "I'll make you

hard again. It's warm with you on top of me and feels good."

"Same here," I said. "Many thanks to you and Jake."

"You're entirely welcome. If anybody deserves a good time, you do."

"I'm glad you and Jake feel that way."

"Don't make jokes about it. You made it happen for Jake and me. Or is it Jake and I?"

"You got me there," I said. "Better ask Jake. He's the grammar expert around here. Jake is all right. I'm glad he knows what we're doing. I'd hate to sneak behind his back."

"Nobody's sneaking. I told you I told him. Or he told me. Same difference. Saddler, fucking is great, but it's no great drama, to use Jake's words. Jake says he can't see one person killing another because of fucking. Like he says, there's no reason why a woman that truly loves her husband shouldn't go off once in a while and get fucked by another man. 'Where's the harm in that?' Jake says."

"Jake is right," I said. "Too bad the rest of the world doesn't agree with him. But let's not talk sex, let's do it. If this is to be our only night together, we don't want to waste it talking."

"Right you are," Rita said.

So there was no more talking for a long while. Rita had been a whore, and would be again when he reached San Francisco, and she knew every trick in the book. Jake was a lucky man to have such a woman. She sucked me off in a way that made me shake all over. I returned the compliment by tonguing her to a fare-thee-well. I guess with an ordinary paying customer she would be mechanical enough—a whore can't respond to every man she dicks—but we were good friends and that made the difference. There was no need to hurry, no need to be nervous since she was pleasuring me with Jake's blessing. And even old man Claggett couldn't interfere because Rita wasn't one of his flock of redeemed whores. That was the best part of it, to be able to screw a good-looking, willing woman without fret or fuss.

Rita let me do anything I wanted. And anything she

did to me was fine. We were friends so there was very little we didn't do. She sat on my face while I licked her. She came in salvos, and there was nothing fake about it. This woman had saved my life, and I should have been the one who was grateful—I *was* grateful—but she wanted to please me more than anything else. I sure as hell wanted to please her.

We talked in whispers though there was really no need. "You surely like your women, don't you?" Rita said. "I mean that as a compliment. Most men don't know how to treat women. You do."

"I surely do like women," I said. "Of all the pleasures in life women are the greatest. What would we do without them?"

"Where would women be without men," Rita said. "A nice man with a big cock. I don't care if he's rich or poor as long as he treats me nice."

"And has a big cock."

Rita laughed quietly. "Well, it's the truth. I've seen every kind of cock there is. Big ones are best, no matter what they say. There may be nothing but fatback and beans on the kitchen table, but if you can look forward to going to bed with a big dick you don't worry about the same poorboy food for breakfast. How are you feeling, Saddler? You had enough of me or would you be wanting more? Just asking, no hurry. Jake says it's all right for me to stay all night. I can sleep in the wagon, but what about you? Comes morning you don't want to be walking in your sleep."

With my hands roving over her body I said, "I can sleep anytime. This is better than sleep." And with that I rolled her on top of me and she put my cock in for me. She straddled me with my cock sticking straight up into her. She lifted herself up and down while I took my ease and let her do the work. Pushing up and down on my rigid cock made her gasp and she came several times. I came after she stretched out on top of me and squeezed her legs together and tightened her cunt muscles. It was like being squeezed by a fur-lined vice. I came until I felt drained.

"Many thanks to you and to Jake," I said sincerely. "If I don't get another fuck between here and California, this ought to hold me."

"You'll manage to get a few fucks," Rita said. "Knowing you, it's bound to happen. I never saw such a bunch of horny women in my life. You'll make out all right."

"I'm satisfied with what I have now. I doubt if there's a woman in the train as good as you. This has been one hell of a night, thanks to you and Jake."

"Jake is good people," Rita said. "If we live through this, we're going to open the finest bordello in Frisco."

Jesus Christ! This night was full of surprises. I had half expected her to say that she and Jake were going to settle down in a rose-covered cottage, with Jake working at some regular, honest-john job, and Rita cooking up hearty suppers for her hard-working husband.

"I hope you make it," I said.

"Don't say it like that. Of course we'll make it. Jake has good ideas but can't get himself organized. He starts a thing but never finishes it. With me it will be different. I'm not Pennsylvania Dutch for nothing. Jake says the word for us is methodical."

My cock was getting hard again; I'd be ready to go again in a few minutes.

"That's what I've always heard," I said. "You get things done. But how about money? You won't get far without money to make the right start."

I felt Rita's body stiffen with anger. "I'm not doing this because I want money from you. If that's what you're thinking, you can go—"

I held her tight. "No dirty talk," I said. "I know you're not. Don't be a horse's ass about this."

"What about *your* dirty language?"

"It's all right for me, not for a lady. Now simmer down, and let's talk sensible."

"All right."

"How far would a thousand dollars take you in Frisco?"

"A thousand would be more than enough. Jake is good with his hands, 'cause of all the trades he's worked at. I can make the curtains, do lacework. We can make a thousand look like ten times that much. You'd get your money back in no time at all. With interest."

"I won't come around breaking down your door to get it," I said.

"But we want you to come around," Rita said. "You'll have the pick of the house. Jake has this wonderful idea of making it what he calls the House of All Nations. Sweet young girls from all over. French, Mexican, Irish, Japanese, South Sea islanders—whatever you want."

"You talked me into it," I said. "I'll be there anytime I'm in Frisco."

"Different rooms decorated according to the different nationalities," Rita said. "That's Jake's idea, too. What do you think of it?"

"Well, I've never had a South Sea islander," I said.

Rita hugged me. "I'm so happy, I could kiss you."

"Why don't you," I said. Then we fucked again. Down there Rita had muscles I didn't know women possessed, and she used all of them on me. It went on like that for hours. This was a night to remember. And wouldn't you know it, she managed to get me up again, except that the only way she was able to do it was to roll me over on my back and take my cock in her mouth. I really didn't think she'd be able to make me come again but, by God, she did it, working on the head of my cock with her mouth, tickling it with her tongue. Gradually, I got hard again. A soft hard-on at first. Rita knew how to make it firm. She took all my big cock into her mouth and sucked it until I was ready to go crazy. I was slow in coming, but she was patient with me. Then I came with a gasp loud enough to wake the preacher, if he hadn't been such a sound sleeper. I soon drifted off into an even deeper sleep.

I hadn't been asleep very long when Jake Steiner's yelling woke me with a start. Jake wasn't a shouter, and at first I thought we were under attack. But it was no such thing; there wasn't an enemy in sight. Jake was standing by the front of Iversen's wagon and yelling at him to come out and fight like a man.

The fight exploded while I was running up the hill to

the wagons. Iversen came out of the front end of the wagon like a human bullet in a circus. I don't know how old Jake was; he must have been close to forty. Iversen, I knew, wasn't much past thirty. Iversen's weight struck Jake and knocked him down. They rolled in the dirt trying to throttle each other. I straightened my gun belt but made no attempt to stop the fight. It was best to get it over with. After that it could go one of two ways. The bad feeling could get worse, or maybe it would just wear itself away.

They were back on their feet, trading solid body punches you could hear at a distance. Jake was a chunky man, but there was plenty of muscle under the lard. Iversen moved faster than Jake, but what he lacked was the real roughness of the Wandering Jew. Old Jake had taken too many hard knocks to be downed by a beached sailor with brass buttons on his coat. Still and all, Iversen was a fair fighter. He had some idea of professional fisticuffs. Jake had none, but he took his punishment and gave back more than he got. I was waiting for Reverend Claggett to show up. I looked around, but he was nowhere in sight.

A hard right from Jake broke some of Iversen's front teeth, causing his mouth to bleed. Iversen's lady-catching smile wouldn't be half as charming after this. Anger made him careless, and he bored in, trying to drop Jake with a flurry of blows. Another man would have gone down under the furious onslaught. Not Jake. He stood like a rock and punched like a man who knew he was going to win. In a few minutes, Iversen seemed to know it, too. He was tiring fast, swaying on his feet. Blood dripped from his nose and mouth, and his defense against Jake's attack was a sham. Jake just knocked him aside and punched him in the head and body. Jake himself was taking plenty of punishment. His left eye was closed, and a dribble of blood leaked from a cut on his cheek. The gut punches he took must have hurt like hell, but all he did was grunt.

Then Iversen, after one last wild swing, began to fall. Jake drew back his big fist to strike again, then decided not to do it. If it had been me, I would have crippled Iversen with kicks after he hit the ground. But that would have been dumb. We needed Iversen, and a crippled man isn't much use as a soldier. After one last look at Iversen, Jake walked away.

Right at that moment Reverend Claggett came down from his wagon. I thought he was going to start in on me for not stopping the fight. "Maybe it's just as well this way. Let me tell you something, Saddler."

"What's that?"

"I know more of what goes on in this wagon train than you think. Iversen and Steiner have had their fight, and that's the end of it. I'll kill the first man that starts up again."

Dr. Ames patched up Iversen as best he could. Some of the broken teeth had to be yanked out with forceps. Ames also gave Iversen something to wash out his mouth with. Iversen looked like a Halloween pumpkin without his front teeth. After he finished with Iversen, Ames followed Jake with his black bag. Jake said he was all right—just a puffy eye and a cut on his face.

"No need to take up your time, doctor," Jake said courteously.

Rita was holding a wet cloth to Jake's swollen eye when I came over. "You mind telling me what caused all that? He's been riding you for weeks and you took it like a lamb. Why the sudden change?"

"It's of no importance, not now," Jake said. "I don't think he'll do it again. If he does, I'll kill him."

I still didn't get it. "What will he not do again?"

Rita answered for Jake. "He came to my wagon and offered me money. I told him I didn't want his money, but he kept on trying. I guess he had been spying on us. He said I'd been with you all night and must have taken money for it. Anything you gave me he would match and double."

"And what did you say?"

"I asked him if he had a thousand dollars. I said he'd have to make it five thousand before I'd even think about it. He said I was crazy and offered twenty dollars. Then, when I told him to get away from my wagon, he tried to come in and grab at me. I didn't want Jake to get into a fight, but I had to tell him about it."

Jake took away the wet rag and inspected his damaged eye with a forefinger. "The asking wasn't what got me mad. It was the grabbing. Of course, there were other things to be settled, too."

I grinned at him. "Iversen looked settled enough, last I saw of him."

Rita said proudly, "From now on, I lie down for no man but Jake."

"Now! Now!" Jake said bashfully. "There's no need to go into details."

Rita's declaration wasn't what you'd call romantic, yet I took it as a declaration of love. I wondered what the future would hold for this odd pair. Somehow I got the idea that they would do all right. Frisco was one hell of a town, the liveliest, most open-handed town on the West Coast or anywhere else. You could do anything in Frisco, provided you didn't do it in the street and frighten the horses. A lot of men and women had gotten a new start in that town.

"Bless you, my children," I said.

Steiner said, "You wouldn't want to come in as an active partner?"

I hadn't given the idea any thought. "Not unless you run a gaming parlor as well. Even then, I'm not much for staying long in cities."

"There will be no gambling," Rita said firmly. "The rich men who come there will come to spend money, not to have it taken from them. Gambling would give the house—our house—a bad name. We have to create goodwill from the first day we open our doors."

"Nothing can stop us now," Jake said, smiling at Rita. "I feel good enough to get married."

Steiner was just joking, but Rita took him up on it. "Why wait till Frisco? Claggett's a minister, isn't he?"

I wasn't sure how legal Claggett was. Legal enough, I guessed. Anyhow, maybe as wagon master he had the same marrying power as the captain of a seagoing ship.

"Why don't you go ask him?" I said.

Steiner said, "I'll do that. You'll be the best man, of course."

"Be glad to."

Claggett was surprised when Jake approached him with the idea. He became angry when Jake asked him if the marriage would hold up in court.

"I am an ordained minister of the Church of Redemption," Claggett said. "I do not condone your ways, Mr. Steiner, but it is better to have you married than living in sin."

"And best wishes to you, too!" Rita said, but she wasn't mad. She was about to get a man of her own, one she loved and trusted. Not even Claggett's sin-hating face could get her down.

I don't know that I ever attended a grimmer wedding. I'd been to funerals that had more cheer to them. The girl in Rita's wagon agreed to be her bridesmaid, and then we got the wedding group together. After some preliminary bullshit, Claggett pronounced them man and wife. Both signed their names in a big, old, battered book that Claggett got from his wagon, his register of births, deaths and marriages. Until Steiner and Rita came along, there had been nothing but deaths filling the pages. Although I have no use for the institution myself, it cheered me to see these two people getting married.

The only one who didn't turn up to stare was Iversen. No doubt he stayed away out of a sense of delicacy. Maggie O'Hara was there and so was Flaxie. Maggie's eyes were filled with scorn; I knew Steiner had made a real enemy of the good-looking, woman-loving jailbird. I thought Flaxie looked kind of wistful, as if thoughts of another kind of life were heavy on her mind. Reverend Claggett refrained from offering his best wishes. Then, as if to show his independence, Culligan came forward and shook Steiner's hand.

"The best of good fortune to you and your lady," the slab-faced Irishman said. Then he went back to his work.

A few of the women had the decency to offer their best wishes. Even Maggie O'Hara came forward and tried to

kiss Rita. Rita pulled away before she could do it, and
Maggie sneered, "You're going to need all the good luck
you can get."

For an instant, I felt like telling Maggie what she could
do with her woman-loving kiss. I held back, though,
because I didn't want to start a gunfight at a wedding. It
was too bad Maggie couldn't be satisfied with Flaxie. I
figured something had happened between them, or maybe Maggie was trying to use Rita to keep Flaxie in line. It
seemed to me that Flaxie wanted to get away from
Maggie but didn't know how to do it. Something about
her seemed to say that she wasn't the same queer breed
as her wagonmate. Besides, there had been that night
with me. Of course, there are women who like to get it
from men as well as from women. It was none of my
business.

Maggie had it in for me, but I couldn't quite figure out
why. Since I had been warned away from Flaxie, there
had been no other nights under my blankets in the
moonlight. In the past, Flaxie had fucked many men, yet
Maggie seemed to reserve all her hate for me. Maybe I
summed up all men for her. She tensed up every time she
saw me. The other men didn't seem to have the same
effect on her though. At no time had she ever displayed
any interest in Iversen, even before he'd had his teeth
knocked out. Now that Steiner had snagged Rita for
himself, I expected Maggie to turn her anger on him. But
that didn't happen. She didn't like him any better, but
that was as far as it went.

Maggie was what she was, and proud of it. I admitted
that she excited me, the way a bronc-buster is excited by
the meanest-spirited horse in the bunch. But I figured
that here was one horse that couldn't be ridden, no
matter what. I was ready to bury the hatchet if she was,
but Maggie's attitude was that she'd like to bury it in my
head.

"Party's over," I said.

THIRTEEN

It took a little more than two days to reach Fort Bridger. There was a long pull to the top of a shaly slope before we could see the fort in the early morning light. It had been weeks since we had seen humans other than ourselves. It would be good to see faces that hadn't grown so familiar. The fort looked solid after life on the move, as if it had been there forever.

A bugle brassed far below, disturbing the quiet of the morning, yet the sound was lost immediately in the vastness of plain and sky. It wasn't summer yet. The sky on that morning was gray, dull, heavy and low, loaded with clouds. Rain began to fall, drumming on the canvas tops of the wagons, which leaked where poorly patched.

The train went over the rise like a huge snake with a broken back. Wind-driven mist blew in our faces, blurring the outlines of the fort. But just to see it lifted the spirits of everyone; for a little while at least, we were back in what passed for civilization.

We had started out before first light so as to catch the soldiers at assembly time. The sound of the bugle said we had timed it just right. The bugling stopped and we could hear shouting in the rain. The gate of the fort was closed and barred from the inside. In more settled areas, the gates of a fort are hardly ever closed. In back of the gate and to one side of it was a spindly-legged watchtower, from which the country could be scanned for miles. The watchtower had a little peaked roof. Up there only one man could stand watch at a time. There was a man there now, so they knew we were coming. He shouted down from the tower and, before we got all the way down, the gate opened and an officer and a squad of men came out. The men all carried rifles at the ready position; to my mind they didn't look too friendly.

I guessed they thought we were Mormons, because there were so many women in the train. The Mormons and the Army were forever at war; it had been going on for years, ever since the Saints packed up and moved clear off the maps. But civilization had caught up with them, and so had the Army.

"Hold up, there!" the officer hollered, a young lieutenant, his holster flap unbuttoned. The lieutenant regarded Reverend Claggett with deep suspicion, a reasonable enough reaction to the gaunt, mad-eyed parson. The first time I had seen Claggett I knew he was bound to get me into trouble.

"Hold up there!" he said again.

Claggett was more accustomed to giving orders than to taking them. "Hold up for what?" he growled, impatient with everything that held up the Lord's work. To the preacher, his work and the Lord's were one and the same.

"We want nothing more than we can buy at the sutler's store," Claggett said. "What do you think we are, a pack of beggars? I asked you a question, boy? Hold up for what?"

The lieutenant knew the men were grinning behind his back, and being called boy in front of the squad didn't make him love Claggett any.

"I'll ask the questions," the lieutenant said roughly, though I could see he wasn't a rough man. "You look like Mormons to me—are you?"

He was wasting his time trying to intimidate Claggett. "Maybe we are, and maybe we aren't," he said. "If we are, what's it to you?"

I liked the way Claggett stood up to the jack-in-office lieutenant. But I would have liked it better at some other time. At the moment, I wanted to stay on the good side of the Army, for what it was worth. As it turned out, it wasn't worth a goddamned thing.

"Are you Mormons or not?" the lieutenant repeated, unsure of how to deal with Claggett. "You people have been making trouble since you came out here."

"The Mormons were here before the Army, before everybody," the preacher said, determined to have it out.

"We're not Mormons," I said before it got worse. "We only look like it because of all the women. This here is the Reverend Josiah Claggett, and he's taking the ladies to a new religious community in California."

The lieutenant wasn't convinced. "Only the Mormons bring women across the Plains in such numbers. Women going west to find husbands go by boat."

"These women didn't have a boat," I said patiently.

"What's your name?" the lieutenant asked.

I told him. I said I was a guide and hunter.

"Mormons have been known to lie," the lieutenant said. "They don't consider it lying if it gets their God's work done."

That was a new one on me. I didn't know the Mormons had a God of their own. Maybe they did. "You know more about them than I do," I said. "Believe me, sir, we are what we say we are."

But the lieutenant stood firm, at least for the moment. "I can't be sure you're telling the truth."

"Get a Bible, or we'll use the Reverend's. I'll swear on it."

"The Mormons don't believe in the Bible."

The lieutenant must have been studying up on the Saints on what they did and didn't do. And he had grounds for his suspicion. For the most part, Mormons look like other humans. They don't all wear chin beards, black suits, round-crowned hats and glum expressions.

Suddenly, I thought of a way out. I called Culligan. "Fetch your bottle," I called out. "Maybe the lieutenant is in need of a drink."

At that hour of the morning, Culligan was red-eyed and stinking of stale whiskey. You could just about smell him from where he was. He reached over the endgate of his wagon, opened a box and from it took a full quart of whiskey, a brand so cheap and bad it could've killed a mule.

Culligan took his bottle and stood beside me in the rain. He blew his breath on the young officer and nearly knocked him over.

"Are you a Mormon?" I asked the Irishman.

"Lord, no," Culligan said. "That's worse than being a Protestant."

Then, so there wouldn't be any more doubt, I called for Maggie O'Hara; the hard-eyed woman-lover came forward with a swagger. In her tight, striped pants, carrying a double-edged knife and holstered pistol, she didn't look like any docile Mormon female.

I think Maggie impressed the lieutenant more than Culligan did. She was enough to impress any man and maybe frighten a timid one. There was real menace in this good-looking woman.

She knew what was expected of her; whatever else she was, she was buggywhip smart. "What the fuck did you call me for?" she asked. She didn't have to fake the hostility. "Do we get into the fucking fort, or do we stand here all day in the fucking rain?"

At that moment, the lieutenant decided that we couldn't possibly be Mormons. He knew what Maggie was. A woman of her breed would have been driven from a Mormon wagon train with whip and club. And if she didn't go, she'd be killed.

I thought I finally had it settled, but Claggett started up again. "I still say you got no right interfering with other people's religious beliefs. You know now we're not Mormons. How about the Jews? We got one Jew in the train. You got any special rules for him, any questions you want to ask him? Can he come in, or does he have to stand outside the gate? Tell me, so I can tell him. I wouldn't want to do anything against Army regulations."

Maybe the lieutenant thought he was telling the truth when he said, "We treat the Mormons the same as everybody else except when they break the law of the land. Polygamy is against the law. Congress has said so, but the Mormons say they have to father a lot of children in order to survive."

"Bullshit!" Claggett said. It was the first time I'd heard him use any rough language. He walked straight into the fort, and the lieutenant didn't try to stop him.

I had to try to get the United States Army back on our side, so much so that I was willing to do a little soft-soaping, a little ass-kissing. I had to be practical. As soon as Claggett was out of earshot I said, "My apologies, Lieutenant. Reverend Claggett is old and tired. For all his quick temper, he's a good man. All his life he's worked for the poor and needy." Naturally, I didn't mention the years when the preacher was robbing and killing.

"Old men get cranky," the lieutenant said.

"That they do," I said. "I'd like to talk to your commanding officer—or are you in command?" That last question was a little of the soft soap.

The lieutenant liked the idea that I considered him fit to command a big post like Bridger. "No, sir, I'm not in command, and Captain Flack is only in temporary command." The lieutenant said his own name was Wakely and we shook hands.

"He'll talk to you," Wakely said, waving me toward the gate.

It was plain that the lieutenant was bored and lonely. I was sure he wasn't married. It was all right for the men to poke the fort washerwomen which was the name they used for the enlisted men's whores, but an officer couldn't stick his dick in the same hole. He looked with longing at all my women, especially at Flaxie, who was walking across the parade ground with Maggie.

Wakely led me across the muddy parade ground. The

men had just been dismissed and were headed for the mess hall. If the fort hadn't been soaked with rain, the news of the 50 women would have set it on fire. As it was, there was many a backward glance as the men headed for breakfast. Fort Bridger was smack in the middle of nowhere, not a town for hundreds of miles. The few white women in Bridger would be officers' and sergeants' wives—corporals didn't rate a wife—and God help the man who poked or tried to poke another man's woman. To the enlisted men they were as untouchable as white plantation women would be to Negro slaves. The man who dipped his wick in the wrong oil could get killed, and sometimes was.

We passed the women hurrying into the sutler's store. Women love to buy things even in the middle of the wilderness. Certainly it would be a long time before they got another chance to stand in front of a counter. A sutler's sold just about everything, and everything cost a lot more than back east, because it had to be carried so far. Some of the politicians were in cahoots with the office-holders who granted permits to the sutlers. A sutler on a big post could get rich in no time at all.

I saw Culligan heading toward the store and knew he wasn't going there to buy sarsaparilla. The Irishman had enough whiskey already to see him to California and back again, but a real drunk never takes a chance on being caught short.

I followed Wakely to the captain's office, and he was there, early though it was. He was old for a captain; in the peacetime Army promotion is slow. If we went to war with Canada or Mexico, he would be a colonel in months. No wonder peacetime officers longed for war. A soldier without a war is like a carpenter without a saw. Captain Flack was about 50, with a belly, a red face and tufts of reddish hair in his ears and nose. Either he shaved without care or had a dull razor, because his face had powdered nicks in several places. One nick still oozed a little blood. He looked like a man who drank a lot, probably late at night in his quarters, drank and listened to the sounds of the fort, dreaming of the wars he'd never fight. The whiskey showed in his red-veined eyes and in the thick, shiny skin heavy drinkers develop as they get older.

He was not glad to see me, or anyone else, though he was civil enough for a man with a hangover. After we shook hands, he showed me a chair and said with barely controlled impatience: "You should get off the Overland and go north on the Oregon. Then you can come back down through central California. It's one long valley all the way south. No mountains to cross, no Indian trouble of any kind. That's what I think you should do."

What he said made sense for any other wagon train except the one I was guiding. The captain had no way of knowing my problems. "We have to go the quickest way," I said. "I was hoping you could give us a small escort for part of the way. I know you can't escort us all the way to California, but the presence of even a small group of soldiers would make a difference. Even the worst band of wagon-raiders has more sense than to attack an Army escort."

"These raiders, who are they?"

I told him about Kiowa Sam and the trouble with him at the start of our journey. I said I expected the next trouble to be a lot worse, maybe a massacre, if we didn't get some protection. I said we didn't have enough men to fight off a determined attack. "Maybe we can fight them off for a while. But that won't stop them," I said.

Captain Flack said he had never heard of Kiowa Sam. "You can't believe all these stories," he said confidently, his big belly pressing against the desk, maybe thinking it was about time for a small drink, just to get his brain working again.

"I think this story is real, Captain."

Flack said, "Some of these old-timers like to give themselves fearsome reputations. That's supposed to make people afraid of them. Mostly it's bluster."

"There's good reason to fear this old man," I said. "Old, bad men are the most dangerous of all. They know they're going to die soon, so they don't care what chances they take."

The captain's impatience showed again. "Then take the Oregon Trail like I told you. We've cleared most of the raiders off that route. It's been working fine."

Again, there was much truth in what the captain said. Raiders with sense tried to keep out of the way of the Army. There was no point getting hanged for the meager possessions to be found in the usual emigrant train. But my train was far from usual. It carried a cargo much more valuable than gold.

"I think Sam would risk it to get at the women," I said. "If he gets them, he can name his own price. A wagonload of women could set him up for life."

"I still can't give you an escort." Captain Flack wiped beads of sweat from his upper lip, though a cool morning breeze came through the window and stirred the papers on his desk. "I'd like to help you, but I can't. I just can't. I'd be forced to resign if I went against my present orders."

"What orders?" I could be impatient too.

"On this very day my orders are to proceed to the Sawtooth Mountains where the Mormons are said to have established a new settlement of polygamists. Every time we think we have the Mormons in line, they move on to some remote place. Now there are rumors about Mormons living in a canyon far back in the Sawtooth range. Instead of obeying the law, they just move on."

"Then you're just marching on a rumor?"

"I'm not marching on anything, not by myself. I don't think up my orders. I just follow them. If the polygamists are there, I am to arrest the men and burn the settlement and crops."

"What happens to the women and children?"

Captain Flack didn't like to be questioned by a civilian. "If it's any of your business, I'm to take them back to this fort and await instructions from my superiors. *They* will get *their* instructions from the Department of the Interior."

Flack's face softened a little. "Listen, Saddler, I have nothing against the Mormons. Some officers do. Not me. If I had my way, I'd let them have all the wives they want.

The more white people out here, the better. But my orders come from people who don't know anything about the situation. I don't know how this whole Mormon thing got started—politicians' wives probably. They say whole bands are moving to Mexico, where the government won't bother them. Good luck to them! I wish they'd all go."

I knew I wasn't going to win, but I had to keep trying. "If they think they're safe in the Sawtooths, they'll still be there a month, a year from now. They only move when they're bothered. There may be nothing in the Sawtooths, Captain, whereas I have a whole wagon train of living, breathing young women. Why can't you give us an escort and then go into the Sawtooths?"

Captain Flack had creases of hangover pain between his eyes. "I can't help you, Mr. Saddler. You look like an experienced man; you must have known what to expect when you started out with these women. If it's any consolation, my patrols to the west haven't seen anything. No activity at all."

I knew the Army would not have seen Sam's raiders. If they worked with a man like Kiowa Sam, they would be a wily bunch, well-experienced in dodging Army patrols. When it came right down to it, I couldn't fault the boozy captain. He didn't look like a fire-eater, a Mormon-hater. He was just a getting-old man, who drank too much and wanted to hang onto his job because it was all he had.

He stood up, his way of telling me there was nothing more to talk about. "The best I can do is give you extra ammunition. I'll have to give you shells that are getting old. I recommend that you test some of them."

I said I would take anything I could get. We shook hands again, but he didn't walk out with me. I got over to the sutler's and found Culligan drinking at the rough plank bar in the far corner of the big room. The sutler was a bearded, burly man with a leather apron and a straw hat with a broken brim. No soldiers were there. Some of the women had gone back to the wagons. Claggett had gone too. But not Maggie O'Hara. She was drinking, keeping as far away from Culligan as she could.

Claggett had forbidden the women to drink, so it looked like Maggie was getting bold.

I got the sutler to set up a bottle and glass for me. I asked him if he stocked dynamite. No, he said, the one thing he didn't stock was dynamite. The Army had no use for it, and there were no settlers to buy it. I swallowed the bad news along with my drink. Maybe it was just as well. It would make the women even more nervous if they knew we were carrying explosives. I didn't offer to buy Culligan a drink; he wouldn't have liked the intrusion.

"We'd better get going," I told him. He threw back his drink, picked up a sack of bottles and went out without a word.

But Maggie wasn't to be hurried. "You didn't get an escort, did you, Saddler?"

"No escort," I said. "We'll have to go it alone."

Maggie snapped her whiskey against the back of her throat. "Our hero!" she sneered.

FOURTEEN

It continued to rain as we started out again. All of northern Utah lay ahead of us, rough country, jagged and forbidding. The rain came down as if it would never stop. With the rain would come sickness. Dr. Ames would have his work cut out for him, but there is only so much a doctor can do on the trail.

The train was silent as we moved away from the fort and down a long grade, keeping to the south bank of a creek. Some of the women looked back until it was out of sight. The only sounds were those of the turning wheels, the creak of harness and wood. And the rain, that goddamned rain! It drummed on the wagons and splashed in the creek. You get to hate rain like that because you know it's trying to kill you. I knew it could well kill some of the women. It starts with a shivering that rapidly becomes pneumonia. There was nothing to be done about it. Stopping and making camp didn't help. We would just lose time.

We moved on through the day and, except for the rain, the going wasn't too rough. Then there came a point where the creek turned sharply, cutting right across the trail. If it hadn't been raining, it wouldn't have been much of a creek. Now, built up by flood water, it roared like a fast-flowing river, overflowing its banks, tearing up bushes and small trees. There was no way to get across it, so we stopped short of it and made camp, wet and cold as we were. It was hard to get the fires started and hard to keep them going when the wood began to burn. I was helping with one of the fires when Rita came up to me and said the girl in her wagon was down with a bad chill, shaking all over and bringing up blood when she coughed.

"I think she has the same consumption her mother died of," Rita said. "Dr. Ames is with her now."

I went to the wagon. Ames was giving the girl spoonfuls of some dark medicine to help stop the coughing. After a while the coughing stopped and the girl fell asleep. I climbed out of the wagon with Ames. "I think she has consumption," he said in his peculiar high voice. "I don't think it's too bad, if she doesn't come down with pneumonia."

"Will she?"

"I'm afraid so."

"Then she'll die."

"That's right."

And she did, early the next morning. The pneumonia started late in the evening. By midnight she was delirious, sweating and babbling. By first light the girl was dead. Rita stayed with her to the end, sponging her face with a damp cloth, talking quietly to her. Rita held the girl's hand until she shuddered and died without ever regaining consciousness.

I'll say this for Ames: he did everything he could. It was no use. He closed the girl's eyes after she died and climbed down from the wagon. His daughter had kept the deathwatch with him, sitting silently beside him, saying nothing. Ames looked very tired when it was over.

During the night the rain had stopped, but it was full day before the level of the creek began to drop. We buried the girl while the flood lessened. By the time the preacher read over her, it was time to take the first wagon across. I took Claggett's wagon because it was the biggest and heaviest and went across easily. Culligan rode with me. After we got across, we strung ropes across the creek and started to bring the other wagons across. We had all but the last wagon across when, suddenly, an uprooted tree came sailing along in the still-strong current and struck the wagon in the center, busting the sides and front wheels. The two women in the wagon were Germans, quiet sturdy women of about 30-years-old—the ones who had prepared Hannah Claggett's body for burial. The tree swept the wagon away, and it turned over on its side in the swift current. They screamed for a moment, but then there was nothing. The wagon came apart under the battering of the tree and the current. I saw one of their faces for a moment; then it was gone.

I told the rest of the train to stay where they were while I rode downstream, followed by Culligan and Steiner. There was no sign of either of them. We rode for a mile, stopping now and then to look for the bodies, but there was still no sign of them. They were gone for good. It would be a waste of time to keep on looking, so we turned back finally, and the wagon train moved on.

The next one to die was Isabel Ames, the doctor's pretty daughter, the short-haired girl with the bossy ways and a real dislike for me. I never did find out what it was she had against me. It wasn't like with Maggie O'Hara. No spark had passed between us.

It started with nothing: a bite from a prairie dog in a hole near where we had halted for the noon meal. As usual, Isabel cooked the meal for her father and herself, and she ate it with him. If we had moved on a few minutes sooner, it wouldn't have happened at all. But Culligan had to work on a wheel that was giving us trouble. That held up the rest of the train, because it was the rule never to split up, even for a short time.

I noticed that the girl had been teasing the doctor, and that struck me as kind of odd. Both were in a nervous, smiling mood. She whispered in his ear and ruffled his thinning hair, making him blush. In her loose canvas trousers and thick wool shirt, Isabel Ames was damn good-looking. Not the kind I favored, though. I like women when they're not so skittish, and not so bossy. The way she fussed over and teased her own father was a caution.

You'd have to describe her behavior as silly; as if some sudden girlish mood had taken hold of her. She rolled on the grass in front of Ames, smiling at him all the time. He smiled back, but it was plain that he was embarrassed, although he didn't want to offend her.

I happened to glance over at her as she stuck her hand into the prairie dog burrow. I yelled at her to take it out. Her hand still in the hole, she turned an indignant face toward me, ready to tell me off. Then she yelped—a yelp, not a scream—and jerked her hand out of the hole. It was bleeding slightly from a small wound. She ran to Dr. Ames, holding it out in front of her.

"Something in there bit me," she said, holding up the hand for the doctor's attention. Some of the women exchanged hard-eyed glances. All that fuss about a bite from a prairie dog. People had died on the trip with a lot less fuss.

Dr. Ames opened his black bag and was doctoring the small row of punctures when Culligan announced that they could move on. I didn't think any more about it until we were camped for the night. I made the nightly count of those standing guard and those in or around the wagons and cookfires. I was getting to the doctor's wagon when he climbed down over the endgate. His face was creased with worry and a kind of mental fatigue. I hoped he wasn't getting sick on us. I jerked my arm away when he grabbed at me, unaware of what he was doing. Then I looked at him again and knew something was wrong.

"What is it?" I asked.

He grabbed my arm again; this time I let him do it. He led me around to the other side of the wagon where the others couldn't hear. There was sweat on his long upper lip, where a heavy mustache had flourished until recently, I felt sure. I felt his hand trembling on my arm.

"Oh, dear God!" he said. He paused until he had control of himself. What he said next brought a trickle of cold sweat from my armpits. "I think my daughter has come down with bubonic plague, Mr. Saddler. She has all the symptoms. I can't be mistaken."

Cold sweat slid over my ribcage. "Can it happen that fast?"

"Yes," he said, trying to fight the tremor in his voice. "It's been more than eight hours since she was bitten. Already she's running a high temperature and the spots are beginning to appear on her face." He sucked in breath before he went on. "I know what the plague looks like. I saw it twice before in Panama, as a young man. There can't be any mistake about it. You're going to have to leave us behind, or the whole train will become infected."

I removed his hand from my arm, but not in a rough way. "You could be infected; so could I. What about other people who have been close to your wagon during the day?"

"I don't know," Ames said. "They could be. We don't know exactly how it spreads. That's why you have to move on right now. Leave us and move on as fast as you can. Do what I tell you, Mr. Saddler. The longer you stay here, the more danger you'll be in."

Ames climbed back into the wagon. I went to tell Claggett, and even his rough-hewn face blanched at the most dreaded word on the Plains—plague!

"I'm going to stay with them," I said. "I have to know for sure if she's got it. Move on about three miles and wait for my signal, three shots fired at five second intervals. Send somebody back when you hear the signal. Tell them not to get too close."

Claggett glanced down the line of wagons. "What does the doctor say we should do?"

"Put up red plague warnings. Flags. Make sure they can be seen. Ames says that's all you can do right now. Get a move on, Reverend, before we all come down with it."

* * *

It was one hell of a lonely feeling to see the wagons pulling away. Word had spread, and the women looked fearfully at the Ames's wagon as they drove their own teams around it, staying as far away as they could. I stood by the fire until the last wagon disappeared into the darkness. It was Culligan's, and he thrust a bottle of whiskey at me before he left.

I hadn't done much drinking on the trip. Now I needed a drink. I felt as if I needed the whole bottle. Uncorking it, I took two big swallows before I stoppered it again. The whiskey burned in my gut without doing much good. There are times when whiskey is like that, and this was one of them. The fires burned down, and it was quiet except for the night wind and the sounds coming from the wagon.

In a while, Isabel's moaning became screams, and she kept on screaming, though whether from pain or terror I couldn't tell. I waited in darkness, drinking now and then, and listened to the dying girl puke away her life.

The hours passed slowly, one after another. Far away on the prairie I could see the fires of the train burning low. The fires winked out, and the sky was streaked with gray. No more sounds came from the wagon.

I had enough whiskey in me when I climbed up to take a look. I had to force myself to do it. Two coal-oil lanterns hanging from hooks threw a yellow glare on the girl's body. Isabel Ames looked like a rotting corpse, her face covered with running sores.

At first, Ames didn't seem to notice me. I waited on rubbery legs, wanting to be anywhere but where I was.

"She's dead," he said quietly, then bent forward and kissed her full on the lips. I waited without speaking until he turned away from the face with a strange, fatalistic look on his pale, middle-aged face.

"We had what we had, and now it's over," he said.

The stench of death was strong in the wagon, because Isabel hadn't died easy. I found myself looking at Ames as if for the first time. The final act of kissing the plague-ridden body had changed him in my eyes. Whoever they were, whatever she had been, there had been real love between them.

"She wasn't your daughter," I said, then stopped. "You don't have to tell me anything." I wasn't prompted by sympathy. I didn't want to hear his story. I felt the weight of too many lives on my shoulders, and there comes a time when you don't want to know any more about them. I had signed on like a drummer-boy larking off to war, and here I was up to my neck in grief.

"It doesn't matter," Ames said. "No, she wasn't my daughter. Her name wasn't Isabel, just as mine isn't Ames. But I am a doctor—was a doctor—and if I do say so, a good one. She was my nurse back in New Jersey. Her name was Jenny Sills, mine is Robert Belknap. She brought such joy into my life, Mr. Saddler. I'm fifty years of age, and until last year I thought my life was over. Now it is, but I had most of one good year in an otherwise miserable life."

Then I remembered the name Robert Belknap. I don't bother much with newspapers except when I'm in a barbershop and have to wait my turn. But I remembered the name Robert Belknap. The wife-killer, the yellow press called him. The newspapers said he had battered his wife to death with a poker, planning the deed with his pretty young nurse, then lost his nerve and fled. The paper said they were being hunted by police all over the country. I don't approve of killing middle-aged ladies—I figured she was middle-aged—but I couldn't see why the paper was making such a fuss over it. It must have been because Ames—Belknap was a doctor. People expect doctors to be better than they are, and want them to pay hard when they do wrong. Or maybe the papers were short of good scandals that week. Belknap didn't look much like a killer.

He looked at me. "Have you ever hated someone so much you found it hard to breathe in their presence?"

"Never that much," I said.

Belknap said, "That's how I felt about my wife. Twenty years ago she was my nurse. I was just getting started and ... well ... we became intimate."

For a wife-killer, Belknap was a pretty delicate fellow.
"I liked her well enough, but I didn't love her," he said.
"When she told me she was pregnant, I agreed to marry
her. It seemed the right thing to do. Too late I discovered
she wasn't pregnant. Well, I was prepared to be philo-
sophical about it—after all, I had my work. I don't know
when she came to hate me. Perhaps it was because she
had to trick me into marriage. There had been broad
hints, but I ignored them. Whatever the reason, she set
out to make my life a misery, and for twenty years she
succeeded."

Again, I tried to stop him. It was no use.

"She belittled me constantly," Belknap went on. "As it
got worse, I kept suggesting that we separate, but she just
sneered at me. I was her husband, and I was going to
remain her husband no matter what. She was going to
make me suffer—her actual word. In time, I grew to hate
the sound of her voice, her presence, everything and
anything about her. On the night she ... died ... I
thought she had gone to Philadelphia to visit her sister.
But she was just waiting for Jenny to stay late after office
hours. She crept into the house and caught us together. I
think now she must have been insane. She tried to kill
Jenny with a poker, but instead I wrestled it away from
her and killed her with it. I didn't just strike her once.
Twenty years of hate went into that murder. You have to
believe that, Mr. Saddler."

"I don't have to believe anything," I said, sick of his
small-town sins.

"You mean you aren't going to turn me in? You're the
law in this train. I'm a murderer."

"Look," I said. "Even if I didn't believe your story, I
wouldn't turn you in. It so happens I do believe it. Where
were you hoping to go when you joined the train?"

Belknap said, "The train was our only hope of getting
away. They were watching all the railroads and ports.
Out on the Plains we'd be lost for months. First California, then Australia, that's where we hoped to go. If we
were lucky, we'd get new names and a new life."

"I won't try to stop you if you still want to go on by yourself. You do what you like, Belknap. You're still Dr. Ames to me. I didn't hear what you just said. Your woman is dead, but I got a lot of live ones to think about. I ask you again. Do you think the plague has spread to the other wagons?"

Belknap forced his mind to return to the here and now. "There's a good chance that it hasn't," he said.

"Can we rejoin the train after you . . . ?" It was hard to say it.

"After we burn her body," Belknap said. "That's what has to be done. If we bury her, animal prowlers may dig her up and spread the plague far and wide. The answer is, yes, we can rejoin the train after we burn our clothes and disinfect ourselves. If the plague isn't there now, we won't bring it with us, if we take the right precautions."

I nodded. After he climbed back in the wagon, I fired three shots, the signal for the train ahead to send someone back within hailing distance. I expected to see Culligan or Steiner, but it was Maggie O'Hara who rode back from the train.

She reined in her horse a fair distance from me. "She dead yet?" she hollered.

"She's dead," I yelled back. "Ames is taking care of the body. We have to burn our clothes and wash down with disinfectant. After that we can rejoin the train. Anybody else sick yet?"

Maggie's horse stood atop a high, grassy mound. "Not so far," she called. "You want me to get fresh clothes for you and the doctor, is that it?"

"That's it."

"I'd just as soon leave you bare-assed on the prairie. But we need the doctor, so I'll be along directly. You didn't expect me, did you, Saddler?"

"That's right."

"You thought I'd be scared to come this close?"

"That's right."

That got her going, not a hard thing to do. "Fuck you, Saddler! I can do anything a man can do, and do it better." Without waiting for an answer, she turned the

horse and rode back toward the wagons, now halted
miles away on the prairie. Belknap called to me from the
wagon. I came close, and he handed me two buckets and
two bottles of carbolic acid to be mixed with the water.

"Take them away some distance," he said. While I was
doing it, he splashed coal oil all over the wagon, soaking
the body and the bedding. I came back.

"That's close enough," Belknap said. The strange look
was back on his face. "Take off your clothes and pitch
them in here. After that you make the solution good and
strong, as strong as you can bear it on the skin. Burn the
wagon before you start to wash down."

I stared back at him. "Why don't I just do as you do?"

He gave me that odd smile again. "I think not, Mr.
Saddler." Before I could stop him, he drew the revolver
from his belt, put the muzzle in his mouth and pulled the
trigger. The bullet blew off the top of his skull, spattering
his blood and brains. After he was dead, I wasn't sure
that I would have stopped him if it had been possible.
Robert Belknap was finished as a man. Keeping him
alive would have meant nothing more than carrying
extra weight.

There was nothing to do but get on with it after I took
the revolver from his dead hand and the extra cartridges
from his pocket. He had fallen beside the body of his
woman. In life they had been a strange pair; in death
they looked like everybody else.

I peeled off my clothes and pitched them into the
wagon. I threw my hat in too. I could find another hat.
That left only my boots and gun belt to be washed, along
with my body. The wagon was well-soaked in coal oil; all
that remained was to strike a match. It went up like a
bomb, with a loud, whomping sound that split the
covers. I turned fast but the fierce heat reached out at
me.

The wagon was still burning as I washed myself in one
bucket of carbolic solution. It stung like hell, so I knew it
was good and strong, as he had ordered. Then, using the
bucket intended for him, I washed myself down a second
time. It might be all a waste of time, because there was

no way I could be sure I wasn't bringing the plague, or that it wasn't already there.

By the time I finished, the wagon—and the bodies—were reduced to a pile of glowing ash. I fired the last three bullets in my pistol and reloaded. Sometime later I heard the drumbeat of horse hoofs coming back and there was Maggie, riding hell for leather. I started out to meet her. If she was afraid of me as a possible plague carrier, she didn't show it. I guess she'd rather die than show fear to any man. She rode up without a moment's hesitation, leading my horse.

She looked down at me, dressed now in nothing but boots. I hadn't buckled on the gunbelt. That would have made me look even more foolish, if that was possible.

"Where's the doc?" she said, instead of giving me my pants. "There was a single shot a while ago."

"Ames killed himself," I said. "He didn't want to live after his woman had gone."

For once, that didn't bring a sneering comment from her. She slung the fresh clothes down at me. "You look kind of limp today, Saddler. Better get dressed before the ladies see you as you really are—limp! You sure you're not going to infect everybody in the train?"

I pulled my pants on. "The doc didn't seem to think so. It may be there now; it doesn't have to come from me." I finished dressing and buckled on my gun. "Let's go."

There was some puzzlement in the quick look she gave me. "You're all washed and clean, Saddler. You could just ride out and leave us. Why don't you?"

I mounted up. "You'd like that?"

"If you'd asked me that question a week ago, I'd have said yes."

"What changed your mind?"

"I can't stand the sight of you, but you got us this far. Maybe you'll get us the rest of the way."

"That's all there is to it, huh?"

Maggie had a mean, gutter mouth, nothing at all like Rita's good-natured obscenities. She told me what I could do to myself. A few things I hadn't heard before—

and that's saying something, since I'm a man of considerable experience in such matters.

"That's what I think of you," Maggie finished. She set off at a fair clip, but it was no trouble to catch up with her before she had gone any distance. All at once she seemed to realize that there was no great hurry. If we were carrying the plague, it would stay with us, no matter how fast or slow we traveled.

FIFTEEN

The plague warning flags still fluttered above the wagons. They would stay aloft until we were sure we didn't have the disease in our midst. Belknap had said that an outbreak would come within a week, if it came. After a week we could be reasonably sure that we were out of danger. But Belknap hadn't been absolute about anything. Not that much was known about the plague except that it struck fast and its victims died a horrible death. Why certain rodents on the Plains carried the plague was as big a mystery as the plague itself. No one knew why it hadn't wiped out the entire country, but right at that moment I wasn't concerned with the state of the country, just us.

I rode to the lead wagon and told Claggett about the death of Ames and the girl. He just grunted. His response wasn't unnatural or unusually hard, given the circumstances. "Two more gone," was all he said at first. Then he said, "What can we do if the plague breaks out in the other wagons?"

"Not much," I said. "If it breaks out in a wagon, then

we leave the wagon and the people in it. I don't know
what good that will do. If we have the plague, it's likely to
kill all of us."

"Most likely it is. Then it's just wait and see. No more
precautions we can take?"

"Nothing that will be of any use."

"You ever been through an outbreak?"

"Not even close to one."

"Me neither. It's not that common, far as I know. How
long do we wait?"

I had been figuring the hours. Jenny Sills—it was hard
to get used to that name—had died in less than a day
after we cut the wagon loose from the train. By now we
were some hours into the second day. But I was just
fooling around with numbers. It couldn't be cut that fine.

"I'd say we better give it a full week," I said.

Claggett grunted again. "It's going to be a long week."

And so it was.

In a way, it was like waiting to be hanged, with just the
smallest hope of getting a commutation at the last
moment. Naturally we didn't tell the women about the
time limit, because it would have tensed them up even
more than they were. Some were holding up pretty good;
others were close to the breaking point after the strain of
the endless journey.

More than a few of our original number had died, and
California seemed no closer, though we were, in fact,
well into Utah and fast approaching the Nevada border.
The plague might or might not come, but there was no
doubt in my mind about Kiowa Sam's raiders. I was still
betting that they would attack somewhere in Nevada. As
the days passed there was less and less reason to change
my mind.

The seventh day passed without the slightest sign of
plague. It was morning, and I rode up to Claggett's
wagon. He stared at me without saying anything. Jake
Steiner knew about the time limit. So did Rita, Maggie,
Iversen and Culligan. I don't know how many others
knew, or what fearful, whispered exchanges had gone on

among the women. Of those who knew for sure, none dared to say that seven days had gone by. To put into words our secret hopes seemed to be risking bad luck.

It took Claggett to say it. The old preacher didn't believe in luck, good or bad, just an angry God. "Looks like we're out of danger," he said. "You think we can take down the plague flags? It will make everybody feel better, whatever lies ahead."

Just as he spoke, I got the feeling that we were being watched. The feeling came suddenly, almost like a pain or a bunching of the nerves. The feeling was so powerful that I looked up in spite of myself. But there was nothing stirring out there in the dun-colored wasteland, not even a buzzard wheeling in the sky. It was a hot, bright morning without a breeze or a breath of cloud.

"We leave the flags as they are," I said quickly.

Claggett had already reached out and was grasping the tall sapling from which his own flag flew. He withdrew his hand and his face grew dark with anger. "Then what the doctor said was a lie? The seven days don't mean anything?"

"No lie," I said. "The danger is over, but we'll let the raiders see the flags. I think they've been looking at them already."

"You know that for sure?"

"For sure? No, a strong feeling is all."

Instead of scanning the hills, Claggett's eyes remained fixed on his team of mules, as if I hadn't said a thing about danger. "If they've been watching us, then they know it's been more than a week since the Ames girl got sick."

"They're not likely to know about the time limit. I didn't know about it and you didn't know about it."

"An old Plains hand like Sam might know about it. If he's been crossing all these years, he's bound to have run into plague. If he has, then he'll know you're running a bluff."

I couldn't give him much of an argument about that. "Maybe Sam knows, but is his word good enough to make men attack plague wagons? Even to get the women, will they figure it's worth the risk? You know anything that scares men more than plague?"

Claggett had his doubts, and properly so. "You're trying to read men's minds, Saddler. All right, you have a point. Maybe some of them will run out on him, not wanting to risk their lives, even for a cargo of women. How many is just guesswork, though, and you know it. Now that we're guessing, my guess is they'll just follow along like they been doing."

This time Claggett and I were on the same side, and it surprised me. "You're not just taking my word they're out there then?"

"No need to," Claggett said. "I got that being-watched feeling myself. I was hunted too long ever to lose it. You're like me in that way, having a nose for danger. If it hadn't been for the threat of plague, we'd have smelled Sam long before now. A big problem is this. Every day that we travel and somebody doesn't die is going to weaken our position."

That was just as true as the other things Claggett had said. Still, I figured the threat of plague gave us some sort of edge. Before the plague killed the girl, we were fair game for Sam's raiders. Now we had some kind of chance, however thin. "Maybe I am reading men's minds," I said, "but it would take a lot to make me attack a plague-carrying train. I sure as hell wouldn't do it for money. Every raider that turns tail is one we don't have to kill."

"Or be killed by," Claggett said. "We've got nothing to lose, but the women have to be told. You see the way their nerves are."

"Let me do it in my own way," I said. "If you do it, you'll make an announcement. The women look hangdog now and have to stay that way for Sam's benefit. The first sign of good spirits will bring Sam down on us."

Claggett grunted but didn't argue.

After that, I rode back and forth among the wagons, as I had been doing for a week. Jake Steiner was waiting for orders to take down his flag.

"Looks like we don't have it," he said happily.

I told him to wipe the smile off his face. "Do it quick. They could be glassing us. Look like we're a rolling mass of pestilence. Do it, Jake. I'll explain later."

I rode back through the train, talking quietly to the women, explaining how they were to behave. Some caught on right away, but others were stupefied by fear and fatigue. That was just fine. Kiowa Sam could be using field glasses or a telescope. Either way, he'd be able to look at us up close. I did my best to keep the relief from showing in their faces, but right then I couldn't be sure how successful I was. They had to be told. It was the only way I could get back some of the fighting spirit we were going to need. I laid it on thick about Kiowa Sam, and that took care of any good cheer there might have been.

We crossed into Nevada late that afternoon, with the fading sun throwing an orange glow on the first real desert country we had seen. To get to the desert we had to traverse a range of bare, brown hills with nothing remarkable about them except the fact that they probably hid Sam and his killers. The women who had never seen the desert before greeted it with startled cries. Even without the threat of raiders, it would have been a grim sight. From the looks of it, it wasn't such a bad stretch, but to anyone who hasn't experienced it before, the desert looks like the entrance to hell. And, for all we knew, that's where we might have been heading.

I kept watching for the flash of field glasses. Nothing showed, but I kept looking, for the light of the dying sun seemed to be all around us, and even the most experienced scout can make a mistake at that time of day.

Now that they knew Kiowa Sam was stalking us, the women didn't have to do any play-acting in their efforts to look glum. Only Maggie still displayed the hard edge of her spirit. I was counting on the mean-eyed woman-lover when the shooting started. In a fight she'd be as good as any man, and maybe better.

Some of the women would be no good in a fight; I wasn't faulting them for that. I was going to have to depend on about 20 women, maybe less. Claggett, Steiner and Culligan would fight like tigers, knowing what they could expect if we were overrun. I had no great confidence in Iversen; I guessed he would fight hard enough. I still wondered why he had chosen to cross the Plains by wagon train. Back in Missouri his reasons hadn't mattered; now they did.

The arms had been parceled out to the 20 women who knew how to use them. Against a determined band of raiders we wouldn't stand much of a chance, but I was still hoping that the plague warnings would have an effect. I could just about see Sam and his men arguing the point in the cover of the hills. Claggett was right. Most likely Sam would know about the seven-day limit; as an old-timer on the Plains, he'd be bound to. Some of the men would believe him, but then there would be the ones who didn't want to believe and the ones who weren't sure. As I had told Claggett, the thought of catching the plague was enough to make the hardest hard case shiver and kick dirt in hesitation. Hell! I was scared shitless myself, come to think of it. I had seen the Sills girl die of the plague, and it was as bad a death as ever I'd seen. Nothing could save you from it once it struck. No serum was worth a damn—you just died. A millionaire in a private hospital died as horribly as a pauper in a charity ward.

The sun went down as we formed the wagons into an oval, which could be taken as a routine precaution in rough country rather than as a sign of panic. If we formed too tight a defense, Sam would be sure to think we were on to him. I didn't want to do that, not now anyhow. At the moment his men were still fresh and lusting for young female flesh. What I wanted them to do was wear themselves out deliberating the ins and outs of the situation. Even in a gang of outlaws, there are men more cautious, more sensible than others. In Sam's bunch there would be crafty men and fools, cowards and diehards. I was hoping there would be a lot of wary men and ordinary cowards.

A strong guard was posted while supper was prepared. This was high desert country, and it got cold as soon as the sun went down. I warned Iversen about walking in front of the fire. Culligan didn't have to be warned, and neither did Steiner. Iversen's face had healed, but he would never be the same. He had grown more sullen, but I couldn't decide whether it was because of Kiowa Sam or the missing teeth. I didn't expect him to snap back at me when I warned him about getting shot by firelight. He muttered something, and stepped away from the light.

Iversen didn't have anything else to say, so I took my plate of food and moved away from the fire so I wouldn't have to look at him. I sat on my heels and ate without much interest. When I looked up, Maggie O'Hara was standing over me, going to stand guard after having eaten. I kept on eating, wishing she'd go away. At any other time the thought of matching words with the woman-lover would have interested me, especially this woman-lover. But with things as they were, I wasn't in the mood.

"I heard what you said to Iversen," she said. "Nerves getting tight are they, Saddler?"

"Go to hell!"

Maggie, cradling her rifle, hunkered down beside me. "That's what's got you jumpy, isn't it? The idea that they'll lay back and try to pick off the men. If they're plague-scared, that's what they might do. Pick off the men at long distance with no danger to themselves. With the men dead, they'd count on the women to give up. Then all they'd have to do is wait and see if there really is a plague."

I set down my plate and looked at her. She was right. That was what I'd been thinking. The women would give up, most of them would anyway.

"I don't know what they're going to do," I said. "That's the same answer I gave the sailor."

Maggie replied irritably, "I'm no sailor, friend. You can talk straight American to me. Pretend I'm a man. It's not that hard."

She was wrong there. It would have been hard to think of her as a man, even if she had been wearing a potato sack. Somehow, the tight pants she thought made her look mannish only served to make her appear more feminine.

"They could try to wear us down by sniping," I admitted. "If they start that, the men will have to ride in the wagons, or else the train has to travel by night."

Maggie found that funny. "You wouldn't like that, would you, Saddler? Traveling in a wagon out of sight, while women protected you."

I grinned at her. "Depends on whose wagon I was in."

Her temper boiled again. "Don't start that fucking shit or we'll have trouble. We came close a few times, so don't lean too hard on me. You and the other men could go all the way. Wear dresses and poke bonnets."

That was supposed to make me mad. Maybe I was edgy. I started to laugh.

"What's so funny?"

"I was thinking of Culligan in a dress."

Maggie stood up, holding the rifle. "You're a hard one to figure, Saddler."

"Then don't try."

"I do what I like. You have to remember that. For what it's worth, tell me this. Are you as tough as you think you are, or is it all for show? The other men I figured out long ago. Open books to me, even old man Claggett. You, you're different in some way."

"What's so different about me?" I wondered what in the name of Christ she was leading up to, if anything.

For a moment she stood looking at me, and I think she was as puzzled as I was. Then she said, "You might just be the first real man I ever met, Saddler. All my life I've listened to men brag about how tough they were. From my drunken father on down the line, that's all I ever heard. When I worked in that whorehouse in New York, it wasn't any different. More than half the men that came there didn't come to fuck the women. The dear darlin's came to talk and show off. I got paid whether they talked or fucked. No difference to me. Some bragged about how rich they were. Some even bragged about their wives and children. A lot of them sounded off about the size of their cocks. If you knew how to do it right, without giving the

appearance of lying, you could always count on a big tip
for telling a man what a big cock he had. I asked Flaxie,
and she said you have a real big one when it's standing. Is
that true, Saddler?"

"Gosh! I don't know. I never got to comparing with
the other fellers."

My lack of response angered her. "You think nobody
can make a dent in you?"

"I have a few dents," I said. "You want to try to make a
fresh one?"

Suddenly, there was confusion in her face; the rifle was
turned on me. I'm sure her sudden bewilderment was
genuine, as if this peculiar conversation had triggered
something inside her—something she had buried and
wanted to keep buried. I didn't want to get shot over it,
and I didn't want to shoot her.

Maggie said quietly, "If I wanted to make a dent in
you, I'd have you begging for mercy. You'd beg for
mercy, and then you'd beg me not to stop. They didn't
call me the best fuck in the Tenderloin for nothing. I'd
break your back, Saddler. I'd break your back, and you'd
be glad to be a cripple."

Maggie stalked away and left me with my plate of cold
stew. Overhead, the stars came out in a blaze of soft,
white light. Ah, the language of romance, I thought. Me
and Maggie O'Hara and starlight on the desert.

Break my back, would she? Well, sir, my back was
there any time she wanted to break it. For a few brief
minutes I was able to forget about Kiowa Sam.

SIXTEEN

I was standing the last watch of the night when a woman began to scream. There was less than an hour to go before first light. The sound, wild and despairing, made the hair stand up on the back of my neck. I knew this was no nightmare, but death in all its finality and ugliness. It came from one of the wagons at the far end of the oval from where I was hunched down with my rifle. Before I straightened up the scream came again.

The two women in that wagon were sisters who had worked together in the same Philadelphia cathouse. Their names were Lily and Julie. Lily was the one who was dead. I climbed up in the wagon, and the other woman wouldn't stop screaming, so I hit her. That stopped the screaming. She collapsed and began to sob, almost knocking over a stub of a candle that guttered in a bean can with holes punched in the side.

Lily had slashed both wrists with a sharp, meat-cutting knife. She lay on her mattress with a peaceful look on her face. For her the trip was finally over. Sometime during the night she had decided that she couldn't stand any more of it. I didn't blame her much, and maybe she was better off.

I called Rita and Steiner, and they took the dead girl's sister to their wagon. "Get some of Culligan's whiskey for her," I said, adding Lily to the growing list of the dead in my mind. I heard Steiner calling for Culligan when Claggett came to the wagon and climbed up into it.

The preacher's face had no expression as he stared down at the dead woman. "God forgive her," he said. "She has done a terrible thing. There is no greater sin than the sin of despair. We'll bury her as soon as it's light, and move on. What else can we do? I'm beginning to think God is angry with me, so many terrible things have happened since we began this journey."

I didn't care how mad God was at the preacher. I hated what I had to say next. "We won't bury her," I said. "We'll burn the body along with the wagon. The sister will have to bunk in with the Steiners or in some other wagon."

At last I had said something that shocked the preacher. His thin lips moved before he spoke. "You want to burn the body so the raiders will think we have the plague?"

I didn't mind his disapproving stare. That was all right. I didn't approve of it myself. "I'll go farther than that, if I have to," I said. "You hired me to get you to California. That's where we're going. It can't make any difference to the dead woman."

"I won't have anything to do with it," Claggett said. "You'll have to do this on your own."

I shrugged. "She's going to need a prayer no matter how she goes."

"I thought you didn't believe in prayer."

"Not your kind of prayer, Reverend. But I used to see the dead woman listening to you while you preached your sermons on Sunday. The least you can do is read a few words over her."

Claggett was sharp enough. "That's not the real reason. You just want to make it look right, if Kiowa Sam is watching."

"That's another reason. It'll do."

Before he climbed down, Claggett said to me, "I don't know if you're a good man or a bad man, Saddler. But I'll do as you ask."

I called Steiner and told him to keep feeding whiskey to Julie until we got the job done. "I don't want her to see it," I said.

Steiner's face was lined with strain. "She's almost unconscious now—shock and whiskey. We'll be miles out before she wakes up."

I said, "Make sure of it, Jake. It won't be easy to face her after it's over. She's not to know about the burning."

Steiner laid a heavy hand on my arm. "We're all part of it. It's not just you."

Sure, I thought, but I'm the one who thought of it. I'm the one who's going to light the match.

"Sure, Jake," I said. "We're all in this together."

I made sure it was full daylight before the rest of the wagons began to move on, leaving me with Claggett and a can of coal oil. Claggett stood in the cool morning, his sparse hair ruffled by the wind, and read from his Bible. Once that was done, I soaked the wagon and set it on fire. Flame and smoke boiled up into the clear air as we rode on to rejoin the wagons.

Everything had been done quickly, the praying and the burning, as if we couldn't get away fast enough. We were turning away from the flaming wagon when I caught the first flash of morning sunlight on glass. We had our heads bowed a moment before, so they must have thought it was safe to glass us from afar.

It must have looked pretty convincing: the dead woman, the burning wagon. Still, Sam was a foxy old killer, and maybe fooling him wouldn't be that easy. But the other raiders had seen the burning wagon, and there was no way that Sam could make them believe that we had burned a woman just to make it look good. The cautious ones and the cowards would be scared.

I knew I was. Maggie's talk about long-range sniping came back to me. The only good cover was out of range of even the most powerful rifle. They would have to get in closer if they meant to do some sniping. Could be that some of them were closer than I figured. No way to know that with experienced stalkers. I could feel rifle sights lining up on my chest. That could've been fact or my imagination. It's a hell of a thing to be stalked like an animal; the hunter has all the advantages. I began to sweat, because I'm no hero. We'd know pretty soon how it was going to be.

If I had been with the train, I might have got it instead of Iversen—me or Claggett, we were the tough ones in our bunch. But we weren't there, so Iversen got it first. The shooters were up ahead, waiting for the train to pass. I was glad it wasn't Steiner or Culligan; they were men too valuable to lose.

Iversen was driving the preacher's wagon, because the preacher had to stay behind with me. We were hurrying to catch up with the train when the first shot boomed and echoed across the hills. I heard Iversen yell as the bullet knocked him back into the bed of the wagon. Then bullets came at Steiner and Culligan, but they were under cover by the time Iversen had finished dying.

Claggett and I ran to the last wagon—Culligan's—and climbed into it. Bullets splintered the thick sides of the wagon without ripping through them all the way. We lay on the floor of the wagon, breathing hard. Culligan lay with the reins in his hand, blowing his whiskey breath on us. I edged up to the front and yelled at the women to keep moving. Maggie O'Hara yelled back that she would drive the preacher's wagon. I yelled at her to go ahead. I knew she was safe enough. They wouldn't kill any of the women unless they had to. Women were what they wanted, and they were no good dead.

The sniping started again when Maggie dropped down from her wagon. At least one of the shooters had taken her for a man, what with the pants, boots and cowpuncher's creased hat. I wondered how pleased she was at being mistaken for a man. Bullets chased her as she ran along the side of the train. Then I couldn't see her any more, but the shooting went on. Then suddenly it stopped. Somebody with good eyes had realized that they had been making a terrible mistake, trying to kill one of the best-looking women in the bunch.

The train began to move faster after Maggie took over the driving of the preacher's wagon. I told Claggett to stay where he was. "I'm going up there with her," I said.

"That's my wagon," Claggett said angrily.

"You don't move fast enough, Reverend."

Claggett knew I was right. His gun hand was the only fast thing about him. "What're we going to do, Saddler? We don't have to guess anymore."

"Right now we stay as we are and keep moving. They're scared to come in, or they wouldn't have started sniping. We still have the scare working for us."

How long it would go on working was the unanswered question. The way things were, we were in a kind of moving standoff. A slow-moving standoff, with the raiders still too scared to attack and the rest of us unable to show ourselves.

I showed myself as I dropped from the wagon, and bullets came at me from behind a long ridge on the closest hill. I was glad they had no cover to shoot from on the other side. On that side the country was flat and ran flat and bare for miles. A bullet tugged at the tall crown of my borrowed hat, but when the next bullet came I was on the safe side of the wagons. But I had to show myself when I crossed the open spaces between the moving wagons. Every time I did, I got shot at. But long-range shooting isn't that easy with a moving target—whoever had shot Iversen was pretty good—and I wasn't just moving, I was running hard.

I came closest to getting killed when I reached the wagon and started to climb up over the endgate. The endgate was up, and that made it hard to get over. They turned all their bullets on me then, and I don't know why one of them didn't find me. I probably would have been killed if Maggie hadn't dropped the reins, grabbed the preacher's Winchester and started blasting in the direction of the snipers. There wasn't a chance of hitting anything—the Winchester didn't have the range—but when someone is shooting at you, it can put you off your aim. Maggie's wild shooting gave me the time I needed to get into the wagon. I lay panting, telling her to stop shooting. "Somebody could get mad and shoot you off the box," I yelled. "You'll get killed if you don't stop."

As I yelled, a bullet tore into the wagon cover not far from Maggie's head. "Sons of bitches!" she yelled, mad enough to pull her belt gun. I jumped to the front of the wagon and yanked the pistol from her hand.

"Quit it!" I said.

She struggled furiously until her anger wore itself out. Any temper left was directed at me. "Don't ever do that again, Saddler. I swear I'll kill you if you do."

I thought it was safe to give her back her gun. "Peace!" I said. "The enemy is out there."

Maggie holstered her gun while I reloaded the Winchester. "What in hell are you doing here?" Maggie raged. "You were supposed to stay in cover."

I grinned at her. "I'm in cover now. I wanted to see how you were doing."

The shooting from the ridge had stopped. Maggie said, "You see how I'm doing. I don't need your help." Slowly, she grinned back. "I was right about the sniping, wasn't I?"

"I wish you'd been wrong," I said. "At least it's out in the open."

"Nobody's out in the open except us," Maggie said. "What do you think they'll do next?"

"Keep on sniping when they think there's a chance of hitting something. Maybe just keep on sniping, hoping to wear us down. They may try something else after it gets dark."

Maggie didn't like the idea that anything could wear her down. "They can just pull it," she jeered. "Let the bastards try anything they like."

The sniping started again, and we ducked our heads, though the bullets buried themselves harmlessly in the side of the wagon. Maggie straightened up defiantly. "Fuck 'em all!" she said. "You too, Saddler, if you'd like to be included."

Another rifle bullet socked into the heavy wood. I

knew we were safe enough for the moment. "Tell me," I said, "are you really as tough as you make out, or is it all for show?"

Maggie grinned. She was a wild, crazy woman I was beginning to like. A lot of strange things had made her what she was, just as they had made all of us.

"I won't bullshit you, Saddler. Why try to bullshit a bullshitter like you. I'm tough enough, I guess. Tough as I have to be."

Another bullet tore into the wagon. "Stay tough for now," I said.

"Just watch me!" Maggie said.

We moved on through the day, and so did the snipers. At first we had to stay close to the line of hills because broken ground strewn with big rocks and slashed by deep ravines separated us from open country. It was hours before we were able to turn the wagons and head out onto the flat. I wasn't sure that they wouldn't attack when they saw the train moving out of range of their most powerful rifles. I got back in the wagon bed and made a slit in the cover and watched the hills as we moved away from them. And then for the first time I saw the raiders, some outlined against the top of the ridge they'd been shooting from, others coming down from higher up on the slopes. It was too far to see much. As we moved farther out onto the flat, they mounted up and began to nudge their horses down the side of the broken hills.

Maggie had seen them too. "They're coming after us but taking their time about it. They're scared all right."

"They'll have to decide after a while," I said.

We traveled on, and the raiders stayed with us, but at a good distance. I stood up on the box and could see them a long way back, eating our dust as we went deeper into the desert. There were a lot of disheartened marauders out there in the heat and glare, I thought. It wasn't going at all like Kiowa Sam had told them it would. Instead of enjoying more women than they'd ever dreamed about, they were eating dust behind what could be a plague wagon.

The sun traveled across the sky as we moved on. In a few hours it would begin to get dark. Night had its protection and its dangers. But they hadn't attacked yet, and every mile put us that much closer to the California line. Right on the other side of the line, right at the end of the Overland, there was an Army post. If we could manage to survive for another few days, there was a chance of running into a patrol. That was the optimistic side of me thinking; the other side knew that Kiowa Sam wouldn't wait that long. The danger of plague had taken the fight out of his men, and Sam would have to find a way to get it back.

Culligan gave it to him, or I should say Culligan's wagon did. Of all the wagons to break a wheel, the last wagon had to. Maybe Culligan had been too busy fixing other wheels to look after his own. I heard the goddamn thing break from way up in front. It broke with a sound like a rifle shot, and there was a crunching, smashing noise as the wagon went over on its side. I jumped down and started to run back. Far out I saw the flash of field glasses, and then the line of raiders began to move faster. Now they were making their own dust cloud. The field glasses flashed again, and I knew they had seen me running. Claggett and Culligan were coming down from the front of the wrecked wagon. The rumble of the raiders' horses was getting closer as they lashed and spurred their animals to run faster. They were still too far out for accurate shooting, but a bullet doesn't have to be well-aimed if it kills you. In seconds, their bullets began to come in closer.

Culligan could run fast enough for a man of his bulk and drinking habits. Jesus! Suddenly, I thought of all the whiskey in the Irishman's wagon. Claggett wasn't doing so good. Moving as fast as he could behind Culligan, he staggered and fell. The raiders were getting the range now, and bullets sang all around us. I didn't want Sam to get the Irishman's big store of whiskey, but there was no way I could get out of helping Claggett. I cursed him for being so old, but I had to let the whiskey go and help him to his feet. His face mottled with anger, he shoved me aside and followed Culligan, making his old legs work as best they could.

Now I could see the raiders plain, make them out as men instead of shapes in the dust. I turned and ran after Culligan and the preacher. I heard Kiowa Sam's wild yell and knew he was out in front of the others. I chanced a look and saw Sam riding straight for the halted wagon. The rest of the raiders had slowed down some, not wanting to get that close to it. By the time Sam reached it, they had reined in and were waiting. I heard Sam yelling at them to come on in: there was no danger. I heard him yell, "Whiskey, boys! All you can drink!" But the raiders stayed where they were, all but three of them, who took their horses out of the waiting line and rode forward.

Culligan climbed into another wagon, but the preacher kept pumping his old legs until he had reached his own. He got alongside, and Maggie reached down to help him up. I got up too, knowing I was the only one who had given thought to all the red-eye in Culligan's wagon.

"They're still holding back from a full attack," Maggie said.

"Maybe not for long," I said. "They've got all Culligan's whiskey. Once they get that down, they'll be brave enough. Some of them will."

Claggett gave out with a biblical oath.

"At least they'll be good and drunk," I said. "The ones that do attack will hardly be able to walk straight. No amount of whiskey will persuade the others."

Maggie grinned fiercely, actually looking forward to the fight ahead. "Then it won't be so bad," she said. "Every man I kill, I'll be thinking of my drunken father and his leather belt. It won't be so bad after all, Saddler."

I knew it would be bad enough.

SEVENTEEN

It got dark. Claggett thought we should keep moving on into the night. Traveling on the flat was easy, even after it got dark. But I said no. It was best to make camp where we were. If we kept moving, they could sneak in from both sides, maybe get in front of us, too. The preacher remained silent after that, and I knew he thought God had cursed his expedition.

This time we formed the wagons into a fighting circle, with the harness animals inside the circle, the cows turned loose. If we survived, we could round them up in the morning. The attack had to come that night, because Sam wasn't likely to stumble over another cache of whiskey. If they didn't attack tonight, they wouldn't attack at all.

We made no cookfires. What cooked food there was had to be eaten cold. Claggett sat with bowed head, chewing slowly on a biscuit and sipping peach juice from a can. Maggie went to her wagon and came back with a canteen of cold, strong coffee. That was another of her peculiarities, drinking cold coffee all through the day.

The coffee tasted good after the slightly rancid meat I'd been chewing. Far out in the darkness I heard them yelling, tanking up on Culligan's whiskey.

"They're working up their nerve," Maggie said quietly.

I handed the canteen of coffee back to her. "That's what they're doing."

She drank deeply from the canteen and stoppered it. "How long do you figure, Saddler?"

"As long as the whiskey holds out," I said. "Then they'll come, those that are coming."

It was going to be a long night, or maybe not so long. At least as long as a boxful of quart bottles. I had divided our force evenly: one half would sleep or rest, the other would stand guard. Claggett and Steiner were with the women on the first watch. Culligan and I were to join the second. The watches were to be short, so there wouldn't be too much strain on the watchers. I thanked Maggie for the coffee and crawled into Claggett's wagon to sleep for an hour. I knew the whiskey would last longer than an hour. From where I lay on the bed of the wagon, I could see the stars through the hoop opening of the wagon cover in the front. I heard a sound, opened my eyes and saw Maggie O'Hara filling the hoop of light. There was a tenseness in her that had nothing to do with the impending attack. Her voice was quiet, "Don't talk to me, Saddler. Just do it!"

She lay down beside me in the half darkness, but when I tried to kiss her she pulled her head away. Then she changed her mind and let me. Her mouth was sweet, with a taste of coffee. We couldn't take all our clothes off. We took off just enough so that it didn't make any difference. It was strange not being able to talk, to make any noise. But that didn't make any difference either.

Maggie's body grew rigid when I put my hand between her legs, so I kept it there but didn't move it for a while. Then she took my hand and put it deeper between her legs. She was sopping wet, as if she had been wet long before she came to the wagon. Yet she resisted when I tried to straddle her. Her resistance, too, passed in a few minutes, and she opened her legs, took my cock in her hands and guided it into her.

Her back arched as it went in, driving deep into her. The cry she gave was almost a sob. I don't know what it was, maybe a cry of relief. I expected her to put all her expert ways to work on me, as she had promised, or threatened, but after the first hostility passed she was as tender as any woman I'd known. It could be that the thought of death had softened her, made her see that there was no need to fight me. I drove into her, but it took hard work to make her come. Coming with a man inside her was what she wanted, something I guessed she hadn't been able to do. I helped her every way I could. I had to break down years of anger and disgust with men. I think the desperation of the moment helped to do it. Maggie seemed to know that she might never get another chance. I counted the minutes in my head without being completely aware that I was doing it. Maggie might be the last woman I might ever enjoy, and I put everything I had into making it good for both of us.

She came quietly. I expected her to writhe under me, dig her nails into my back. But her orgasm was quiet, and she kissed me hard while she was coming. I hadn't come yet, so I made her come again and again. Women are lucky, the way they can keep coming until they are exhausted. I think Maggie was worn out by the time I couldn't hold back any longer. She had had many men in her during her life, and she knew I wanted my own come.

"Come, Saddler," she whispered into my ear. "Come now—I want to feel your hot juice."

And so I did, spurting my juice inside her. I couldn't be sure what she thought of me, if she'd forgiven me for fucking Flaxie. For all I knew, she might still hate me. There was no way to tell. I wasn't even sure that she might not try to kill me with that double-edged knife. It lay close at hand with her short-barreled revolver. But after I came she did nothing but relax, so maybe I wasn't going to get knifed or castrated after all.

I thought she might run off after her sex experiment with me. Some half-forgotten instinct had made her come to me. She wanted to prove something to herself. We were all so close to death she knew she might not have another chance to prove anything. I had been wanting this fierce-tempered woman since that first night in Claggett's wagon. But I had given up hope because of her relentless hostility. But here she was on what might be our last night on earth.

The way she fucked, I could well believe that she had been one of the best—if not the best—whores in the New York Tenderloin. She pushed my head down between her legs, wanting me to do to her what she had so often done to Flaxie. I was gentle with her because I have to admit I was afraid not to be. She seemed to like the way I tongued her because she sighed with contentment. She reached down and held my head with both hands, running her fingers through my hair. When she came she came as quietly as she had when we fucked in the regular way. She squeezed my face between her legs.

"Oh Jesus, Saddler, I'm all confused," she whispered. "Things got so turned around in my life. You know I love Flaxie, but . . ."

I had nothing to say to that. Circumstances had made her a woman-lover and I felt sure she wouldn't change at this point in her life. I really don't understand woman-lovers, but I could see that loving someone like Flaxie wouldn't be so bad. Everybody needs sex and you do the best you can.

"I think we better leave off," she said finally. "The bastards will be coming soon. We don't have much of a chance, have we?"

I could be straight with this tough woman. "Maybe, maybe not. All we can do is make a fight of it. You have any regrets about this trip?"

"Not a one. Anything is better than jail. How about you?"

"Nobody lives forever. I don't know if you still hate me, have changed your mind enough to like me, or if you plain don't give a shit about me."

"Well, you're not the ruthless bastard I thought you

were. I guess I like you all right. Is that good enough for you?"

"It'll do," I said.

Out in the dark the yelling was louder. They were full of whiskey now, and some of them sounded willing to risk anything to get at the women. I told the people on the first watch to stand their ground. The attack had to come in minutes. I turned and saw Maggie take up her position beside Flaxie on the other side of the circle. She hugged Flaxie for a moment. I didn't know how much of it was woman-love or just love. It didn't seem to matter. We all need love, no matter how or where we get it.

I stood up and moved around the circle of defenders, talking quietly. Jake clapped me on the shoulder and said he hoped I'd be able to make it to San Francisco. Jake seemed to have no doubt that he and Rita would survive. If they had to die, it was best to go out thinking that way. Rita kissed me, then let go. Culligan was down on one knee, his rifle ready. He was in a cold fury at having his whiskey stolen. He didn't know that maybe his whiskey would make it possible for us to live through this. Some of us. He didn't look at me, and I had no words for him. Claggett was the last one I spoke to. "If I get killed and you don't, head straight for the California line. I think tonight will decide it. Whatever happens will happen now. If you get it and I don't, I'll do my best for your women."

Claggett looked surprised. "My women!"

"That's who they are, Reverend. They still look up to you."

"I don't mind that," Claggett said, and that's all he said.

Everyone knew what they had to do: fight to the end. No stylish plan was called for. Drunk as they were, the marauders would come straight at us. It was some consolation that Sam wouldn't be able to cook up any fancy plan of his own. His men were too drunk for that. Sam was, in his way, as desperate as we were. I had no more orders, no more advice to give. Shoot and keep on

shooting I'd said, until you're down to the last bullet.
Then fight with anything you can find.

We waited, tense in the darkness. Out beyond us, they
were working up to a frenzy of drunken lust and rage. I
was counting in my head again. That was nerves. I made
myself stop. I wouldn't have been half as jumpy if it
hadn't been for the women. Sam's men would have to
kill some of them; the old killer must have accepted that
by now. I guess he was hoping to pick up whoever was
left. But he had to be crazy and desperate to settle for
that.

They were moving out around us now, but I couldn't
see a thing. Then a rifle cracked and flashed and they
opened up from all sides, screaming and yelling as they
fired. The night exploded with gunfire as they came in for
what they hoped was the kill. Then there were dim
shapes behind the flashes, and I yelled, "Open fire!"

Flames jetted from the wagons. The yelling was
drowned out by the shooting on both sides. During a
break in the noise I could hear Kiowa Sam urging them
on. The attack wasn't as heavy as I expected it to be, but
it was heavy enough. If they hadn't been drunk, they
would have done a lot better. Suddenly my women—
Claggett's women—began to yell themselves, as if all the
months of tension were tearing loose inside them. It rose
up into a scream of fear, anger, and desperation. It
chilled my blood to hear women scream like that.
Suddenly, I knew we were going to win. It would be
bloody, but we were going to win.

Drunk, staggering, still yelling, they came on through
our fire, some dropping to the ground under the hail of
bullets. A woman got hit with a bullet in the face. She
jumped, fell down and died without a sound. The
woman's death seemed to drive the others crazy. They
fired and reloaded as fast they could pull the trigger or
work the loading lever.

The night was filled with death and gunsmoke and hot
lead. And still they came on, running, lurching to their
deaths. I felt another woman dropping beside me. There
was no time to see who she was. Maggie yelled her hate

when a bullet brought Flaxie down with a soft, helpless cry. I jerked my head around and a bullet sang past where it had been a moment before. I knew from Maggie's scream that Flaxie was dead.

We were holding firm on my side; they were breaking through on the other. Rita took a bullet in the arm and shifted her handgun to the other hand and kept on firing. I heard Claggett cry out, a gasp more than a cry, and knew he had been wounded. They broke through on the other side, and we turned to face them as they came howling through between the wagons, some falling under our fire. I spotted Kiowa Sam, and he spotted me at the same time. I jerked my rifle to my shoulder, but before I could pull the trigger four or five women turned their guns on Sam and he fell, blasted by lead.

Claggett was wounded again, and I killed the man who fired the shot. Somebody jumped me from behind. I threw him over my head and shot him in the back of the head. Maggie's rifle was empty; she yanked at the belt gun and started blasting. A wounded raider came at me with a big Bowie knife, and Maggie shot him twice in the chest. She was yelling something at me when a bullet drilled her through the heart. She stood for a moment looking at me, holding her chest with her left hand. I don't think she actually saw me. She fell and lay still, with Flaxie a few feet away.

And then, as quickly as it had come, the attack was broken. We shot at the few raiders left as they ran into the dark. We killed a few before they got to their horses. I heard them—not many—riding away into the night. I knew they wouldn't come back. Sam was dead. They'd be heading for places where the Army couldn't find them. The sound of the fleeing horses died away, and it was quiet again except for the moaning of the wounded.

I ordered torches lit, then the lamps in the wagons. Claggett had died during the last moments of the attack. Maggie was dead, so was Flaxie. Culligan was wounded but alive. Steiner was binding up the wound in Rita's arm. Nine other women had died; six had been wounded. One died later. We had lost close to half our people since starting out from Missouri. Now, at long last, it was over.

We buried our dead at sun-up. Since Claggett was among them, it fell to me to read the prayers. I didn't feel foolish doing it. Not silly at all. We had come a long way, but there was still a fair way to go. I didn't know what the remaining women would do when they arrived in California. I had done my best for them, but from now on they would have to make their own way in the world. I guessed they'd be all right. Men were looking for wives all over California; even the plain ones would have no trouble finding a husband.

This time we put crosses over the graves of our dead. Then it was time to move. We were running short of water, but a river was marked on the map. We pulled away in bright sunlight. Before the distance became too great to see, I turned and looked back at the crosses standing stark in the glare of the desert.

"Goodbye, Maggie," I said. Then I thought of all the others who had died, and I said goodbye to them too.

As we moved on, Jake turned to me and said, "I guess you're the leader now."

"Yeah," I said. "I guess I am."